Copyrigh

All

The characters and events   ny
similarity to real persons, livin   ended
L

No part of this book may be reproduced, or stored in a retrieval system,
or transmitted in any form or by any means, electronic, mechanical,
photocopying, recording, or otherwise, without express written permission
of the publisher.

ISBN-9798680955796

Cover design by: Anne Bone
Library of Congress Control Number: 2018675309
Printed in the United States of America

*This book is dedicated to all those who have suffered trauma
and have found a way to love and live again. Courage and
bravery comes in many different forms.*

PROLOGUE

Here I am, getting off this big boat, and thinking about the new life I am about to embark on. I hope I have made the right decision to leave my old life behind. Only time will tell, I suppose.

I watched the sunrise over the horizon this morning, and thought of my mother. She always told me to see each day as a new day of hope. I have so many hopes, the main one being that Harry will be standing on the quayside, waiting for me as he promised. Then, I hope that his family will accept me. Above all, I hope that by leaving my past behind, I will be able to live a peaceful existence.

PART ONE

Scotland

CHAPTER 1

November 2017

Laura and Iona sat each side of the elderly lady, who seemed to be lost within the crisp white hospital sheets that covered her frail body. The old lady had lapsed into an unconscious state, and her pigeon chest rose up and down slowly as her shallow breaths came and went.

'She looks very peaceful, Mum,' whispered Iona, gently stroking her great-grandmother's wrinkled hand. The skin seemed to be almost transparent, littered with brown liver spots; an indicator of a life long-lived.

'I know, love, but I really hope she hadn't lain for too long before they found her. I feel so bad now, that I didn't visit when I meant to last week. Poor Granny.' She reached for her grandmother's other hand, which lay under the hospital blanket. The hand was warm, but limp. She took it into both of her own hands slowly rubbing, almost as if she was trying to rub some life back into her.

'She is a good age, Mum. Eighty-nine, and she is really remarkable, still living on the croft, and looking after herself.'

'Well, she wouldn't have it any other way. I know Dr Mackie tried hard to get her to consider going into the local home, but she wouldn't have any of it. But maybe now, she will have a second thought about that.'

Iona smiled, wondering if her mother really understood that her eighty-nine-year-old great-granny, Elsa, was unlikely to leave this hospital alive. Iona was well aware of the signs, given that she was four years into her training to become a doctor. She had recently been on this actual ward, as part of her student observations at Aberdeen Royal Infirmary. Little had she known that just a few weeks later she would be here as a visitor.

Laura leant forwards so she could speak into her granny's ear. 'Granny, can you hear me? We are here, Iona and me. Oh, Granny, what did you do to yourself?' She reached out and smoothed the face of the woman, the face that had a large bruise beginning to show across her cheek. She looked across at Iona. 'They say they found her beside her bed. Think she may have taken a turn. It's just as well that Maisie Campbell took a look in, and found her. Thank goodness for posties, and that it wasn't at a weekend.'

'Yes, she couldn't really have been lying for too long,' Iona replied, 'or else she would have maybe ended up with hyperthermia. Thank goodness you persuaded her to have the heating put in and that she actually had it going. November in Deeside wouldn't have allowed her to lie for too long.'

Elsa's breathing seemed to take a shudder and then her eyes fluttered for a moment. Laura stood over the bed. 'Granny, it's me, Laura. Can you hear me, Granny?' The old lady's eyes opened slowly, her eyelids fluttering, but seemingly having trouble at staying open. A smile slowly developed across her wrinkled face, and then slowly the eyes closed. Another shudder of breath, and then nothing.

Iona stood and felt for a pulse, and shook her head. 'Sorry, Mum. She has gone. We better call for a nurse. I'll go and get someone.'

Laura sat back on the seat, and found her eyes glistening with tears. She looked at her grandmother's face, now, it seemed, as though her skin had softened, and she did look at peace. She had known this woman the whole of her forty-four years, and it would indeed be strange not to have her in her life any longer. She had had a peaceful death, and that brought some relief and comfort to think, that and at least she hadn't died alone. Was it only just few hours ago that she had been sitting drinking her morning coffee and browsing the internet on her iPad, when her phone rang? It was Dr Mackie, telling her that Elsa had been found by Maisie and was being transported to ARI. She had been galvanised into action, managing to get hold of Iona, and then making the hour journey from her home at Broadsea, a small town on the Moray Firth coast, into Aberdeen.

Iona appeared back in the room, accompanied by a young-looking male medic and an older nurse. He inclined his head to her before taking Elsa's hand and checking for a pulse. He spoke in a deep voice, confirming that indeed life was extinct, and looked at his watch to check before recording the time of death. There would be some formalities, he told them, before he turned to hand over the responsibility of this elderly woman's body to her relatives and the nurse. The nurse had compassion scripted across her face; death wasn't unknown to her. She went across and placed her hand carefully on Laura's shoulder. 'I'm sorry for your loss. It was very fast, and at least you were beside her.' Her soft tone was indeed a comfort. 'I can leave you with her, take your time. There is no hurry,' she reassured Laura, and nodded to Iona before she quietly left the room.

Laura looked across at Iona. 'I don't think she suffered, did she?'

'No, Mum, I don't think she did. She was very comfortable and she didn't die alone.' Iona stopped for a moment and realised that this was the first death she had witnessed. She knew that she would probably witness many more in her future career, and doubted that many would be so peaceful.

'What do we do now?' Laura looked towards her daughter for

advice. Given her connection with medical matters, she imagined she might have the knowledge. 'Do we need to contact an undertaker and get things going, do you think?'

'I think that they will move great grans body to the mortuary, and then the undertaker will take it from there. Did great gran tell you what she wanted to happen, when she died?'

'No, you know what she was like. She never spoke about things like that; in fact, you know she was closed off from speaking about anything to do with emotional things. Poor Granny, I have often wondered why she was so reserved. You know what I mean, about speaking about things.' Laura paused, suddenly realising something. 'Oh goodness, what about, Bella and the cat?' Bella was Elsa's ten-year-old border collie. Her companion, who everyone had tried to talk her out of getting when the then seventy-nine-year-old determined woman had announced she needed to have another dog, after her previous collie had died. They all told her that it was too much work to train a puppy at that age. But as usual, Elsa had ignored advice, and told them in no uncertain words that she was quite able and fit to do so. She went on to prove them wrong, and herself right, and as Bella grew she became her watchful and constant companion.

'I suppose we should make our way out to Birch End to see what we need to do. Can you come too or do you have to get back to uni? I will need to give your grandad a phone as well, he'll be wondering. He wanted to come with me, but I know he had a bowls competition on this afternoon and I didn't want him to miss it. You know how he takes it all very seriously and especially as he is the captain of the team.' She smiled warmly when she spoke about her dad. Grant, now aged seventy, was still very active and continued to be a constant support to her.

'Yes, I can come, Mum. I wouldn't let you do this on your own. I didn't have any lectures today so don't worry, I was just revising in the flat.' Laura was immediately grateful that her daughter had decided to go to Aberdeen University rather than one further afield. She was now living in a flat share with two other students from her course, and she suspected rightly that Tony, one of them, was more than just a flatmate, but was waiting for her daughter to confirm this.

'That's good. Shall we go and see what we need to do, then, and let the staff here get on with looking after Granny?' Laura stood up and leant over and planted a kiss on her grandmother's forehead. 'Goodbye, Granny. I hope you are meeting up with Grandad, and Mum. I am sure they were waiting for you. God bless.' She found the tears gently slipping down her face. She was not sure whether they were for her grandmother, or for her mother who had died when she was a child just before her tenth birthday. She still felt the sadness of that loss even though it was thirty-four years ago and she barely could recall her. Nevertheless, it was times like this that reminded her that she didn't have her mother to comfort her.

CHAPTER 2

It was a good three hours later before Laura turned off of the narrow road into the gateway of her grandmother's croft. The gravel driveway was full of holes and dips and you had to negotiate carefully at slow speed in order to avoid damaging your car. The track was narrow, and lined each side by silver birch trees; hence the croft's name of Birch End. At the end of the track sat a set of buildings – the cottage, and two stone steadings – that appeared to be sitting on a ridge with a panoramic backdrop of Lochnagar and the Grampian Mountain range whose granite rocks were even now peppered with white.

'It never fails, does it?' Iona commented while her mother negotiated around a rather large pothole. 'Just to see it, it, never fails to remind me of the times we used to come and stay when we were little. That smell and that view, but no sound of barking and a bouncing dog coming out to meet us, that different.'

'Yes, I wonder where Bella is?' Laura drove up to the front of the cottage and turned off of the engine, gazing as she did so through the windscreen to see whether there was any movement. She took her time to get out of the car and stretch; the hour-and-a-half drive out to Glen Gavin took a toll on her back, and she needed to loosen the muscles that had seized up. Laura stretched her five-feet-six-inch body, and for a moment swung her arms around. She had a slight build, taking after her mother, she was always told by her dad. She couldn't remember herself, but not only was she told that she was of the same build, but that was also where she got her thick, slightly wavy shoulder-length brunette hair, oval face and small, pointed nose. The latter had always seemed to be the bane of her life; she had wished as an adolescent for a slightly wider and less pointed nose.

'Have you got a key?' enquired Iona, as the younger woman marched towards the heavy wooden blue front door, which was, in fact, the only outside door into the two-storey granite cottage.

'Yes, it's in the bag of Granny's effects that they gave me at the hospital. Here it is.' She reached into the plastic bag and pulled out the rather large key, which her daughter fitted into the mortice lock and twisted. Laura couldn't recall any other time that she had had to unlock the door. Normally it was open, and even when she spent time staying during school holidays as a child, her granny never bothered to lock the door.

They now walked through the door, which opened immediately into a small hallway. A door was placed on each side, with a narrow corridor that led towards the back of the house where a small bedroom and bathroom was placed. The narrow, steep stairway directly in front of them led to two bedrooms. Iona opened the door to the left, which led into the large kitchen, which was always considered to be the main room of the cottage. The kitchen ran the length of the house, with windows at each end. At one end sat an old pine table, one where at least three generations of Kerrs had sat around and ate and passed the time of day. The old range had been replaced several years ago with an electric cooker, although there had been quite a fight at the time, as Elsa had taken some time to be convinced that it would mean she didn't have to clean it out and keep it going every day. At the same time,

Laura and her father had managed to persuade her to have electric storage heaters installed, and thankfully the house and room were quite cosy.

Iona filled the kettle and switched it on. 'I don't know about you, Mum, but I could murder a cuppa.' She opened the fridge to find that it was well stocked, including fresh milk. 'Looks like Granny must have had a recent delivery, from the amount of food in here. Or otherwise she hasn't been doing much eating of late.' She was searching through, checking dates on the ham and lump of cheese.

Laura looked around the room. So many memories and she didn't think much had changed in her forty-four years apart from the heaters, cooker and of course the fridge freezer. The table was still covered by the once colourful oil cloth. On it sat the wooden place mats and the salt and pepper, which she remembered had been a gift to her grandmother from a holiday trip to London when she was a teenager. Around the table were six chairs, all with padded cushion seats, covered many times when they became threadbare. The current ones had been there for at least ten years, but she supposed they had been sat on less over the years, as Elsa lived alone.

Beside the back window were two old armchairs, facing each other and looking rather shabby. Both had rug throws over them. One was clearly Bella's chair as there was strong evidence of lots of white dog hairs on the rug. Laura could just see her granny and her dog sitting happily in the chairs on winter afternoons. There was no television, as again Elsa was absolutely determined that she had no need for one, and as long as she had her radio she was happy. She had reminded Laura that there was no signal anyway, and she didn't need any of those satellite dish things that had seemed to have sprung up on the other houses in the Glen. To her mind, technology was not required to keep her occupied or entertained.

While Iona made the tea in the old-fashioned brown teapot,

which had been part of the surroundings for as long as either of them could remember, Laura went across the small hallway to the other room on the ground floor. It had once been the sitting room, or the 'room for best', but had over the past eight or so years become Elsa's bedroom. She had had to admit that getting up in the night to go downstairs to use the toilet had become a little too much, so they had moved her bed into the front room. As Laura looked around she found herself becoming tearful again, as she looked at the bed with its rumpled sheets, and the imprint of her granny's head on her pillow. She couldn't help thinking that this time yesterday her granny was alive and sleeping in her bed. At least there were no signs to indicate there had been any struggle before Maisie found her on the floor beside her bed this morning.

She looked around the room. In the corner was the sofa, which also provoked many memories. She remembered it as being the most uncomfortable sofa in the whole world. She felt it now and, yes, it was still hard. No wonder it had survived so long. On the mantelpiece sat many photographs. Laura picked up one and gazed at it. She had done so many times during her life, but it always fascinated her. It was a black-and-white photo of her grandparents, Elsa and Harry, with a small child between them. The small child was her mother Estelle. Next to it was one of her on her own wedding day, smiling happily into the lens with her dad Grant beside her, looking so proud. There had once been another of her wedding photos on show, that of her and Gus, both looking so happy. But she supposed that her grandmother had removed it when she and Gus had divorced nearly ten years ago. Goodness me, where had all those years gone? Laura glanced at the other photos on show, ones of Iona and Liam her youngest, when they were little. So many happy memories.

'Tea is on the table, Mum!' shouted Iona from the kitchen. 'And I made us a couple of cheese and ham sarnies.' Just as Laura sat down at the table to pick up the sandwich the phone rang. Iona answered it, and passed it to her mother. 'It's Maisie,' she told her.

Laura broke the news to Maisie about her granny's death and listened to the story of how Maisie had knocked this morning and, when there was no answer, she had gone in and found Elsa unconscious on the floor. She had waited until the ambulance had taken her away, and then she had taken Bella with her. What did Laura want her to do with the dog, she asked. Laura hadn't really thought about what she was going to do, but she supposed she would need to take Bella back home with her, and then think about what she would do in the long term. So she arranged to pick her up later, when she was on her way back home.

Once she hung up, she remembered that Bella of course wasn't the only animal to look after, and then just by magic, she noticed that Tammy the tabby cat was meowing on the window sill, her white nose up against the window pane, with a look of hunger. Oh, and of course there were the six hens that would need looking after, too. Thank goodness there were no longer sheep on the croft, nor the two cows that once kept things ticking over. A dog, cat and six hens were enough to be going on with....

'I suppose what I need to do is to go back home tonight, and collect some clothes and then come back tomorrow. I can feed the hens, it won't harm them to stay in the coop for another day, and the cat can be fed in the steading.' She spoke her thoughts aloud; clearly her mind racing over the tasks she had to do over the following few days. 'I can pick up Bella and drop you back into Aberdeen if you want.'

'Mum, I'm not letting you drive me all the way back to Aberdeen tonight, and then drive another hour up to Broadsea. What if I come home with you and maybe you could drop me off at the station at Huntly tomorrow? I would come back here with you, but I have to finish an assignment to hand in for the end of the week.'

'That's what we will do, then. I have to register Granny's death, and sort out the funeral. Oh my goodness, just when I start to think about all that needs to be done. Yes, I think I will be better placed being here where I can find what I might need.'

Iona stood up and collected the dishes from the table. 'Well let's get going, then. It's getting dark and the roads might get slippy if the frost takes. I can drive, Mum. You have had a long and stressful day.'

It didn't take too long to feed Tammy and the hens and make sure they were settled for the night. Iona made sure the cottage was locked up and they set off, hoping that Maisie wouldn't keep them too long when they stopped to pick Bella up. Maisie was very helpful, but also liked a wee gossip and she would no doubt want to know what plans Laura might have for Elsa's funeral.

Thankfully, when they arrived at Maisie's, Charlie, her husband, informed them that she was out attending a community council meeting, so they were excused an interrogation. Bella became overly excited once she recognised Laura, and was happy to be placed in the back seat of the car.

CHAPTER 3

The drive home was uneventful, although Laura was grateful that Iona was doing the driving. She felt exhausted. It was as if all her energy had disappeared. They agreed to stop off at the chip shop for a fish supper rather than cooking. Iona insisted that she would go in and buy their supper. It always took a good while, as Bob who owned the business cooked everything to order, and it allowed Jenny, his wife, to interrogate customers as to what was going on in their lives.

Laura sat back and waited and gazed around her. Broadsea was a rather sprawling village, which snaked around a sandy bay. A small harbour was positioned in the middle of the bay; it had once been home to a local fishing fleet. Nowadays, it offered moorings to a few local boats, whose owners took their boats out for leisure, rather than to make a living. There were several small shops. Most were like Laura's small business, very driven by the seasons, and were closed during the winter. The local Co-op supermarket incorporated the post office; she supposed that they were lucky to still have a post office; there once had been two banks, but both had closed a couple of years ago. The supermarket did well, and had a fairly good selection of groceries; but you would have to drive to Huntly If you wanted to get a big shop. Laura tried hard to use the local shops, otherwise she would feel like a hypocrite, but sometimes it was just too difficult to get all she wanted in the local shops.

During the season the local caravan park brought in more business, certainly the ice cream and sweet shop soaked up the tourists. The fish and chip shop was the only takeaway in the village. There had once been a Chinese takeaway, but it didn't survive the winter months, so the business closed up. The premises were still empty, and people were complaining that they were becoming a bit of an eyesore, annoying many of the residents. The Broadsea Arms was the only pub, and it too struggled in the winter. In the summer it did a rare trade, especially given its position on the seafront. It had commandeered part of the sea front and added some picnic tables, so families could sit outside and enjoy a drink and a meal, letting the children play in the sand while the parents relaxed.

Just two houses along the road was Laura's small premises. A double-fronted shop, which doubled as a tea room and gift shop: Broadsea Gifts and Tea Room. Laura loved it. It was her pride and joy. She had also been thrilled with flat above the shop, which was now her home. She loved her flat, especially the view from her sitting room that overlooked the bay. She also adored her bedroom, which was the second room that overlooked the bay. On winter nights, she loved nothing better than lying in her bed listening as the storms battered the Moray Firth. At the back of the flat there was another bedroom, a kitchen and bathroom. Over the three years she had lived here, she had made it her own. It was comfortably furnished in an eclectic way. She had a good eye, and had scoured the area for bits of furniture that she rubbed down, recovered, and indeed each piece seemed to have been chosen specially to fit into a certain place. Upscaling had now become fashionable, but to Laura, she thought it made sense: why spend loads of money on new furniture when you could make something old, look like new? The outcome of her endeavours was that anyone who entered the bright flat relaxed immediately.

Laura had worked hard to build up her life after the very painful divorce. When she had met Gus nearly twenty-five years ago, she had fallen in love with him. He was then a good-looking, hard-working lad, and as well as being lovers they were also best friends. Gus was just a couple of years older than her and lived in Inverness. Laura had met him when she was at a wedding of one of her friends, and she was immediately smitten with him, just as he was with her. They married just one year later, and lived in Inverness, welcoming first Iona, and then two years later, Liam. Gus had a good job as a plumber, but then set up on his own business. Laura became his book keeper, as well as working part time in a local gift shop. They seemed the perfect family.

It was when Iona had just celebrated her tenth birthday that the image of a perfect family was shattered. Gus had told her that he was leaving her, and wanted a divorce. It had been a huge shock, especially when he admitted that the reason he was leaving was because he had fallen in love with someone else. Laura couldn't believe it; she had had no idea. She knew the old adage that the wife was the last to know, and this proved very true. It turned out the affair had been going on for over a year. Sally, the other woman, was younger and an Australian who had been back packing and working in the local gym. Laura had known that Gus had become a regular visitor to the gym, and had even encouraged him to do so; he had seemed much fitter and happier. Little did she know that the fitness and smiles were because he had a new and younger lady.

The eleven months until the divorce was finalised, were hard. It was so painful for Laura. She was angry and humiliated. Especially when she discovered that Sally was pregnant, and Gus was going happily around Inverness puffing his chest out, and announcing to the world that he was going to become a father. The divorce was messy, but she did have one small victory in her mind: that was when she handed him his books and accounts. He didn't find out till he opened the bag that they were all shredded. Eventually they agreed on a deal; Laura would get the house, and he would walk away with the business. The house held so many memories, and she was lucky it was at the height of the housing boom, so she got a fair amount of money. Laura decided to move back to Broadsea and stay with her dad, who welcomed her and the children. His four-bedroom detached house, where Laura had grown up, was like a beacon of light and security. She certainly made the right decision: just as she sold the house, Gus announced he was moving to Australia with Sally to start up a new life. For her, it had been a relief that she did not have to witness him snuggled up with his new wife and family, but for Iona and Liam, it was painful.

Grant, her dad, had been wonderful. He had welcomed his daughter and grandchildren and had become the male role model for them. He was insistent that there was plenty of room in the house for all of them, and there was no reason why her and the children not to make it their home. They did so, and Laura would be forever grateful to him. There had been times when she fell into a hole of depression, and it was her dad who had persuaded her to seek counselling and not allow Gus's rejection of her to define her future life. She did so, and was able to come out and start to look to the future, but sometimes she still found that her confidence dipped and she still struggled with her self-esteem. There was one thing that she was sure of; she would never allow herself to be in the same situation, which of course meant she wasn't ever going seek another relationship. There was no way she was going to allow the possibility of further hurt, or of someone abusing her trust.

The teenage years had been hard for her children. Iona was someone who just focused on her school work. She had a determination and steeliness in her, to focus on her dream of becoming a doctor. She was a hard worker, and again Laura was thankful to her dad who had masses of patience and had sat with Iona many times and helped her do her homework. Grant's view was that he was delighted to help her, especially after he had retired as an accountant, and had plenty of time on his hands. Liam had found it harder. He had missed his father and while Gus had kept in touch, it wasn't the same. When she had bought the shop and flat, Iona had left to attend university, and Liam had chosen to remain with her father. She had found it strange to be living on her own for the very first time in her life, but it had helped to have them both just around the corner.

What had thrown Laura was when, just over a year ago after Liam had reached his eighteenth birthday, he had told her he wanted to go and live with his father for a while. She understood his need to do so, but waving him off at Aberdeen Airport the day he left had shattered her yet again. He seemed to be doing okay, though, and she tried to speak to him via Facetime as often as possible. He told her that he was not sure how long he was going to stay. She wondered whether he would ever come home, as he seemed to be enthralled with what Australia could offer him.

It was her father again who supported Laura to purchase the shop and flat. She had been able to use the money from her divorce settlement which her dad had helped her to invest. So she was incredibly lucky that she was able to purchase the property outright, which allowed her the opportunity to build her business without the anxiety of making enough money. She was in fact doing okay, and she believed that the next season would be busy, as for the past two years she had built up a trade of customers who came frequently to enjoy her homemade cakes and scones.

It seemed ages until the car door opened, and a rather irritated Iona appeared, passing the very hot packages across to her mother. 'Honestly, that woman never changes!' she yelled. 'She should be recruited by MI5, talk about bloody nosy.'

Iona turned the ignition and drove off at speed, although she hardly got to change gear up to three before she was breaking as they came to a halt outside of Broadsea Gift and Tea Room.

'I should have thought, I could have walked along and got the kettle on, while you got the chips.'

'Kettle, Mum? Please tell me you have either some gin or a bottle of wine. I think we both deserve a drink tonight, don't you?'

A little later, both women had eaten their fish suppers and were on their second glass of wine. Laura had lit the wood burner, which was her most favourite thing, especially on a cold night like tonight. Iona had helpfully taken Bella out on the beach for a run. She returned shaking sand from her coat, something Laura would have to get used to.

'I have been making a list,' she told her daughter. 'One of the first things I will do in the morning is to phone Aunty Vi. I should have done it tonight, but I think I will leave it until tomorrow.'

'How is she doing,? Is she still settled in the sheltered housing flat? How old is she now?'

'She seems fine. I did take Granny to see her about a month ago. She is just coming up eighty-six, in fact it's her birthday next month. She still as bright as a spark; as she says, it's her body that's letting her down. Her arthritis is really making it difficult for her to move around, but she seems happy enough. It's been three years since she gave up the house and moved into the sheltered housing complex. It's a pity she's so far away or otherwise Granny would have been able to visit her more. They enjoyed seeing each other, and I am sure Aunty Vi will be sad, they have been sister-in-laws for such a long time. The only ones of that generation left.'

'Well, for Aunty Vi, she will only have us now, I suppose. Sad that she never married. I will do my best and try to go down to Dundee and visit her more often. I take it she is still as out-spoken ever?'

'Even more so; she seems to have lost whatever filter she once had.' Laura yawned. 'Well, sweetheart, I think I am going to turn in now, I am feeling knackered and it was a good idea to open the wine. I switched the electric blanket on in the back room, so it should be nice and cosy for you. Grandad will come over in the morning and join us for breakfast; he's dying to see you before you go back.'

CHAPTER 4

A very sprightly and cheery Grant arrived the following morning. He was very happy to take an excited and bouncy Bella out for a morning walk on the beach, while Laura cooked breakfast. Laura watched from the sitting room window as her dad walked quickly, throwing a stick; he seemed to really enjoy being with the dog. It was crossing Laura's mind that maybe that might be the answer to what she was going to do with Bella; maybe between her and her dad they would manage her to provide her with a home. From the look on both of their faces when they returned to the flat, it was definitely something worth considering.

Over breakfast, Iona brought her grandad up to date with her studies and gave him a very potted version of her life in Aberdeen. Laura was sure her dad was well able to have an open mind, but clearly Iona wanted to share only some of her life with the elderly man. To Laura, her dad hadn't seemed to age at all. His hair was snow white, but then it had been for as long as she remembered. He had thick hair, and a ruddy complexion; a result of years of living by the sea he always said. He had what might be referred to as a smiley face, and his eyes shone, especially when he caught sight of his beloved child and grandchildren.

Grant always had reflected that he had done okay, bringing up Laura single-handed after her mother died when she was such a wee girl. Devastating, it had been. He could still remember how it felt on that winter's night, when he had opened the front door thirty-seven years ago, to be faced with a police officer. He was given the heart-breaking news that Estelle's car had skidded on black ice, and had hit a tree; she had been killed on impact. Every 5th December, he found himself still thinking of that night, and always placed some flowers on the bend where her life ended. It had been a hugely dark time in his life. If it hadn't been for Laura, he didn't think he would have been able to keep going; she had been the reason he got out of bed every morning. She was his life's work.

'So then, Laura, you've decided to go across to the Glen to stay?'

'Yes, I think that would be best, Dad. It would mean I could start sorting out stuff, and getting things organised.'

'Are you sure you wouldn't want me to come as well? I can easily do so. I've only got a few things I would need to change this week.'

Laura smiled across the table and shook her head. 'It's okay, Dad. I know you have your outing this week with the bowling club, and I can manage. Perhaps, though, once we get a date for the funeral you could come over then, and I am sure I will then need a bit of a hand to sort things out.' She felt a wet nose nudge her under the table. 'Oh, miss, you are being very cheeky if you are thinking I am going to feed you any treats, just because Granny did.' Bella looked at her with such sad eyes that she found herself picking up the edge of a piece of bacon that was still on her plate, and feeding it to her.

'There you are then, Mum. That looks like you have a friend for life and have started something.' Iona laughed. 'You'll regret it.'

'I know, but poor doggy, she must be wondering what is going on. I think we might have another mouth to feed permanently,

Dad.' She looked across the table at her father, while stroking the dog's silky ears.

'I was thinking that this morning. I think we will manage her, Laura. She's getting on herself, and we couldn't abandon her. How many cats are there now?'

'Just the one, Tammy. He's getting on too, not sure how he would settle though but we can see. The hens are a different matter though; I have no idea what we can do with them.'

'I shouldn't worry, lass, there will be someone happy to take them off of your hands. Good layers if I remember rightly. Anyway, we can get that sorted. What a blessing that it's November, at least you don't have the shop to worry about, and it will give you a bit of time to sort your granny's stuff out. Poor Elsa.'

'How long is it since grandad Harry died?' Iona asked, as she buttered another piece of toast. She was thoroughly enjoying having a big cooked leisurely breakfast instead of a piece of toast on the run.

'My Grandad died just when you were a year old, so twenty years ago. Granny's been on her own since then. She of course looked after Grandad for about five years before he died; he became quite frail even though he was only seventy-six when he died. No age at all when you think of Granny.' She waggled her head, motioning across the table. 'Present company provides evidence of that, eh Dad? You are just a spring chicken compared with Granny. I remember Granny always saying that she was sure it was all the soakings Grandad got working on the croft, and his job as a postie. He used to cycle everywhere, he wasn't like Maisie is today with her little van. He only had his bicycle.'

'Another world, wasn't it, when you think about it. Nobody thought anything of walking or riding bikes for miles. Well, think about it; it was three miles into the village from the croft, so that was six miles every day, plus at least another ten delivering around the area. I remember your grandad as a fit man. It was only after he retired that he started to get problems. That's why I am keeping busy,' Grant told both women as they smiled indulgently at him.

'You're fine, Dad. I don't think of you as old, and you keep fit with your bowling and walking. Plus you love organising the village quiz nights; that, I am sure, keeps your mind active.'

'Anyway Grandad, you don't look a day over sixty,' chimed Iona. 'You're still the most handsome man I know.'

'Oh get away with you, both of you. Now lass, you give me a phone tonight to let me know what's happening.' He turned to Iona. 'And you, young lady, just behave yourself and don't break too many boy's hearts with your beautiful smile…and don't forget to warm your stethoscope before planting it on anyone.' This was a standing joke between them from the day Iona left home to go to university. Home for Iona was always her grandad's house, where her childhood bedroom stayed the same and was always waiting for her.

While Iona cleared the breakfast table and washed the dishes, Laura went online to check out what she needed to do to register her granny's death. A task she hadn't done before. She had the death certificate, but realised she might need other documents. She had no idea if her granny had left a will, but she supposed that as her closest living relative she would be the one to inherit what she had. Laura wasn't expecting much, really, apart from the croft which had been in the Kerr family for at least four generations as far as she knew. It suddenly struck her; goodness, there she was worrying about a few animals, but whatever would she do with Birch End?

It didn't take too long before the car was packed with enough clothes and belongings that Laura could stay for an extended period if necessary. At least her dad could keep an eye on her house. Bella was panting in the back of the car, anticipating another trip; she wasn't really used to a travelling in a car, but it didn't seem to bother her too much. The black-and-white collie seemed more fascinated about looking out of the car window and spotting another dog, which triggered a yelp and bark.

Iona laughed when she saw her mum place her iPad into the seat pocket. 'I don't think you'll be getting much use out of that,' she said, 'especially given that Granny didn't do any on-line anything, and the signal is rubbish.'

'Well, that's why last year when I went across for a few days, I purchased a dongle, so I can get Wifi. It's not that fast, but it does mean I can connect with the world. Granny was fascinated when she saw my iPad and what it did. I did suggest she got one, but you know what she was like; she tutted and looked at me as if I had suggested she took a flight to the moon.'

Iona laughed. 'She was quite a character, wasn't she? So stuck in her own little world. Do you think she had ever been on an aircraft in her life?'

'Probably not, taking her to see Aunty Vi, and stopping at the large Tesco's in Dundee was enough to send her into an anxiety crisis. I suppose it was just being so isolated up the Glen for so long. She even stopped going into Deebank for her shopping over ten years ago. Thankfully Maisie and a couple of other neighbours did that for her. She did become a bit of a recluse, sadly, but she was so thrawn, and she just seemed to want to stay in her own small world.'

Iona looked at her watch and anticipated that she would be in time to catch the train from Huntly to Aberdeen. Her mum was a careful driver, but she supposed that was understand-able given that her own mother had been killed driving a car. The roads across country were quite narrow and winding, so they always had to leave plenty of time to get somewhere. 'What did Aunty Vi have to say, when you told her about Granny?'

'She responded just as I expected, without much fuss. I think the older women in our family are stoic and feisty; maybe they were products of a much harsher life than that as we know it. They certainly have always been very independent women. Aunty Vi never married, she always said she was married to teaching. She did well, though, becoming a head teacher, and still likes to think of herself as such, but has swapped the school for the sheltered housing complex. I think she certainly rubs some of the other residents, and probably the warden, up the wrong way with her domineering ways.'

'I know. I was really cringing when I went down with you last year. Goodness, she seems to think she is running the place. I just felt for warden and that other lady who was in to organise some activities for the residents.' With that, Iona checked her bag and reached into it to get her purse, ready to purchase her train ticket, as her mum negotiated the car into the drop-off space outside the small rural train station. She leant over to hug her mother. 'Bye, Mum. Give me a text or a ring once you sort out when the funeral will be. The sooner you find out the better, so I can organise my rota and stuff. And, Mum... take care of yourself, I haven't seen much sign of grief yet...' She smoothed her mother's cheek. 'Just give yourself a bit of time, I know you loved your Granny.'

'Thanks, love, just you get yourself off and get your ticket before the train gets here.'

Laura watched her daughter stride over towards the ticket office. Her long legs glided along the pathway; her long fair hair fell loosely around her shoulders. She was so proud of her daughter, so caring and loving, and to her mind also beautiful, although she had to admit she was biased. More than anything, she was pleased she seemed to be doing so well in her life. Iona was much taller than her, taking after Gus, who was tall and slim. She did, though, have the same eyes as her. Their eyes were, they had been both told, their greatest feature.

Brown. Like amber, she had been told many times.

CHAPTER 5

Laura already had a loose plan in her mind. Firstly she would get herself ensconced into Birch End, and then she would have a look through some of her granny's paperwork, to see if she could find maybe her birth or marriage certificates. If she couldn't, then she might find something else she could take to the registrars tomorrow to register her death. She would also give the undertaker a phone, hopefully to get a potential date for the funeral. That was something else Laura was hoping to discover: whether Granny had left any instructions for what she wanted to happen. She had never discussed it, and the only thing that she thought might be a guide was that Grandad had been buried in the local churchyard, and somehow she thought Granny might want to be laid with him.

Once she had unpacked her car, she let the hens out; they were definitely looking as though they had had enough being in their run and coop. They quickly made their escape and ran for freedom, clucking and flapping as they did so. Tabby was also pleased to see her, and almost tripped her up as he weaved in and out of her legs. She almost dropped the four brown eggs that the hens had gifted to her.

The cottage had a musky smell, so Laura decided to brave the cool air and open a window just to let some fresh air in to penetrate the kitchen. After putting the kettle on, she unloaded the fresh food she brought with her. Taking a more critical look around her, Laura realised that her granny hadn't been able to do much cleaning recently, and there were several signs of decay. That might be one of her first jobs – giving the bathroom and kitchen a bit of a clean – before she started on her other tasks. She had brought some bedding with her, and gathered it up and decided that she would make up one of the beds upstairs. She would need to check that the beds weren't damp, and when entering one of the two upstairs bedrooms, she thought that was unlikely as the storage heater was blasting out heat. It almost felt as though the room was too hot. She wondered when her grandmother had last climbed the stairs. Possibly it had been some time ago and she wouldn't have thought to adjust the heaters. Goodness, the last time she stayed overnight was last April, to celebrate her granny's birthday. Chances were the storage heater had been blasting out heat all through the summer. Oh well, at least there were no worries about damp mattresses.

It was late afternoon before Laura completed a clean of the cottage, which included stripping her granny's bed. That led to her shedding some tears, as she caught the smell of her granny's soap when she collected up the bedding to place in the washing machine. There was one thing that the elderly woman had been fastidious about, and that was her personal hygiene. This included the weekly changing of bedding. Every Monday morning without fail, the bed would be changed and a clean nightdress would be placed under the pillow. Towels, tea towels, in fact anything that had been worn or used would be washed. When the weather allowed, it was then hung out to dry on the back green, and during bad weather it was hung in the drying rack which was suspended to the kitchen ceiling and had a pulley which allowed access. Laura had had many discussions with her granny about the latter method not being really the most sensible, given it took quite a lot of strength to pull the rope to get the rack back up. She couldn't help smiling as she recalled the way her granny had just given her one of her looks. That was enough to tell her that it was not worth any further discussion.

It looked like the bedding would be blowing on the outside line tomorrow, as by the time the washing machine had finished its cycle it was almost dark. It was dark by four in the afternoon this time of the year, but according to the weather forecast it would be a bright day tomorrow. Laura then just remembered to gather the hens up, and make sure that they were safely penned up for the night. They had been quite compliant, thankfully, almost as though they had had enough of foraging for the day.

With a mug in her hands Laura sat in one of the arm chairs and after a while took up the large box she had found under her granny's bed which appeared to contain lots of papers. She opened the box and started to pick out various documents. It did feel a little strange, almost as though she was prying, but she had to do it. The top of the box contained a number of utility bills. Some dated back to several years. She placed them on one side: at least she knew who Elsa's energy supplier and her account number were.

The next paperwork was documents relating to other official correspondence. Some of it related to her grandmother's pension. Another helpful item she would need. As she worked her way through the box, she didn't find anything that gave her any clues about what her grandmother's wishes were. She at last found an old tin, which looked as though it had contained sweets or chocolates. The tin itself looked like it was from something in the fifties, purchased as a memento from a holiday somewhere. In fact when she looked at closely she could see faded letters outlined: *Present from North Berwick.* It took a little tugging to get the lid off, and when she did so she was rewarded with other folded pieces of slightly faded paper. The first she opened was her grandfather Harry's death certificate.

She noted that it was dated September 10th 2000. It gave his cause of death as pneumonia.

The next piece of paper she found was a newspaper cutting, and when Laura opened it out, it took her breath away. It was a piece that had appeared in the *Press and Journal* dated 7th December 1983, two days after the death of her mother. Alongside of the write up of how a car had left the road and a young wife and mother had been killed - was a photo of her mum. One she still had tucked away in amongst other photos of her. She had looked so young, but of course she had been, she had only been thirty-three years old. She was so young, and so bonny. Laura could see the resemblance to herself; she smoothed the newspaper out and studied her mother's face. She looked kind, she reflected. From all she had been told, that was exactly right; many people had told her over the years how Estelle had been a kind, thoughtful and funny woman. One of her lifelong regrets was that she never had the chance to find out more. She had had to use her imagination to think what it might have been like to have her mother in her life, especially at special times, like her wedding day and the day the children were born. The sadness never seems to go away, but she supposed that must have been the same for her poor granny. Estelle had been her only child: such loss. Laura couldn't recall how her grandparents had reacted at the time. She was in a state of shock herself and doubtless they had been too.

Before she delved into any other bits of paper she decided to take a bit of a break. Perhaps she would empty one of the plastic cartons, which contained one of the homemade ready meals she had brought with her into a dish, and put it into the oven to heat up. She had also brought a couple of bottles of wine with her, and so she made the decision that before she found any more reminders from the past, she would pour herself a glass of wine to enjoy with her supper. Although it was still only early evening it was pitch black outside. She always forgot about the darkness in the Glen – no street lights, only the light of the moon to guide you on a night. She could also hear the wind get up and starting to whistle as it spun across the hills. Not a night to venture out, she thought.

After she had eaten and consumed a large glass of wine, Laura returned to the tin box. There was an envelope which she opened and removed from it a small written note. She recognised her grandmother's spindly writing, and took a breath as she read it.

To whom it may concern.

I Elsa Kerr, born on the 8th April 1928, do leave all my possessions and worldly goods including Birch End, Glen Gavin, to my granddaughter Laura Simpson. I hope she will look after it, and carry on the Kerr legacy.

I don't want a big fuss for any funeral. Just bury me with my Harry who was both the love of my life and my saviour. Without Harry I wouldn't have lived a long life. I was born a Catholic, but don't let any priest near me, they can never be trusted. Just something simple, a few words beside the grave will be fine with me; maybe the sound of the bagpipes would be nice.

I appoint my granddaughter Laura Simpson as my executor in all matters pertaining to my estate.

Signed: Elsa Kerr Dated 1st December 2000

Witnessed by: Violet Kerr 1st December 2000

So, it seemed that she had found her grandmother's will. She wasn't sure how well it would stand up in any legal system, but at least it had been witnessed by her Auntie Vi. There was one really positive piece of information, and that was she now knew her grandmother's wishes. This meant that she could now organise the funeral as a quiet graveside affair, rather than as a church service. She was surprised to learn, though, that her grandmother had been a Catholic; this was the first she had known about this. She clearly had had an issue with a priest along the way, given how she had phrased *"Don't let any priest near me."* That seemed a strong statement. Maybe Auntie Vi would be able to shred a little light onto this.

Laura was well aware that neither of her grandparents were church-goers. Religion wasn't anything they discussed. Her own mother hadn't been religious either, but had got married in the Church of Scotland, and so when it came time for her funeral she had had a church service. Laura remembered that the church had been packed out, and that there were even people standing. It had been surreal to walk past them all as she followed her mother's coffin out of the church. She shivered just thinking about it, and recalled how it felt, with everyone's eyes on her. She had tried hard to be brave and not cry. She did not want to upset her dad; he had cried a lot since the policeman had given them the news. Laura let her mind return to those weeks and months after the accident. It had been a horrible time. Everywhere she looked reminded her of her mum, and that she was no longer going to come through the door with her happy smile. She often wondered if losing her mum at such an early age had added to her lack of confidence, and anxiety. She worried sometimes about silly things, she knew, things she couldn't do anything about. But it was as though her mother's death had left a legacy behind, that of expecting another catastrophe to be waiting to strike at any moment.

Setting the will to one side, she delved into the box again. This time she found the death certificates of her great-grandparents, Duncan Kerr who died in 1968, aged sixty-nine and Grace Kerr who was seventy-four when she died in 1970. Laura never knew her great-grandparents. She only had a few photos of them, but no doubt Auntie Vi would be able to enlighten her about them. Goodness, maybe Auntie Vi was the holder of lots of information that she hadn't really thought much about, up until now.

Another sip of wine, and the next very faded piece of paper she opened out was her grandparent's marriage certificate. Oh me, this is lovely, she thought, as she started to read it. It seemed they were married in a civil register office, in Edinburgh on 5th May 1948. Harry's address was Birch End, and his occupation was recorded as a Crofter. Great-grandad Duncan and Grace were noted as his parents. Laura's eyes widened as she read the details of her grandmother. Elsa Wouters was aged twenty. No occupation was recorded, but what made Laura's eyes widen was that Elsa's address was recorded as Klapdorp 25, Antwerp, Belgium. Her parents were recorded as Dr Martin Wouters and her mother Estelle Wouters. They were both recorded as being deceased.

Well, blow me down, she thought. Just then the phone rang, and Laura got up to answer it. It was her father, checking that she was okay. Laura shared what she had discovered in the box. 'Did you know that Granny had come from Belgium, Dad?' she enquired.

'No, I didn't, your mother never spoke about it. I do recall that I asked her about her other grandparents, and she said she had never met them and they had died in the war. Now I do recall her saying that her parents had met during the war, but it was all a bit of a no-go area to speak about it. I suppose, lass, that it wasn't too surprising, as after the war lots of folk didn't speak about it. So its news to me too. Shame you can't ask her, isn't it? But you know, even if you had done, I am not convinced Elsa would have told you if she didn't want you to know. She was closed off in a lot of ways. So what are you going to do about the funeral, lass?'

Laura put the receiver under her shoulder as she poured herself another glass of wine and took it back to the easy chair. 'I will speak to the funeral director tomorrow morning; I am sure he will arrange the time and deal with the lair being opened and all that. I am going to head into Deebank tomorrow morning and register her death, now I have some documents. I haven't discovered her birth certificate yet, but maybe I won't.'

'Quite likely you won't, love. She could have lost it during the war; she would have more than likely had an identification card then. Maybe you'll discover that. Who knows, you might be related to half of Belgium.'

They spoke about several other things, and then she realised how tired she was. She supposed that she had had a long day. After saying goodnight to her father, she let Bella out for a final pee before trudging up the stair to a very cosy bedroom. As she floated off to sleep, she couldn't help but wonder how her grandparents had met, and how Elsa had ended up travelling from Antwerp to spend most of her life living in a Scottish glen.

CHAPTER 6

Laura slept well, and probably would have continued in her deep slumber if she hadn't been awakened by a wet nose prodding her hand. There was a short time delay before her conscious mind spun into action, and she realised where she was, and opened her eyes to come face to face with a rather eager black-and-white dog. 'Good morning to you too, Bella.' She reached out to smooth the top of the dog's head. Then, turning to look at her alarm clock she realised why she had been abruptly awoken: it was nearly nine o'clock. This, she suspected, was at least two hours past the normal time of Bella getting up and on with the day.

Laura was still a little sleepy as she made her way down the stairs, letting Bella out for a pee, before then making her way to the bathroom to do the same. The bathroom window was frosted up; it was certainly the coldest room in the house, having been added on at some point in the past.

Once she had a mug of tea and Bella had been fed her breakfast, Laura took a little time to browse the news, check her emails and Facebook on her iPad. All the time she was half thinking about what she needed to do today, making a mental list. Number one was to go into Deebank and visit the registrar, to register Elsa's death, followed by the visit to the undertaker to sort through the arrangements for the funeral. This was now much easier given she was aware of her grandmother's wishes.

Before all of that she needed to sort out some breakfast, have a quick shower, and then deal with the hens.

Thankfully she had completed all of those initial tasks before she caught sight of the small red postie van driving towards the cottage. She went out to meet Maisie, who was making her way towards her carrying some mail, and trying to cope with the welcome that Bella was bestowing on the visitor.

'Well hello there, Laura, how are you bearing up?' She strode across the yard, her small rotund body moving quickly. She handed Laura a couple of brown envelopes, and then stood back, waiting for a reply.

'I am doing okay, thanks Maisie, just trying to sort out some things of course. Thanks again for helping my gran; I don't know how she would have coped without you. It certainly meant she could stay here, rather than go into care. A subject we were not allowed to discuss with her, I must add.'

'Oh, I know, she was a very independent woman was your gran. Talk about doing things her way, I think I learnt early on, that she wasn't going to do it any other way.' Maisie stopped for a moment seemingly contemplating how to phrase the next question. 'I suppose Birch End will be yours now. Any idea what you will do with it? Blimey, I think it's been in the Kerr family for generations, and poor Elsa sometimes worried about what would happen to it.' She stopped and gazed around her. 'It needs a lot doing to it, mind you.'

'It's a bit early for me to think about all that, Maisie. It's all come about a bit quick.' Laura realised that of course Maisie was fishing, so that she could transfer that news to the village. 'No doubt I will have to have a good think. Firstly though I have to organise Granny's funeral.'

Maisie's ears pricked up. 'So any ideas when it will be, will you be having a service in the church? I canna say I have ever seen your granny in the church mind you, but then she was rarely seen in the village at all, these past few years.'

'I will be sorting it out later, but no it won't be a church service, as you say she wasn't a church-goer and whatever it will be it will be quite simple. I hope you will manage to come though, Maisie, as you and a few others were who my granny relied on as friends and neighbours.'

'Aye, of course Charlie and I will be there. I am sure that Ted Mclean, and Jenny and Sid Topping will be there too to pay their last respects. We used to take it in turns to look in on Elsa, and certainly Ted used to take her backwards and forwards to the village when she needed to go.' Maisie looked at her watch, realising she needed to get on; there had been an odd complaint made about the wait for the post, and so she was careful not to spend too long chatting along the way. 'Just give me a call when you get things firmed up, and I will let the others know, Laura. Look after yourself, lass. Your gran was a lovely lady and I will miss her.'

It didn't take long to register Elsa's death; it was all very straightforward. She was also relieved when the registrar told her that she would be able to inform the pension people, so one less job for Laura to have to think about. The next on the list was the undertaker. Jim asked if she would like to view her granny's body. It took a little moment but Laura shook her head. She had been with her when she died, and didn't need any other viewings. The undertaker was very helpful and had already been in contact with the Council to arrange the opening of the lair, so that Elsa's body could be placed with her husband. He was also happy to arrange for the notice to go into the paper, and helped her form the words needed. Lastly, they agreed that the funeral would take place the following Tuesday, in five days' time: apparently it was much easier to arrange a funeral if it was just a burial. What, he asked, was she planning for afterwards?

This was something that Laura had spoken to her dad about

the evening before. The options were that they could arrange for one of the hotels in the village to provide a funeral tea, or they could invite people back to Birch End. They agreed that it was unlikely that many people would attend apart from the immediate neighbours. Elsa had been very much someone who hadn't had a group of friends, and so it was not likely that there would be hordes of folk attending. When Laura informed him that they would invite folk back to Birch End for a cuppa and a sandwich, Jim was very forthcoming in recommending one of the cafes who did outside catering. That was a little of a relief for Laura, as Elsa's kitchen was not really set up for catering. Armed with this information, she made her way to the café, and firstly ordered a latte, before arranging with the café owner an order for Tuesday. Given the funeral would take place in the early afternoon; they agreed that the owner would drop off the order at Birch End in the morning.

After sampling a large cheese scone to accompany her coffee, Laura decided she had made a good choice. She had probably over-ordered, and they would likely to have an overload of sausage rolls and cake, but it felt the right thing to do, for Elsa.

There was one last thing on her list to do today, and that was the visit to the solicitor who she had arranged an appointment with before she had left the house. Laura had used a solicitor for her divorce and purchasing the shop, but apart from that, she really didn't have anyone who she would necessarily consider as her own legal advisor. She had decided this morning that it probably made sense to speak to a local one, and luckily they were able to fit her into their appointments list. She found their office easily, and was reassured by the professionalism of the solicitor, who introduced herself as Susan Williams. Laura needed some confirmation that Elsa's written wishes would be considered legally acceptable, and was somewhat relieved when Susan advised that they would be. She suggested that it might be helpful if Laura could find any other legal documents, such as the deeds of the Birch End, although she would do a search if not. It would, she was informed, take some time for the estate to be dealt with, but at least Laura felt she was on safe ground. It was by now afternoon, and it felt like that was enough for one day. She was feeling rather tired: she supposed that all this sorting out was quite emotionally tiring. So she headed back up the road to the Glen, and decided that she would take Bella for a walk along the river before it got dark.

Bella was certainly happy to see her. After she had donned her walking boots and her woolly hat, they set off across the field behind the cottage where there was a pathway that led through some woods, before it came out alongside the River Dee. This wasn't part of Elsa's estate; the banks and the fishing rights to them were owned by the local laird. It was a path that Laura had walked all of her life. As a child she had spent time staying with her grandparents during the school holidays. Her dad had always encouraged her to keep in contact with them, and it was rather exciting to stay with them when the croft was working at full pent. She recalled when she and Elsa would take the dogs – there had always been two border collies when she had been a child, and they would take them down to the river on a warm afternoon so they could cool off. On the occasional really hot summers' day, Laura was allowed to paddle in the shallow River Dee too. She now stood on the exact spot where they would do this, but currently the river was in full spate; so there was no chance for either herself or Bella to paddle now. The autumn colours were fabulous, though. Some of the trees had lost their leaves, but these were now providing a brown and yellow floor covering. The late afternoon sun was shining onto the river as it rushed and splattered over the rocks. The wind had dropped, and now the air was still, with just the sound of the river and birds filling the void.

Laura found a large rock and sat on it, while throwing the stick for Bella to fetch. As she gazed around, Laura's memories of the happy times she had spent here rose up. She could visu-alise her granny now, sitting beside her, doling out the home-made lemonade and the large slice of her special apple cake. Just for a moment, Laura felt her granny beside her: *So, Granny, what do you think about it all, I wonder*? A sense of sadness crept over her, realising that she would never see her again. While it had been some time since she had accompanied her granny to this place, she knew, it hadn't been that long since her granny had walked the same pathway, and maybe even had sat on the same rock. She just hoped that wherever she was now, she was at peace.

That evening Laura didn't have much motivation to do any-thing apart from speaking to her dad and Iona. She had sent Liam a message, and was still waiting for a reply. She was a lit-tle disappointed that he hadn't replied, but then she told her-self the time difference may have not helped. Surely, though, he would send her some sort of reply to let her know he had re-ceived it. She was determined she wasn't going to contact him through Gus – he hadn't really been a fan of her grandmother, finding her, as he had put it, a bit odd.

Laura was missing the television. She found it strange to be somewhere without access to one. It was often on in her flat, even if it was in the background. But not having access to it, and with her Wifi not being good enough to watch much on her iPad, she took herself off to her bed much earlier that she would usually. Maybe she wouldn't manage to stay here all on her own until after the funeral, but it would be silly to drive home. She made a decision that if her dad was okay about it, she would get him to come over at the weekend. She knew his bowls outing would be over by then, and she would welcome his company.

CHAPTER 7

The weekend passed really quickly, especially after the arrival of Grant on Friday evening. Laura, pleased with his company, cooked one of his favourite dishes for his arrival. Toad in the hole; this was indeed a family favourite, and this one was special as the sausages were from the local butcher, renowned for making their own tasty and meaty ones. Laura had insisted that her dad leave Broadsea before it was dark, as she worried about him driving across country roads in the dark. He would never admit it, but she knew that his eyesight at night was not as acute as it had once been. It had been a relief to see the headlights of his car driving down the driveway. They had spent a very companionable evening, before launching into sorting the cottage out over the following two days. Laura had realised that there could be more folk attending the funeral than she first thought. She had had visits by several of the folk who lived in the Glen, as well as some folk who knew her gran from Deebank. Laura's two closest friends had advised her they were coming too, and Iona had called to say that her flatmate, Tony, was coming with her. Laura was looking forwards to casting her eye over the so-called flatmate: she was sure that he was more than that to Iona.

So over the weekend her dad helped her to move Elsa's big bed back upstairs to the other bedroom. This in fact had been Elsa's original bedroom. The two old armchairs that matched the uncomfortable sofa had been stored up there, and she realised that no way would she have been able to transport the heavy and bulky furniture down the narrow stairway on her own. They had to take a break once they had managed it, with a cuppa and a piece of cake before they started the big clean up.

The more furniture Laura moved around, the more she realised that Elsa had been struggling for some time. The amount of dust and muck that lurked behind and under the bed and chest of drawers proved that nothing had been moved since it was placed there all those years ago. Thankfully, the heavy Victorian wardrobe had remained in its original position, in the upstairs bedroom. They still wondered how on earth it had been transported upstairs in the first place, and the idea of trying to move it seemed impossible. Elsa hadn't been that bothered, and she had been happy to hang a few of her clothes she required on the rail that Laura had bought her when they had originally moved her downstairs. There was no doubt, though, that nothing had been cleaned or hoovered for some considerable time. Once all the furniture had been removed and the whole house hoovered, and cleaned from top to bottom, it not only looked better, but smelt better also.

The bathroom had a special going over, and Grant insisted on giving it a coat of paint, especially where there were signs of dampness. He reckoned it was due mostly to condensation. The bath had been removed a few years ago, and an electric shower installed. It had initially taken some convincing and cajoling by both Laura and Grant until eventually Elsa had agreed to the shower. After it had been installed, she had mentioned more than once that it was much better than trying to get in and out of the bath. It had been a bit of a relief to know that Elsa wasn't stuck in the bath, and the shower cabinet had been fitted out with rails so she could manage it securely. Once Grant had finished painting, it did indeed look better.

Now the sitting room was back to its original state, and it seemed to be okay. The fireplace was still in working order: Elsa was always meticulous in ensuring that the chimney was kept swept. She was insistent that she always wanted a back-up in case there was a power cut. They found some logs and coal in the steading, so a fire was lit, just to ensure it was okay. Laura looked around and was thankful that they had changed the room back to the original sitting room: it was just as she recalled it as a child.

Auntie Vi was going to be collected by Iona on the morning of the funeral. She was going to stay overnight, and Laura would take her back the following day. They decided that Grant would move upstairs to sleep in the reinstated bedroom, and that meant Auntie Vi could have the back bedroom and be close to the bathroom. They realised that in fact that had been Vi's bedroom when she lived at Birch End, so no doubt it would bring back some memories. Whether they would be happy ones, who knew.

The night before the funeral the cottage looked lovely. Even Bella was delighted to lie in front of the coal fire. It was cold outside with what seemed to be a hard frost, but the forecast for the following day was that was to be bright and sunny. Thank goodness for that – a burial in horizontal rain was not much fun. Laura had received two lovely bunches of flowers, one from her long-time friend Val, and the other from Hamish McKenzie, the local laird. That was a bit of a surprise, as he had very little to do with neighbours and spent more time in his other residence than his Highland estate. Grant wondered what was behind that, as he was pretty sure Elsa had very little to do with him. She owned the croft, unlike some of the other residents of Glen Gavin. He couldn't help being a tad suspicious of why he was making the gesture now. He didn't voice his thoughts, though; Laura had enough to contend with at the moment, and was working so hard at ensuring that Elsa's final send-off would go without any hitches.

CHAPTER 8

The morning of the funeral was indeed very bright and sunny, but bitterly cold. Nevertheless, it brought with it a sense of relief that the winter sunshine would make the whole event easier to deal with. The cottage looked lovely; the dark furniture gleamed after extensive polishing, the scent of the flowers penetrated throughout, and when the café owner dropped off the food for the get-together afterwards, both Laura and Grant were impressed. 'Goodness me, lass,' Grant said, peering into the box of sandwiches, sausage rolls, scones and home bakes. 'They have certainly done a fine job here. Let's hope plenty of folk come back after, otherwise this will go to waste.'

'We will just need to ensure we eat it, Dad. In fact we could have a few of those sandwiches for our lunch. I am pleased they also have given us the loan of the big teapot and crockery.' Laura pulled a large metal teapot out of another box and started laying out cups and saucers onto the table. 'They even have loaned us another kettle.' She paused for a moment and looked around her. 'I can just hear Granny saying, make sure we don't waste anything.'

Iona eventually arrived, having phoned to say she had been held up. Seemingly Auntie Vi had been faffing about, and it had taken much longer than expected to load her into the car. She had sent a text to say that it looked like she was intending to stay for longer than one night, given the amount of clothes she had packed. Another text arrived to say please don't ask Tony too many questions; that implied that she was a little wary of introducing Tony to her mum and grandfather, goodness knows why.

If Laura had been with her she would have had an insight as to why that text had arrived: Tony had already been exposed to an interrogation by Auntie Vi on the journey from Dundee. She had asked him every question she could think of. Questioning him on his family background, his current circumstances, and she had even got him to admit to her that yes, he and Iona were more than flatmates. That admission had almost caused Iona to swerve the car. She hadn't even shared that with her mum yet, and no doubt Auntie Vi would make the announcement before she had the chance to do so.

That was in fact exactly what happened. She didn't even have the chance to introduce Tony, before her elderly great aunt did so, announcing as she got out of the car, 'Iona's young man is very nice. Such a handsome young man, maybe we will end up with two doctors in the family, Laura, wont that be handy.'

Laura couldn't help smiling at having her suspicions confirmed. She noticed her daughter's blush, but also a slight incline of her head to convey her apology. She welcomed Tony, who was indeed a good-looking man, tall and dark with a strong jaw line, and kind warm eyes. 'It's so nice to finally meet you, Tony.' She dispensed with the handshake and gave him a hug. 'You are very welcome, and thank you so much for coming with Iona and supporting her.'

'It's no problem, Mrs Simpson. I am pleased to finally meet you too.' He moved across to shake Grant's hand. 'And you must be Iona's grandad, I have heard so much about you. Lovely to put a face to the name at last.' He gave Iona a cheeky grin just to make the point.

'Just make sure you call us by our Christian names, Tony. I am

Grant, and Mrs Simpson over there goes by Laura. She tells everyone to do so, isn't that right, lass?'

Laura was in the process of hugging Iona, who was whispering in her ear how sorry she was and had intended to introduce Tony as her partner today. But of course Auntie Vi got there first.

Auntie Vi's case was unloaded and she then inspected, and confirmed, that she was very happy to be sleeping in her old childhood bedroom. She also was delighted when she realised that the bathroom had been fitted with aids that meant she could manage it without any help. The comment she made about how lovely it would be to spend a couple of days in her old childhood home didn't go unnoticed. Once all of the inspection was completed, there was just time to hand them a cup of tea and a sandwich before the funeral hearse made its way slowly down the drive.

'Oh flip,' said Iona, trying not to laugh. 'Poor Granny, she is certainly getting a bumpy ride home. And then she's going to have to do it again in a wee while too.'

Auntie Vi was a little put out that there was no funeral car for them to follow the hearse. 'Why on earth not, Laura?' she enquired. 'Was it to do with the money? Because if so, you only had to ask, you know, if you were short.'

'No, it had nothing to do with the money or costs, Auntie Vi. It was just that Granny had left a note with her wishes. It was very clear and she said didn't want any fuss. You must remember that: you even witnessed the note.'

'Oh, that wee note. Well, not wanting a fuss is one thing, but surely, Laura, it's the decent thing to do is it not, for the close family to arrive in a funeral car? How are we supposed to get there?'

'You can come with Dad and me, and Iona and Tony will follow us. We are only going to the graveside after all, and it's a mile along the road, Auntie. I just didn't think it was necessary.' Laura felt a little put out, as she hadn't given it much thought that it would cause any issues in taking their own cars. It literally was just over a mile to the cemetery, and hardly seemed as though a large car was worth it. She decided she wouldn't get into any further discussion about it, and helped her aunt into the front seat of her father's car, before looking across and catching a wink from him. That smoothed her concern. She then ensured that Bella was locked securely in the house before the small possession started off.

The piper was waiting for the funeral cortege to arrive, and started playing a lament as Elsa's casket was unloaded onto a trolley. Laura was quite surprised by the number of folk gathered at the gate of the cemetery, who bowed their heads in respect as the funeral director led the way along the pathway to the open grave. Laura and her dad helped Auntie Vi, who found walking a little difficult, and the last thing any of them wanted was for her to fall. It took a little time until everyone reached the graveside. Jim, the funeral director, stepped forward. It had been previously agreed that he would lead the short committal. He called on Laura to say something, so she took a deep breath and stepped up beside the graveside and began.

'My dear Granny, Elsa Kerr, has lived a long life. She has lived here on Deeside since she married my grandad, her husband Harry, in 1948, and has never left Glen Gavin since. Granny loved the countryside, nature and said she had no need to seek other places to go. She was a kind, gentle soul, who was very private. She was a woman of few words, but the words she spoke always had a meaning. She didn't suffer fools gladly, but as a child I never experienced her raising her voice, even when I managed to break her most favourite jug. Believe me; I wouldn't have been so forgiving.' Laura paused, listening to a titter of laughter. 'Granny loved her animals, especially her dogs, and she always said they were the most faithful friends you could have, they never speak any ill.

'So.' Laura paused again and felt tears welling up; she swallowed and took another deep breath. 'So, I will miss you, Granny. I will always hold you in my memory. I hope your journey wherever you are brings you peace, I know..' She found tears rolling down her face, and Iona moved to her side, so that she could place her arm around her mother, '...I want you to know, Granny, that you were well loved.'

Jim thanked Laura, and asked Iona to step forwards and read the poem that Laura had found, tucked away in a small book of poetry that had been in her granny's bedside table. It must have meant something to her, and so it seemed appropriate for it to be read now.

When I come to the end of the road,
And the sun has set for me
I want no rites in a gloom filled room
Whey cry for a soul set free?
Miss me a little – but not for long.
And not with your head bowed low.
Remember the love we once shared.
Miss me, but let me go.
For this is journey we must all take.
And each must go alone
It's all part of the master plan,
A step on the road to home,
Laugh at all the things we used to do.
Miss me, but let me go.

Iona read the poem very well, her soft Scottish lilt bringing the words to life. Hearing it read here seemed to sum up her granny, and brought on a fresh set of new tears.

Jim took over then and made the committal. He invited Laura to be the first to throw a rose into the grave, and others followed her. The piper started up and again and the small gathering listened to the sound of the pipes as they seemed to bounce and reverberate off the surrounding hills.

It was a cold day, but the sun shone, and the autumn colours seemed to signify that it was the right time for her granny to leave them. It had been a very simple service, but again that seemed to fit with the simple life that she had lived. Laura wiped her eyes and blew her nose, and then asked Jim to announce that everyone would be welcome to return to Birch End for a cuppa and some refreshments. She had counted nineteen people, and thankfully she had more than twenty cups so all was well.

Once everyone had crowded into the cottage it was full to the brim. Iona and Tony helped to fill the teapot and hand around the cups and food. Several of the folk had come up to offer their condolences to Laura, and she was comforted by seeing her own dear friends who hugged her tightly, and said that they would just have a quick cuppa and then make their journey back to Broadsea. Bella was banished to the steading, as she kept getting under everyone's feet, and nearly tripped up an elderly man who had known Elsa he said, for the past forty years. Laura could hear Bella barking, but she was safer out there than in the cottage, and once everyone left, she would no doubt enjoy hoovering up the crumbs that people were dropping on the floor.

The guests began to thin out, leaving just a handful in the sitting room where Auntie Vi was holding court. Iona arrived in the kitchen to fill up the teapot again, laughing as she did so. 'Goodness me, I think Aunty Vi has definitely lost her filter. You ought to have heard what she had just said to Maisie.'

Laura looked up as she removed the last of the sausage rolls from the oven where they were being heated through. 'Don't tell me, she is being rude to poor Maisie.'

'She has just told her that she remembered her granny, who when she was a young girl would lift her skirts for any man.'

'Oh, for goodness sakes, I don't think I even want to guess how Maisie took that. '

'I think it is the first time I have ever known Maisie to be lost for words.'

Tony appeared beside Iona, carrying an empty plate. Laura was impressed by the way he had just got on with helping without any fuss, as though he was part of the family. 'Please don't tell me that she has insulted anyone else in there.'

'Well, she is now sharing her views on religion, saying that all priests and vicars are cheats and child abusers.'

'Right,' said Laura as she wiped her hands on a tea towel. 'Iona, could you bring the rest of those sausage rolls through? I am going to put an end to her holding court, before she does any further damage.' Angus Mckay was an elder of the church, and his wife was the organist, so she could only but imagine what they must be thinking.

Thankfully by the time Laura reached the sitting room, Grant had intervened and moved the conversation away from religion onto the weather. Auntie Vi looked pleased with herself, and it struck Laura how much the elderly woman enjoyed causing a stir, and clearly she knew exactly what she was doing. It had one result, and that was to spur folk to think about leaving. They all thanked Laura, and told her just to let them know if they could do anything. Jane Spark, who lived at the other end of the Glen, had offered a solution to her hen problem: she said she would be very happy to take them and add them to her brood. That was one thing ticked off of Laura's list, and they arranged that she would collect them the following day.

Once everyone had left, leaving just the family members, Iona and Tony insisted that Laura sit down while they washed up. She didn't argue, feeling as though the energy had left her body, and she sat on the hard sofa, plumping up the cushions to try to make it slightly more comfortable. She was pleased to take the weight off of her legs, and realised she probably hadn't sat down since she ate breakfast.

'Well now, Laura, I think that went off really well; just the ticket,' Grant told her. 'Don't you agree, Vi?'

'Yes, I suppose that it was okay, and you were absolutely right not to have a church service, Laura. Elsa would have been rolling in her grave if you had. She had no time for religion at all; she always was very clear on that. Now I think I need to go and use the facilities. Perhaps you could give me a hand up. I think I will stay an extra day, Laura, I could do with a little break and now I am here, I might as well stay for two nights, rather than rushing back tomorrow. That will be okay, won't it?'

Laura was pleased to help her auntie into her bed later that evening. Iona and Tony had left to return to Aberdeen. Iona had given her mother a huge hug, and told her not to let Auntie Vi run her ragged. She told them that Iona must bring Tony to Broadsea for a weekend, or just out for a meal, so they could get a chance to speak properly and get to know him under better circumstances. He had announced that he would love to visit them, and put his arm around Iona's shoulders, looking to her for confirmation that she would arrange the visit. She had nodded to him and then hugged her grandfather, telling him to be careful when he returned home the following day. He hugged her back, and told her to stop being bossy. That brought a smirk to Tony's face as he had mumbled, 'That would be a first, if she stopped being bossy.'

Sitting beside the now dying embers of the fire, Grant and Laura enjoyed a nightcap. He nursed a single malt, while she sipped a Baileys. 'It's been a long day, hasn't it? Are you okay, Dad?' she enquired, noticing that he looked exhausted. 'You have helped so much in the last few days with all the moving of furniture and painting, I hope you haven't overdone it.'

He shook his head before taking a sip of the amber liquid, and swilling it in his mouth before swallowing. 'Not at all, lass, I can easy stay a few more days if you need me. Especially now as it seems you will have a house guest for an extra day.' He nodded towards the back of the house where Auntie Vi's loud snores could be heard. 'Now don't let her bully you, or else she will be moving in and you will be running around her left right and centre.'

'I will not, don't you fret. She will be to Dundee on Thursday, but I suppose I can't blame her, it's been ages since she has been here. It must be strange for her, returning to the place she was born and brought up. So, I am happy for her to stay the extra day. Once I get her back home, I will just come back and spend a couple of days here sorting through Granny's clothes, and see what is worth saving and put it down to the charity shop. I am sure there are some clothes up in that huge wardrobe that might be vintage.' She took a mouthful of her drink, relishing the smooth taste. 'I plan to get home sometime at the weekend. I will bring Bella and Tammy with me. I am not sure what he will think about travelling in the car, but I will pick up a pet carrier when I am down in Dundee. Are you sure you don't mind giving him a home, Dad?'

'Not at all, lass, he'll be a bit of company for me. Plus I have a garden, where he can get in and out of. I just hope he will settle with me. I am happy for Bella to come to me too, you know. Especially when you open the shop again; she won't like being shut up in the flat. Look at the racket she made this afternoon when she was shut in the steading. The poor creature's not used to being shut in.'

'I know, but she's made up for it since she got back into the house! Look at her now lounging in front of the hearth.' Hearing her name being mentioned brought the dog's head up, looking to both of the humans, before she placed it back down again and returned to her slumber. 'I think she will be okay with me, but if she can come to you during the daytime in the season, that would be great. But Dad, you will need to keep on with your bowls and activities; we can maybe work it out between us. She is a good dog though, and I am sure she will settle down and enjoy walks on the beach. It might be good for us both, I certainly will need to get out more and the walks will do me no harm. Anyway I think it's time for me to get to bed. I am pleased with how it went today, I think Granny would approve.'

'I know she would, lass. You got it just right; it suited your granny down to the ground. No fuss, just a few words, a bit of poetry and the sound of the pipes. She couldn't wish for a better place to lie, in the middle of the hills which she loved so much.'

CHAPTER 9

Laura was up and about early; she hadn't slept well. Partly, she supposed, that was due to having Auntie Vi in the house and being a little concerned that the elderly woman might struggle in a strange environment. She had just taken her a cup of tea, and had found her sitting up in bed gazing around the room. 'You know, Laura,' she said, pointing to the wall, 'that wallpaper has been on those walls since 1960, This was your mother's bedroom. You know that, don't you?'

'Yes, I know, but I didn't realise it was that long ago since it had been decorated. When was it that you moved out, Auntie?'

'Oh that was in 1952, when I got my place at teacher's training college. It was so exciting being in Aberdeen, the big city. I had some fun; I could tell you lots of stories that would make your toes curl!' She laughed, as she reviewed a memory in her minds' eye. 'That's when your mum moved down into this bedroom, she would have been just two. She was a pretty little girl and very compliant. She used to love sleeping on the camp bed in here when I came home during the college holidays. That was something I could never understand, why Elsa didn't just move into this bedroom, instead of taking over the front sitting room like she did.'

'She was very definite about wanting her own bed, and it was just too big to get into here.' Laura recalled the conversation she had had at the time, and how Elsa had also said that the back room held too many memories, and she didn't think she would sleep soundly in it. Laura hadn't questioned this, but took it that because it had been her mum's childhood room, there were just too many memories.

Laura was just setting the breakfast table, while Grant made the scrambled eggs that Auntie Vi had ordered, when her mobile rang. She picked it up and was incredibly relieved to see Liam's name flash up on the screen. 'Hello stranger,' she answered. 'I have been worried, Liam, are you okay?'

'Yes Mum, I'm so sorry, but I have been up country with some mates, and just got back. I had left this phone at Dad's, as he has bought me a new one.' There was a pause. 'Sorry, I meant to text you my new number, but will do right away. I just got your messages about great-granny. That was sudden, then. Have you had the funeral and all that?'

Laura went on to give him the details, and listened as he outlined what he was doing. He certainly seemed to be having a great time. He had, he told her, got a job in a bar and the hours meant he had plenty of time to go to the beach in the daytime. He mentioned several times how great his dad and Sally were, and he was enjoying playing footie with his two young half-brothers. Laura couldn't help but feel a tug of irritation, but was determined not to allow that to spoil this conversation with the son who she missed terribly. She should be happy that he was settled and enjoying having a good relationship with his father, but it rankled. She passed the phone to her father so he could have a quick chat with his grandson, but after a few cursory remarks Grant handed it back. Liam told her that he would text her his new number, as this one was no longer going to be in use. He promised as always to keep in contact, but she knew from his tone that she would not be on the top of his list.

Auntie Vi made herself comfortable at the top of the table

and tucked into her scrambled eggs on toast with a relish that demonstrated she still enjoyed her food. She was not a slim person, and Laura had thought many a time that her weight didn't lend itself to helping with her arthritis and mobility. She would never dare to raise this, though. They heard a car arrive, and Bella started to bark and get excited, much to Auntie Vi's annoyance. Laura got to the door just as Maisie reached it with some mail. They exchanged some words, and while she would have been happy to have stayed longer to chat, Laura managed to extract herself, telling Maisie that her dad had just made her breakfast and it was getting cold.

Carrying the mail back through, she glanced through the small pile while she tucked into her eggs. There was one from Elsa's bank confirming the details of her bank accounts. It was as Laura had thought: there was a savings account with a just under twenty-five thousand pounds, and a current account with a couple of thousand. Grant had helped Elsa set up the savings account when Harry had died, as well as organising all her bills, which were paid via direct debits. Elsa didn't spend much. Laura opened the next letter, and read the contents with a growing astonishment. 'Well I'll be dammed!'

'What is it, lass?' Grant and Vi both stopped eating and regarded Laura with some concern. Clearly whatever the letter contained had shocked her.

'It's from Hamish McKenzie. He wants to buy Birch End,' she told them. 'He says that he will send his land agent round to speak directly with me, and he will be able to survey how much the property and land is worth.' She took a large breath. 'But then goes on to say that he suspects that given the decay over the years, the property will be under the market value, but he would be,' she stopped again, 'and listen to this bit… he would be happy to take it off of my hands. Cheeky bugger! Goodness, Granny isn't even cold in her grave yet, and who does he think he is?'

'They have always been the same, those McKenzies,' Vi piped up. 'Always been arrogant buggers, think that because they own most of the land around here, that they can run rough-shod over everyone else. Mind you, it is not the first time that he tried to buy it. Do you remember, Grant, after Harry died; he approached Elsa then saying he would take it off of her hands.' She peered across the table. 'I hope you're not going to sell it to him, Laura.' She sat up straighter in her chair, and waved her fork at the younger woman. 'In fact, I hope you're not going to sell it to anyone. This has been in our family for nearly two hundred years.'

'I don't know what I am going to do with it, Auntie Vi. To be honest I haven't given it much thought. I know I can't live in it, but with the money Granny has left me, I certainly don't need to rush to make a decision just yet.'

'Quite right, Laura. It's not the time to think about this yet, and Vi, she will have to do what is right for her, I can under-stand your view about it being in the family for so long, but there isn't anyone who can take on the croft.' Grant's inter-vention closed any further discussion and advice from Vi, who looked mollified but ready to dish out her views. 'Now, ladies, before I leave this afternoon, why don't I treat both of you to lunch in the village?'

*****

It was later in the afternoon after her father had left, and she and Vi made themselves comfortable in the sitting room in front of a blazing fire. They had enjoyed a lovely lunch and neither thought they would need more than a snack for their supper. The thought of not having to cook supper was bliss for Laura, who couldn't be bothered to think about cooking a meal for them both. There was no TV to distract them, and she had already suffered from her aunt's disapproving look and tutting when she checked her Facebook page. So she put her iPad to one side and focused on her aunt.

'You know, Auntie Vi, I never realised that Granny was from Belgium, not until I found her and Grandad's marriage certificate. She never had an accent, for some reason I just assumed she was born in Britain. I know that she met Grandad in the war, and I remember my mum saying that her parents had been killed in the war, but not much else.'

Vi sat back in chair, and seemed to shuffle her bottom to get more comfortable before she answered. 'Elsa and Harry did meet at the end of the war. I was just fourteen when the war ended, and Harry didn't get demobbed until around the beginning of 1946... if my memory serves me right. I do recall my mother getting a letter to say that he was coming home, and that he had been working at a hospital up near Hannover, in the north of Germany. You see, Harry was part of the medical corps – did you know that? – and I think he had something to do with looking after some of the people who they found in that awful concentration camp. You know the one, Belsen.'

Laura was very surprised to hear this. 'No, I didn't know anything about Grandad being involved in that. Goodness, how awful. Surely that's not where he met Granny.'

'To be honest with you, Laura, I don't know exactly where he met Elsa. When he first came back home he told our parents very little about what he had seen, like most soldiers returning from war. I think they had been told to keep things to themselves. Harry was changed, though; he wasn't the light-hearted and fun brother that I remembered before he left for the war. I remember my parents being worried about him; he was quiet and withdrawn as though he had the weight of the world on his shoulders. I suspect that many men returned like that. Goodness knows what he saw and had to do during his service. After a while, he seemed to come to himself and started to help Dad with the sheep, and it seemed to help him come out of it a bit. I remember teasing him when letters started to come back and forth, with a foreign stamp on it. It must have been well over two years that the letters kept coming, and he just got on with day-to-day work. Of course, as you know, he managed to get the job as the postman, which meant that we didn't see how often the letters arrived. He did seem secretive about who he was corresponding with, and when asked he would just say someone he met when he was overseas. He would colour up, though, so my mother and I guessed it was a girl.

'I do remember the night when he announced that he was going to get married; my mother nearly had a hairy fit. She was astonished when he announced this, given that there appeared to be no girl on the scene. He then explained that he did have a girlfriend but she was in Belgium and she had managed to get permission to travel to Scotland. He was intending to meet her at Hull and then travel up to Edinburgh where they were going to get married. Well, the roof nearly blew off with my mothers' fury, how dare he treat them like that? Why couldn't he bring her here first, so they could meet her, and then get married here in the Glen? What would people think? She had ranted on and on. He just said it was all arranged and that's how it was going to be.

'My mother didn't speak to him until he returned from Edinburgh with Elsa on his arm. She was such a wee young woman, and she looked even smaller against Harry's tall frame. She looked gaunt, you know, as though she had been through it. She had curly shoulder-length dark hair in those days, and was small boned, I think that made her look even more fragile. Funny enough, but I do recall, I couldn't help looking at her hands, she had such graceful hands, with her long fingers. Goodness though, she was bonny.' Vi hesitated for a moment. She closed her eyes as if she was back in that moment, meeting Elsa and seeing her for the first time. 'It was her eyes that looked hollow, and seemed to hide a story, and she was very quiet and shy and well…vulnerable. Well, my mother took to her immediately and clucked about her, and took her under her wing. She could speak very good English and so that was no barrier, although she didn't say much at all. When we heard that all of her family had been lost in the war, that was the final hurdle as far as my parents were concerned. Harry was forgiven, and he and Elsa settled down to married life. Whatever Elsa had been through was never discussed, but I do remember hearing her having nightmares. She used to cry out and looked awful in the morning, and I remember asking my mother what was wrong, and being told to mind my business and not to ask Elsa any questions. It wasn't unusual in those days, that any upset was just put down to the war.

'Whatever happened to Elsa, and how they actually met remains a mystery to this day, Laura. They had a good marriage, and when your mother was born it brought them real joy, and I think it also brought Elsa some peace. I don't think that I heard the nightmares after Estelle was born. It was in the past, and you know if someone wants the past to remain in the past, then who are we to question it?'

CHAPTER 10

Laura was quite relieved when she eventually deposited Vi back to her sheltered housing flat. She was fond of her aunt, but goodness me couldn't she talk. On the journey she had given Laura a running commentary on what she should do about Birch End, and was insistent that she should tell Hamish McKenzie to go to hell. The journey back was much easier, and after stocking up with a few things from the supermarket, she was pleased just to drive and listen to one of her favourite albums.

She had a plan. Once she had unloaded the shopping, and given Bella a quick walk, she would then tackle Granny's wardrobe. There were no hens to sort out as, true to her word, Jane had arrived the previous day and carted the clucking hens away. Laura had decided not to give much thought to Hamish McKenzie's offer, and would think through all the options and talk to Iona and her dad before she made any long-term decisions. She was just returning along the path at the back of the cottage when she spotted a Land Rover parked in front of the yard. A man was sitting in the driver's seat, and once he caught sight of her, he got out and walked towards her, extending his hand.

'Good afternoon, you must be Laura Simpson. I am Donald Cameron, Mr McKenzie's land agent. I am pleased to meet you.'

Laura was taken aback, and found her own hand being crushed

before she could extract it. She took a step back to put some distance from this uninvited person.

Before she could say anything the loud voice boomed out, 'I thought I would just call in and introduce myself, and perhaps we could make an arrangement for me to have a proper look around.' He stood and turned towards the cottage. 'Clearly I will need to do a full survey, it does appear that there will be a lot of work to undertake before this is brought up to the standards of the estate's other properties, but we will, I am sure, be in a position to make you a reasonable offer.'

Laura was stunned and took a moment to find her voice, she took another step back. Looking this man up and down, she chose her words carefully so there would be no confusion as to what she had to say. 'I have absolutely no intention of selling Birch End to Hamish McKenzie.' He now looked equally stunned. 'You will not be getting any access, or undertaking any survey. I am astounded that you think that you can call in here, two days after I buried my granny and expect me to be grateful that that you might make me a *reasonable offer*. So now I would like you to leave my property and you can inform Hamish McKenzie, that Birch End IS NOT FOR SALE!' With those final words she marched past him, calling Bella to her side and stormed into the cottage, slamming the door behind her, leaving a rather bewildered land agent wondering whether he had got the wrong message from his boss, who had told him that the family would be eager to offload the rather dilapidated cottage and land. He would certainly report back that it would appear that that wasn't the case.

Meanwhile, in the kitchen, Laura was walking round and round the kitchen table, cursing under her breath, how bloody dare he, the arrogant bugger. Whatever she decided now about the future of Birch End, she would certainly ensure that Hamish bloody McKenzie did not get his bloody hands on it. It took her another half an hour, a cup of tea and a phone call to Iona before she calmed down. It was then she decided that she would return to her original plan and climbed the stairs to begin the assault on her granny's wardrobe. It was not going to be a straightforward task, she decided; the clothes hanging on the rail would be easily removed and sorted into piles, but it was what was contained at the back of the wardrobe that might take much longer. There was one box which contained photographs. Some were in albums, while others were placed haphazardly in packets, and envelopes. Laura took a minute to scan some of them and they looked like there were many family photographs dating back to her great-grandparent's day. She decided that this was a task that needed some time, and she placed the box to one side; she would take this back home with her and take time to sort through them. She wondered if Auntie Vi would want some, and maybe she would find some of her mother when she was a child. Yes, definitely not something that could be rushed.

Delving into the back of the wardrobe again, she found yet another box; it looked as though it held all sorts of things that Granny had saved. Searching through it she found an assortment of old birthday cards, mementos of past croft activities. She found a rolled-up document and when she opened it she found what appeared to be the deeds for Birch End. She scanned it, and put it to one side with the photographs; she would read it later. At the bottom of the box, she found a small package of what looked like four letters; these were bound with a rather faded blue ribbon. She looked at the address on the front and realised that they were addressed to Mr Harry Kerr, Birch End Croft. Goodness, could these be the letters that Auntie Vi had spoken about?

She extracted the top one and saw that the postmark was dated April 1948. She was careful to remove the rather thin airmail paper, and sat on the bed to read it. She realised immediately that it was written by Elsa.

Dear Harry,

It was lovely to get your letter, and with the money for my fare, are you sure you do not mind travelling to Hull to meet me off of the boat. I have looked at the map and it is a very long way to come for you. But I think I will be grateful as I am rather anxious about travelling so far on my own.

I cannot wait to see you again, and I so hope that I will not be a disappointment to you, and that we can resume what we started. I don't think it has really hit me yet that I will be leaving all of the life here behind and start a new life with you, my lovely Scottish man. You will always be my rescuer and I am looking forwards to you being my lover too.

It was good to hear that you have made all of the arrangements for us to get married. Have you told your parents yet about me? I hope that they are going to be alright about me becoming their daughter-in-law. I cannot wait to see your Birch End, if it is half as stunning as you describe it will be wonderful to be there. You tell me that it is a peaceful location and that is something I yearn for after all the troubles I have had.

I am just now finishing off the arrangements for the house and then I can leave the memories behind, just as Doctor Peeters advised. I am determined to follow his advice, he has helped me so much over the past two years. Sofia and Lucas are telling me that I am doing the right thing. I will miss them, they have been so kind to me, but I am lucky to be getting a new start in a place where new memories will be made, and I must keep the old ones at bay, just as Doctor Peeters advises.

So my Scottish love, I am going to end now so I can get my letter to the post office, there are still queues to get it sent via the airmail system. I will see you in just a couple of weeks.
All my love
Your
Elsa

Goodness me. Laura sat back down on the bed, and re-read the letter. She carefully folded the letter and replaced it in the faded envelope, taking care not to damage it. This, she realised, was something very special, and she would want to share this with Iona.

Picking up the other letters, she counted just three, and wondered why it would seem that her grandad had kept these. There must have been more. She was tempted to read all of them, but realised that it was getting dark – and Bella appeared in the doorway, a silent reminder that it was time for her supper. She would take these downstairs with her and read them later. She felt excited to learn more about her grandparents' love.

She looked again into the back of the wardrobe and saw that right in the back buried under a box of what appeared to be shoes, some clearly her grandad's, there was a suitcase. It was very old-fashioned, and not large, but as she removed it she realised it was heavy. It was made of leather, and had two clasps that had locks. She humped it onto the bed and tried the locks but they seemed to be locked, although the locks looked a bit rusty and didn't seem to have been used for some time. I wonder what this contains, she said to herself. Right; she would take this downstairs with the letters and would ponder on it after both she and Bella had eaten their supper. She would then light the fire in the sitting room and see what other treasures she might find.

****

Settling in front a roaring fire, which if Bella was not careful of, she would feel her fur being scorched if she got any closer, Laura picked up the letters again. She had decided that the suitcase could wait until the morning, as she would need to go into the outside shed to find some tools to get into it. She had sent a text to Iona a while ago, and heard her phone ping with a message. It was a reply, agreeing that it was exciting to find the letters and she looked forward to reading them.

Laura decided she would try to read the letters in date sequence, and the first appeared to have been sent in March 1946. She recalled that her Auntie Vi had said her grandad had returned home at the start of 1946. Being extra careful in removing the paper from the envelope, especially now when she knew how these would become so cherished in the future, she began to read.

Klapdorp 25
2000 Antwerp
Belgium
16th March 1946
Dear Harry

I hope you are well, and that your journey home was not too arduous. I am sure that your family are very relieved to have you back home, and hope that you are getting back into working with your animals.

I am with Sophia and Lucas, I cannot thank them enough for replying to my letter. I thought that maybe they hadn't survived, but it was just they had moved to another apartment, and thankfully the person who found my letter delivered it to them. When they wrote to tell me that they had a room I could stay in, then I felt a wonderful sense of relief. It was not the same after you left, Harry, I missed our talks and missed your kisses even more. Once your group had left, then there were some new ones arriving, and many of us were able to return to our towns.

It is very strange to be back in Antwerp, nothing is the same, yet everything is, if that makes any sense. I haven't been back to the house yet, Sophia tells me that there are families living in it. I am not sure how to go about things. Lucas is going to help me try and sort this out, I have no doubt it will take much time. There are still many food shortages, and I am being careful not to take too much from Sophia, but she has my ration card and so at least that helps. There are long queues at shops that much hasn't changed. There is a sense of sadness mixed with relief, no more jackboots marching around the streets, and the blessed Nazi flags are no longer waving. Life is very strange.

I am so grateful now that my mother was such a stickler for me learning English, what would I have done, my Harry, if I hadn't been able to speak to you in English, and now I can write to you as well. I think it would have been much more difficult if I had to write in Flemish for you to understand.

Now that you have an address to write to me, I hope that you will do so, Harry. You are very special to me, and I hope that you did mean it when you said that you loved me, and would do what you could to make sure we would be together. I love you very much.

With love
Elsa

Blimey, Laura sighed. This is so interesting. So wherever her grandparents had met then, it didn't seem to have been in Antwerp, as Elsa said she had returned. She was intrigued to find out more. The next letter wasn't in an envelope but folded up,

Klapdorp 25
1st September 1946
Dearest Harry
I hope this gets to you in time, and you like the birthday card I made. I would have liked to send you a present too, but I wasn't sure what to get you. Sophia suggested that I knit you a hat, but I am hopeless at knitting, my mother thought it was more important that I learn to write, read and do arithmetic rather than sew or knit. So instead I send you my love.

I do love it when I receive your letters, dearest Harry, the way you describe your Birch End sounds wonderful. Your little sister Violet sounds fun, I am sure she doesn't mean to tease you so much. It is so good to know about you getting the job as the postman. At least you will get my letters a little earlier.

There is still no news about the house. An old friend of my family has introduced me to someone who might be able to help me. It is something I wish I didn't need to deal with but I know I must do so. I have my first meeting with Dr Peeters next week, it is so good of him to take an interest in me, and I hope that it will help me. I sometimes find it very hard, my dearest Harry, but I am determined I am not going to burden you with my poor mood. I just want to remember our lovely walks and talks.

Please have a nice birthday and I hope that I will be able to spend next years in your arms if all goes well.
With love
Your Elsa

So, a little more of a story began to unfold. This Dr Peeters, mentioned again, made Laura wonder what her granny was suffering from. Also there was another reference to the house. She assumed that her grandad had some reason for keeping her a secret from his family, and what happened to all of the other letters, as clearly there had been regular letters, yet there were only four remaining. She reached to read the last one

Klapdorp 25
1st January 1948
Dearest Harry

Thank you so much for the lovely surprise. What a wonderful Christmas present and I am so pleased that Sophia persuaded me to not to open it until Christmas morning. The ring fits perfectly and YES, my dearest man, I would love to marry you. Are you absolutely sure that you want to do this? I know it has been so long since we saw each other, but I am sure that I love you.

There have been so many times when I had thought I would never reach another Christmas, and I am so pleased that I have. I have survived, that is what Doctor Peeters keeps reminding me. Not only have I survived but now I am an engaged person, thank you my

Harry.

The work I am doing with him is very hard, but Sophia believes it is helping me, she says I am not making so much noise at night as I did when I first came to stay with them. I am following his advice very well, and am so fortunate to have him to help me, when so many others do not.

Lucas thinks we have a breakthrough with the house, and that things are moving. I will be so pleased when it is all sorted out, I will let you know if we have the progress I am hoping for.

Well my dearest Harry, my hand is getting tired, I have been writing a lot today, as Doctor Peeters has spurred me on, and with your proposal I think I can start to believe that I do have a future where I might find some peace.

Have you told your family that you have asked me to marry you? I do hope so, Harry, as when I get to meet them I don't want there to be any unhappiness. I know you don't want to create a fuss, and will do whatever you think is necessary. I hope that tonight that my dreams will be of you my dearest.
With all my love
Your
Elsa

Wow, Laura exclaimed, her grandad had proposed, and for some reason she had not clocked her granny's age, but of course she would have only been twenty when she got married. She could not even imagine what this young girl had gone through, but clearly this Dr Peeters was some sort of psychological doctor, as from what Elsa had indicated, he was helping her with her nightmares and survival. What on earth had her grandmother gone through, she wondered, and at such a young age. Maybe she would never find out what had happened to her. She wished she was here now so she could ask her. There was never a time during her life when she recalled

Elsa making any reference to what she had experienced during her early years. She never referred to it at all but then, to be fair, neither had anyone else.

Looking at the clock, she thought it was time for bed. She glanced at the locked suitcase with even more fascination of what it might contain. Of course it might be just a load of rubbish, but in the morning she would make sure she got the case open to reveal, she hoped, more about her grandmother's early life.

*****

She was indeed up early the following morning, not having slept so well. She couldn't help thinking about what she had read, and her mind was too busy to have a good deep sleep. Once Bella was let out and she had a quick shower, she rummaged through the tool box in the shed until she found a suitable implement to prize the suit case open.

It didn't actually take a lot of pressure to do so, and she lifted the lid, her heart racing slightly with excitement to see what it held. There were several large bounded notebooks. On the front of each one was a number; she opened the first one, and recognised her grandmothers distinctive writing. She read the first paragraph.

I don't really know how to start writing this journal, but Doctor Peeters has advised me that it will help me to deal with what has happened to me. He has said for me to start at the beginning and write it all down. Then, when it has been written and he and I have discussed it, I am to close the book and place it into a locked place and let it remain there, in the past, where I can close it away from my memory. He says that at the moment the past is part of my present, and I need to change that so that I can live in the future. So I will do as he suggests, and I will try and write all of what I remember, so here I go…

PART 2

Antwerp Belgium 1940

CHAPTER 11

Elsa's story

U p until I was twelve, I think I would say that I had a prefect life. My father Martin Wouters was a kind and gentle man. He was a doctor, and while he had a very good list of patients who paid him well for his advice and treatment, there was also a constant stream of those less well-off who would seek his help. His surgery was on the ground floor, in the front room of our three-storey house at 45 Ramstraat. Papa ensured that those who could not pay for treatment attended in the early morning, before his wealthy patients were up and about. It wouldn't have been unusual for Papa to be called out in the middle of the night, and when this happened, we would all be awakened by loud banging on the front door.

Mama was not such a gentle being; she was I would say the stricter of my parents. Whereas Papa would allow me to do some things, Mama would not. Mama had been a school-teacher before she married, and she held education as the most important part of life. She also held strong ideas about equality, and made sure that I received the same level of education as Derk, my older brother. In those days, I suppose it wasn't often expected that girls should be treated in the same way as boys, but Mama was very certain that they should be.

'How else had I been given the chances I had if that had been different?' she would tell us. She had grown up in Brussels, and once she had qualified as a teacher in English, she had got a job in a private school in Antwerp. She used to tell me that she loved being able to fill children's heads with knowledge, and see how they flourished. So it was no surprise that as soon as I was old enough, she started to fill my head with such, and lit the fire of a passion for learning. She was convinced that it was important that everyone was able to speak more than their native language, and so my brother and I were taught English and French, so that we would be able to grow up and be able to widen our worlds. Not just the Flemish world we lived in. Antwerp's residents usually spoke French and Flemish, and while my father was an educated man, he chose to speak primarily Flemish. This, he said, was to ensure the local people were able to engage with him.

My bedroom in Ramstraat was on the third floor; our house was I suppose quite large. On the top floor were our bedrooms, the middle, our living space, and the ground floor Papa's work space. His surgery was situated in one of the front rooms, and across the hallway were the reception and waiting room. I suppose, looking back, they were furnished quite fashionably, with several comfortable wingback chairs around a large coffee table. The receptionist, Rachel, sat in the corner behind a small desk. I always thought she sat like a sentry guarding the several metal filing cabinets, which held the patients' records. My Papa's consulting room always held a fascination for me, with his large rosewood desk, behind which he would sit across from the patients. I liked to sometimes climb onto his examination table and play at being a patient. He would scold me laughingly if he caught me.

The two smaller back rooms were where his dispensary and his study were situated. I loved his study, because it smelt of his pipe tobacco, and it was small and rather cosy in my mind. The walls were almost covered with bookcases, with medical books spilling out from the shelves. It was also the only room where he was permitted to smoke, as Mama had banned him from doing so in other areas, as she said: 'The smelly pipe was responsible for stinking up the drapes, and furniture.' There was just one other smaller room on the ground floor, a cloak-room which had a toilet and washbasin.

On the middle floor, the kitchen was at the back of the house, and it could also be accessed directly by steps from the back garden. Mama had insisted that this was built when they moved into to the house in the early days of their marriage, as she didn't want to have to keep clumping up and down the main stairway to get to the back garden. The garden held a special place in Mama's heart, somewhere where she enjoyed being, and caring for her plants and flowers. I think that the kitchen was probably the hub of the house. It was painted a bright lemon, and on the days when the sun shone into it, it seemed the brightest of all our rooms. The deep sink was beneath the back window, which looked out to our long garden. Mama had had a yellow blind with purple flowers on it made, and this framed the window nicely. Our cooker was a large range. It had a double use, as it also provided some heat to a large tank for our hot water. Sometimes the rattling of the pipes would wake me up, as my bedroom was over the kitchen and next to the bathroom. Some cupboards ran along the wall, above which were shelves which were full of plates and jars. In the middle of the room was a long, scrubbed pine table, with six wooden chairs. The table had seen better days and held the scars of many years of chopping vegetables, as well as some scorch marks from scalding dishes placed hastily to avoid burning fingers.

Also on this floor was our dining room, which held a large, polished table and eight chairs. The sideboard was almost as long, and held my mama's precious set of china crockery that had been a wedding present from her parents, who had died when I was just a toddler. The last room was our sitting room, which looked out towards the street. It was comfortably furnished with warm colours and two sofas that faced each other in front of the large decorative fireplace and surround. There were several other armchairs dotted about the room; two were placed at angles in front of the large bay window. It was where I loved to sit and read my books, and watch the comings and goings of our neighbours and arrivals to my papa's surgery. When Derk and I were little, we used to love hiding behind the thick drapes and wait silently for our parents to look for us, then leap out and scare them. We had many happy family times in that room, with games, and watching Mama and Papa dancing to records played on our very swish gramophone.

There were four bedrooms on the upper floor. Mine and Derk's were at the back of the house; they were smaller and allowed the family bathroom to separate the walls between our rooms. Mama and Papa had the large front bedroom, and the other was kept as the spare bedroom. It was kept for guests, although we rarely had anyone to stay overnight. Occasionally during Christmas Grand-mama Helena, Papa's mother would come and stay; she preferred though to remain in her family home, in a suburb on the outskirts of the city. Even more infrequently Mama's cousin Nina and her husband Lars would visit; they lived in the countryside and farmed some animals. Mama always became sad when she spoke about Nina, who had been unlucky, and not been able to have any children. I liked it when Nina did come to stay; she would always ensure that I had the softest and sweetest of the fruit she brought from the farm. I think she had a special place in her heart for me, and Mama used to accuse her of spoiling me, although I did not object to this at all.

My bedroom was decorated with wallpaper on which pink roses climbed a wall. Whenever I awoke early and knew that Mama and Papa were not up and about, I would make up games and count the roses. I kept all of my dolls and toys in their own place along my shelf that ran along one side of my room. My china doll tea set was my most favourite item, and I would often line my dolls up, and play afternoon tea, just like the one I had been taken to by Grand-mama in a posh café one afternoon. I was even fortunate to have a large doll's house, which Nina had carefully furnished for me, even to the point of making tiny curtains. I would spend hours playing alone with my toys and using my imagination to create a story for my dolls and my favourite bear.

Derk, four years older than me, was quite different from me, and it wasn't just because he was a boy. He liked to be out and about, and had a bicycle, which meant he was often out of the house more than he was in. It did cause some family arguments, as Mama would lose patience with him when he was late for meals; she always insisted that we all eat together around the large dining table. It was, she used to say, important that we shared meals together so that we could converse and discuss things that were taking place in our lives. Derk often arrived at the last minute looking dishevelled, his hair uncombed and clothes muddy, and even the occasional hole in his trousers where he had been caught up on something. Mama would shriek at him to go and scrub his hands and face, and only return once he was clean and presentable. He would scowl at her, and follow her instructions, often with a poor attitude. Papa would only intervene if asked to, and I often spotted him, with a slight smile on his face, as though he supported the wild urchin that Mama insisted their son was becoming.

I, on the other hand, was very different. I was much more what could be described as a home bird. I loved my home, and especially loved spending time with my father. I would creep into his study when his surgery had finished, and snuggle up on the easy chair where he sat to enjoy his pipe, and read the newspaper. He used to tell me that I was prettiest girl he had ever known, and I would beg him to put his newspaper aside, and tell me one of the many stories he made up for me. He would laugh and ruffle my long dark curly hair, and tell me to scoot off and help Mama set the table, or find something to do. He always made me feel that indeed I was the prettiest girl in the world. Of course I wasn't, I was I think quite plain. I was of small build, and quite skinny. I also had thick curly dark hair, and it was often tangled and would really hurt when Mama insisted that she needed to brush it out, and admonished me for letting it get into such a state. I also had quite sticking out ears, although thankfully my hair covered these, but my pointy nose couldn't be covered. Mama said I had the same nose as her mother, my grand-mama, who I had no memory of. I often wished she had had a different nose, so that I hadn't inherited the same one as hers.

We were a quiet family overall. Like many of the families of my parents' circumstances and status we had help in the house. Mama did all of the cooking, but we had a young girl called Sophia who worked for us. She would come in every day from her home and help Mama with the housework and general tasks around the house. I liked Sophia: she was only a young girl, just a couple of years older than Derk, and I often thought that he behaved differently when Sophia was around. I asked him once why his face became red when Sophia was helping Mama with the food, but he just became irritated and told me not to be so stupid. But I did know that there was some difference in him but backed off from asking him, as clearly my questions made him uncomfortable.

Our family was supposed to be Catholic. I say supposed to be: we didn't attend the church on any regular basis, just at Christmas and other important days of the year. Mama and Papa did not expect or force us to attend Mass, and I think I was grateful for that, as when we did attend a church service I found myself becoming extremely bored with the procedures, which seemed to last forever. Both Derk and I did attend Catholic schools, though; mine was just a short walk away and run by nuns, while Derk had to take the tram to his, and he would often mumble that he couldn't wait until it was time to leave school and go to work. What work he was thinking of was never explained, as Mama would demand that he pay more attention to his studies and less time gallivanting around the city on his bicycle. Papa would also tell him to think about his future and work towards it. But if anything, I think that Derk was only interested in playing sport and physical activities, rather than any studies. He, I believe, was a disappointment to our parents, especially to Mama, who put so much store into study and learning. I was happy to learn, and so I suppose I was compensation for them, and they had great hopes that I would maybe follow them into one of their occupations.

While I liked learning, I did not like the nuns who taught me. They terrified me on the whole, with their rulers that could swish across your knuckles without a moment's hesitation. They accused us of day-dreaming and not paying attention. There were one or two who were kinder, but they appeared to hold the view that children could only learn if they were in fear of their teachers. I didn't have much time for the local priest either, who would appear occasionally and bore us rigid with his sermons and talks. To top it all he had terrible smelly breath, and when he came close to you your instinct was to cover your nose. If you did so, and it was noticed by an eagle-eyed nun, and then you were in for it once he had left. They were not all horrible, of course. Sister Margerite and Sister Mary were quite nice, but they were unquestionably in the minority. Nevertheless, I did try to enjoy school, and certainly enjoyed spending time at the breaks with my friends, Dominique and Adele. They lived in the next street and we were invited over to each other's homes to share a tea and play in the gardens many a summer afternoon. Their parents, Lambert and Cecily, were good friends of my parents. Lambert had been childhood friends with Papa, and was also a doctor, but worked at the hospital as a surgeon.

So, we were just getting on with our lives. Papa and Mama busy with their roles, and Derk and I just ordinary children. All that might have continued if it hadn't been for what was happening in Europe. When war was declared in Europe at the end of 1939, Belgium decided that it would remain neutral. This was truly understandable, given what had taken place just twenty-one years previously, when the First World War had finished and Belgium had been so terribly affected. It was also understandable that the leaders of Belgium would initially try to protect their citizens from yet another terrible conflict. Papa was especially vocal about war never solving anything. He knew better than anyone, as it had taken his own father and his older brother from him, when he was just a teenager. All that changed, though, when in May 1940 the German army moved into Belgium and occupied our country.

CHAPTER 12

There was a great deal of upset on that Tuesday morning, when it was announced over the radio that the German occupation of Antwerp had taken place. Mama and Papa were distressed, and Papa especially was furious. I don't think I had ever seen him so angry.

'How dare they, Estelle, we have kept out of their damn conflicts and now they just walk in and take us over. What are our leaders doing, for God's sake? How did they allow this to happen!'

Mama was quiet, but I noticed that she was very sad too, as she brushed away a tear and patted my fathers' arm. 'Please, Martin, let's not frighten the children too much. I don't think that we will send Elsa to school though. Not until we work out what is happening.'

'I agree, and as for you, young man –' he addressed Derk, '– you are to stay in the house today as well.' Derk had completed his formal education, and had been due to start an apprenticeship with the local garage; this would allow him to continue to practice his most crucial passion – that of playing football. He hoped that he would maybe be able to play this professionally at some point, but Papa had insisted that he also focused on getting a trade, and so, somewhat reluctantly, he had settled for an apprenticeship as a mechanic with a local garage.

Derk looked at Papa, his eyebrows raised. 'Really, Papa, surely I should go and at least speak to Mr Smett, and see whether he would wish me to start work today?'

'No, you will remain in the house, young man. I will telephone Mr Smett, and let him know that you will not be attending today. As far as I can make out, people are being advised to remain in their homes. So please, on this occasion, my son, do not disobey me.'

'I wonder whether Sophia will come in today. I have no way of contacting her, so I do hope she will stay with her family.' Just as Estelle finished speaking the back door to the kitchen opened to admit a rather flustered Sophia.

'Sophia, are you alright? I was just saying I hope that you wouldn't try and come in today.' Estelle went to the young girl and helped her into the room, and removed her jacket. 'Do sit down, and Elsa pour poor Sophia a cup of coffee and put some sugar into it. She looks as though she has had a shock.'

Martin went over to assist his wife, taking into account how pale and shaken the young girl was. He bent down in front of her. 'Take some deep breaths, Sophia, and wait just a few moments to settle down.'

It was several minutes before Sophia was able to compose herself, and tell them that there were tanks and German soldiers everywhere. The *Grotte Markt*, the main square which she had to come across on her way to Ramstraat, was now flying the red and black flag brandishing the Nazi emblem and it was horrible to see them. She had kept her eyes down and hurried past them and thankfully the streets around the Wouters's house were more or less the same as usual. 'I did think about turning back, but then I was almost here, so kept going,' she told them, her voice still slightly weakened. 'Oh dear, Dr Wouters, what on earth is going to happen to us now?'

The front door bell sounded, and all present looked at each

other; there was a real sense of apprehension. Martin looked at this watch. 'It is probably Rachel arriving. I will go and open the door, and then I suppose we will see whether anyone arrives for this morning's surgery.'

'Tell Rachel that she is to come and have a cup of coffee before she starts work. I am sure the poor girl must be very anxious.' A few minutes later Rachel, Papa's very efficient receptionist, arrived looking upset. Rachel lived just three streets away in an apartment. 'Rachel, come and sit down. Elsa, please pour another cup of coffee. Rachel, you look as though you haven't slept.'

'Oh, Madam Wouters, I am sorry, you are right. I haven't slept. I was awoken by the heavy movement of traffic in the early hours, and when I looked out from my window I could see tanks and vehicles streaming along the main road.' She lifted the coffee cup to her lips, holding it with two shaking hands. 'I walked very swiftly here, but I suppose now that will mean that David will now not come home.' She placed the cup shakily onto the table, and searched for her handkerchief, which she used to dab her eyes. 'I am sorry, Madam. I try not to think about him and where he might be, but seeing those Germans arrive today, fills me with no hope.'

'Now Rachel, we cannot give up on hope.' Mama busied herself with starting to clear the breakfast things away. 'David may be somewhere quite safe. We know that many of the Belgian soldiers have managed to escape. Goodness, Dr Wouters was telling me just last night that he had heard that some have joined with the British forces. So please do not give up hope. Now drink your coffee and then I am sure my husband will need you down at the surgery.' Mama turned to the other young employee. 'Sophia, you and I will clear up the kitchen, and then we will have a think about what else we need to get down to this morning. Elsa, you are to go and tidy your room.'

Once all had been given their orders, mama had excused herself, I had waited a while and then went to find her. I found her in her room looking down at the street. She looked worried and quite sad. She turned and beckoned me to join her; we stood quietly taking a moment to reflect. 'Are you worried about Rachel?' I asked.

'Yes my darling I am. We can only pray that David is safe, please keep this to yourself, but Papa has heard that there were many casualties in the Belgian army, let us just hope that David isn't one of them. They were so happy when they married just last year, it is such a shame that they have been so cruelly parted. We just have to hope Elsa. We must never lose hope.' Mama placed her arm around my shoulders and hugged me as we continued to watch the street. Estelle excused herself for a moment,

CHAPTER 13

May 1940 – December 1940

T hat first six months of the occupation saw many changes within our household. One of the main changes was that the number of occupants of the house at Ramstraat increased significantly. Within just a few weeks of the occupation taking place, Mama and Papa made several important decisions. These were based on keeping those they loved and cared about safe. So, Papa's mother Helena moved from her home in a suburb of Antwerp, to take up residence in the spare bedroom. She had initially been reluctant to leave her small comfortable home, but saw the sense on what her son was saying about pooling their resources. This had become even more important given that the citizens of Antwerp needed to register with the city authorities, and receive vouchers to purchase food on a ration system, and food was beginning to become less available.

Within just a few weeks of that dreadful day when the Germans took up residence in the city, Papa and Mama had taken time to consider all the unused space in our home, and decided to ensure that we used it in the most effective way. Firstly, the cellars were tidied out, and the large space they provided would lend itself to providing them with some safety should the British start to drop bombs. The cellars stretched the full width and length of building and were accessed from a small passageway that led down a narrow stairway, from the hallway beside Martin's dispensary. There was also a second entrance that could be accessed from the back garden. Once the cellar, which had not been really used to any useful purpose apart from storing rubbish, had been cleared, they realised that they could possibly use this space for numerous purposes.

The cellar was made up of three spaces, separated by thick brick walls. One of the sections ran from front to the back of the cellar, and there was a very narrow and small hatch that allowed access into the confined space, which really only amounted to about a metre wide. There were no windows in this part of the cellar; the only light came from two air vents at either end of what was the front and back of the house. Mama recalled that the first time she had viewed the cellars before they moved into the house, they had commented about what a waste of space this was, and could never see how this part of the cellar could ever be of any use. Papa had agreed, as he had crouched down on his knees to shine a torch through the small hatch to see whether there was anything contained in it. The only thing they had thought that it might be useful for was to secrete their valuables, as it would be easy to conceal them in this space.

The other two spaces were much larger and also lighter. There was a wall between the front and the back of the cellar. There was one small window at the front and one at the back, which did allow some light into the area. They decided that this could be put to some use. So first, there was a job to keep Derk busy, and that was to whitewash the walls. There was no electricity in the cellar, so it was considered that if the walls were all painted white, then it would increase the light.

While Derk was set to his job, Mama, assisted by Sophia and me, tackled the top of the house. The loft space was also large, and could only be accessed by a ladder that was pulled down from the loft entrance. The ladder was quite sturdy and when pulled down stood just to the side of the entrance to Derk's bedroom. It meant that once it was extended, he had to walk behind it to gain entrance to his room, but we thought that wouldn't be too difficult to do. The loft was a wide, open space, with two small windows towards the back to let in some light. That was their only purpose, as neither had the mechanism to open to allow any air to penetrate. The loft held lots of pieces of unwanted furniture. Some of it had been in the house when they had purchased it all of those years before, and instead of getting rid of it then, they had decided to pile it up in the loft, just in case it might come in handy. Eighteen years later, it would certainly do so. With the help of Derk and Sophia's friend Lucas, we managed to manoeuvre a couple of small beds, three mattresses, a couple of small tables, two small armchairs and two rather dusty rolled-up carpets, down the stairs so that the two rooms in the cellar could be furnished. This left a couple of beds, chest of drawers, a wardrobe, and another two chairs in the loft space.

After the loft had been swept and cleaned, the rugs beaten to an inch of their life to remove years of accumulated dust, it seemed to be just what Mama and Papa had envisaged. They then had sat the family down, and invited Sophia, Rachel and Lucas to join them and shared their idea with them.

Papa addressed the group as we sat around the dining room table, most of us looking a little anxious about why we had been summoned. 'Now then, firstly I want to thank you for helping us sort out the cellar and loft space. You have all done a marvellous job, I have to say. Estelle and I would like to put a proposition to you.' Everyone sat up a little bit straighter, even Grand-mama, who had already been taken into her son and daughter-in-law's confidence about what they were planning, and had thoroughly agreed with them. 'We know that it is becoming more difficult to move around the city easily. Sophia, after you told us that your family are intending to leave the city, and go and stay with their relatives in the country, and you didn't want to leave, for very good reasons…' Papa paused and smiled, looking towards Lucas as he did so, '…we thought that it might prove helpful if we created some space, and you could move in and so could maybe use the loft as a bedroom.'

Sophia let out the breath she hadn't realised she had been holding in. 'Oh, Doctor Wouters, yes please, that would be wonderful! It would mean that I could continue to work for you, and it would be a real help to my family not to have to worry about me.'

'That is good, then.' Papa turned to Rachel.' And we thought that maybe you, Rachel, could also move in and share the loft space with Sophia.' He watched the look of sheer relief flood over the face of the young woman, who had been nervously clutching her handkerchief in her hand and weaving it in and out of her fingers. 'We know that it is really difficult for you, Rachel, especially as there is no word of David. So we thought that it might be a little safer if you were under our roof, so you didn't have to worry about the journey here every morning and evening.'

'I don't know quite what to say.' Rachel dabbed her eyes. 'I cannot thank you both enough. I have to admit that I am quite frightened on my own in the apartment, especially now that I know that there are some people in the apartment building who are actively helping the Nazis. It makes it very uncomfortable, and so I would absolutely welcome moving in here.' She turned to Sophia, who was at least five years her junior. 'I am sure we will manage, won't we?'

'We certainly will I suppose that it would be alright, for me to call you Rachel, rather than Mrs Cohen, then,' Sophia asked, 'seeing as we will be sharing a room.'

'Lastly we have Lucas here, and I have to say, Sophia, that since you introduced Lucas to us, he has been a huge help to us all.' He smiled towards the young man, who was in his early twenties. Lucas had been seeking work since he had returned to the area, having been in France, where he had worked on a vineyard. Once war had been declared, he had made his way back to his country of birth, only to find that his family had moved on. He had no address for them, other than being told by a neighbour at the apartment building where they had lived that they had left some months ago to travel north. Since then Lucas had been living mostly rough, finding spaces to sleep and along the way had met Sophia, who had shared food with him and who had then asked Mama whether she needed any help in the garden. Hearing Lucas's story had meant that he was given some work, and now, Papa informed him, he was welcome to have some of the cellar as his own space. Hope-fully they would only join him downstairs if there was any bombing.

Lucas responded with a huge smile, and a nod. He glanced across the table at Sophia and winked; this was better than he could have hoped for.

****

So the Wouters household had become a very busy and at times noisy place. Lucas had helped Mama transform the gar-den. It no longer had a lawn and tidy pretty flower beds, but had been dug up to allow the planting and growing of a variety of vegetables. The apple and pear tree at the end of the garden shielded blackcurrant and gooseberry bushes. And right at the back of the garden, Lucas had managed to build a chicken coop, which now housed four brown-speckled hens. They were incredibly treasured, as they had become a very prized possession for the Antwerp residents. It had become Elsa's job to feed them, something which she quite enjoyed, but her other job she was not so fond of, that of cleaning them out. She had taken a real liking to them, and had named them all, gaining a promise from her parents that they would not ever be eaten. They had, of course, a much better use: that of producing four brown eggs every day, which were put to very good use.

Lucas was a good worker, and often in the evening he and Derk, who was now over sixteen, would sit on the bench in the garden and discuss a whole range of topics. He turned out to be a calming influence on Derk, who was becoming more and more frustrated by being penned in, and unable to go about his business as he would have liked to do. He was slightly pleased that he was still able to go to the garage every day and learn about car mechanics, but still found himself cursing the Nazis who prevented him from playing his beloved football. Having Lucas living in the household gave him someone to vent this to. He didn't want to burden our father, who seemed to be working longer and longer hours. He now often saw patients in the evening, as there were fewer opportunities for people to access medical advice, and so his skills were even more in demand. Apparently a large number of professionals had left the city to seek other places to live, which they perceived to be safer, and the knock-on effect meant that there was a higher demand for medical services. Derk had listened tonight to Papa telling us how it seemed that as food was becoming less available, it impacted on people's immune systems, making them less able to fight diseases, and so hence they were seeking medical help more often. This had incensed Derk, and if the Nazis hadn't invaded then this would not have happened, so he had even more reason to be angry.

The other big change in our family household was that Mama was conducting my education. Both Mama and Papa had decided that the risks of me going backwards and forwards to the school were too great. There had been reports of young girls being approached by German soldiers, and either touched or intimidated. It wasn't a hard decision, as of course Mama could revive her teaching skills. It wasn't just me that took part in the morning lessons that were held around the dining room's large table. My two friends Dominique and Adele Van Holden had joined us. The two families were thinking as one when it came to concerns about their daughters going out and about in the community.

Mama had added another language to teach, that of German, which had raised the eyebrows of all the children. 'Why, Mama, are we going to learn German? Do you think that they may make us all speak it soon?'

'Well I hope not, Elsa, but I think that I would be useful to have some understanding of the language. It might help if you know what they are saying to you. Just to ensure that if they instruct you to do something you understand it, so there is no confusion.' This was something that worried Mama, because she had witnessed a German soldier shouting and ordering a woman to turn around and return to her home, but the poor woman couldn't understand him, and this resulted in him hitting her and her falling to the ground. It had been a very difficult event to witness, and at that point she made up her mind that she would teach me some of the language: it just maybe would help to keep me safe.

We three girls enjoyed spending the mornings together, and Mama did her best to ensure that we didn't spend the time chatting, but concentrated on the work she set us. It was around September time that we were joined by two extra pupils who lived just across the road. Sarah and Martha Tasma had not been pupils of the Catholic school, but had attended the Jewish school some distance away. It came about after a visit to Papa's surgery by their mother Ruth, who in some distress was worrying about her daughters attending school, given the increase in assaults on Jewish people. Papa had diagnosed Ruth as suffering from severe anxiety, and after she had left the surgery he had sought Mama out, and discussed the idea of Sarah and Martha just coming across the road to join in our lessons.

Mama had agreed immediately, and rushed to find her coat to go and knock on the door across the road to speak to Ruth and her husband Jacob. He now conducted his legal business from the family house, again due to the concerns of making the journey to the office he had used for the past ten years. It was considered safer to try to not be seen out in the streets. They hadn't really had much to do with the Wouters family since they moved to their house, just a couple of years before. Their usual doctor was now some distance away and Ruth hadn't felt it safe to travel to see him. The couple carefully considered the offer. Mama reassured them that the teaching she could provide would be generic, and not focus on any religious aspect. It would be good for all of the girls, she argued, to have some company. The girls didn't know each other, apart from occasions when I had waved to them across the road. It was decided that Martha and Sarah would indeed join the morning lessons, and Mama reassured their parents that she would keep them safe in her care.

So the little school at number 45 Ramstraat became a busy and at times noisy affair. Mama loved it. It allowed her to practice her love of teaching and sharing her knowledge with this small band of girls. Both Martha and Sarah were welcomed into our small circle. They were somewhat younger than me and my friends, and we took to helping them with some of the tasks that mama set. I enjoyed this, and relished in being able to have younger children who I could boss around. I was kind to them, though, as I quickly picked up both girls' sense of nervousness.

****

Christmas of 1940 was a fairly sober affair. Food had become more difficult to get, and Papa was unrelenting in his view that they should not buy food from the black market. It incensed him that people were profiteering, when others were going without. He saw this more than others in the household; as some of the patients he observed were struggling with finding enough food. He had taken the decision that he would not charge them for his services, if they couldn't afford it. The patients that were wealthy and still making and earning money, would, he decided help to subsidise those who could not, even if they were unaware they were doing so. Consequently, the word was being passed around that if you needed to see a doctor then Dr Wouters was the person to go to.

Sometimes in place of monetary payment came the odd gift, some onions or apples from a garden, and Papa always accepted them, realising that the person who was giving them wanted to hold on to their pride, and felt better that there was an exchange taking place. One local butcher, who was struggling with paying when Papa had lanced a particularly large boil, had delivered a piece of gammon, and this became the centre of the Christmas Eve dinner.

Mama and Papa had done their utter best to try to keep the household upbeat. They had ensured that St Nicholas had visited me and I, at nearly thirteen, was delighted that the tradition was continued, even if there were fewer presents than usual.

Even with the restraints, the traditional celebratory meal that was held on the Eve of Christmas was fulfilling. The household were aware that while Rachel did not celebrate this festival, she was willing to share it with them. Everyone tried hard to close the curtains, and lock the doors and try to ignore what was taking place outside. The sadness and worry, though, could not be fully ignored, especially for Rachel who had still not heard from her husband. Lucas too, had no idea where his family were. They were all determined that for a few hours they would make it a jolly affair.

Christmas morning saw Grand-mama insisting that the family attend Mass. Neither Mama or Papa were keen on going, but to keep the peace and respect the elderly woman they agreed to do so. Derk was resolute that he was not going to attend, and at nearly seventeen our parents decided that the fight to get him to comply would require too much energy. He and Lucas would stay at home with Rachel, who advised the others that she would prepare lunch.

The family took the short walk to the church, although it took a little longer than usual due to Grand-mama's inability to walk fast. She mumbled about how silly her son was, to not have a car when he could easily have afforded one.

'It's like this, Mama, why would I need to own a vehicle when I can walk to all of my patients, and even if I need to attend the hospital, it is still within walking distance? Or I can take a tram.' Papa said that with a smile on his lips; he knew that his mother detested trams, and if she had to take transport then it was likely to be a taxi.

The church was full by the time we arrived, and we were able to find some vacant seats towards the top of the church. Why these were still vacant became clear when they saw who was sitting in the two front rows. German soldiers all spruced up in their uniforms. Sitting immediately behind them were several well-known local people, who were regarded as helping their occupiers. Collaboration was now becoming something that many citizens of Antwerp were coming to despise and loathe. Who could they trust?

The service commenced with Father Francis leading the service, and who in my eyes droned on for far too long. I couldn't help gazing around the church, and my eyes focused on the backs of the German soldiers. It had been a bit of a surprise to see them here. I hadn't given much thought that they could follow the Catholic faith, or any faith.

At the end of the service, Father Francis stood in the doorway to greet and shake hands. The German soldiers were the first to stride out, their heads high, not looking sideways at the rest of the congregation. The dislike for them by most of the congregation was palpable, and surely they would feel it too. At the church door, Father Francis was almost bowing to them; he smiled and held their handshake just a little bit longer than necessary. He was almost falling over when he greeted some people, smiling and speaking to them in, as I would describe it, his thin whining voice. It was our turn to be greeted, and while Grand-mama was greeted with a level of respect, both Papa and Mama could not miss the lack of sincerity behind the smile that was given to them.

'I see that you are missing of one of your family members,' the priest proclaimed. 'Where is Derk? He is not ill, I hope?'

Mama answered quickly. 'No, Father. He didn't feel he wanted to come, and he is old enough now to make his own decisions.'

The priest stood back for a moment, ensuring that he had an observant audience from the queue waiting behind. 'Well,' he exclaimed, 'when is a seventeen-year-old boy viewed as being old enough to make his own decisions, I ask you?' He looked Mama up and down for a minute. 'And I understand that you have taken it on your own back, to remove your other child from our school. And, I am led to believe, that you have set up your own school.' He drew breath. 'Also, and even more interesting, Madam Wouters, you have taken on the teaching of children who are not even of our faith.'

'In my mind, Father Francis, children are children and all deserve to have an education.' Mama stood up to look the dumpy middle-aged man in the eye. 'Regardless of their faith, or family background.'

Before any further comments could be made, or his wife could reply with an even louder retort, with what he could see would be an angry response, Papa stepped in. 'Thank you, Father, we are holding up the queue. A good day to you and we hope that you have a peaceful time.'

He took Mama's arm and steadied her, and taking his mother's in his other hand, he guided them away from the church. Papa reminded his wife as calmly and quietly as he could that they were being watched, not just by their compatriots, but by several German soldiers who had been listening to the exchange, and seemed curious about whom this family were.

Once they had returned home, and ate the lunch, nothing was said until Grand-mama excused herself, saying she was going to her room for a rest. Then Mama let forth with her anger.

'Did you see the old hypocrite, the way he was sucking up to those Germans, all smiles and simpering? I don't trust that man not to be part of the welcoming committee to them. How dare he make those comments about me teaching! Clearly he was referring to Martha and Sarah. He is a nasty little man, who hides behind his cassock.'

My eyes had widened. My mother was clearly angry and didn't have a lot of respect for Father Francis, which I was rather thankful for, as it gave credence to my own thoughts about the man, and mine were not unique. I hoped that going to Mass this morning was not going to spoil the rest of the day for us all.

'Now, my love, let's not let the man spoil the day. I have heard that Father Francis is very busy, visiting those who can ensure that the church receives funds and food, to keep it going. It is nothing surprising, is it?' Papa looked across the table and seemed to realise that I was all ears, and didn't want to influence me at a young age by his and Mama's views of the church. Neither had a lot of time for it, but in respect for his mother they would follow what was expected and pay it lip service. But as with most things, he wanted his children to have a mind of their own, which was one of the reasons he hadn't insisted that Derk attend church with them this morning. He addressed me. 'Now, my darling girl, would you like to play a game of cards? Go and see if Sophia and Rachel would like to join us and we can have some fun.'

I didn't need a second telling, and as soon as they thought I was out of earshot, Papa turned to Mama and said, 'I am in total agreement with you, my love, but let us be a little careful about what we share in front of Elsa. She doesn't need to know all of our worries. I have heard that indeed Father Francis has plenty of meetings with various people of our occupying force, and making sure he is supplied with the best of whatever is available. But let us now enjoy some family time. I will go and root Derk and Lucas out from their hide-out in the cellar to join us.'

CHAPTER 14

As I had become the most excellent of observers and an even better eavesdropper, I saw and heard that Mama and Papa were becoming more concerned about what was happening in the city. Every day brought more concerns. One March evening, it was late, and Papa had only just returned from his shift at the hospital where he helped out now and then.

'How was it tonight?' Mama had asked.

'It was busy. We had two young children brought in, suffering from acute diarrhoea, and desperately dehydrated. They should have been treated much earlier, but their parents were frightened to take them to a doctor, as they could not afford to pay. I was furious when I heard that they had sought medical help two days ago, but turned away from a doctor as they couldn't pay the fee he was requiring. Whatever happened to the Hippocratic Oath, I asked myself.'

'Will they recover?'

'Hopefully now some fluids are being administered. It's the poor quality of the food even when they do get it. The parents told us that they had all been ill, but the children don't have the immunity they should have. It makes me so angry, Estelle; this morning I had two patients attend my surgery. Both had minor complaints, and both spoke about how well the German government is managing the city. One of them even went on to say that he was in total agreement with the city paying money to the German government, as they needed the funds to ensure that they were able to look after all of the citizens under their care. I was astounded, I can tell you. I think he was quite surprised that I didn't jump to agree with him. I bit my tongue. I have to say, I would have liked to have ordered him out of the surgery, and taken him off of my list. But what did I do, but usher him out and tell him to return for a further check-up in two weeks.'

'My darling, you were absolutely right to bite your tongue. Sometimes I think these collaborators are nothing more than Nazi spies. They cannot be trusted at all, and are waiting for people to argue against them and then report them. I know it is hard for you, but please, darling, just keep doing what you are doing.'

'I was having a chat with Lambert; he was doing an extra shift at the same time. We were thinking about those who cannot access medical treatment, like the family with the two children. There are many more like them out in some of the poorer areas.' There was a pause. 'Before you say anything, I know I already treat some patients for no fee, but Estelle I must do more.'

She asked him what he was planning, as she understood that he clearly had an idea of some sort.

'Lambert and I are going to speak to another two of our colleagues who feel the same, and we are going to go and set up a couple of mobile surgeries in the poorer areas. It seems the right thing to do. If people cannot safely come to us, then we will go to them. I think it will help me when I am faced with those patients such as this morning. I will smile and nod, and know that with the money they are passing to me for their fee will help me fund some those who are suffering in this terrible war.'

Just two days later the morning lessons were interrupted by Sophia, to say that two men had arrived and needed to take an inventory of what was in their garden. Mama looked at Sophia with a look of puzzlement. 'What on earth do you mean?'

'Just as I said, Estelle, two men, who apparently are from the town authorities have arrived saying they have the power to do so. Dr Wouters is in the middle of his surgery so Rachel asked me to fetch you.'

Mama instructed us to continue to work on the arithmetic she had set us, while she dealt with the two visitors. I couldn't help myself and crept out of the room so I could stand at the top of the stairs and observe her. She met them at the bottom of the main stairs. Both were wearing armbands that signified that they were part of some bureaucratic organisation. Many groups had sprung up under the German government administration. The two men nodded to her, and one stood upright to stare at her as she descended the stairs.

'What can I do for you?' she asked, looking them up and down and returning the stare with some distain.

'Madame, we are undertaking an inventory of what each household is growing in their gardens. We have instructions to do so.' He seemed to sneer for a moment. 'Just to ensure that all the citizens in Antwerp are not withholding vital supplies.'

'When, can I ask, was this particular order made? It appears to be very invasive to citizens, does it not, to demand to see what we have in our gardens?'

The second man stepped forward. He looked slightly familiar but she couldn't place him for a minute. It was when he spoke that she was able to identify him: Albert Du Pont. He was, in fact, one of the members of the church and helped Father Francis. Evidently, he now had a new position as one of the so-called helpers to the German government. 'Madam Wouters, please do not create a difficulty here, we are doing our job and anyone who will not comply, or allow us access will be reported to the relevant authorities, and well, I am sure you do not wish to cause trouble for your household.'

Mama looked him up and down, thought for a moment that she would just tell him to bugger off. But then she really didn't wish to bring any trouble to the house, especially if it might impact on Papa's practice.

'Oh, for goodness sakes come on then, follow me, and please be quick as I am in the middle of teaching my daughter.' She made a quick decision that she would not enlighten them about the other girls in her little class. They followed her up the stairs into the kitchen where Sophia and Grand-mama were taking their morning coffee; Grand-mama glared at them as they passed through. Down the outside steps they followed her into the garden, where Lucas was planting some cabbage plants.

'You have a large garden here, madam. Do you employ this man as a gardener?' He pointed his pen towards Lucas, who had stopped what he was doing to look at the men. Thankfully, Sophia had already quickly warned him that they were about to get this visit.

'No, he is not employed as a gardener, just a friend helping out.' she told him, but then immediately had the thought that maybe she should have said Lucas was employed.

The smaller of the men approached Lucas and asked for his name and address. Mama intervened. 'He lives with us,' she told them. 'I thought you were here to take an inventory of our garden, not an inventory of who is in the house.' She waved her arm and gestured at the garden. 'Please carry on. As you will see we are growing vegetables, and these are for our own use. Any surplus is shared with others, especially any of my husband's patients who are poor, and do not have enough to eat, unlike many others in our city who seem to have plenty to eat.' She emphasised the last words looking both men up and down, as they seemed to be well fed.

The two men walked to the end of the garden noting down the fruit trees and bushes, and stopped when they came to the chicken coop. 'Madam, you have chickens I see.'

'Well, that is exactly right, that is in fact…chickens.'

'Madam, do you know that you have failed to register that you have these chickens, and that it is necessary, for all livestock to be registered with the relevant authorities.'

'Really, well that is a surprise. You see I have had these hens for some years, long before any one was in the least bit interested as to what we have in our garden.' Mama allowed the small lie to fall from her lips without a moment's hesitation.

'We will note this down, and if it is required that these are handed over for food supplies then you will be informed.'

Mama was aghast. She could not believe what she heard. She took a deep breath to try to settle her temper before she answered. 'Herr Du Pont, my chickens are not being grown for food, they are but my daughter's pets, and so I will not be handing them over to your administration at any time. Do I make myself clear? I cannot believe that even your superiors are that lacking in food supplies that they would take a child's pets from her. Surely the German government are telling us how compassionate they are towards the citizens of Antwerp.' She drew breath. 'And you, Herr Du Pont, are a man with Christian beliefs and would not, I am sure, bring yourself so low in taking a child's pets from her.'

Du Pont and his colleague were left rather stunned and speechless by her outburst. They had not heard before that chickens could be considered as children's pets. Getting himself together, Du Pont responded, 'We have taken a note, madam, that you have three chickens. You are advised that should you get any more 'pet's' that you are to inform the relevant authorities.' With that the two men turned and walked towards the steps that led back to the kitchen. Mama ushered them up through the kitchen, and back down the stairs where she opened the front door and bid them both goodbye.

She watched them walk along the pathway consulting their notes and speaking quickly to each other. How bloody dare they! What on earth had things come to that they needed to register chickens, for goodness sake. It unsettled her, though. It was an intrusion into their small household bubble, and she hadn't liked the way they had looked Lucas up and down. She would speak to Papa after lunch. She also realised that the men plainly could not count, as there were of course four brown hens, so if the worst happened then at least one would be saved from being captured.

****

Later, when Mama shared her concerns with Papa, she was careful to try to make sure that I did not overhear them. She spoke to Papa about the fact that the hens had become my pets, and that I had little else in my life to give me any real pleasure at the moment. It wasn't just about the chickens, though, that Mama was keen that I didn't overhear, it was her concerns that the two men would return, or worse we would get a visit from a Nazi soldier poking about and asking too many questions.

'We have nothing to hide, my darling,' was Papa's response. 'I hardly think that they will bother too much about our chickens. Lucas is here, and has registered with all the authorities, who have a note that he is resident at this address. I know what you are most concerned about, my love, and that is whether he might be ordered to go to work in one of the German factories, which of course may happen. We should develop a plan, should we not?'

'What sort of plan are you thinking of?'

'I am keeping my ear very close to the ground, and sometimes hear things that are being planned. Please do not ask me how. I do not wish you to know more than is absolutely necessary. But if I hear that there is likely to be a round-up, or things change, then I think we should get both Lucas and Derk to leave the city, and go and stay with Nina and Lars and help them on their farm. We can always advise anyone who comes to look for them that they were needed to help grow food in the country. I think we will have a chat with the two of them and let them know that this may happen in the future and to be ready.'

'Surely the fact that Derk is working in the garage would mean he wouldn't be required to leave? He has after all not even reached eighteen years old yet. He is still a child.'

'Well, I do not think we will risk it. Working in a garage is not considered that helpful to the Nazi regime, unless it is mending one of their vehicles. Plus, my love, you know that as the lack of petrol hits harder, many like me have garaged their cars and that means that there will be less need for cars to be repaired.' When he saw the realisation appear on her face, he hugged her to him. 'In the meantime, let's just ensure that if they come back and capture our chickens, we manage to hide one, eh?' He smoothed her cheeks and planted a kiss on the end of her nose.

CHAPTER 15

I celebrated my thirteenth birthday by having a small tea party. April was the beginning of spring, and the day started with sunshine which shone through the gaps in my bedroom curtains. I remember jumping out of bed and pulling back the curtains, to gaze down to the back garden, seeing the green sprouts of plants that were poking their heads up, just above the soil.

Dressing quickly, I ran to the bathroom to clean my teeth and comb my hair, not even minding the tugs of the comb through my curly hair; today Mama would not complain. My first job was to go outside and let the hens out. I had been rather concerned and worried when last month Mama had had the visit from those two men. Mama had told me a small lie, telling me they were checking the vegetables, but I had overheard her telling Grand-mama about them threatening to make us hand over the chickens. So every morning since that visit, I made it my first job every morning to check that they were still all accounted for.

Lucas emerged from the cellar, rubbing his hair dry. He had a cold water tap in the cellar and washed himself there, even though Mama had told him to use our bathroom. But I think he did not wish to intrude.

'Good morning, Elsa, and a very happy birthday to you…wait one moment!' With that Lucas turned back into the cellar, and returned a moment later to pass me a small, wrapped package.

'Can I open it now?' After his nod of agreement, I carefully untied the string that bound the brown paper wrapping. Inside I found a small wooden carving of a chicken. 'Oh, Lucas, did you make this? It is lovely, thank you so much! I will treasure it.' I reached up and put my arms around the wide shoulders, and gave him a big hug.

Clutching my small gift, I climbed the stairs to reach the kitchen, where Sophia was busy making the breakfast. 'Look, Sophia, what Lucas has made for me.' As I showed the young woman, I soon realised that of course, she would already know that he had been working on this gift for me, given that they seemed to be spending longer and more frequent time with each other.

Sophia smiled, wishing me a happy birthday and returned to stirring the oats she was making for the family breakfast. Papa, closely followed by Mama, came in carrying a wrapped present and an envelope with a card. I rushed over to them, to be embraced by both at the same time, making a huddle between us all, and causing us to laugh and hug tighter.

After the birthday greetings were made by each member of the household, I sat down at the top of the table with a small pile of presents in front of me. I had to wait until everyone was present before I was permitted to open them. There was a surprise gift from Grand-mama, who gave me a very pretty sapphire brooch; this, she told me, was a family heirloom, and should be treated as such. Grand-mama told me, that as I had now officially become a teenager, it was the right time to receive it. It was a lovely brooch, and I immediately pinned it onto my dress and told her that I would cherish it. A pretty slide and a new hairbrush were gifts from Derk. Rachel had knitted me a cardigan, and Sophia presented me with two linen handkerchiefs embroidered with my initials. It was Mama and Papa's present that caused me the most excitement, though, and that was a book. It was a novel called *Ballet Shoes,* and written in English, which I knew would provide me with several hour's enjoyment. I thanked them all by getting up and kissing each on their cheeks, although Derk wasn't over impressed by this and quickly wiped his hand across his cheek.

In the afternoon the four girls who shared my lessons returned dressed in their best dresses, to share a birthday tea. Dominique and Adele presented me with a small box of chocolates, causing me to almost squeal in delight when I saw it. Chocolate was one of the precious indulgent items that had almost disappeared from life, and each chocolate would be eaten with sheer pleasure, the taste relished and enjoyed. Sarah and Martha handed me a package which contained a small silver bracelet. I was taken aback with the gift, which seemed to be an expensive item and much more than would be expected.

Martha, the elder of the two girls, answered this question before it was verbalised. 'Mama and Papa wanted you to have this to also say thank you, Elsa, for being our friend and allowing us to be part of your class. '

Mama told me later that she too had been taken back by the gift. But she explained that she had realised that the family of these two little girls were already feeling the impact of the Nazi regime's tightening up restrictions on what Jewish residents could do. She told me that it made her sad to think that even Jewish children were suffering from these strange and unkind rules. She conveyed to me that I should value the small silver bracelet, as it would remind me of how friendships could cross the divide of prejudice.

CHAPTER 16

I t was the end of October, and there was little to do in the evenings so, I usually went to bed around nine o'clock. I found myself taking longer and longer to fall asleep these days. My mind was always alert to the comings and goings of our household.

I could hear Rachel moving about in the attic above me. She often spent her evenings in the large room, busily knitting in one of the big comfy armchairs in the corner. Wool was difficult to find these days, so Rachel found any old knitted garments and unpicked the wool so she could re-use it to create something that could be worn. She was excellent at making hats and gloves, and Mama had encouraged her to continue, saying that they would all need these with the winter coming. I was aware that it was becoming more and more difficult for my parents to secure adequate food, and I had overheard Mama telling Grand-mama just yesterday that she didn't know how they were going to manage this winter as fuel was becoming very hard to find.

I was also very aware of Rachel's anxiety, and being able to keep her hands busy by knitting helped her. I came to know why she was so fretful, and why the young woman rarely ventured outside of the house. My skill at eavesdropping had continued to develop. It was something that I was now well accustomed too, now that my parents seemed to believe that

I should be excluded and protected to what was taking place in the city. I listened to my brother's conversations with our parents and Lucas, and heard that there were some frightening things happening on the streets. It seems that anyone who was known to be Jewish was especially at risk from being abused, and the sad thing was not only by the Germans but by some of the residents of Antwerp. My family were united in its protection of Rachel, and I remembered the day when she was summoned to the town hall to have her card identity card stamped with *Jew*. It had been very upsetting, and Rachel had been trembling when she had returned and Mama had given her a little glass of her precious brandy to help calm her.

Sometimes I worried about my papa going out, especially at night, which he seemed to do more often now. I knew that he was going to visit some sick people who were poor, and he also helped at the hospital. I often lay awake until I heard him return home, and climb the stairs to his bed. Only when I knew he was safely home could I allow myself to fall asleep. I knew that Mama also worried about him, as I had overheard her just a few days ago asking him to be more careful and not take any more risks that he was already doing. I had been a little puzzled by his answer, that if they didn't try to help these men, then he would never be able to live with himself. I wondered what men he was referring to. At times I thought that Ramstraat 45 was becoming a house of whispers and secrets. It was proving arduous to be the youngest person in the household.

Even Sophia had become more secretive, although I believed that was more to do with Lucas. One morning during the summer, when I had awoken very early, I took myself down to the garden and I spotted Sophia creeping out of the cellar. I was about to shout to her, but something stopped me; there was something in the way Sophia was acting that told me she didn't want to be caught doing. After that event, I had carefully watched Sophia, and there was definitely something going on between her and Lucas.

Then there was Derk, who I knew was unquestionably involved in some kind of secret life. I had listened when he had told our parents he would sleep in one of the spare beds in the cellar, so he wouldn't disturb them if he and Lucas played cards late into the night. This, I knew was untrue, as while he did sleep in the cellar, I had observed him creeping out of the little concealed gate at the end of the garden which led to the small pathway along the backs of the houses. I wondered where he could be going so late, and knew our parents would be livid if they found out. I decided not to confront him, but to watch him closely.

It seemed as though it was only Grand-mama who didn't behave in any way to cause concern. She was living a very quiet life, spending her time more often in the sitting room listening to music on the gramophone, or listening to the radio. The most exciting part of the day for her was mealtimes. She did at times look at what was on her plate, and raise her eyebrows towards her daughter-in-law, as if to ask, is this all I am getting? Mama was careful that any food we did have was shared equally, but often it was less than Grand-mama would wish for. Mama just cut off any questions before they could be raised by reminding everyone around the table of how fortunate we were to have this food, when so many had so little.

I heard the sound of my papa climbing the stairs; thank goodness he was home. I could now allow myself to go to sleep. I was just about to drift off when I was brought fully awake by the sound of raised voices. It was Papa and Derk. I got out of bed and went to the door to listen.

Papa's voice was loud, but then it was as if he realised that he might be overheard, so he lowered it somewhat, meaning that I had to carefully open the door just slightly, so she could hear him better.

'How dare you be so stupid? Don't you realise that if you get caught they will kill you?' he was saying.

'But Papa, I cannot stand by and not do anything. Don't you realise that there are others who are trying to do what they can to fight the blasted Nazis. We are being very careful, Papa, I promise.'

'Oh so careful, that I found you creeping along the back path just now. You must tell me exactly what you are up to, Derk, and more importantly who you are up to it with. Now come down to the kitchen so that we do not disturb the rest of the household. I want you to tell me everything. Do you hear me? Everything.'

Well, I thought, what on earth is Derk up to? Could I dare creep down the stairs and listen at the kitchen door? No, I decided that might be a risk too far. So I took myself back to bed and lay listening for any sounds that might alert me to both Papa and Derk coming to bed. But I found my eyes closing. I tried hard to prevent myself falling asleep, but in the end I couldn't prevent it when my eyes became too heavy to resist.

The next morning I watched my family, trying to work out what was going on, and certainly there was something taking place. There was a distinctive atmosphere. Derk was getting ready to leave for work, when Papa told him to make sure he was back before dark, as he and Mama wanted to speak with him.

Derk looked annoyed, but nodded his head in agreement. I would do my best to be present when this meeting took place.

Mama seemed rather distracted that day. She kept repeating herself during the class; that was unusual and even Dominique commented on it. At lunch, I noticed that Mama only ate a very small portion of her soup, and seemed to have difficulty swallowing. When I had asked her if she was feeling unwell, she had responded in the negative, telling me that she was fine. That was clearly untrue, as whatever was going on, she certainly was not fine.

That afternoon, I sat in one of the armchairs in front of the sitting room window, a book in my hand, but I wasn't reading it. I was watching out of the window. I saw Derk cycling towards the house and dismount so that he could carry his bicycle up the steps to the front door. I stood up immediately. I was going to ensure that I kept my eyes on Derk, to observe where this conversation with our parents would take place. When I reached the top of the stairs, it was in time to see Derk deposit his bicycle in the back hallway, remove his cap and coat, and make his way up the stairs where he met me.

'What's happening?' I enquired.

'What do you mean, little sister, there is nothing happening,' he told me. I sensed he was trying to be casual in his answer.

'Yes, there is something going on, I heard you and Papa last night.' I stood in front of him to prevent him making his way to the kitchen. 'Tell me please, Derk. It isn't fair that I am left out of everything.'

He pushed his way past me, and shook his head. 'There is nothing happening, and if there is anything happening, then no doubt you will be told when it is considered to be in your interests. Now I need to have a coffee, I have had a hard day.'

I was fuming. So I would have to return to watch silently. It was after the evening meal that the meeting took place in Papa's study. Once my parents and Derk were ensconced in the room, I tiptoed down the stairs, and carefully placed my ear to the door.

My mama was speaking about Derk putting not only himself, but the whole household, at risk. Surely he realised how dangerous it was to get involved with the Resistance. I couldn't really hear his reply, but could hear Papa tell him that he understood why he wanted to help others, but he was so young. That if he was caught, then he would be taken to *Breendonk*, which I knew was the prison that the Nazis were using to interrogate anyone involved in the Resistance.

Derk had raised his voice so I could hear his reply. 'Papa, I know the risks, but we have to do something to fight back. Look at what is happening around us. Mathis and Victor have a very good established group, and are very careful about any infiltration. I want to be part of it, please do not insist that I am not. Surely you can see that we need to do this. Papa, can we not all do something to help, I am sure that everyone in our household will keep a secret. If you hadn't caught me last night, I was going to come and speak to you both about helping anyway. We have a plan of how we can help the British airmen who get stranded, and there is a route and a whole network so that we can help them get across the borders to Spain. Papa, Mama, I have an idea – please just listen to me.'

It was then that I became aware that someone was coming down the stairs, so I leapt back into the shadows. It was Rachel, coming to finish off a task in the surgery. Once she had disappeared into the room, I thought I had been too close to being discovered, so I quietly made my way back up the stairs and went to my bedroom to contemplate on what I had heard. Goodness, Derk was involved with the Resistance; my first thought was, good for him. I was proud of him. Yes, he was placing himself in danger, but at least it felt like he was trying to do something to change their world. I would have to carefully watch and listen to see what my parents would do next.

****

I found out the following day. It was a Sunday, so Derk was not going to work, and the family breakfast lasted a little longer than that of weekdays, as we tended to spend a more leisurely time. Papa announced that it had been decided that Derk was going to spend some time with Nina and Lars at their farm in Lint, and that he would be leaving the following day. Derk looked as though it had been agreed without his agreement, but seemed resigned to do as he was bid. Grand-mama asked the most questions, and was told that as the Germans were beginning to make noises about young men being sent to work for them in the factories, it would mean that Derk would be safer living with Nina in Lars in the country. It seemed to be a reasonable excuse, but I didn't miss the look that took place between my parents: that wasn't the real reason, and I knew it.

CHAPTER 17

I helped Sophia clear the breakfast table before it was time to set up the dining room for the morning schooling. It was 5th December, and in other years I would have been getting excited for the festival of Saint Nicolas visiting tonight with sweets and goodies. This year, we had taken the decision that we would not celebrate this, mainly due to the fact that sweets and goodies were in very short supply, and Papa especially thought that it was indeed insensitive for us to do so when others had not enough to eat. The onset of winter was depressing enough, and although I accepted and agreed with my parents, I would miss the fun of marking a key day in the build-up to Christmas. I assumed that even Christmas would be more low-key than last year. I thought I was now old enough to accept and adapt to this, and Mama had reminded me not to expect much this year, as each day brought more shortages.

We had been careful with harvesting our garden produce, and on the shelves in the cellar were several jars of blackcurrant jam and gooseberry jam, as well as bottled pears, apple and tomato chutney and various pickled vegetables. Sophia and Mama had worked hard to avoid any waste: even vegetable peelings were put to good use to make stock for soups. So, I reasoned with myself that I was being selfish to even think about wishing for treats. But it was not easy, and the longer this war went on, the more depressing it became.

Mama had been called down stairs by Papa, and neither Sophia nor I had taken much notice of the summons, both being caught up in washing the dishes. The kitchen door was flung open to admit a furious Mama, who almost danced into the kitchen, she was so incensed with fury. She was quickly followed by Papa, his white coat that he wore during surgery times flapping in the aftermath.

'How dare they!' she raged. 'How dare they, the conniving, deplorable, revolting, excuses for bloody men!' She took an intake of breath, and wiped away tears that were beginning to stream down her face.

I could not recall ever seeing my mama so upset or angry; it was quite scary to see her in such a state. 'Mama, what on earth has happened, what men?' I asked, throwing the tea towel to one side to go and approach her, hoping that as I got closer she would be a little calmer.

'Estelle, my dear, please calm down. Look, you are frightening the child.' Papa attempted to place his arm around her, but she swiped it away.

'How can you just stand there, Martin, and let them dictate to us, and tell us what we can and cannot do in our own home. I am sickened by this bloody regime.' She furiously wiped the tears from her face, picking up the discarded tea towel to wipe her face. She turned to me. 'I am sorry if I am upsetting you, but...' and she turned to glare at Papa, '...you will learn of this soon enough. Those two horrible individuals, the ones if you recall attended our garden some months ago to take an inventory. Damn them, they have returned with a new edict, that my little school as they snidely referred to our lessons, must now not include Martha or Sara. Martin, it was the contempt that they showed when they referred to the girls as those two Jew girls.'

'Mama, are you saying that Martha and Sara will no longer be able to come for their lessons every day. Why on earth not?'

Papa came over to me and placed his arm around my shoulders, trying to convey some comfort in what was becoming a grim start to a day. 'Elsa, apparently the German government have a new dictate.' He drew breath before he continued, almost as if he could hardly bare to say the words. 'That is, that no Jewish children are permitted to attend any non-Jewish school. So they came to inform us that Mama has to stop teaching the girls.'

He was interrupted by Mama. 'Well, I have decided to disobey their stupid new law.' She stood up, her hands on her hips with a determination that signalled that she was indeed going to do as she wished. 'It is beyond belief that they treat the Jewish people as they do, and now they wish to interfere with a perfectly private tutoring scheme. I will not have it, so there.' She stamped her foot to make the point.

'Estelle, we have to discuss this, there are others in this household who may suffer if we ignore this instruction.' He was thinking of Rachel, who more and more had to deal with snide remarks and black looks from some of his patients. He was already concerned that they might have to consider whether she could continue in her present role, as the grip on the hate for the Jewish population grew tighter.

'There will be no further discussion.' She faced him, looking at him directly as her eyes were filled with tears, mostly I thought from anger and frustration. 'Sara and Martha will continue to attend. Hasn't their family already suffered with Jacob being stripped of his legal practice just a couple of months ago? That was the family livelihood, and now he is reduced to trying to get enough work from other Jewish families. We cannot, or I cannot, tell them that their children are no longer welcome. So I will continue.'

'Mama, couldn't we just say that Martha and Sara have come to spend time with me, say playing a game or such like, and you are no longer teaching them? If we are really careful, perhaps we could beat these horrible laws, by looking as though we are obeying but we are really not.'

'Yes, you are right, Elsa, let us think about how we could get around them, and play a little game with them.' Mama sat down at the table and picked up the mug of coffee that Sophia had thoughtfully poured for her. 'I think though, that we do need to protect Dominique and Adele, as while I think that their parents would be supportive of me continuing to teach, I don't wish to cause them difficulties.'

'Remember, Estelle, that Albert Du Pont and his cronies will no doubt be keeping an eye on the coming and goings of who comes to us every day.'

Now that we were thinking about how to get around these rules I suggested, 'How about this then Mama: why don't you still continue as normal to school, Dominique, Adele and myself in the mornings, and Sara and Martha come across in the afternoon. Then if they turn up to check in the morning, they will think you are following the rules.'

'Yes, that might just work.' Mama smiled a little now that a plan to get around the laws was forming. She wasn't naïve not to have worked out that it wouldn't be her who would receive the reprisals but the Tasma family who would be in biggest amount of trouble. So while we wanted to flout their stupid laws, we did need to be careful. 'We will ensure, though, that we have a system in place so that we can demonstrate that I am not teaching them, but you are entertaining them with some games. Will they be intelligent enough to work out that your entertainment is also helping the two young girls to learn? Well, I think not.' She drained the rest of her coffee, and looked across at Papa. 'Will that work do you think, Martin?'

Her words were met with a reassuring smile from Papa. 'I think that might just work, as long as we are all very careful.'

'Right. In the meantime, I will go and visit Ruth and Jacob and explain what we are going to do. Of course they may not agree, but I wish them to know that they have at least our support.

****

So the dining room at Ramstraat 45, became a little changed. In the morning Mama continued to school us three girls, and on just three afternoons Sara and Martha attended and Mama was assisted by me. Ruth and Jacob had argued that they felt that they were placing too much strain on Mama for her to continue for five days, and were overwhelmed by the offer. They felt it might work better if they came for just three days. Sure enough, just two weeks following the first visit of Albert Du Pont, he returned and found that the two Jewish pupils were no longer in attendance. So he seemed to be bolstered up, thinking that he, and his so-called official comrades, had sorted out yet another problem and had ensured that the Wouters were complying with the law.

It was, however, the way he had looked Rachel up and down that sent a shiver down Papa. We heard about more attacks taking place in the streets against the Jewish population and so, as I was later to discover, he decided that they must act soon or risk something nasty happening to Rachel.

CHAPTER 18

January 1942 to March 1942

I was really struggling to keep warm, as were most other people at the beginning of 1942. Mama kept reminding me that I was lucky, as I didn't have to leave the house, and we were still able to have some of the rooms heated. While I moaned and groaned a little, it was Grand-mama who had the most to say on the matter. We now ate our meals around the kitchen table, as while it was significantly smaller than the dining room table, the kitchen was somewhat warmer. Grand-mama would arrive for meals dressed in her old mink coat which, she told me, had been inherited from her own mother and, I whispered to Sophia, it smelt quite rotten. Nevertheless, it helped keep her a little warmer.

Most of the daytime activities in the house now took place in only in two rooms. The kitchen was the main focus, and the other was the sitting room, which because it was south-facing, captured any sun that did appear between the clouds, and helped to lift the temperatures ever so slightly. The fire in the grate was kept going during the day, but kept low to save fuel. The dining room was now not used, so morning lessons took place around the kitchen table, and in the afternoon I entertained Martha and Sara. The kitchen had become the real hub of the house there was something reassuring about that, as though our household were acting as a team, not only to beat the silly rules and regulations, but now to also beat the winter. Extra blankets were distributed to the bedrooms, and Sophia and Rachel found that the loft space was exceptionally cold, so as well as extra blankets they placed their coats on the top and went to bed wearing layers of clothing, looking more as though they were leaving the house to go for a walk than retiring for the night.

The snow fell across the city and made it really quite difficult to get around. It didn't prevent the queues that continued to form to purchase food and other essentials. The German authorities had a grip on all supplies, and there was certainly no food waste within the Antwerp population.

Papa had a small fire burning in both his surgery and the waiting area. Rachel had told him that she would be able to manage without one in the waiting room. However, Papa's waiting room was now forever busy, and so he felt it necessary that the patients seeking his assistance because they felt unwell should at least be able to feel comfortable while they awaited his consultation. He was becoming increasingly concerned about his patients; many were beginning to show signs associated with lack of food. Apart from some of his wealthier patients, those who didn't seem to share the same moral compass as his own. Many of these particular patients appeared happy to pay money to the ever-increasing numbers of black market racketeers, so that they could continue to purchase the best of food and goods. He suspected that they also had warm houses with blazing fires burning in every room.

Morning surgery was over, and once Rachel locked the front door, and they both climbed the stairs to the kitchen for lunch they were both greeted with a very busy and somewhat cosy kitchen. Dominique and Adele were just finishing up their lessons, and getting ready to leave for their home. Papa reminded both of them to ensure they were well covered, so they didn't get too cold as they made their way the short journey to their home.

Once the girls had left, the rest of our household bunched up around the table to consume a large bowl of vegetable soup, dipping the fresh bread that Sophia had baked that morning into it. We chatted loudly between ourselves.

After lunch it was Papa's routine to retire to his study and take a little time to catch up with any paperwork, or sometimes he found himself becoming drowsy and was forced to take a little nap. His study was cold, but he wrapped a rug around himself to keep some of the cold at bay. He told me that could not recall a winter as cold as this, and he did worry about safeguarding our family's health and wellbeing. It was one of the things that kept him awake at night. Getting fuel was becoming a stressful activity. Lucas had managed to source some from various sellers, with a very clear instruction from Papa that on no account should it be with anyone considered to be involved in the black market.

I decided to pay him a visit, and waited a little time for him to get himself settled. I knocked on the door, and heard him tell me to enter. Poking my head around the door, I asked, 'Can I come in, Papa?'

'Of course, my love, you are more than welcome. Have you come to chat, or have you a particular requirement of your old papa?'

'To chat, Papa, if that is okay, and I hope I am not disturbing you.'

'Not at all, so come and snuggle up in the chair here.' He moved to one side to create some space for me to slip into. The space he created was not large, so it was probably just as well I was very slim. 'Now, let me share my rug with you.' He moved the rug that was round his legs so that we were both encompassed underneath it. 'So what would you like to chat about, Elsa?'

'Papa, do you think the Nazis will always be here in the city?' I asked, moving my head so I could watch his profile as he considered his answer.

'I hope not. It is not a question that I can answer for you, I am afraid. But let us hope that the British and the other Allies can free us in the future.'

'Papa, I know that you listen to your radio, I can hear it. Do we have to keep it secret?'

Papa took a deep breath. 'Well, not the radio in the sitting room, Elsa: that is still permitted. But yes, you are right, I, do have another radio, and I listen to the BBC every day. It is better that you do not announce that to anyone, as no doubt our German friends would not like to learn that many people in the city are tuning in to hear about what is happening in other places.' He placed his hand on my face and touched my nose with his finger. 'It is not for you to worry your pretty little head, though, my sweet girl.'

'What are they saying, Papa? I promise I will not tell anyone, and I would not mention a thing to any of the girls.'

'Britain is doing its best to fight the Nazis, and some of our own brave men have formed the free Belgian forces, and are in Britain as we speak, getting ready to come and take our land back.'

It was a surprise to hear this. 'Oh Papa, do you think that Rachel's David might be one of those brave soldiers?'

'Let us hope he is, my love. Now are there any more questions or can I just get back to smoking my pipe?' I shook my head and gave him a kiss on his cheek before leaving the room.

The conversation had left him realising that I was nearly fourteen, and that he couldn't shield me from reality. I know that he too hoped that David Cohen was safe and well. There were so many concerns at the moment, and I was very aware that he tried hard not to show his anxiety to the rest of the household, but at times it was hard. He very much believed that it was his job to keep us safe and protect his family.

I felt a little relieved. I too worried about Rachel's David. I wondered if I should tell her about the free Belgian soldiers, and reassure her that maybe he was alright. Then the thought entered my mind that maybe I should not say anything, as it might get her hopes up, plus hadn't I just agreed with Papa that I would keep the knowledge of his radio secret? Oh, how I hated this war. It had even caused my toes to have chilblains, which irritated me beyond belief. Never before could I recall being so cold, especially at night even with the extra blankets that, while heavy, did not seem to keep the coldness at bay.

Grand-mama was asleep on the sofa in the sitting room. Her legs were propped up onto a stool and she had her mink coat covering her. The fire glowed, and I carefully placed another small log onto it. Precise instructions were followed: only putting one small log onto the fire, just to keep it going. I longed for the time when we could have a blazing fire again, the sort that penetrated the whole room rather than just the immediate area in front the hearth. I took one of the rugs and wrapped it around my shoulders and sat in my favourite chair in front of the window. It was nearly dark, and soon it would be time to draw the heavy curtains across. Until then I could gaze out to the street below. The snow was continuing to fall, and it looked as though people were struggling to walk along the pavements, and had now taken to walking in the middle of the road. Oh, I did wish that we could go out and sledge, or have a snowball fight in the park as we had the last time it had snowed so heavily. I felt so hemmed in. This blessed war, how I was coming to hate it more and more. I could understand why my parents were so strict about me not going out, as it was to keep me safe, but I yearned to go and look in the shops or to go and visit the cinema. Now my life seemed so small. Thank goodness that I had the girls every morning to share my studies or otherwise I would find it really lonely.

I could see Lucas making his way along the road. He was pushing and pulling his bicycle along the road. It looked like a real struggle, as the wheels kept sticking in the thick snow. He looked frozen, his heavy outdoor coat covered with snow, and his peaked cap looked more white than grey. On the back of his bicycle it looked as though he had a bag of logs...thankfully. I envied Lucas and Sophia as they still left the house at least once a day to source food or fuel. Lucas saw other people, and sometimes if I caught him at the right time he would tell me about what had seen on the streets. Only yesterday I had overheard him telling Sophia that he had seen a young man beaten by two Nazi soldiers when he had failed to stop. He said everyone on the street had looked away, and no one had dared to intervene. Lucas had been angry about it, and I wasn't sure whether he was angry about the poor young man being beaten, or about himself not being able to intervene.

I allowed my thoughts to wonder what I would do if I witnessed something like this. Mama and Papa had always held strong views that we should always help others, and this was inbred into both Derk and me, but how could we do anything to help people now? I was proud of both of my parents for doing what they did, my Papa helping people with his medical knowledge and Mama teaching me and the girls.

A loud snort reached my ears, and I turned to see Grand-mama wake up and look around her, appearing to take a moment to gain her senses as to where she was. She looked to me. 'Goodness, Elsa, is it still snowing? It's getting dark so for heavens' sake close those drapes. It will help to keep the cold out.'

I did as I was bid, and went over and sat beside her. 'Are you warm enough, Grand-mama?'

'Yes, my child, I am at the moment. Thank goodness I brought my coat with me when I moved in here last year. I would think it would prove quite impossible to get across to my house now, and get anything. Is it nearly time for a cup of café do you think?'

This was my grand-mama hinting that she would like me to go and get her some. I was happy to do so; after all, at least I could be a help to her.

As I crossed the hallway to the kitchen and entered, I realised that I had interrupted some sort of household conference. It really annoyed me, as clearly I was been excluded, yet again. Around the table sat my parents, Sophia, Rachel, and Lucas who had recently arrived and was rubbing his hands together to revitalise circulation.

'What am I missing?' I enquired, looking them all up and down and waiting to be told to disappear.

'You had better come and join us,' retorted Mama, an acquiescence that they could not exclude me from this discussion. She nodded her head towards Papa, to infer that he should allow me to join them.

'Sit down, Elsa. We were discussing the situation of the increase of attacks against the Jewish people.' He looked at Rachel, who was looking quite upset and scared. 'I have been concerned for quite a while about Rachel's safety, and this morning we had a rather distasteful situation which has raised my concerns. One of my patients, who will remain nameless, made some very nasty comments to Rachel, and then asked me how long I was going to go on employing her. She insinuated that she was friends with some Nazis, and that maybe they should be aware that some doctors, were continuing to employ Jews.' He watched this information soak in, and Sophia must have mirrored my own look of distress. 'Now Estelle and I have had a plan in the background for some time, and we think it may be time to put it into action.'

We all stared at Mama and Papa, waiting to hear what the plan was. Mama continued, 'Rachel, we all love you as one of our family, but we are very alarmed that one day the Nazis might just turn up and demand that you are removed. What would be even more disturbing would be if they said that you could no longer live here with us. We know of other situations where this has happened. So we want you to leave the city.'

Rachel looked shocked and frightened. 'Do you mean you want me to just leave? But where will I go?' She was struggling not to cry.

Papa leant across the table and took her hand to steady her. 'We think that it might be safer if you went to stay on the farm with Nina, Lars and Derk. They also have some contacts who are getting Jewish people out of the country to safety, and so they will try to help you. We are very anxious about what is happening, and I have been informed that the Germans are taking more and more Jewish people away on trains. So we want you to be safe, Rachel.'

'But what if David comes to find me, and I am not here?' she asked, now not able to prevent the tears flowing down her cheeks or the shaking of her body.

'My dear, if David comes to find you, I think he will be relieved that you are somewhere safe, and to be frank, I no longer think that staying here is providing you with safety. With this terrible weather we think that might aid your travel. Derk is coming to visit tomorrow, and he can escort you back to the farm. It is the right thing to do,' he said in a reassuring manner, rubbing the back of her hand to emphasise this.

So it was decided that tonight would be the last evening that Rachel would be share the evening meal. We had decided not to make a big thing of it, and Grand-mama was just told that Rachel was going to leave to stay with friends, not that she was going to stay with Nina and Lars. We had all agreed that it was best not to share the plan with her, as although Grand-mama didn't go out often; she had been known to forget that she wasn't supposed to share things, and so to protect us all, she would be excluded from this plan. I was secretly pleased, that I was now part of the inner circle and they were treating me more as an adult, rather than as a child.

****

The next morning Derk arrived. He stomped the snow from his boots, and shook his cap. We were all pleased to see him, and he brought us up to date on the news from the farm. They were quite isolated so hadn't had any visits from officials for some time, he told us. They continued to feed the animals, and he had made several friends in the area. That piece of news raised worried looks between our parents. They didn't ask who the friends were, but I think they surmised that he was still dallying with the Resistance. He had left the small truck he drove on the edge of the city, and had walked and taken the tram to the centre. He told our parents that he was being careful and the truck was parked in a forest track that was well hidden. It had been a little difficult to drive with the snow, and he didn't want to wait until later, so after eating a quick bowl of soup he suggested that Rachel and he left.

We all hugged Rachel, and tears were streaming down all of the faces of the females in the room. I hugged her tight, and told her that if David came looking for her we would make sure that he was looked after. I would miss her very much, but I understood the need for her to leave, and wanted her to be safe more than anything.

I also hugged my brother, who surprisingly returned my hug with even more force. 'You stay safe and well, little sister,' he told me, holding my face in his hands, 'and do what Mama and Papa tell you.' I bobbed my head, and hugged him again, telling him to also stay safe. It had been some time since we had held each other closely, and I felt a sense of strength emanating from my big brother, who seemed to have developed a layer of muscle since he had been working on the farm.

Just in case there were anyone who was watching the house,

Derk and Rachel left by the small hidden gate at the end of the garden, and waved to us all as they reached it. It needed a bit of force to get the gate open as the snow had drifted against it, but they eventually managed, leaving the rest of Ramstraat 45 sad, and anxious that Rachel would be alright.

****

With Rachel leaving her post as the receptionist, it left a gap. Who was going to take over her role? We did not wish to employ someone from outside, and so it was decided that Lucas would take on the job. He was an intelligent young man who could easily pick up on the tasks that were required. He also had a very pleasant manner, and could be courteous and respectful. It would, we agreed, also provide some protection for him, as he would have an important job, and therefore be spared from any German government requests to work in one of their ever-growing number of factories. So, that made perfect sense. He was indeed greeted warmly by the patients; the older ladies were quite taken by his quiet presence, and the men were content that he was always respectful. There were several comments which riled him: some expressed their view that they were pleased that the Jew girl had been dismissed. He just smiled at them, while thinking how awful it must have been for Rachel to have to have been on the receiving end of these looks and comments. One day when this was all over, he hoped that he would never have to be in these ghastly people's presence again or, better, he could tell them what he actually thought of them.

CHAPTER 19

The terrible winter weather at last departed, and in April all of the city residents were relieved when the spring sun began to penetrate the skies and begin to warm them. It had left its toll, with people suffering from the results of such a long cold spell. The Wouters were rewarded with the news that they had definitely made the right decision to help Rachel to leave, as anti-Jewish sentiments increased. We had received the news that she was being helped to make the long journey out of the country. We didn't know how, but were assured that she was amongst friends and that was enough for us. I remember thinking thank goodness she was safe, and I sent a thought that if there was any such thing as a God, then could he please watch over her journey.

It had been a bleak time, and Papa continued to move around the city in the evenings to administer to the sick and poorest. He rarely shared what he had seen or who he had met with anyone, even Mama. I still lay in my bed waiting until I heard him return. I had just celebrated my fourteenth birthday, and my parents decided that as I was becoming a sensible young woman they would provide me with a special treat and take me to the cinema. It had been a regular outing before the war, but I had not been allowed to go since the German occupation. My parents had indeed shielded me, but had relented after I had told them that my biggest wish was to go out to visit the cinema.

It was a rather strange experience; it had been so long since I had been up to the centre of the city, or even been on a tram. It was as though I had entered a strange city. It had a very peculiar atmosphere, assisted by the red flags with the horrible swastikas fluttering in the breeze. There was evidence of German occupation and presence everywhere it seemed, even though the city was still being administered by the collaborating council officials. I thought back to before the war, when I would travel on the trams frequently, to visit the cinema or go with Mama to visit the shops. Now, many of the shops we passed looked forlorn, their window displays limited to just a few items, emphasising how few goods were available to purchase, even if you could afford it. When a German patrol car passed it left me with a sense of uneasiness; it felt intimidating and scary. Nevertheless, being out and about, brought with it a sense of elation. I was so looking forward to watching a film and experiencing an outing after all those months being confined to Ramstraat.

The outing gave me a huge boost. Now that the radio was officially banned, there was little to distract and provide entertainment. Papa still listened covertly to his own radio that was secreted in the cupboard in his study. No one in the household mentioned it, and I didn't think that my Grandmama was aware that it existed. She had been enraged when the Nazis had announced that radios were now banned; it had been one of her most favourite daily routines, to spend an afternoon listening to it, and now she could no longer do so. She complained every day, that it was criminal, that they were depriving so many people from a little daily respite from what had become a dreary existence. While we all agreed with her, we now just listened and bobbed our heads in agreement, rather than adding our own frustrations with the ban, which seemed to tighten the grip even more on what we could and couldn't do.

Just a week after my birthday outing, another happier event

gave our household a little reprieve; this was when Lucas and Sophia announced their intention to marry. Their announcement was met with a cheer and toast from the diminishing stock of alcohol that was used now very sparingly. Even I was allowed a small glass of the fiery liquid to toast the couple. They informed everyone that they had booked an appointment with the registry office to marry the following month, and hoped that all of us would be able to join them.

Sophia had been to visit her family, who were living in a small village in the north, close to the Dutch border. She had taken a couple of days off the previous week and made the journey. It had been the first time she had visited her family since they left. She had returned looking quite unhappy; it seemed that her parents had not been overjoyed with her news, and wanted her to wait until the war had ended before she married, and they were especially not happy with the news that she wasn't to marry in a church. Her visit to them had been arduous; it was not easy at all to travel out of the city, and she returned disheartened that she hadn't been given her parents' blessings. However, she would dismiss their views and marry her lover as soon as she could. She told me that she felt that our family were more her family than her own flesh and blood. She had smiled when she told me how Lucas had reassured her that they would eventually come round, and made her smile telling her that once they got to eventually meet him, they would be bowled over by his personality and looks.

Sophia had shared with me that she had reflected to herself that at least she had been able to visit her parents, whereas Lucas was still unaware of where his family were. So many families had lost contact with each other; there were so many people on the move throughout Belgium. She told me that she wished that she had been able to grant one of her parents' wishes and marry within the church, but she couldn't bring herself to approach their local church, and especially the rotund Father Francis, with his bulging eyes and stinking breath. Sophia occasionally accompanied Grand-mama to Mass – either she or Papa did so, to assist her as she seemed to have a deeper devotion than the rest of the household. We had all agreed that someone would need to do so, given that Grand-mama had more of a problem with her mobility: it had lessened as she had become frailer. Mama, though, had put her foot down, and declared she would not set foot into the church again. This was mainly due to having to be in the same building as Albert Du Pont and his fellow collaborators. News often reached them, via Papa's patients, of some of the more unpleasant behaviours of some members of the church and their leader, Father Francis. Only yesterday, Lucas had heard two women in the waiting room gossiping about how Albert Du Pont had been seen visiting at least two young women, who he claimed he was helping. But it seemed that the two women had a different story – that he was threatening them. If they didn't grant him favours, then he would ensure that their husbands would find out when they eventually returned home from Germany where they had been sent to work in the factories.

That had made Sophia's blood boil, and cemented for her their decision to marry via a civil service. The date was set for the beginning of June, and Mama had surprised her today by presenting her with a roll of very pretty material. She had been touched and delighted and set about shaping it into a dress that would become her wedding dress. It was a lovely shade of pale green with very small white flowers dotted about. She would enjoy making this, as sewing had become her liberator; it had become the outlet for her creative juices.

****

The eve of the wedding came upon them, and there was a great deal of excitement in the house. I was extraordinarily excited, as this was perhaps the most excitement that I had had since the start of the war. I had assisted my mother to make a cake: it was somewhat a rather diminished affair, because there were so few ingredients about. However, we had improvised, and in the end we had managed to produce something, that would mark Sophia and Lucas's day. Sugar was rare, so we picked some pretty flowers from the one remaining flower bed in the garden and decorated the cake with them in lieu of icing. The wedding ceremony was to take place in the afternoon; then we would celebrate with a meal in the evening, with a small piece of beef that Mama had managed to secure from the butcher, accompanied by some fresh vegetables from the garden. One of the remaining bottles of wine was already in the cellar to keep cool.

The morning of the wedding day was a busy affair. Lessons were cancelled on that sunny Friday morning, and this allowed me the space to help Sophia get ready. The bathroom was made available to her so that she could bathe, and preen. Lucas was banned from entering the house, and instructed by me that he was barred from entering, or to try to peep at his bride before they left for the ceremony. He had smiled and patted me on my head, looking down at me, saying he would not dare to disobey my orders.

I had been given the special honour of being Sophia's bridesmaid. I was taking my role very seriously, which made the rest of the household smile; they hadn't seen me so happy for so long. I had practised styling Sophia's long auburn hair before the big day, and had so enjoyed doing so. Several styles had been tried before we had come up with the current one, that of pleating her hair and then twisting it and pinning it carefully so it created a look of sophistication. Or, that's how both Sophia and I viewed it. I helped Sophia get dressed; she shyly had put on the silk underwear that was a gift from Mama, and had carefully folded the silk nightdress that was edged by fine lace, that was also part of Mama's gift. She had been taken by surprise by such a lovely gift. Mama had smiled, and whispered to her that every young woman on their wedding day should feel silk against her skin. That comment had made Sophia blush, and I could only imagine how the nightdress would look on her when she went to bed that night. It caused me to wonder what exactly went on, that made both Mama and Sophia seem so skittish.

Sophia had been overcome with the generosity of our family. First she had been summoned to Grand-mama in her bedroom and presented with a necklace. This was one chosen from her rather large jewellery box, and seemed to hold a green emerald; she had initially tried to refuse the gift, saying she couldn't accept such a lavish item. Grand-mama had brushed her reticence away, telling her firmly that she wished her to have it, it was a mark of thanks for the kindness she had shown her.

No sooner had Sophia recovered from this kind gesture when was called into the sitting room to find Mama, Papa and me waiting for her. I presented her with a lovely bunch of spring flowers, bound in a green ribbon to match her dress. When Papa stepped forward and presented her with an envelope which contained some francs she was overcome, especially when she knew that they had given Lucas some money just the day before. 'Surely this is far too much,' she told them.

Mama had stepped forward. 'Not at all, Sophia. We regard you as one of our family and we are delighted that you are going to be married to another one of our adopted family members today.' She had held the young woman's hands in hers. 'And you have been such a help and so loyal to us. We cannot thank you enough.'

Papa stepped forward and placed a kiss on her cheek. 'Now then, young lady, do not destroy your lovely make up by tears, or else I will be in trouble from this young and very excited person here.'

Shortly afterwards our small possession made our way down the stairs to the front hallway where Lucas was waiting. He was spruced up in a suit that had once belonged to Papa and adjustments had been made so that it fitted him like a glove. Henry Smeet was waiting outside with his large car that he used occasionally as a taxi, and welcomed the six of us to squeeze into it.

The ceremony was a speedy affair, and was completed almost before we could think about it. Sophia could not help but reflect that a wedding Mass would have meant more, but when Lucas kissed her and whispered his love and welcomed her as Mrs Neefs, she seemed so happy. She told me later that she realised that the most important thing was that now she was married to the man she loved.

It was a very jolly affair back at Ramstraat. Papa opened the wine, and the couple were toasted, and wished future happiness. The meal became a cheery and noisy affair. I was delighted and uplifted by the event. As I gazed around the table at the people who meant most to me in the world, for the first time in many months I felt a sense of wellbeing. I remarked to myself later, as I lay in bed and went over the day's events, that I would remember this day for a long time to come, and it would bolster me in the days to come.

CHAPTER 20

J uly brought with it some long sunny days, and it allowed me time to help Mama in the garden. Now that Lucas was working alongside Papa, it was necessary that we helped out to keep the flow of vegetables and fruit to provide us with a constant supply. In the morning we continued to follow the routines, with Dominique and Adele spending the morning with Mama schooling us. The girls and I really enjoyed spending this time together, and while the level of how much we actually learnt could be questioned some mornings, it provided us with a sense of normality in a world that was raging out of control. Our little group was shielded from many of the atrocities that were impacting on so many. On three days of the week the visits by Martha and Sara brought another little brightness into the household. I looked forwards to seeing them, and I was aware that my parents watched and commented that I was like a little mother hen, the way I fussed and clucked about them.

It was a Wednesday afternoon; the younger girls were visiting and being entertained by me in the garden. The little girls were helping me pick some fruit, and they were delighted to be doing so. Life in the Tasma household was sombre, and anxious. The increasing number of attacks on the Jewish community were causing them real fear. There were stories circulating that some people were being rounded up and put on trains; where they were being taken wasn't clear. The girls' parents were very grateful to our family; they told us that we were the only people providing their children with some semblance of normality. When they returned from their afternoon visits, they seemed happier, and acted more like children.

A visitor entered the house: Father Francis had arrived, bustling in and requesting to see Grand-mama. Lucas had asked him to wait while he ran up the stair to find Mama, who was busy peeling potatoes in the kitchen. She was a bit taken aback when Lucas told her he had left him waiting in the hallway. 'Well, I suppose we better see if Helena wishes to see him.' She wiped her hands, and marched into the sitting room where Grand-mama was dozing in her chair. She came to when Mama approached her, and was equally surprised when she was informed that Father Francis had come to visit her.

'Why?' she asked.

'Who knows, Mama, but firstly do you feel up to seeing him? I can just tell him that you are resting.'

Grand-mama sat up and preened her hair a little. 'Oh, Estelle, of course I must see Father Francis.'

Mama turned and huffed, as although she did not agree, she could not argue with her elderly mother-in-law. She stomped down the stairs, steeling herself to meeting the priest and having to allow the obnoxious man into her home. He saw her coming down the stairs, and it was quite clear to him that he wasn't being welcomed with open arms. This was something he wasn't used to happening; he was used to being not only welcomed with open arms but being treated with total respect.

He was shown up to the sitting room. Mama left them, but grimaced, as Grand-mama requested some coffee be brought in. Although it was rather petty, Mama whispered to me that she was considered spitting in his cup, but of course she did not do so.

Grand-mama recounted to us later what took place between the priest and her, and it answered many of the questions we would have about this visit.

'This is a surprise, Father,' Grand-mama had smiled. 'I think it must be the first time that I have had a visit from you. What is the occasion, I must ask?'

The priest lowered his growing rump on to the sofa, and sat forward, passing his hand through his thinning grey hair. 'Madam Wouters, it just that I haven't seen you at Mass in the last couple of weeks, and I wondered whether you were well.'

'Yes I am well, but it was only just two weeks since I attended Mass, Father. It has been longer before. I find walking a little more of a challenge these days.'

'I hear that Sophia and Lucas have married. I have to say, Madame, that I was rather surprised that they did not see that it would have been more appropriate to have married within the church.'

Grand-mama had bristled slightly; was this the reason for the unannounced visit, she had wondered. She was ready to defend Sophia, of whom she had become increasingly fond over the past few months. 'Well, Father, I think that they just didn't want too much fuss. We are in difficult times, are we not?'

'Well, yes, times are very different, but still no excuse not to be married within the faith.' He had paused. 'And there are other changes here too. Doctor Wouters' receptionist is no longer here, I hear. Whereabouts has she moved to?'

Before Grand-mama could formulate an answer, the door was pushed open to reveal Mama carrying a tray with two cups of coffee balanced on it. She had refrained from adding any sugar or any other refreshments. Handing a cup to each, she turned to leave when Grand-mama spoke. 'Father Francis was inquiring about Rachel, Estelle.'

That brought Mama to a complete halt; she looked down at the man, giving him a hostile look. 'Really, Father, why would you want to know anything about Rachel? You have made it perfectly clear in the past that you have no interest in anyone who doesn't follow your faith.'

The priest had shuffled in his seat slightly, causing his cup to rattle in the saucer. 'I had just heard that she was no longer working here, and wondered where she had gone, that is all.'

'Well, please do not spend any further time wondering. Rachel has left the city to live with friends in the country. So, as I said, please do not concern yourself with her whereabouts. Enjoy your coffee.' She told me later that she had hoped he would choke on it, but it perturbed her: what was this all about?

A little while later I was helping Martha and Sara wash their hands in the kitchen sink; their hands, were rather stained by juice from picking blackcurrants. After I had dried their hands, Mama and I were ushering them out of the kitchen and down the stairs when the sitting room door opened to reveal Father Francis, who stepped out and looked the two children up and down. 'So these are the two girls.' He focused his eyes for a moment on the yellow stars that were sewn onto their coats, as required now by all of the Jewish population.' So, Madame, I see that your little pupils are still attending your lessons, even though I understand that this has been forbidden.'

I could see and sense Mama getting angry. 'Well, that is where you are wrong, Father, the girls are not my pupils, and they are friends of my daughter. They come here to spend time with her, and I will make this very clear to you, Father, they are *not* my pupils, but our guests. Children who need, I would suggest, a little respite from the terrible things that are happening. 'She turned, and ushered the bewildered children down the stairs where I as usual would accompany them across the road to their home. I felt the tension, and I had not liked the way that Father Francis was looking at my two little friends. It worried me.

Mama had been furious she had turned back upstairs where the priest was standing watching. Sophia had described to me later how she had heard mama say 'I take it, Father, that your visit has been completed, and so I will escort you out.' There was a moment of standoff, both glaring at each other, their dislike tangible. She had breathed a sigh of relief when she shut the front door behind him, but told us that she couldn't dispel the sense of anxiety that she felt in pit of her stomach. She didn't trust the man, and wondered what the true purpose of his visit had been.

CHAPTER 21

I was sound asleep, but it was interrupted by loud banging and shouting. Opening my eyes, I rubbed the sleep from my eyes, and glanced at my clock that sat on the small bedside table. It was ten past five. What on earth was going on at this time in the morning? The sounds didn't seem to be coming from our house. Pulling back the covers I placed my feet into my carpet slippers that were strategically placed beside my bed so that I was able to put my feet straight into them and avoid the coolness of the lino. As I opened my bedroom door, the sounds became louder; definitely some shouting. Tiptoeing, across the landing I knocked on my parents' bedroom door, which opened almost immediately. Papa's hair was standing on end, and he looked disturbed.

'Elsa.' It was the only word he uttered as he moved quickly across the room to re-join Mama, who was standing at the window, her hand across her mouth and her eyes wide, as if, whatever she was viewing was beyond her comprehension. I moved across the room to join them and looked down to the street. I could see two lorries and several Nazi soldiers standing beside them. My eyes were drawn to the front door of the Tasma family home: it was hanging from its hinges, it having been, it would appear, destroyed. Mama placed her arm around my shoulders and drew me towards her. I wasn't sure whether I was being comforted or whether the comfort was for Mama.

A few seconds later, we saw Ruth appear. She was being escorted by two burly soldiers, and she was weeping. A moment later, we watched as my two little friends were pushed roughly by another two soldiers; both girls were crying. They were followed by Jacob, who was hauled down the front steps; he was struggling, shouting to please leave his family. Take him, he pleaded, but please, please, spare his family. There was a slight struggle, which resulted in him receiving the butt of the rifle across his head. His body slumped, but he just managed to hold onto his balance and remain on his feet. It was Martha who reacted when she saw her father get hit: she evaded her captor and ran towards him screaming Papa! Papa! Before she reached him, the soldier grabbed her by her hair, picked her up, and threw her into the back of one of the trucks. We heard the sound of her scream as she hit the floor. Jacob was poked and prodded, a rifle in his back and forced to climb into the back of the truck. I could hear the sound of Martha and Sara's terrified screams and cries, penetrating the air.

The two groups of soldiers stood for a few minutes, chatting and laughing between themselves, before two climbed into cab while another secured the back of the lorry. It then drove off, leaving several more soldiers to return into the house, and shortly after they reappeared carrying several items. Shocked as she was, Mama recognised the painting one was carrying; it was, she knew, one that was immensely valuable.

I was trembling and weeping. 'Papa,' I asked, 'where are they taking them?' My face was awash with tears which fell swiftly down my face to drip from my jaw.

'I don't know, Elsa, but I have heard that they are moving some of the Jewish people out of the city onto trains.'

'My God, look at the bastards!' cried Mama, pointing to the soldiers who were clearly looting our friend's house. We could hear the smashing of furniture, and then a moment later two of the bedroom windows were smashed, allowing the soldiers to throw some more items down, to be grabbed and placed into the back of the second lorry.

'Come away, both of you.' Papa drew us both away from the window and we followed him down to the kitchen, where Sophia had already filled the kettle and had it on to boil. 'We saw them, too,' she told us. 'How could they?' She also started to weep, using the corner of her apron to wipe her face.

I felt my heart quicken and my breathing becoming stressed. I needed to get out into the cool air, away from this. I wanted to run and run, and not stop. The sound of my two friends' screams were still ringing in my ears. Stumbling out of the kitchen door, my legs barely kept me up as I navigated the stone steps; missing the last one entirely caused me to fall. Mama was behind me and helped me to my feet. 'Oh Elsa, my dear.' She half carried me to the bench beside the entrance to the cellar. 'Come sit down, you have had a terrible shock. We all have.'

I sat beside her, and burrowed my head into her, as I cried, my voice breaking. 'But, *why*, mama? What have they done to deserve any of that?'

'They have done absolutely nothing, my love. Nothing other than be of the Jewish faith, that is all that is needed for them to be treated so appallingly. It is outrageous.'

'Will we see them again, Mama?' I sobbed, looking at her for some sort of reassurance that what we had just witnessed was going to be some sort of huge mistake, and the family would return.

'I don't know, I really do not know. Let us hope that one day we will see them again. Now come, my sweet girl, let us take a moment to sit quietly and send them love wherever they are.' As we sat on the bench on that summer morning, the peace was only interrupted by the sound of a bird calling to another. 'Look at the sun coming up, Elsa. We will think of Martha and

Sara every day when we see the sun come up, and send them our thoughts. One day this will all be over, and let us have a little ritual between us shall we.' I looked at her and nodded. 'When we see the sun rise each day we will take a deep breath, and know we are one day further on the path to peace. It will bring hope. Will you do that for me, my darling girl?'

'Yes, Mama, I will. Every day when I see the sun rising, I will take a breath and think of peace and hope, and I will think of Martha and Sara.'

****

The household sat around the kitchen table. I was still very tearful, as was Sophia. Grand-mama had joined us; she had only discovered what had happened when she had appeared a short while ago. She had always been a deep sleeper, and so missed the dramatic event. When she listened to the account of what had taken place she was horrified and immediately became distressed: she was very fond of the two girls, and couldn't grasp quite why the Nazis could be so cruel to perfectly decent people. Just as she raised her cup to take her first mouthful of weak coffee, she stopped and voiced what others had already thought. 'You don't think that their removal has anything to do with Father Francis's visit yesterday do you?' She then went on to reflect again when had taken place and what he had appeared to be interested in.

Mama banged her cup on the table. 'It is what I have been thinking, too. It would be such a coincidence, that he has never called to see anyone here before yesterday; and yet the day following Tasmas are taken. I think not. I think that obnoxious monster is at the bottom of this. He was asking questions about Rachel's whereabouts, and then he saw the girls. The absolute bastard, calling himself a man of God. He is only a Nazi spy as far as I can make out.'

'Mama,' I sobbed. 'Was it because Martha and Sara came to us, that they were taken?'

Before Mama could answer, Papa stepped in and answered. 'No, my sweet, I am sure it had nothing to do with us. There have been several round-ups of Jewish families over the past couple of weeks, helped I may add by some of the city police.' He looked around the table at the rest of the household, and it was as if what had taken place this morning had spurred him into making a decision that had been lying heavily on his mind over the past couple of weeks, and even more so in the past two days. As he studied the people sitting around the table, who were most dear to him, he seemed to have realised that he couldn't keep them all safe, no matter what he did. He couldn't shield them from the terror that was taking place around them.

'It is time,' he told us. We all turned towards him, watching him, as it seemed a thousand thoughts were flashing through his mind, and he was gathering them together to make a cohesive narrative. 'You are all aware that the most crucial for me is that you are all kept safe, and I have tried to do my best to do so. I have shielded my loved ones from some of the worst atrocities that are happening just beyond our street, but after this morning's debacle, I now see that we can no longer sit back and accept what is taking place. It is abhorrent what has taken place with our friends and neighbours, but I think that it means I need to take action. I can and will only do so if I have your support, and perhaps more important, your absolute loyalty and discretion.' He had turned searching around the table at our faces, one by one, we all nodded in agreement.

'You all know that I have been joining my colleagues some evenings to establish a mobile surgery. This has been very successful, and I believe we have helped many of our community. We have treated whoever has needed it, regardless of their religion or culture. What I have witnessed is a determination and forbearance amongst many of the Belgian people, who have made me proud and honoured to be one of them. But, it is now not enough. I have been asked to help with the

Resistance, brave men and women who are doing their best to disrupt our tyrants, and I have been asked if I can assist them.' His attention was drawn to Grand-mama, who had seized her handkerchief and pressed it to her mouth, as if to prevent herself from uttering a cry. 'I have been thinking it over for some time, but now after today, my mind tells me I have to help.'

'What sort of assistance are you thinking of, Martin?' Mama had become very animated as she listened to Papa; seemingly, her previous distress was now being directed to thinking of how they could fight back.

'They need my medical skills,' he answered, stretching his fingers. 'They of course have some members who are injured in the action they are taking, and cannot of course attend the hospital or other medical practitioners, as they do not know who can be trusted. The Nazis are always desperate to locate and capture members of the Resistance, and so they need doctors like me to help. The most pressing thing is that they currently have an injured British airman, who is presently in a safe house. They have a system set up for the rescue of airmen, and a route made up of safe houses that allow them to be transported to Spain…a similar route as our dear friend Rachel took.'

Grand-mama perked up. 'So, she is safe?' she asked.

'Yes as far as we know she is. Thank goodness.'

'Wait one moment,' interjected Mama. 'Does that mean that Nina and Lars are involved too?' She didn't add her son's name, as she already knew he had been involved at some level with the Resistance while at home, and suspected that this had continued.

Papa did not answer, but looked across the table at her. His look told us all that he knew more than he was sharing with us. 'So, getting back to the injured airman, I managed to visit him last evening, and his injuries are extensive, and he will not be fit to travel for some time. So,' he hesitated, swallowing before he continued, 'I am proposing that he comes here and he stays down in the cellar. Of course we need to take every precaution, and put that odd useless space in the cellar to work. He would be mostly in the main part of the cellar. Neighbours are used to seeing the oil lamp in there, so it will not raise any interest, but if we have any visitors, then he will move into the confined space and stay there until it is safe. I am asking an incredible commitment from you all, of course, and will only carry this through if you agree.'

All of us replied at once that of course we agreed. I felt a little bubble of hope fizz up inside me. It didn't remove the horrible pain from what had happened earlier, but if we could all help someone who in turn had placed their own life at risk, then it seemed the right thing to do.

Lucas stepped forward and reached out his hand to shake Papa's. 'I am right beside you. I wish to help in any way I can. Firstly, I will go down to the cellar and work out the best way to conceal the small hatch that is the entrance to the concealed room. We must of course use the back gate; again, I will go and do what I can to think of a way that when we use the back gate, while making it would seem to others that it is not in use, if that makes sense.'

'Papa, I too wish to help. I can help to nurse the airman when he comes, but what will we say to Dominique and Adele?'

'Well now, I think we may have to make some adjustments,' he told me. 'It may be that we have to decrease the amount of times the girls attend their studies. We will use what has happened to the Tasmas, as the reason, in that we are now going to limit our contact in our home with people from outside. So I know that you will miss your friends, but if we are hiding an airman we have to be ultra- careful, not that I would suggest the girls would tell, but it is not fair to involve anyone else.'

It only took a moment for me to process that this would mean that not only had I lost the friendship of Martha and Sara, but was also going to lose the company of the two friends I valued so much. But I realised the magnitude of what my father was asking from us all, and I would always do whatever my papa thought was necessary, so, I held my tongue.

CHAPTER 22

I wasn't asleep when Captain Johnny Paxton was carried into the cellar. I may have been dowsing when I heard some sounds of disturbance, getting out of bed I crept down stairs. I crept into the cellar and Papa saw me, but didn't send me back to bed. So I watched as he helped the young airman onto the bed and started taking his vital signs. The two silent Resistance men disappeared quietly through the back gate, which was closed after them by Lucas, putting the old bench he had found across it, and adding some branches as camouflage.

It had been agreed that less movement in the house would be safer, so apart from Lucas and Papa, everyone was in bed. The one thing that was of some help to their night-time movements was that Papa was a doctor. He could argue that he was needed out with the curfew hours, and so any person who might be interested in Ramstraat 45 would put any disturbance down to him doing this work.

Johnny Paxton had become tangled up in a tree when he had to bail out of his aircraft, just less than a week ago. He had been rescued and taken first to a hidden farmhouse where he was taken care of, but it soon became apparent that he needed medical assistance; his leg clearly had been broken in his fall, plus it was suspected that he had internal injuries as well. He had been secretly transferred to the city and taken to another safe house, where Papa had met him and assessed his injuries. A fractured tibia, as well as several ribs, was also diagnosed. As far as Papa could assess, there were no internal life-threating injuries; the bruises and cuts could be dealt with, but the leg needed to be set and placed in splints, and it would be several weeks before he would be fit enough to make the gruelling and dangerous journey to Spain.

Now that he was in the cellar, Papa was able to treat his injuries. Johnny was given a sedative while his leg was manipulated and placed in splint. His torso was bound, and his cuts cleaned – one of them needed a couple of stiches. He was made comfortable, and Lucas advised Papa to get some sleep. He would remain with Johnny to take care of him for the rest of the night.

****

In the morning, I awoke and crept over to my parents' bedroom door to do my usual listening. I heard my Mama's voice asking about the airman, and my Papa reply, 'Yes he will survive, as long as he rests. Estelle, I do hope we have done the right thing in bringing him here. It is an awful lot to ask for everyone in the house. I hope that poor Elsa is not even more upset by us not having Dominique and Adele here any longer. She has been so affected by the events of yesterday.'

'After yesterday, I do not think our daughter will ever recover fully. She loved those little girls, and while we cannot give her a clear answer, you and I both know that whatever their future is, it isn't likely to be good. I think she is resolved to help, and bless her in that, she is only fourteen, but we cannot shield her from the war any longer. The war came to our street yesterday, and has left a huge weeping sore. Even your mother has voiced a steely pledge, that whatever happens we will know that we have done our best to help. She is quietly furious about Father Francis. Both Sophia and I counselled her against racing to the church and giving him a piece of her mind. We have all agreed that should that despicable priest come visiting again, he will be sent on his way with the message that Helena is resting and seeing no visitors. It still makes my blood boil when I think of him; the more I think back to his visit, and the sneaky way he behaved, I have no doubt that he reported the girls to one of his shit friends, or maybe even directly to one of his Nazi masters. I can't help thinking about that poor family, and wonder where they are at this moment. One thing that will be certain, they are not sleeping soundly in a comfortable bed.' I caught the sound of her of punching her pillow and sighing deeply. 'There is one other thing that will be certain: I will never, ever set foot in a Catholic church again, for the rest of my life.'

The morning brought another sunny summer day, although there was just a tinge of autumn in the atmosphere. I returned to my bed, and lay for a while to review what I had heard. I was still feeling quite sleepy and a little strange. It had taken me some time to fall asleep last night: every time I had closed my eyes all I could see was Martha as she was dragged by her hair and thrown into the back of that lorry. I could still hear the girl's screams, and I found myself trembling and weeping again. Even when I had managed to eventually fall asleep, possibly because I was so exhausted, I had not slept well: my dreams were infiltrated by images of Nazi soldiers chasing me, and throwing me into a lorry. I took a while to look around my bedroom, seeing all the familiar items. It gave me a sense of safety and comfort.

After lying a while, I got up and dressed quickly, and went to check out whether the new visitor in the cellar had arrived safely. I was told by Sophia that he had, and that Mama was down in the cellar at the moment taking him some breakfast. Lucas had gone to change and ready himself for, as he now described it, his day job.

I went out through the kitchen door, and stood for a moment, looking at the sun as it appeared just above the roofs. I took an intake of breath, and sent out the thought that it was one day closer to peace, and hoped my two little friends were safe. I felt a tiny bit better for doing this, and hoped that there was a magical invisible line that would transmit my thoughts both to the girls and beyond to the universe. I made my way down to the cellar and slowly opened the door, to see Mama beckon me in. The injured airman was introduced to me; he looked a little bruised and battered, but had a crooked smile, revealing that amongst his other injuries, he seemed to have lost a couple of teeth. His face and chin were covered with a ginger beard; it wasn't long, but it matched his flop of ginger hair. I was initially quite shy, but when I spoke to him in English, it brought a huge smile to his face, lighting up his whole face. 'Well, young lady,' he said, 'that is a relief to be able to speak in my own language, you speak it exceptionally well.'

Mama smiled. 'Yes, I am pleased she is able to converse so well, and while you are here she can practise.'

That was how the friendship between Johnny and I began. During the ten weeks he remained our guest in the cellar, I would spend periods of time visiting him, playing cards and teaching him board games. It passed the time for both of us, and it enabled me to practise my English. Johnny was exceptionally grateful for my company. His injuries were healing but he was getting restless. He mentioned more than once that he realised how his presence was placing the family in severe peril, and Papa had reassured him time and again that they were all willing to assist him. There was one very strict rule, and that was he must stay within the cellar, day and night, and not to go outside in any circumstances. It was also made very clear about what he had to do if he heard the signal, of three hard bangs on the floor above him. Then he was to remove himself quickly into the concealed area, shuffling through the small hatchway and staying silent until he was released. He had practised this with some difficulty shortly after he had arrived, and while it was rather claustrophobic, he suspected that he might have more small, confined places to hide in, if he was to eventually escape to freedom. During the ten weeks he was with us, he only had to evacuate into the hiding place on two occasions, when he was informed afterwards there had been a visit from some officials who wanted to inspect the garden area. On those two occasions, no one had actually entered the cellar, so he hadn't felt under threat, but he was relieved once he was let out.

Papa, he reflected, had helped him tremendously; not only had he set his leg, but he had then shown him exercises so that it could be strengthened. He was now able to use it without pain, and also had worked on his fitness by using the cellar to exercise. He had been given the green light that his journey could continue, and that he would be collected at some time during that night.

I spent the evening in the cellar with him; we played our favourite game of cards, and drank a very weak cup of something that, although it was called coffee, didn't taste as such. We spent the evening chatting and I voiced what we had both been thinking.

'I will miss you, Johnny,' I told the young man, 'and do hope more than anything that you get home safely.' I knew that he came from a place called Southampton, and that it was on the south coast of England. Johnny had told me that he had three younger siblings, and had been courting a girl for the past two years, and he had spoken lots of times of his intention to ask her to marry him when he got home.

'I will miss you too, you have been a great companion, and when this is all over, I hope we can meet up again.'

We bid goodbye by a hug, and I felt his strong arms around me, and hoped that he would make it home to his family. I went to bed knowing that I must not ask any questions about his progress. The golden rule in the whole business of what they were doing was that the little you knew the better. None of the female members of the household knew anything about the Resistance, not who they were, or when and how they moved about the city. It was deemed necessary for them to know as little as possible for their own safety and that of the brave people of the Resistance.

CHAPTER 23

We continued our day-to-day business at of Ram-straat 45, keeping as low a profile as possible in the community. Of course Papa's daily surgeries continued. He smiled and dealt professionally with the patients he secretly loathed, and welcomed those who he knew was suffering greatly under the Nazi regime. Lucas became his right-hand man; he helped him in and out of the surgery. He was bright, and Papa taught him how to measure and dispense the medicines, as well as how to assist him when he was undertaking a procedure. He would, Papa said, make an excellent doctor. His calm manner not only aided him to focus on the job in hand, but also enabled patients to feel comfortable and relaxed.

Mama busied herself around the house and garden, trying to make do and mend. She also rarely went out, other than to occasionally go to try to purchase something that the household needed. Sophia helped out by assisting everyone; it was her role to go out to try and secure food when needed. She always said she didn't mind standing in the queues, as it allowed her the opportunity to listen in to the gossip. Some of what was said outside was pure supposition, some rumours, wild, ideas, of what was taking place. Other times, what she heard was useful, and she was able to share with the household. Grandmama and I led a very quiet life. I had become bored, and still had moments of sheer despair, especially when I experienced the recurring visions of the two young girls. Grand-mama and I developed a close friendship, and now the radio was no longer permitted she was often at a loss of how to spend her time. Card games became part of our daily routines, and we developed games of our own.

As a household we were very committed to following the rules, so that we didn't bring any unwanted attention. It had been decided that Grand-mama, would attend Mass on a regular basis, so that Father Francis would have no excuse to come calling. Mama, true to her word, refused to attend, so Sophia and Papa took turns to accompany her. Grand-mama described how she painted a sugary smile on her face when she came into contact with the priest, or any of his minions, as she referred to them. Papa was also wary of creating any over interest in our lives and shook hands, but spent as little time in their company as they could safely get away with. He reported that still a number of Nazi soldiers attending, of whom he noted that some were wearing the uniform of the Gestapo, and who were shaking and smiling the hand of the priest as though they were all cosied up together.

Since Johnny had left, there had been a few very short-term guests in the cellar. I was only aware of their comings and goings because I helped to deliver food and water to them. I knew that they were receiving medical treatment from Papa – some sported various slings and cuts – but I didn't pay them the same attention as I had Johnny. I didn't ask questions: this had become the norm for all of us. Papa patched them up, and a few days later they were whisked away in the darkness.

****

I celebrated my fifteenth birthday very quietly. There were no guests in the cellar so Dominique and Adele were invited to a reduced birthday tea. Food was sparse, it being the third year of occupation. The Nazi occupiers took any surplus food to Germany, leaving the city citizens struggling to find enough to eat.

It was just a few weeks after my birthday that a very unex-
pected guest arrived. It was late at night and the household
was awakened by loud banging on the front door. This brought
fear radiating throughout, as it could mean that we were being
awakened by the authorities, or Nazis, so we quickly became
alert. I got out of bed to join my Mama at the top of the stairs,
looking down as Papa went to open the front door. As he did
so, two people fell through it, a man and a woman. The man
spoke in Flemish, asking for help. His wife, he told us, was
in labour and had been for a very long time and she needed
help. Indeed the woman did seem as though she was barely
conscious and her stomach protruded massively to confirm
her pregnancy. What drew our attention was that both were
wearing the yellow star on their coats, so this was definitely
a risky situation, given that there were very strict rules about
the treatment of Jews. Many had been removed from the city,
many others were in hiding, but clearly this was an emergency.

Mama rushed down the stairs to assist Papa, and make a space,
and together with the man they helped carry the woman
into the surgery. After ensuring that the drapes were tightly
closed they were able to then put lights on. Papa examined the
woman and realised that there was unquestionably a serious
problem that needed immediate action. He told the man that
his wife needed an emergency operation to deliver the baby.
The man pleaded for Papa help them, so with a look at Lucas,
who had appeared looking somewhat dishevelled, they set
about making an emergency operating theatre in the surgery.

Meanwhile, Mama ushered the man up the stairs and into the
kitchen, where he was seated while we boiled kettles of water
needed, we were told, to assist with the birth. Mama managed
to find out what had brought them to our door. The story he
revealed was one of distress. He gave his name as Ruben and

his wife as Rebecca. They had been in hiding for several weeks after the family they were living with were arrested and taken away. He had no idea where they had been taken – on one of the many trains, he thought. Ruben and Rebecca had been hiding in some attics and had managed to stay hidden, and were hoping that once the baby was born they could try to leave the city and head south. However, when Rebecca's labour had started, it had gone on and on and he didn't know what to do. He had left her, and gone to find some help. Thankfully, the contact he had was able to advise him about Papa, that he was known to help those in trouble; hence the knock on our door. It had been a hairy journey from another part of the city; all of the time he had struggled with helping his wife, while trying to remain under the Nazi radar. Mama had reassured him that her husband would do his very best, and that both were most welcome to be with us.

I helped my mama cut some bread, and find some blackcurrant jam to spread on it, before placing it in front of the man. He looked as though at first he would refuse this, but the hunger in his stomach reacted before he could contemplate that, and he grabbed for food, and ate it quickly. I wondered when the last time this man had anything proper to eat. He looked gaunt and thin. Mama cut another piece, and placed it in front of him. No words were spoken.

While Sophia sat with Ruben, Mama beckoned me to go with her. 'We had better see if we can sort out something for his poor child,' she told her. 'Let us find a couple of towels that we can cut up to use as napkins, and goodness me, what do we have that could fit a baby?'

'Oh, I know exactly, Mama,' I cried. 'What about my dolly clothes? I haven't used them for years, but they are still in my cupboard. Some of them for made for that big doll that Grandmama gave me.' We found the small pile of clothes and held them up.

163

'Yes they might just work, at least in the short term. 'Now then if we empty one of your drawers we could use that as a small crib, and let us find some bits of bedding that will make it comfortable.' We worked away to do so, and then just as we completed our task, we heard someone climbing the stairs. We went out to find Lucas carrying a small bundle wrapped up in towel.

'It's a girl he,' told us, 'and a healthy one at that.' We both raced over to look at the tiny screwed-up face buried in the towel. 'I am taking her into meet her father.'

Ruben took his daughter into his arms and gazed down at her. He started to weep quietly; the wonder of seeing this small being who he had helped create was overwhelming. 'Is Rebecca okay?' he asked, and received a positive reply from Lucas, who informed him that Papa was fixing her up, and once she had recovered consciousness he would come and fetch him and the baby so she could be introduced to her mother.

Once Rebecca had recovered from the sedation she was given, she was introduced to her baby. She was delighted to see and hear that her baby was healthy. They would have to be moved, though, as it was now getting light, and they would have to vacate the surgery. Neither Mama nor Papa thought it right to place them in the cellar; Rebecca needed somewhere warm and comfortable to recover, even if it was for short time. I volunteered my own bedroom, especially as the emergency crib was currently in there. Mama was grateful, but decided that mother and baby could use Derk's bedroom, and so we quickly sorted out the bedding and moved the temporary crib next door into my brother's vacant room.

By the time we got mother and baby settled it was daylight, and Ruben was shown down to the cellar so he too could get some rest. We were a very exhausted household as we tried to navigate our way through the rest of the day: as well as the loss of sleep, we were all very conscious that if they were dis-covered, our guests would pose a serious risk to us all.

I was very taken with the small baby, who I crept in to see at regular intervals. The baby would be named after Ruben's mother; her name brought tears to my eyes. The baby was to be called Martha.

Of course it was too high a risk for the family to remain for long at Ramstraat 45. Efforts were made to try to dampen down Martha's wails, so that no patients could wonder why a baby had joined our household. Papa disappeared one after-noon, then returned to inform us that he had made arrange-ments for some help for the family, so that they could make the journey out of the city, and hopefully to freedom. What he hadn't shared with us was that the Resistance members he had spoken to had taken some convincing to help, as while there was sympathy, they felt that there might be other Jew-ish groups that could be better placed to help. It was only after some pleading from Papa, for whom they had utter respect, that they relented and agreed that they would put a rescue into motion.

The family needed to be ready for moving two nights later, and that prompted the women in the household to rally around to gather some clothing for the baby. Sophia stayed up late into the evenings, sewing some vests and small night-gowns; we all remarked that we could have done with Rachel and her knitting skills.

On the evening of their departure, the family moved down to the cellar. All of us spent a little time with them, wishing them well, and having a final cuddle with little Martha, who I for one thought was the most beautiful baby in the world. I was sorry to see them leave. I would have welcomed having the baby live with us, but knew that was far too dangerous. I was reminded again how having them in the house was put-ting us all at risk, and I wanted no repeats of what happened to

Martha's namesake. I couldn't sleep that night; my mind was racing, thinking about the family, and hoping that they would make their escape. It was not the best night for the attempt, as there was a full moon, and that rendered these types of operations much more risky. I gave up on trying to get to sleep, and got out of bed and drew my curtains back so that I had a good view of the back garden. As I settled myself down, I spotted a movement at the bottom of the garden. Squinting, so I could get a clearer vision in the darkness of what was happening, I could just make out Lucas. He was at the end of the garden, opening the back gate, and then I saw someone else enter and follow Lucas up the garden. I pressed my face to the window to try to get a clearer view, and just as I did so, the person looked up, and saw me and waved his hand. It was my brother Derk. I felt my heart beat just a fraction faster as I waved back. What I really wanted to do was to rush down and greet him with a big hug, but knew that was not permitted. We had not seen Derk for several months; well, to be more accurate, I had not seen him, but maybe my parents had.

I kept watching and it was just a few minutes later that I saw Derk lead the little family along the pathway, where they disappeared through the back gate. Lucas worked at covering the gate again and then shortly after I heard him climb the stairs to the attic. So my brother was still involved with the Resistance. This confirmed what I had thought, but I had no idea that he had been visiting our home during darkness to help our special guests on their journeys.

The following morning I rose from my bed before anyone else, and tiptoed down the stairs to check in the cellar. There was no sign that a baby had been anywhere near it. I had mixed feelings. I would miss little Martha, who had felt so tiny and snug when I had held her in her arms. Now I felt an emptiness. I was getting used to people leaving, and I sat on the bench by the cellar door to listen to the birds as they called to each other. As I peered up to the sky, I saw that it was cloudless. Maybe it was going to be another hot, sunny, July day. I watched the sun appear over the roofs of the city, its glow changing the colour of the muted sky as it did so. I sent my thoughts to both Marthas and hoped that they were both somewhere safe. Looking towards the sun I closed my eyes, taking a long deep breath, sending my thoughts to them as well as chanting to myself: another sunrise closer to peace and bringing hope. Goodness, I thought, I just so wished that it would come soon.

CHAPTER 24

I would always remember my sixteenth birthday, not for the celebration, but for the lack of it. I had been awoken by Mama on my birthday, and although she smiled when she wished me happy birthday, I noticed immediately that her smile did not reached her eyes, and so I knew something was not right.

'What is it, Mama? I asked, searching her face for some inkling of what might have happened.

'Elsa, we have guests.' Mama stood by my bed, and her hands seemed to be trembling a little. 'I am sorry, my love, but we have several guests, and all have been badly wounded and are suffering.'

'Really, Mama, is it more airmen?' I couldn't help but find that my mind went straight to how Johnny had been the most injured of all of our guests.

'Not this time, we have three men from the Resistance who have been shot. Papa had to operate during the early hours, and remove bullets. We know that the Nazis are searching for them, so we have to be extra careful. So, could you get dressed, as you will be needed to help with the household tasks. I am truly sorry, my love, this is your birthday and now it has been spoilt.'

'It's okay, Mama.' I climbed out of bed and embraced her, to reassure her that birthdays didn't really matter that much, not any longer when we had so much else to cope with.

The three men had various wounds, and when I carried some coffee and bread to them, they all thanked me profusely. They were of various ages; one looked more my age, while the other two were in their late twenties. They sat quietly, alert and ready to dive into the concealed place if needed. They would no doubt be incredibly careful, as if they were discovered then it was certain that they would be taken to the dreaded Breendonk Prison. It had gathered a reputation over the past year as a place where those who ended up there were tortured, and then often murdered. The Resistance had been causing the Nazis considerable trouble over the past few months. Action had been directed at disrupting as much as they could, and they had become real thorn in the side of the oppressors . Of course, if they were captured, then it meant that others who might have assisted them were also no longer safe and would no doubt suffer. My family were well aware of the danger we were in, but so far we had escaped the attention of the Gestapo, who were leading the pursuit of these brave individuals.

At breakfast poor Papa looked washed out; he had of course been up most of the night, and now he was due to carry on with his surgery. Lucas looked equally tired, but as he was younger he didn't struggle with these nocturnal events quite so much as Papa. 'They will be leaving tonight,' Papa told us. 'They have a safe house where they can wait until their injuries heal. I have done what I can for them, and so, can we all be exceptionally careful today, as we have never had three guests at the same time before.'

Lucas inclined his head towards Papa. 'They have been warned, and I have shown them how to get into the space; they have been instructed not to smoke, and we will remove any cups or implements as soon as they have finished using them, just in case we need to move fast.'

I perceived a real sense of apprehension circulate around the room. I wondered what these men had been involved in, and suspected that, whatever it was, the Gestapo would be desperate to hunt them down. The day was very tense. When I wasn't helping Mama and Sophia in the house, then I spent most of it in the armchair in front of sitting room window. Watching the street was another very important task. I was informed that if I saw any Nazi patrols in the street, then I was to alert and advise the men to get into the hiding place. My eyes focused on the house across the road where the Tasmas had once lived a quiet peaceful life. It was occupied now by a Flemish family who had literally just moved in, and had taken over the property without any thought for the people who had lived there before. I didn't quite understand how they could have been given this property, but they had; just a few weeks after the family had been taken, this new family had moved in and taken up residence. The windows had been mended and some furniture brought, and they seemed to have settled in. I knew they had several children, and apparently where they had previously lived had been bombed, so they had just taken up residence. Like others in Ramstraat, they kept themselves to themselves. I knew that the mother had brought the children to Papa's surgery once, but I didn't know what had transpired. Papa had just commented that she seemed a quiet woman. Just as my mind was wandering I caught sight of two Nazi vehicles entering the end of the street. They stopped and several soldiers clambered out. One, who appeared to be an officer shouted orders. I could just about make out what he shouted, and it was an order to start the search.

I flew off of the chair and bounded into the kitchen. 'It's the soldiers! They are searching the street!' I shouted to Mama and Sophia, who had been startled by my sudden entrance.

Sophia immediately rushed down to the cellar to tell the men, and help them into the small space. It would be tight with three of them in it. I followed quickly and passed them a bottle of water. She shut the hatch, and between us we dragged the old sideboard in front of the hatch to help disguise the entry. We looked around and once we had reassured each other that there was nothing to suggest that anyone had been recently lounging around on the bed and chairs, we made our way back up to the kitchen and steeled ourselves.

Mama had gone down to warn Lucas, who was in the dispensary making up some cough medicine for an elderly woman who was waiting in the reception room. Papa was with a patient, and so unaware of the concern. The surgery was just coming to an end, so apart from the elderly lady there were no other patients waiting.

I went to find Grand-mama, who was resting in her bedroom. Once I had passed the news to her, she took herself off into the sitting room where she picked up the novel she was reading, and did her best to look as casual as possible.

It wasn't long before we heard a commotion down in the hallway. Several soldiers had entered the house, led by a very officious officer. He spoke to Lucas, who explained that Doctor Wouters was in the middle of a consultation with a patient. That didn't prevent the officer opening the door to the surgery and marching in. Thankfully the young female patient was fully dressed, and just about to leave. Papa asked that the patient could be allowed to leave, and this was permitted, the officer looking her up and down, seemingly admiring her body as he did so. She thanked Papa, and scuttled off.

The officer addressed Papa, and informed him they were searching houses seeking fugitives who had committed a crime. He didn't ask if he could search, just informed him that his soldiers would be searching his whole house. Papa remained calm and told the officer, that of course they were welcome to search his property, he had nothing to hide, he was a medical practitioner and that was his profession.

The soldiers marched through the house, opening doors, cupboards, and anywhere else where someone could hide. Two marched into the sitting room where Grand-mama looked surprised and demanded to know what they were looking for. Neither soldier answered but just ignored her while they looked around the room. Once they had confirmed that there was nowhere to hide in the room they left and continued their search. Sophia, Mama and I sat around the kitchen table, and continued to chop vegetables. We stared as the soldiers looked around, opening the larder and throwing some utensils to the floor as they checked for any hidden door behind them.

They then moved into the garden. Two went into the cellar, while another two searched the garden. We three women held our breaths. Mama carefully looked out of the window, where she could see the bottom of the garden, and hoped that Lucas's covering of the back gate would work so that it would appear not to be used. She could see the soldier even raking through the hen house, before appearing to be satisfied that there was nothing there of interest, and returning to the steps where they could hear him conversing with his two comrades, who were still in the cellar.

A few moments later they reappeared, and giving us the benefit of a smirk as they passed us, they and their officer left the house. I was shaking, and went to the sitting room to see if Grand-mama was okay, before I carefully looked out of the front window, watching as they continued their search along the road.

Grand-mama reassured me that she was fine, but would be even better if she could have a coffee. I went to get it for her, and found Mama and Sophia hugging each other in relief. It had been a close call, and the men would need to remain in the hidey hole for a while yet until it was deemed safe for them to come out. Papa and Lucas arrived shortly afterwards, having locked the front door. We all sighed, a huge breath of relief, and I for one hoped that the men would disappear into the night as soon as possible. The men were kept in the concealed space for the rest of the day, and only released after dark. They were all relieved to be out, but more relieved that the room had saved them from discovery and arrest. They thanked all of us, and waited until the middle of the night, until Lucas let them through the back gate, where they crept out into the darkness to find refuge in a safe house.

That event left me feeling rather more anxious than before. I could not help my mind taking me to places that I had to consider: what might have happened to us all, if the men had been discovered? I found that more and more I found sleep eluded me until the early hours. I often lay listening to the sounds of the night, hoping that we would be spared any further searches. I found myself thinking too about what Derk might be getting up to, and sent a silent prayer to keep him safe.

****

The following month saw a number of air raids by the Allies, targeting the factories on the edge of the city. Some of their bombs went astray and caused injury to civilians, and Papa was kept busy, going out and helping in the hospital. We found that the cellar came into its own during these raids, as it provided what we had initially planned it would do: protection from air raids. We could hear explosions, and while it was frightening, it was also reassuring, as it signalled that the Allies were definitely stepping up the pressure.

Papa still had his radio, although now it was carefully hidden, but he tried to listen to the BBC when he could. It was in June that he heard that the Allies had landed on the beaches of France, and he had rushed to share this news with the household. 'Just think,' he announced, 'maybe this is coming to an end and we will be free of this horrible tyranny.'

The increased number of air raids meant that this increased the chance that more Allied airmen would need rescue. Just a couple of weeks after the Allies had landed on the French coast, Papa received a message to say that another guest required help. So in the middle of the night, another injured airman was deposited in the cellar. This time he was a Canadian, who had a nasty head injury which needed several stiches, and Papa was concerned that he could be concussed. Papa stitched him up and dressed the wound. He explained the rules, and the airman introduced himself as Hank, and was very grateful for the help.

I was very taken with Hank. I had never met a Canadian before. He was tall and I thought exceptionally handsome. I just loved his accent and tried to ensure that if anything needed taking to him, then it was me who did so. I think Hank was equally taken by me, or so I gathered from the way he looked and smiled at me. My hair was now shorter and my curls made it bounce on my shoulders as I walked. I had also filled out, and although I remained small of stature, my hips and bust certainly announced that I was a young woman. I found, for the first time, that I was being flirted with, and my goodness didn't I just enjoy the attention. I found that for some reason that my body seemed to be behaving in an odd way, and when I had taken Hank some food, I found my hips swinging as I turned to leave the cellar, knowing he was watching. It was a funny sort of feeling. When I saw him I had butterflies in my stomach, and my heart beat just a fraction faster.

Hank was to remain for two weeks before his stiches were removed and he was moved on. The evening of his removal, I made a special point of brushing my hair and pinning it back with two pretty clasps as I delivered food for him.

'So, Elsa, this is my last meal I will receive from you.'

I placed the plate on the small table and turned, making ready to leave, even though I really wanted to stay. But I was a little embarrassed and I felt my face redden.

Hank stood up, came over to me. 'Well, I want to just say thanks to you for all you have done. You are a very special lady, and maybe when this is over, I'll come back and see you. Would you like that?'

I looked up into his hazel eyes and whispered, 'Yes I would like that,' adding, 'Please.' Before I could move, he reached down and almost lifted me off of my feet and kissed me fully on the mouth. I felt his lips against mine, and smelt the tobacco from his breath. I didn't quite know what to do, apart from press my lips back. He put me back down onto my feet, and ran his finger down the side of her face, smiling and bidding me farewell.

It was my first kiss, and I found myself all of a-tremble as I made my way back to the kitchen, where I excused myself so I could go to my bedroom to sit on my bed to recall the sensation over and over again. I did not even try to fall asleep that night until after I had seen Hank being whisked away in the darkness by my brother. I wished them both a safe journey, and lay in bed to await sleep to overcome me.

CHAPTER 25

The summer of 1944 was exceptionally hot. It caused further problems for the residents of Ramstraat, as the house was hot and stuffy. Sometimes the water system didn't function properly, so as well as increased food shortages, now water came and went without notice. All the used water was collected and thrown on the garden, to try to keep the vegetables and fruit healthy. No one dared use such a precious commodity for any other reason than essential usage.

Sophia had received news that her father was unwell, and her mother had asked her to try to visit. An olive branch had been offered, especially when her mother added that it would be also good to meet her husband. Mama and Papa urged them both to go. Travelling had become a big issue for everyone, but their papers were in good order, so they should manage without too much difficulty. It was just the beginning of August when they agreed that they should do so. I hugged them both and waved them goodbye, some parts of me wishing that I could accompany them. A visit to the countryside seemed idyllic, compared with a hot and sticky city. Sleep was almost impossible, and there had been a couple of occasions when the cellar was empty and I had taken myself down there to try to sleep where it was cooler.

It was just one of these nights when I had struggled to sleep and had only done so into the early hours, when I and the others in the house were awakened by loud banging. I looked at my clock; the hands were at five thirty, and the banging became louder. I heard Papa go past my door and down the stairs to see who it was who clearly needed the door opened.

I got up quickly to join Mama to see what the fuss was about. I hadn't quite reached Mama, who was standing at the top of the stair, before I saw a number of soldiers enter the house. Papa was being held by his arms as he was dragged into the surgery. 'Mama, what's going on?' I watched several more soldiers climb up the stairs towards us.

'Get dressed, 'one ordered Mama and me, his voice loud and intimidating.

Quickly I returned to my bedroom and dressed in the clothes I had worn on the previous day. I felt myself shaking. The door then flew open and a young soldier told me to follow him. I did so, and found Mama and Grand-mama sitting at the kitchen table. Mama was dressed in day clothes while Grand-mama was still in her night attire. Grand-mama looked stoic, and was clearly not going to be intimidated by the three soldiers who stood over us.

I wondered what was happening to Papa, and hoping that whatever this was about, he was not being treated badly. Thankfully, the cellar was empty. If this had taken place yesterday, then it might have been a very different story. Mama asked the soldiers several times what was going on. There was no answer, as they stood over us, their presence menacing. The atmosphere changed as two Gestapo officers entered the kitchen. One spoke to the soldiers in German; I was able to make out that he was telling them to go down to the cellar and rip it apart. I looked at Mama, and could see that she too was experiencing severe fear. This was not a routine visit. The three soldiers disappeared, leaving the two Gestapo officers. They appeared threatening; just being in their presence created a fear I had never before experienced.

One spoke, his French accent good. 'We have received very good information that you, madam,' he addressed Mama directly, 'and your husband and your family have been aiding the Resistance. Is that so?'

Mama shook her head. 'You have been misinformed, I am afraid. My husband is a doctor and has always just helped people who need medical treatment. Nothing else.' Her voice was shaky, although she tried to cover this up by the way she held her shoulders, and she looked at the officer directly in the face.

The officer sneered. 'Oh, I think your doctor husband has been treating many people, those who he should not have been treating. You have a son, have you not?'

I saw my Mama's eyes widen; now I could feel the coldness of utter terror penetrate my body.

Mama answered, 'I have a son, Derk, but he is not here. He lives and works in the country.'

'I have to tell you,' the officer raised himself up, balancing on the balls of his feet, and seemed to be enjoying imparting the information, 'that your son was shot dead this last evening, during an operation on a certain farm. I think you are very aware of the owners of the farm, madam, and what they were doing. He did not comply with instruction. Our intelligence has determined that he was not the only member of this family who involved in assisting the enemies of the German state.'

I could not quite comprehend what he was telling us. Surely this was wrong. Surely, Derk wasn't dead. The Gestapo were known to lie, and surely he was lying now as he stood over us. He was playing with us, surely he was. One of the soldiers reappeared, and spoke quickly in German. It was too fast for me to understand it all, but I caught the odd word about concealed room, and that seemed to confirm whatever the officers were expecting.

He stood over us. 'Come. All of you are to accompany us for further questioning.' He motioned for us to stand and do as he ordered. I glanced at Mama to get some guidance of what to do. Mama looked resigned and stood, the sign for me to do the same. Grand-mama did not do so, though; she remained sitting.

'I refuse to be ousted out of my home by you,' she rebuffed his demand, folding her arms to indicate she was not going anywhere.

He turned and looked down at her with distain. 'You, madam, will do exactly as you are told. Now get up and follow your family, or else you will be dealt with.' The last words were delivered with utter contempt. He inclined his head towards the two soldiers who had re-joined us from their search: the soldier grabbed Grand-mama by her arm and pulled at her, but she continued to resist. Turning to the officer she shouted, 'If you have killed my grandson, then you can kill me too, you evil bastard.'

Before anyone could intervene, the Gestapo officer withdrew his pistol, pointed it at her, saying, 'That can easily be done,' and he fired the pistol at her head. There was an explosion, with blood splattering across the room, including over the young soldier who was attempting to pull the old lady to her feet. Grand-mama slumped immediately. I didn't realise that it was my own screams that were filling the air: my lovely Grand-mama, her life wiped out in a second. Mama was also sobbing loudly as we were pushed and pulled out of the house, and thrown into the back of a vehicle and joined by two soldiers. The Gestapo car was parked also, and the two officers got into the back and were driven away. There was no sign of Papa. Had he been killed to, I wondered, causing, another outburst of sobs, and a terrifying sense of fear and distress.

Mama and I were taken directly to the feared Breendonk prison. We were thrown into a cell, already inhabited by two other women who, from the state of their bodies had been there for some time already. I clung onto Mama, clutching her hand tightly, desperately frightened about what was going to happen to us, and wondering where Papa was.

Mama whispered quietly to me as we sat together on one of the hard benches which were deemed to be some sort of sleeping area. 'Just try and stay brave, Elsa. I do not know what they will do to us. They are evil… poor Derk.' She started weeping, and I tried to comfort her, my own grief numbed by what I had witnessed. How could these evil men do such a thing to an old woman who did not do anything to warrant being shot like an animal? I could not even allow myself to consider what had happened to my brother; it was all far too much to handle.

****

Mama was taken several times for interrogation, and each time she was taken from the cell created a terrible foreboding for me. I was terrified that it would be the last time I would see her. It seemed as though it was hours before she was returned, bloodied and battered. I tried to comfort her, and was helped by the two other women, who managed to assist Mama to lie on the bench to recover. It was evident that she had been beaten, but to me it was a relief that at least she had returned, and she was alive. Mama whispered to me that she had not told them anything, before she drifted into a sort of trance state, the shock of what she had endured not allowing her to communicate.

I had no comprehension as to how long Mama and I had been in the cell, but when the door opened to reveal one of the warders, I half expected that they had come again for Mama. But it was not for Mama; this time, it was for me. I felt my whole body shake as I walked in front of the female warder down the dark and dismal corridor. There was an open door in front of me, which the warder pushed me through, into a room where there was just a metal table and two chairs. I was pushed down onto one, and then the warder stood behind me. I did not know who the other chair was for, but this was soon answered by the appearance of the same Gestapo officer who had murdered Grand-mama. I began to shake uncontrollably. My whole body reacted to the terror that this man had brought into my life, and the panic of what he would do to me.

He sat in front of me, staring intently. He asked the same questions over and over again: what were the names of the people who were involved in the Resistance? I shook my head, telling him over and over that I did not know. I had no names; I never saw any of the men from the Resistance. He banged his fist on the table, shouting in my face that I was lying. I was crying so hard, shaking my head, I didn't know anything. He stood up and grabbed me by the hair, pushing my head back, screaming into my face to tell him the truth, and he might just spare my father's life. I looked into his dark eyes that appeared possessed, his hatred projected at me. I just wished I could give him a name. I didn't know any, I told him: if I had a name, I would give it up to save my papa.

He slapped me hard across the face, the blow forcing my head back so much that I fell from the chair. He got up, his face distorted, his eyes almost black with rage and hatred, dragging me up and slinging me back onto the chair. If only I had a name. I sobbed over and over again that if I had a name, I would give it up. 'Please,' I begged, 'don't hurt my papa.'

He slapped me again, hitting me hard across the face. The blow forced my head back, so that I again was propelled off of the chair onto the hard floor. I felt myself being dragged back up onto the chair by the warder, my face and head stinging from the pain and shock. Still he continued to badger me for a name. This terror seemed to go on for ages; more slaps, my head was stinging from the pain as my hair was pulled from its scalp, but still I could not give him names. In the end, he seemed to run out of steam. Maybe he believed me that I did not know any names. He stood up, looking down at me with such contempt, and then turned and left the room. I was hauled to my feet by the warder, and pushed back down the corridor to the cell, and thrown into it.

Mama took me into her arms and checked me over. I was sobbing quietly, my body shaking and mouth dry apart from the metallic taste of blood, from my mouth which had been caught by his hand. One of the women handed a cup with a little water in it, and Mama gently helped me sip some. I tried to tell Mama what had happened, but I didn't need to describe it; she had suffered worse at the hands of that revolting man.

CHAPTER 26

The days at Breendonk were long and exceptionally difficult. The noise in the prison penetrated every fibre of my being. Screaming, shouting, and swear words I had never heard before, all became normality to this strange place that we were imprisoned in. Mama and I found out that our two cellmates, Delphine and Rose, had been there for a couple of months. Both lived in Antwerp, and had been imprisoned due to their apparent disobeying of the rules. Delphine and been found to be helping the Resistance, while Rose had been caught stealing from a German soldier who she had been pleasuring. She told us that she had been forced into selling her body when her husband and child had been killed in one of the air raids. She had been left penniless and homeless and was very ashamed by what she had to do. Often, in the night, I would hear Rose weeping and calling out in her sleep; the names of her child and husband, I assumed. They were both very kind to me, and comforted me when Mama was taken out of the cell for interrogation.

Food was almost non-existent. A bowl of some sort of stew was given to us daily. That and a hard piece of bread. Occasionally we were given an extra ration of some sort of gruel; it certainly didn't do anything to reduce our hunger – my stomach constantly growled for more sustenance. A bucket of water was delivered each day; this was to provide us with something to drink, and for all our other ablutions. The water bucket was very precious, as we knew that if the guards wanted to, they could just forget to replenish it, and the lack of water would have been unthinkable in that crowded cell. We were given something to wear, although the items we were given could not be described as clothes. I had a long sort of dress, made with some sort of hessian material; it was scratchy and uncomfortable. There were two pairs of knicker and vests. These were almost threadbare, and I could not help thinking who else might have worn them before me. We had little choice, and we did our best to try to do something about our personal hygiene. We tried to save a little water in the bucket each day, and took it in turns on a sort of rota system to use it to try to clean ourselves. Also we dipped our knickers in it, in an attempt to try to keep the dirt at bay.

The toilet was a bucket in the corner, which had to be emptied once a day. Each of us took turns at being the one to empty it. It was a job I detested, as on the days when it was almost overflowing, it proved a real challenge to carry it along the corridor to the sluice room to empty it. The cell stank, a mixture of urine, sweat and just sheer dirt infiltrated and settled into our noses, until we almost got to a point where we became desensitised to it and it didn't bother us.

Nights were the worst. I found any sleep I did manage lying on that hard bench was infiltrated by terrible dreams. I kept seeing the face of Grand-mama, bloodied, her mouth open in a silent scream. I would awaken with a sense of dread and terror. My whole body felt as though it was not part of my head. In my head I could hear that piercing sound of the gunshot as it reverberated around the room, and I could smell the sickening blood mixed with the smell of cordite from the gun. I knew Mama was suffering too. She often wept quietly, trying to protect me from my grief, but nothing could protect me from what I had seen and experienced. There were times when I just felt numb, as though I was in a dream, and I was outside of my body. It was a strange feeling, especially if a shot was heard;

then I found myself believing I was back in our kitchen again, and Mama had to hold me tight until I stopped screaming.

We had received no word about Papa. We didn't know whether he was also in Breendonk or if he was even alive. When she thought I was asleep I overheard Mama telling Delphine that she was scared, as Papa did know the names of some of the men from the Resistance, and no doubt he would have suffered more than she had. She had gone on to say that, knowing her husband, he would be unlikely to have given up any names lightly, even if he had done so, which she doubted he would do under any circumstances. She had wondered whether he was even aware that both his mother and his son were dead. It was frustrating and distressing not to know whether he was okay.

What seemed like another act of torture was that there were some days when executions took place. We could see them if we stood and reached up to look out of the small, barred window that admitted a small amount of light into the cell. Whatever these men and women had done to deserve being led, then blindfolded, before they were mown down in a hail of bullets? It left us shocked and disturbed. Mama and I had no real appreciation of how long we had been in the prison, when one morning we witnessed a line of men, standing and waiting for the order to end their lives. We both cried out when we realised that one of the men was Papa. I fell down, burying my head under the thin blanket on my bench, not wanting to see the inevitable, while Mama did witness the death of her beloved husband. Delphine did her best to comfort us, but there were no words that could ease the pain and horror of knowing that my dear Papa had been murdered for just trying to help others. I suddenly realised that I now only had my mama left. The rest of my family had been wiped out.

One of the sounds we started to hear more often was that of planes flying over the prison. It seemed that they were much more frequent and there were more of them. A regular topic of conversation between us was to wonder whether the Allies were making progress, and we hoped that they were doing so, and that we would be freed. Sadly, it did not come soon enough for Delphine, as one day without any notice she was taken out of the cell, and joined the line of people who were executed in the square outside of our window. We were shocked and saddened, but also terrified. Would we be next?

Between us we had worked it out that it must be about the middle of September when one morning the cell door opened and Mama and I were ordered out. We thought that the end had come, and we were going to be taken to be shot. But no, we were pushed and shoved to join a queue of several other women, and taken out to the courtyard where we were ordered into the back of a lorry. We held hands tightly, trying to give each other courage and strength to face whatever we were going to be forced into.

The journey was relatively short; we were unable to determine where we were being taken, as a tarpaulin was pulled tight over the back of the lorry to prevent us seeing, or probably more likely to prevent us from being seen. We felt the lorry shudder to a halt, and a few minutes later the tarpaulin was lifted and the back was opened up. We then realised where we were – at a train station, one Mama recognised as being on the outskirts of the city. We were bundled off and led along the platform to where a train stood. It certainly wasn't a passenger train, but more like one to transport goods, or maybe even cattle. There were other people already in a line on the platform, all bedraggled, men, women and children. Some were wearing the yellow star, and carrying small suit cases. There were others like us, just wearing the uniform of Breendonk prison. There were many soldiers with their guns ready waiting, daring anyone who objected to being there to make a fuss or a run for it. Grisly looking dogs were also watching us, their handlers ready to release them if anyone didn't obey orders.

Mama and I stood in front of the opening to the freight car, then we were instructed to enter. We did so accompanied by around twenty other women. All crammed in, the heat of the morning created a feeling that the air was being sucked from us. There was hardly room to move; the atmosphere was horrific, the fear palatable. The smell was rotten. As the train began to move off, I wept quietly. I had heard about the trains, but no one had been able to be sure of where they ended up. It would seem I was about to find out.

CHAPTER 27

I lost all sense of time. I only knew the movement of the train, as it rattled along the line. The clattering sound attempted to hide the sound of the women in distress. Mama and I had manoeuvred ourselves so that we managed to sit against the side, Mama gripping my hand tightly, as if the fear of letting go might mean I would disappear from sight. There was one smelly bucket in the corner to use. I tried desperately to hold on, but in the end gave up and squatted over it to relieve myself. Others did the same. There were just a few open hatches which let some light in, but more importantly some air. I knew it was night, as darkness had descended into the carriage, and in the end I dropped off to sleep with my head resting on Mama's shoulder.

I was awakened suddenly by the jerking and squealing of the train's brakes as it drew to a halt. I could hear some shouting and dogs barking. We stood up and waited. It felt as though it was an interminable time before the door was slid open and we were greeted by soldiers waving their guns and ordering us to disembark. We did so and looked around, disorientated, hungry and thirsty, to see where we were, the sun blinding us after being in such dim conditions. There were lots of people, many dressed in ordinary clothes, but wearing the yellow star. Others were not, but looked as though they had been travelling for some time. The women from our carriage were dressed in the Breendonk prison clothes.

A Nazi officer shouted orders and we began to walk. I was so thirsty and hungry, but there was no offer of either food or drink. We walked and walked along a road lined on each side by a forest. We had no idea where on earth we were or where we were going. On the way, some people fell by the wayside and the guards who were escorting them, oblivious to their suffering, instead just kicked and screamed at them to get up. At least one middle-aged woman didn't or couldn't; she appeared to have no strength to do so. The guard took less than a moment, before he turned his gun and shot her. Witnessing this seemed to drive the line of bedraggled, frightened people onwards. Moving just that little bit faster to avoid being the next victim.

Eventually we came to an entrance of what was clearly some sort of camp. Around the edge was a high wire fence, and at the entrance was a sign: Bergen Belsen. We followed the trail of people through the entrance. I heard Mama murmur, 'What kind of hell have they brought us to?' Indeed, there seemed to be hundreds of people within the camp; mostly they were wearing what looked like some sort of striped uniform. Some had their heads shaved, and this made them appear ghoulish. There were men, women and children, all of whom seemed to be oblivious of the line of new inmates joining the camp.

It took some time to record us. We had to stand to give our names, and then we were handed what seemed to be a bundle of material. We were then sorted out, the people wearing the stars sent one way, while Mama and I, and the women we had travelled with, were sent another way. We carried the small bundles we were given past several huts; it appeared as though the camp was divided up into sections. Eventually we reached a hut and were ordered to stop; the woman guard shouted that this was where we were to stay, instructing us that we would be called to a roll call at seven the following morning.

Our group of around twenty women entered the long, thin

building. It had windows on each side. It appeared to have been built as a temporary structure, with a tin roof and thin walls. Inside, the first thing that hit me was the smell of dirt and people. There were a number of women already inside, and we were directed to the middle of the long room, where there was space. There was a narrow passageway in the middle that separated the two sides, with some low wooden stalls lining each side of the wall; these were covered with dirty looking straw. These was to be our beds. There was not much spare space, so we walked along until we found a part which looked unoccupied. Mama sat down and looked around. 'What is this place?' she wondered. We could hear languages that we didn't recognise; evidently these women were from several different countries.

I undid the bundle that I had been given. Inside was a thin woollen blanket, and also some clothes. They were not new. They included a long grey coat that looked as though it had seen better days; its elbows were threadbare, and it was far too big for me. Mama had a thin black one. I also found a grey skirt, a blouse and some rather large panties. I thought that even though none of the items would fit me, they might be more comfortable than the prison clothes that I was wearing. There was also a metal cup, bowl and spoon. I took the cup and asked, 'Mama, is there any water do you think? I am so thirsty.'

One of the women who was lying on the other side of the room called out. 'There is a bucket over there.' She pointed to the end of the room where a metal bucket sat, next to a small pot-bellied stove. I almost ran to fill my cup and drink the water that eased my throat. 'Be careful!' shouted the woman. 'We are only permitted one bucket full of water each day.'

Mama went across to the woman, who seemed to be troubled by her back as she struggled to sit up. 'What is this place?' she asked her, realising that several of the other women who had travelled with them were also waiting for an answer.

The woman explained that they were in what was deemed to be a women's camp. They all would be given jobs. Some, she explained, were marched off the camp every day to work on the other camp that they had passed several kilometres along the road; others were given tasks here. She described how they were given one meal a day, delivered to them in the evening. This was usually a very thin soup or stew. 'You are lucky,' she told them, 'if you find a piece of meat or vegetable in it. We use the stove to heat it up, and then we get some bread. The bread is divided into two portions; we eat one with the soup and save the other piece to have in the morning. It is too long at time,' she told them, 'to just have the evening food, we need something for the morning too.'

'What about the toilet?' one of the new arrivals asked.

'There is a latrine, out behind the hut,' she told them. 'It is one of the jobs you might be allocated.' She screwed her face up. 'Not a job any of us look forward to. Before you ask, there are some buckets of water that are not so clean so try not to drink it, and we use it to try and maintain some sense of cleanliness. But sometimes the guards decide that someone has committed some misdemeanour, and they are removed. Some of the bitches,' her voice dropped in a conspirator manner, 'are vile and cruel, you will soon find out which ones. Best advice I can offer you is to keep your head down, and don't bring attention to yourself. Oh, by the way, keep any of your possessions safe, if you have any, because there are always some people who will grab them and use them as collateral, if they get a chance.'

It was a dismal situation, and I tried to remain close to Mama at all times, watching and waiting to find out what job we might be allocated the following day. After a visit to the latrine, where the flies dive-bombed me while I hovered over a disgusting opening where not only could you see, but smell, what the previous person had deposited, I crossed my fingers and prayed that I would not be the one to clean it out.

****

Those first few weeks were incredibly difficult. Just learning the rules and living in such crowded conditions were hard enough, without living with the fear that you might have committed some petty infringement of the rules, and then suffer the consequence. These were often dished out by one of the female guards, who wasn't German, but I discovered was Hungarian. Mama and I had been allocated work in the kitchens, which we were both grateful for. I supposed that we might have been given a job like this as we were somewhat fitter than some of the others, and the kitchens were quite some way away to get to across the huge camp. We worked hard all day; different tasks were given to us. Sometimes it was to chop the turnips and potatoes for the so-called stew. Other times we were tasked with distributing the weak and tasteless stew into the buckets that were then taken to the huts.

Along the way to the kitchens, we passed other parts of the camp and saw many, many people looking very weak and thin. Most of the people like this were in the section of the camp for the Jewish community – men, women and children. It was the children's faces that haunted me most, that faraway look they held, as though their eyes were empty. I wondered if anyone looking at me would think the same. I was just going through the motions of life, although it could hardly be described as living, more like existing.

At night, I would snuggle into Mama, the thin blankets covering us as we lay side by side surrounded by other women. A heaving group of humanity bundled together in our own private hell. It was during the night when I allowed myself to feel the pain of my grief. Images of Grand-mama still tormented me; these were now joined with my last sight of Papa, the blindfold around his head as he stood tall in front of his executioners. I had no image of Derk, only a fantasy of what he might have looked like as he ran, mown down in a blast of bullets.

I knew Mama also used the night to let her grief come to the surface. We held each other while our tears soaked the straw beneath us.

The only positive thing I could hold onto was that at least I had access to some outside air. The camp was situated within a large forest clearing. Every morning I practised the ritual Mama had advised, that of looking towards the sunrise, taking a breath and chanting silently that it was one more day towards peace and hope. I didn't know if I actually believed this any longer, but it had become a ritual, and if I didn't follow it, I couldn't help thinking that that might just bring further misery, if that was even possible. Hope. Hope was all that was left.

Winter descended on the camp. The thin walls and tin roofs offered little protection from the freezing conditions. We huddled together with all the other women at night, our dirty bodies acting as incubation for the bugs and fleas that crawled over us freely. The small stove added nothing to the cold conditions; fuel for it was limited. One of the women was so cold that she suggested that they dismantle the wood from the bed bench for fuel, and sleep on the floor. She was overwhelmingly told by the others that sleeping on the hard, earthen floors would be worse. Finding extra wood for the stove became an obsession for the women. Some found ways to bargain; no one questioned why they returned clutching several pieces of wood, where it had come from or from whom. Or what they had had to give in exchange.

I could not remember ever being so cold. No matter how much I burrowed into Mama's back and even wearing all the clothes I possessed made no real difference. I recalled how I had moaned when I had been cold in my bed in Ramstraat. If only I had known what I would face in the future, I would have relished that type of cold, buried beneath the cosy blankets in that soft bed. Now every day was a struggle. Many of the women developed coughs, and these disturbed us all in

the night, with their hacking and coughing. Often loud sobbing was heard in the darkness, past memories of someone
or something littering somebody's consciousness. Fear and
desolation were in abundance; fear of the guards, but also fear
of the conditions that sucked away our depleting energy.

As the winter eased, and we began to move into slightly
warmer climate, it brought a little relief. There seemed to
be more and more people arriving at the camp. The kitchen
became chaotic with the number of food buckets that were
filled. What was concerning was that while more and more
buckets were filled, the contents contained less vegetables,
and rarely any meat – just more liquid. After a cold winter,
there was less ability to summon any energy and with less
vital food, it became even harder to get through each day.

No one knew what was taking place in the rest of the world.
We were in a bubble of sheer survival. I wasn't even shaken
when two women started to fight one night. What they were
fighting over I had no idea, and how they had summoned any
energy to do so was a wonder to me. Now the smell and the
sight of people who were shrivelling in front of me held little
concern. It was as if the daily grind only allowed me to see one
step in front of me. My eyes may have focused onto another
human being, but I didn't see their suffering or struggles: I was
too busy focusing on staying alive, and doing my best not to
let any guard to focus their attention onto me.

It was a world of loneliness, which I thought was rather bi-
zarre, given the living conditions. But loneliness it was, even
though you were surrounded by a mass of humanity; you
were on your own. Even having Mama beside me didn't wipe
this feeling out. When I looked at Mama, I saw a strange, thin
woman, her once sparking eyes empty and sad. There was little flesh on anybody, and while Mama had never been well
covered, now her ribs could be felt when I held her.

The conditions in the camp seemed to worsen. There was even

less food, and water also seemed to be less available. More women in the hut were becoming ill, and it didn't even faze us now, when one was found to have died in the night. Her body was removed and more space was created. Walking to the kitchens became more of a struggle. It was the same distance, but it felt as though the length had doubled. The stench that permeated through the air was accepted. Most of us realised that the smell was connected to death, and it now held less revulsion. It was part of this desperate life we were living.

****

Something seemed to be happening in the camp, I did not know what, but there was a change in atmosphere. The guards seemed restless and more likely to strike out. Gunshots were heard more often, and food was becoming even scarcer. Then it disappeared altogether. We were not called to attend the kitchen; no one, it seemed, was able to rise from our beds.

My seventeenth birthday came and went. I don't think either I or Mama registered it; by this time both of us were suffering from extreme hunger. Mama became terribly weak. I tried to assist her, finding some water I would help her sip it, but she could hardly grasp the cup. The smell of death was in the hut, but I didn't have the strength to find out who had left this world. How long I lay beside Mama, I had no idea, as I was drifting in and out of consciousness, the thirst and hunger causing my body to shut down. I held Mama to me, trying to send some strength and energy into her body. Mama was quiet, and she was cold. I remembered trying to warm Mama, but her body was cold. I drifted deeper into unconsciousness. There were some points when I felt myself above my body looking down, my mind in a state of delirium. I saw images of Papa float in front of me. I reached out to him, but he disappeared, to be replaced by Grand-mama, her face bloodied. I felt, rather than heard, something pull at me. A feeling of floating, then something cold on my lips, as wet dribbled into my mouth.

Water.

The sound of a voice, calling me, telling me I was safe. Telling me to open my eyes. I tried to do so, but my lids were too heavy. The voice, calling out to someone, 'This one is still alive, but barely, help me.'

I felt myself being lifted, slowly. I managed to open my eyes and looked into a pair of deep hazel eyes, they were kind, I remembered thinking. 'Mama,' I called. 'Mama.'

The voice – it had a strange lilt to it – telling me I was safe. He was sorry, but if that was my Mama, then she was dead. Mama dead! How could that be? I felt myself being carried, carried along by the owner or those kind hazel eyes and the lilting voice. I found myself drifting again. There was some sense that I was safe but I didn't know how. I allowed myself to be carried in arms that held me tightly. Carried to where I did not know, or care. I heard the voice again. 'You'll be alright, lass, I will see you will be okay. Harry will make sure, if it's the last thing I do.'

CHAPTER 28

Harry

My dearest Elsa, I have, as you requested, written what I remember of that day when I first met you. I hope that it will help you and Dr Peeters to "fill in the missing gaps."

That day when we entered that hell camp will remain with me for ever. We had no warning. A message came down the line that the medical corps had to make our way urgently, seemed that the front line had discovered one of the camps we had been hearing about. More medical help was needed. When we got there, we realised that this wasn't just some ordinary work camp. You knew it was something different by the smell that hit you before you even got to the gates. When we did get through the gates, the sights that hit us were from some horror film; it went beyond any horror you could imagine.

The camp had been liberated two days previously, and so some work had already started. There were human beings, well some didn't look particularly human, just walking skeletons, eyes protruding out of almost translucent skin and bone. There were hundreds, if not thousands wandering about, looking bewildered and lost. The forces that that had got there before us were trying to do something for them. A food station had been set up, and water distributed. But it was all too little and too late for many. How could another human do this? It made my blood boil to see it. The smell, we soon found out, was from the corpses that littered the camp. Some of the officers were directing mass graves to be dug, and the bastards that had caused this hell were being made to carry the corpses and put them into the huge pits.

Our job was to search through some of the huts further into the camp, to see if there were any living souls there who needed medical attention. My mate Jimmy and I went with a bit of trepidation. Christ we had seen some sights since we landed on the beaches in France, men blown to smithereens, arms, legs, heads, some we were able to patch up and send them to camp hospitals, but none of that prepared me for what I was seeing now.

We found some huts, they were separate from the main camp, and went into one. There were a couple of dead women, but no one alive. We expected the same in the second hut, there were some bodies lying on the raised benches, we guessed they had been dead for a while from the look and smell of them. Then further along the row there was another two, clasped together, looked as though one was nothing more than a kid, clutching another woman who was clearly dead. I was just about to pass by them, when I saw some movement from the young one. I shouted to Jimmy to come and help. I reached in and felt a pulse, it was weak, but the heart was still beating. It took a moment for me to unclasp her hands from the other woman, she murmured, mama, or something like that. It was hard to understand her, she was so weak, and I presumed she was probably close to death.

We got the bottle of water to her lips, and she swallowed some, and seemed to come around for a minute. She was weak as a kitten, her dark hair matted, and you could see it was alive with lice. She was as thin as a rake, her face all hollowed and skin stretched tight over it, her hands such long fingers. She seemed to come round again, this time I understood that she was asking for her mother, this other woman who she had been clutching, must have been her. I picked her up, she was as light as a feather, like lifting a doll, I could *feel the bones of her as I rushed her out of the filthy hut, and with Jimmy running in front of me, we got her to the medical tent that had been erected and was full to the brim with folk milling around. Once we got her into it, I shouted to one of the doctors and he found a space for me to put her onto. She looked like a wee dolly, so small, her limbs like sticks, they were so thin I think they would snap if any pressure was put on them. I didn't want to leave her, but was instructed to do so, and go back and look for anyone else alive.*

Jimmy and I did, but we found no one else still living. We helped out giving some food and water to some of the other poor blighters; they could hardly swallow anything, but grabbed what we gave them and shoved it into their mouths. We had orders to help move some of those in the medical tent up to the German camp, a couple of miles up the road. Seems like that camp had been used to house the Nazi bastards. Rumour was, that some of those evil shits that had caused this horror had scarpered up there and had escaped. God, if I could get my hands round their necks I would make the bastards suffer.

The camp up the road had medical facilities, and the Red Cross had turned up with some help, so some of the barracks were being turned into hospitals. Our Lieutenant McCrae told us that we were going to be stationed there to help out, that was fine by me. Maybe doing something to help would get rid of the overwhelming helplessness and anger I was feeling.

We loaded the trucks up with those who were going to the hospital, and I again found I had the young lassie in my arms. She was still unconscious, but still alive. I carried and placed her gently in the back of the truck with others, and gave the shout to the driver to drive carefully and slowly up the road.

The German camp seemed to be a hive of activity; folk were doing their best to deal with the influx of all these poor creatures. I made sure that my lassie was in good hands before we headed back to collect more.

What a terrible few days. Lieutenant McCrae told Jimmy and me that our duties were to help out at the hospital. I was happy to do so, pleased to be away from that stinking hell hole of Bergen Belsen. Seems that as well as the poor buggers starving to death, the bloody camp was full of typhoid and that was killing them too. There were several deaths in the hospital, and even those who had made it were dying of the disease. Then we realised that they were also dying from being fed. It was only when more doctors turned up, and told us that it became clear that their systems couldn't cope with food, and so we had to go canny with what they had to drink and eat.

I kept my eye on the ward where the young lassie was. She was still alive, and I was told that she seemed a little more with it. Apparently, she had come to a few times, and been given some water and managed it. Just a few sips, but then she would be out of it again. When I went to see her, I found her still asleep. She had had her hair cut short, the nurse told me that they hadn't any option, as she was alive with nits and fleas, so they had had to treat her. She lay in that bed, looking like a little elf, her small features, a wee pointed nose, and her ears looking as though they were too big for the rest of her head. Seems though that she had come too enough to give them her name, it was pinned at the end of her bed, Elsa Wouters, aged 17.

It was during one of my check-ins that she woke up. I leant over her, and smiled at her. 'Well, lass, you are still with us,' I told her. 'Thank goodness for that, my name is Harry,' I told her. Her eyes focused on me, and they were big and a greyish blue, her eyelashes long and curved, I thought they were quite unusual. 'Do you remember me finding you,' I asked you, but you shook your head. So you can understand me then?' and you nodded, it seemed to take you all your strength to do so. I wondered how you ended up there, and if you could understand me, where you had come from.

I don't know how to describe it, but a strange thing seemed to have happened. Call it what you want, destiny, or meant to be, or something like that. But there was a connection; I needed to keep contact with this lassie. Thank goodness the British Army allowed me to stay in Hohne Camp to do so.

CHAPTER 29

Slowly, I started to recover. It was very long process and I had no idea of the time or how long I had been in the hospital. I did know that I was lying on a bed with a mattress, and that I was covered by clean sheets that smelt of soap. I knew that the people around me came and checked my pulse, and gave me small sips, first of water, and then some warm fluid that tasted of goodness. This was different: they were helping me, and not hurting me. I found myself in those early days drifting in and out of consciousness. My sleep was peppered with memories, and I didn't know where my mama was. Occasionally, I grasped a snippet in my minds' eye of being carried along by strong arms. But it had no context to it, just a fleeting snippet.

I had a visitor, this man called Harry, in his soldier's uniform with his lilting voice, who came to see me. It was those kind hazel eyes that aided that snippet of a memory. These were the eyes I remembered. He was tall, and when he bent over to smile at me, his whole face lit up. His cheeks were a ruddy reddish colour, and he had what my papa would have referred to a rough complexion, his chin looking as though there was a fraction of a beard appearing. I found it hard to stay awake for too long in those early days, but gradually I began to be able to keep my eyes open for longer, and take in my surroundings.

It was on one of those days when I was propped up on my pillows, and I could see the other patients, and the doctors and nurses busying themselves around the long ward, that I saw him striding down the ward towards me. His face lit up when he saw that I was not only awake but sitting up.

'Well now, look at you,' he said. 'You are looking a million miles better today.'

I very tentatively returned his smile, trying to form the words in my mind before speaking them. 'I am feeling a little better, thank you.'

'That now, is just the tonic I needed. Its Elsa, isn't it?' I bobbed my head. 'And it says at the bottom of your bed that you're seventeen, is that right?' I nodded again.

'And you are Harry?' My voice was still very weak so it was quite hard for him to hear me.

'That's right, Harry Kerr, from Glen Gavin, in Scotland. I am twenty-two years old. So not much older than you.' Although I remember he told me later that he could not help thinking to himself that he felt more like middle-aged after what he had experienced. 'Now tell me, where did you come from? Your English is very good.'

'I am from Antwerp in Belgium,' I answered, my thoughts transferred instantly to my home. 'My mama taught me English.' I felt the sorrow and grief overwhelm me when I thought of Mama, and a tear started to make its way slowly down my cheek.

'I am sorry about your mother. That is who you were with when we found you, wasn't it?' He reached over, and gently wiped the tear away; he seemed to care and understand my grief.

I nodded, but could find no words to reply. I knew Mama was dead, and that was the last person in the family. Now I was on my own, but didn't have the strength to do anything about mourning them. That would come later.

Harry was attached to the men's ward in an adjoining build-ing. He helped with their care, shaving, and washing their thin bodies, helping them begin the terrible journey back to phys-ical health. He told me that it was rewarding in strange way, as they began to make their first steps on their own. They sadly still lost many of those who had been rescued, as their bodies couldn't function, and gave up. There were many who were Jews, some, it seemed, had been in other camps. They stood out, as they had what became known as the Auschwitz tattoo. The news of what the Nazi regime had done had filtered out into the world. Some might be considered lucky to have had been moved from the death camps, where so many were sent to the gas chambers. Those who had survived that first terror camp had ended up in Belsen, and at least some had survived. Harry told me later that he couldn't process how the Nazis and that sick, mad little man Hitler had dreamt up those terri-fying camps.

Every day, Harry would visit me. The nurses on the ward smiled when they saw the tall, well-built Scotsman appear. They also witnessed my response too; I had started to look for him. I was now up and able to walk unaided. I still needed careful treatment; the doctors told me that after being so long without food and water it would be a slow return to health.

I was told that I was ready to be discharged to another build-ing, one for the displaced people. Work was being done by the Allied forces with the Red Cross, to try to repatriate all of us who had been taken so far from our counties. Some people were taking much longer to be able to return, and I was one of these; I had no family to return to.

The summer months arrived and brought just a little hope. I was now able take short walks. I did so around the camp. Re-membering Mama's words about looking at the sunrise, and thinking about being one more day towards peace and hope, held a bittersweet feeling for me. If I was really honest, I did not believe I would ever find peace again, even though I knew that the Germans had now been beaten, and Europe was now supposed to be at peace. Each day I became just a fraction more physically able to walk a little further, and I was able to eat larger portions and keep them in my stomach. My limbs now had more flesh, and my pot belly had settled a little as my muscles began to grow and repair. It was my mind that was fractured. When I closed my eyes at night, sleep evaded me, to be replaced with a film of memories, Grand-mama, Papa, Derk, and now dear Mama. I sometimes awoke screaming, my arms flaying about as I tried to escape from unseen assailants. At times I found myself back in the horror or the camp, or at Breendonk, or in our kitchen with the sound of the pistol as it fired the bullet into Grand-mama. These visions came unbidden, without notice, without my knowing when they would raise up and incapacitate me, so I would find myself sobbing and shaking uncontrollably. I wasn't alone with these experiences. Many of those who shared the building with me had similar outbursts. One of the Red Cross doctors told me that one day they would pass. I just wondered how long it would take.

The bright spot was Harry. Thank goodness he was still at the camp. He made sure to seek me out often, and we would take a gentle walk around the large camp. Some of it was on the edge of a forest, and so greenery helped to calm and settle me. Harry didn't pry, he gave me space. I rarely told him anything of what I had experienced; I didn't want to inflict that on him. I did tell him about my family; slowly and tentatively I told him about my early life. That time before the world exploded and Hitler decided to create havoc across the continent. Harry told me about Glen Gavin, where his family were safe and well. He described the farm or, as he called it, the croft. Birch End it was called. He described the Scottish hills and countryside; it sounded peaceful.

Harry made me smile with his stories. Not only about his homeland, but also about what was happening in the barracks. It sounded very much as though the men enjoyed the banter between each other, and he hinted now and then to being the brunt of the banter. This seemed to be about going to see his wee lassie. I liked the idea of being his wee lassie.

We became closer when, one day on one of our walks, Harry caught my hand in his. I didn't pull away. It felt nice. Safe, and a warm feeling. He was so much taller than me; he looked down and I had to raise my head to look up to him. On that first time when he held me close to him, and reached his head down to kiss me on my lips, I experienced such a strong sense of belonging. It was as though we fitted together, although, given our different heights and builds, I had no idea of what we looked like. It just felt right.

Harry was careful with me; it was as though he treated me like a delicate piece of porcelain. He restored my respect and I started to trust in another human being.

Harry told me, much later on, how he had realised that he had fallen in love. He had been getting used to being teased by his mates for visiting me so often. He couldn't wait each day to see me. He told me that I was pretty, especially now that my face and body had started to fill out. My unusual eyes, he said, now had some life in them, and now and again the smile I awarded him actually reached my eyes. What was so intriguing was how well we seemed to fit together. I was tiny against his large frame, and he felt protective and wanted to keep me safe. He did not know what I had seen and experienced on my journey to Belsen, but he did know that he wanted to make sure that for the rest of my life, I would be safe and loved. He loved me, his sweet lassie.

Harry had had no idea of how long he would be at Bergen before he would receive orders to return to Britain. Most of his mates were chaffing at the bit to get home, but he wanted to stay, if he could have his way. The troops were being de-mobbed, and the enlisted men who were intending to remain in the forces were being moved about. Rumour was that new battalions would be taking over this camp and making it into garrison headquarters. The British were here stay in Germany; they would keep the peace. Harry knew that staying in the forces wasn't for him. He was destined to return home; the army were not for him. He had had his fill of fighting; he just wanted to be back in his Highland home, but he wanted me beside him.

The winter of 1945 was cold, but for me the accommodation in the displaced persons building was a luxury compared with the previous year. I had received some clothes, and these actually fitted. I was very grateful for the leather boots I had been provided with. Knowing that they were not new did not matter; my feet were warm and dry and that was sheer luxury. I knew that it took time to trace people, and I didn't even know whether Sophia and Lucas had survived, but they were, I realised, all I had. I had given the Red Cross my address in Ramstraat, but there had been no word of anyone claiming me. Given my age, I was permitted to remain while the search went on.

In the meantime I had fallen in love with my big, strapping, lovely Scotsman. I believed him when he said he wanted to be with me, and that one day we would be together forever. It was a hope we both had, but whether we would achieve that wish, I didn't know.

CHAPTER 30

Harry heard that his unit were likely to be shipped out and back home within the next couple of weeks. He had been reluctant to tell me. I had been improving and looked, and felt, so much better over the past few weeks, and I knew that he was worrying about upsetting me. We couldn't quite contemplate that we would be apart from each other, and he had tried to find out whether I could return with him to Scotland. He had even wondered whether he could get the garrison's padre to marry us, but when he briefly raised the idea with the padre, he received a distinctively cool response. He had been informed that as he was a serving soldier, he would need the permission of his commanding officer to get married, and he, for one, would recommend that this should be refused. Harry had had to clench his teeth as he listened to the padre lecturing him on the difficulties of such a union, and how hasty he was being to consider committing to me, a woman who he had rescued. The padre had pontificated about it was likely that what Harry was feeling was deep sympathy, and taking into consideration of how they met, that was understandable.

Harry's knuckles had been white by the time the padre had run out of words. It had left him feeling furious and frustrated. He was certain that what he felt for me was not just sympathy but real love. Still, he was a member of the British Army, and still under their rules and regulations, so he had no other option but to follow them.

When the final order came advising that his unit was due to move out at the end of the week, Harry felt deep sense of sadness. It was the end of January, and cold, with snow on the ground, making it difficult to find somewhere private for us to be with each other. He met me as planned outside of my accommodation block; I was wearing the warm, long coat on that I had been given, plus my leather boots. I was also wearing my woollen knitted hat and gloves that had been a Christmas gift from Harry. He had had to do a deal with one of lads from another unit, who seemed to get his hands on all sorts of things, for the right price. Now what he saw was a small woman who had almost disappeared under the hat, which it turned out was far too big for me. However, I had been overcome when he had presented it to me just a few weeks ago. If he had given me a diamond, I don't think it would have been any better. The warm clothes were worth much more to me, and actually having something new was a very special present.

Taking my hand in his, he had rubbed it as though he was rubbing strength into it. We walked. It was late afternoon, and the winter sun was going down beneath the trees, and the snow was crisp under our feet. We walked around the Round House, a building that had once been the SS Officer Mess. It was a grand building, and one which they believed held many secrets about what the regime had been up to in the area. As we walked we talked. Harry reassured me that he would not forget me, and I shyly told him that I would be his, forever. He gave me his home address, and begged me to write to him, and let him know as soon as I heard any news about contact from Belgium.

He had pulled me into a doorway at the back of the building, where we were sheltered and shielded from sight. Reaching down and taking my face in his hands he kissed me deeply. The kiss went on, and on, in the end I had to slightly pull away as I felt a tingling of passion, and was not quite sure how to handle it. We kissed again, and I experienced our passion rising, so that we both felt the heat rise in our bodies. We were far too wrapped up in our outdoor clothes, to be able to respond to the passion in the way we realised we wanted to. Harry withdrew, and told me that while he would love to continue, he had too much respect for me. He wanted me badly, but he also wanted our first time to be somewhere more fitting than at the back of a building. He pulled me to him, and told me again how much he loved me, and that we would, he assured me, find a way to get married and spend the rest of our lives together.

We walked back to my accommodation block and he hugged me to him to say a final farewell. It was painful for both of us. The pain I felt was a very different type of pain than one I had experienced before. It wasn't the pain of grief, but of separation. This time, I hoped the separation would be temporary, and there would come a time when I would be with him again. That gave me hope that, just maybe, I might find some future happiness, a concept which had become totally alien to me.

Harry's unit was due to leave very early the following morning, and so I made sure that I was awake, dressed and standing at the gates of the garrison, when the convoy passed by. I searched for his face, and just as a truck rounded a bend, I caught sight of him standing at the back, waving frantically and throwing me a kiss. I could hear the jeers of his companions as he did so. I watched the convoy until it disappeared from sight, and then slowly walked back. The sun was just beginning to show its head over the horizon, and I took a deep breath, and sent a thought that I hoped that it would not be too long before I could be with my Harry.

Just two weeks later I got a message from the Red Cross. They had had a reply and had found Sophia, and she was able to offer me support and accommodation. There was some paperwork to undertake, and a range of strong emotions flooded my mind, relief, excitement, but also an overriding sense of fear of what I would find in my old city.

CHAPTER 31

The journey from northern Germany back to Belgium was not easy, but it was, I reflected, far more comfortable than the journey that had taken me there in the first place. I had been given some money, a travel order, and clothes. My emotions had taken me by surprise when I said goodbye to the many people who had helped my recovery. I told them over and over again how grateful I was for their help. I was driven to the rail station by two women from the Red Cross; they were incredibly kind, and when they both hugged me tightly as they helped me board the train, I found my face awash with tears. I found a seat and waved as I started the first leg of my train journey. I would have to change trains at Hannover Hauptbahnhof, and I was quite anxious about making sure that I got on the right train.

As I gazed out of the windows, we passed the bombed-out buildings of towns as the train rattled through. The thought came to me that the villages and the countryside looked beaten. There was an atmosphere of depression, and when the conductor came along the corridor requesting to see tickets, I couldn't help but feel my pulse race, and had to remind myself that I had nothing to fear from them any longer. There was also a sudden realisation that I had never travelled by myself before. My parent's protection of me, of always insisting that I remained in the house at Ramstraat, or travel with an adult, now seemed such a long time ago. I supposed that I would get used to travelling alone now that, as far as I knew, I was the only survivor of the Wouters family.

Thankfully, after a lengthy journey, I reached Antwerp Central and the train screeched to a halt. I looked out of the window but couldn't see much of the platform due to the engine's release of steam and black smoke. Collecting my bag, I made my way off of the train, and stood for a moment, before I heard my name being shouted. Turning to the direction of the call, I saw Sophia racing towards me, her arms outstretched to throw them around my body, pulling me into a tight embrace.

'Oh my goodness.' Sophia held me at arm's-length, to appraise me. Both of us had tears running down our faces. 'Oh Elsa, I didn't think I would ever see you again.' She reached for me again and hugged me tightly. 'Oh bless you, come, we have much to speak about.'

I was amazed at the changes in the city as we walked from the station to the apartment that Sophia and Lucas were living in. Klapshot was a street in the old quarter, not far from the Cathedral and *Grote Markt*. Sophia talked non-stop, telling me that Lucas was at work but was looking forward to seeing me later. He had managed to find work in a local shop; it didn't bring in much money, but enough to pay for what they needed. I looked around, trying to get my bearings; it all looked so strange, but one of the most positive things was that there were no Nazi flags blowing. They had been replaced by the Belgian national flag. People in the streets looked weary. We passed some shops where there was a queue, and Sophia told me that there was still a shortage of food, but rationing made it a little fairer. I was able to reassure her that I had been given a ration card, and noticed a flash of relief pass over her face.

We had reached the narrow street of Klapdorp, a street with shops on both sides. Sophia stopped at number 25, and retrieved her key from her bag. 'Here we are, it is nothing special,' she told me, 'but we are so happy you can stay with us.'

The front door opened to a very narrow steep stairway, common in Belgian buildings. I followed Sophia up to the first floor where she used another key to unlock another door. There was a steep step into what was a square room with a window on one side. It was furnished with a small wooden table and four wooden, slightly rickety chairs. There was a cooking stove in the corner, and some shelving on the wall. There was a small recess area at the end of the room, which had a curtain pulled across it. Sophia pulled the curtain back to reveal a bed. 'This is yours.'

Sophia invited me to follow her. There were a couple of small steps leading to a small narrow passageway; she motioned to the right, where there was a sort of cupboard area, which contained a sink and a water tap. 'We are fortunate,' she announced. 'At least we have running water.' The back of the apartment gave way to a large room; the first part had a rather battered sofa, its covering threadbare and faded. There were also two chairs; one looked as though it had lost its feet, and wobbled as they passed it. At the back of the room there was a large bed, and a chest of drawers. The room was lit by two small windows, one at the front and another at the back. The room was quite dreary and cold, but Sophia rushed to light the stove. 'It will soon make the room cosy,' she told me.

Sophia turned to look at me. 'Now you sit down, you look tired. I will boil the kettle and make some coffee.' She bustled around, checking the fire, before disappearing back into the entrance room that was also the kitchen. I heard the kettle being filled and then the stove being rattled. As I waited I looked around me. The apartment certainly wasn't the best, but I was both pleased and relieved to be here. Compared with what I had experienced, it was, I reminded myself, a palace.

After a while, Sophia returned carrying a tray, which she placed onto a small round table. She poured two cups of coffee, and apologised for not having any milk or cream. I took the cup and sipped the hot liquid. It tasted of coffee, which was so pleasant that I didn't need milk or cream, and was grateful for the caffeine it contained.

Sophia sat on the sofa. She hesitated for a moment, then spoke. 'I am so sorry about your family, Elsa. It was so awful to hear about your Grand-mama, and your father. Lucas still rails at himself for not being with your papa, instead we were still with my family. Oh, what a shock it was when we returned and learnt what had taken place.'

'Tell me,' I pleaded. 'I have often wondered what had happened after we were taken. What happened to my grand-mama, do you know where her body was taken?'

'Well, by the time we returned, her body had been moved. Do you remember Lambert Van Holden, Dominique and Adele's father? He had been astounded at what the Nazis had done, and arranged to have her body removed and buried. She is in the cemetery.' She watched my face as I took in what she was telling me. 'I can take you and show you her grave soon.' She stopped, her voice wavering. 'Lambert also cleaned the kitchen, but I have to tell you, the house had been looted. The walls, all those lovely paintings your family owned were ripped off and taken, the furniture broken, and your grand-mama and your mama's jewellery boxes were missing. So the bastards took everything of any value, and destroyed most of what was left. But wait for one moment.' She went into the back room and rummaged in the chest of drawers, then returned a moment later and offered her hand. 'They missed these, though. I grabbed them when I found them, and now I can return them to you.'

I held my hand out, and Sophia placed into it the small silver bracelet that was the gift from the two little Jewish girls of the Tasma family. I wondered whether any of them had survived. The second object was the small sapphire brooch, the family heirloom that had been a gift from my grand-mama on my thirteenth birthday. That now seemed a million years away, so much had happened over the past five years. I closed my hand, holding both objects tightly. It wasn't much, but it meant more than I could verbalise. I then allowed the tears to come, and I suspected that there would be many tears yet to fall.

Over the next hour Sophia described hers and Lucas' life over the past nineteen months since they had last seen each other. Once they discovered what had happened at Ramstraat, they realised that if the Nazis returned, they too were in danger. They were not sure either who they could trust. The Van Holdens gave them some shelter for a couple of days, and then they made their way back to Sophia's family, and waited out the end of the war. Sophia could not help but join me in expressing our sorrow: so much grief that could very easily overwhelm us, if we allowed it. Perhaps it was just as well that at that moment Lucas returned from his work, and swept me up into his arms, welcoming me with hugs and kisses.

'I am so pleased you are here,' he told me, wiping tears from his own eyes. 'You must stay with us, and we will look after you, so we will,' He looked over at Sophia for confirmation.' We will take care of you.'

The evening meal was more than sufficient and I passed Sophia my ration card, and felt a little less guilty for sharing their food supplies. I was exhausted; the long journey and the emotional reunion had combined to suck my energy. I was happy to retire to the box bed; the mattress was soft and I felt myself falling into a deep sleep almost immediately. My dreams started. They had become rather repetitive: faces of guards, Nazis, SS Officers, the walking skeletons of the people in the camp, my parents reaching for me, and then disappearing before I could reach them. I was unaware that I was screaming and crying out for them, until I felt arms around me. I was drenched in sweat when I finally awoke in the arms of Sophia, who held me, reassuring me that I was safe.

In the morning, I apologised profusely for disturbing them. Lucas and Sophia immediately responded by telling me that I had nothing to apologise for. They understood that whatever I had suffered, it was totally understandable for me to have nightmares. I was not to worry.

I tentatively asked what had happened to my family home. I saw the look that passed between the two. Lucas answered falteringly, rubbing his chin as he thought how he would phrase this. 'I am sorry, Elsa, but it is occupied by several families. There are so many people without homes or money that many have just now taken over empty buildings.' He watched as what he told me registered with me, and I suppose my face now told a story before I had to say any words. More loss! 'But we will see,' he tried to sound a little upbeat. 'We will see, now you have returned, how we can try and get it back for you.'

CHAPTER 32

The next few months were intensely difficult for me. I just felt a tremendous sense of fear and anxiety all of the time. I tried to dismiss these feelings. I told myself that I was safe, and that the Nazis had been defeated and Antwerp had been returned to a peaceful city. It was just that... I didn't feel safe.

Sophia and Lucas accompanied me to Ramstraat one Sunday afternoon. It was a sunny afternoon in late May, and I had been back with them for nearly three months before I could summon the courage to return. Sophia held my shaking hand as we entered the street, and we walked slowly along the pavement until all three of us stood outside my family home and stared. Its appearance was evidence that it had been damaged. The window of what had once been Grand-mama's bedroom was boarded up, as were some parts of the two front ground floor windows, that had once been Papa's surgery and waiting room.

Lucas went to the front door and knocked loudly. He had to repeat this several times until, eventually, it was opened by a youngish man. Lucas spoke to him, turning and pointing towards me, apparently advising the man who I was. After what appeared to be a fairly short and slightly heated exchange, the man shook his head and slammed the door in Lucas's face.

I stood and observed the building, the place which held so

many memories of my early life. Now I was not permitted to enter. Who were these people who had taken up residence, and were dismissing our request to go in and see if there was anything left of my previous life and family? How much more could I bear?

****

The visit to Ramstraat escalated my trauma. Memories floated around my mind; the nightmares became more extreme. I now tried hard not to fall asleep, and only did so once exhaustion overwhelmed me. I was jumpy and anxious. Just a car backfiring was enough to send me racing for cover, only to discover a few moments later that I was shaking and soaked with sweat, my heart racing and feeling as though it would burst from my chest. It was becoming almost impossible for me to leave the apartment. Lucas and Sophia were terribly worried and concerned for me, and did not know how to care for me. The only time I felt a little calmer was when a letter arrived sporting a Scottish postmark. I would take the letter and close the curtain across my box bed, so I could read it in privacy. Letters brought all of us a little respite.

Lucas made contact with Lambert Von Holden. He explained the concern they had to for me, fearing that while I had survived unspeakable atrocities, he was uncertain whether I could survive life. Lambert listened carefully, his face full of concern. He would make some enquires within the medical circles, he informed Lucas, and get back to him.

It was a couple of weeks later that we received a message: Lambert had spoken to a Dr Peeters, who was undertaking some ground-breaking work with survivors of the war. He remembered Martin Wouters with affection and respect. He would like to meet me.

I was willing to attend a meeting with Dr Peeters, especially after Lucas informed me that he had known Papa. The meeting was arranged at Dr Peeters' home, which doubled as his consulting office. It was a small house, just a ten-minute walk from the apartment. Sophia accompanied me. It was a silent journey, tense with anxiety, and both of us were grateful when we found ourselves at the door without me turning around and running for cover.

I remember little of that first meeting with Dr Peeters. I do recall the warmth of welcome I received from him, and he reminded me that we had met, once before, when I was quite little. I didn't remember this meeting, but it allowed me to feel just a little more open to accepting his help. The one other part of the conversation that stuck in my mind was when I heard him say that it was normal to be suffering in the way that I was. That many survivors of the Nazi regime, who had terrible acts inflicted on them, were also suffering like me. He wanted to help me, and if I allowed him to do so, then I might be able to find a way to live life again,

Those first meetings with Dr Peeter were not easy. He talked gently with me about trauma, giving me information and reassurance, explaining that what I had seen, heard and experienced had left sores inside of me, and these were weeping. The grief and shock of losing all of my family had not hit me yet. I was, he advised, still in a state of shock and processing all that had taken place. I felt terribly fragile and vulnerable. I was fragile, both physically and emotionally. At times I felt as though it would be easier just to give up, allow what the Nazis had failed to do, and just die. It was the letters from Harry that kept me alive. They were banal, full of simple events, the sheep being sheared, the calf that was born. The first chicks hatched, and the pictures he painted of normality and peace. Could I seize that? It was his reminder of his love for me, and that one day I would join him, that gave me the will to hold onto life.

As part of the recovery I needed, Dr Peeters told me to allow my grief to be processed. I spoke about Grand-mama, and with

Sophia's support at hand, I at last entered the cemetery where Grand-mama's body had been placed, thanks of course to Lambert Van Holden. He had kindly ensured that her burial place had been marked, so that when I stood before it I saw Grand-mama's birth had been recorded, as well as the date of her death. I laid some flowers on the spot, but felt numb. It was impossible to comprehend that this was where dear Grand-mama was. I sent my love to her wherever she was, and hoped that her spirit was at rest. The visit to the grave was part of my journey to recovery, Dr Peeters told me. I have to say that I was not convinced, but I was willing to follow his guidance.

The day-to-day life of Antwerp continued. Food shortages were still in evidence, lines of people queueing for their rations had become normal. Sophia made tasty and nourishing meals. My physical health was still fragile, starvation had caused long-term harm. Sophia was careful about the food she cooked, ensuring that it was as healthy as possible. Some days, eating felt almost impossible, but with Sophia's gentle encouragement, I managed to swallow what I needed to rebuild my health.

The first anniversary of the end of the war in Europe brought considerable reflection. The celebrations were muted, as more information and knowledge had surfaced relating to the numbers murdered by the Nazis in the concentration camps. Many of the Jewish community, who had once lived and worked in peace in Antwerp, had disappeared. For me, it was not a celebration. The most significant anniversary was the 13th April: that was the day when the British had liberated Belsen, and Harry had found me. I reflected as to whether I should change the day of my birthday from the 8th of April to the 13th, as that was the day when I was given a second chance of life. When I had shared that thought with Dr Peeters, he had smiled and noted that it was one of the most positive statements I had made with him. Perhaps I had just turned a corner.

CHAPTER 33

The Van Holden family tried to be as helpful as possible. Dominique and Adele had managed to resume their lives. Dominique, the older of the two, and a year older than me, was working in an office of one of Lambert's friends. Adele, at seventeen, had enrolled in a secretarial course. They were both affected by my fragile state when they met me the first time I was invited to join them for tea. I tried hard, but they could not be protected from the sadness that I displayed, and it left them feeling guilty that they had remained safe with their parents. They tried hard to encourage me to visit them more often, and to engage in some social events, but I was just not able to do so. Dominique had raged at her parents for the injustice of what had happened to her dear friend. They had been so distressed when they had heard the news that their old teacher, Estelle, my mama, had not survived but delighted that I had. They questioned, now that peace had been restored and they were rebuilding their lives, whether my survival would mean that I too would one day enjoy the life that they were beginning to experience.

One day when I made my way across the *Grot Markt* with Sophia on our way to an appointment with Dr Peeters, I caught sight of a man who was bent over and limping and who walked close to us. I recognised him, and a depth of fury rose up and almost engulfed me: it was Albert Du Pont. The collaborator! Sophia felt the tension, as I stopped, and she then realised why.

'So he survived!' I cried, pointing to him. He either did not realise he was the subject of interest, or he had become used to fingers being pointed at him.

'Yes, yes he did. He, as you will see is no longer the fit man. Part of the punishment reprisals, when it was handed out to those who had helped the Nazis. He was allowed to live, but he will never be allowed to forget how he assisted the evil Nazis to persecute the people of the city.' Sophia caught my hand, and with some encouragement we continued on our journey.

'What happened to Father Francis?'

'He too was deemed responsible for helping the regime. I am not entirely sure what happened to him. He just disappeared, and there is a new priest at the church now. Neither of us would consider going to church; not now, not ever. '

Lambert and Cecily Van Holden held a special place in their hearts for me. They suggested to Sophia and Lucas that I could move in with them if it would be of any help. This offer had been thanked but rejected; I wanted to remain where I was. They tried hard to offer me what they could; one such thing they were doing was to support Lucas in his exploration of my inheritance. As well as the property of Ramstraat, which was technically mine, there were also other financial assets my family once had, that were rightfully mine. There was not only the house on Ramstraat but of course Grand-mama's property, which she had owned and lived in before the war. It was not an easy search, but eventually they tracked down Papa's lawyer, Marcel Maes. He had returned to the city fairly recently from Switzerland, where he had escaped to during the occupation. Thankfully all of the records and files that had been in his office had survived. His office had been fairly small, and had not been subjected to the looting that many others had. He had resumed his business, and was delighted that someone with an interest in the Wouters family had made contact.

Lambert and Lucas had made the first tentative enquires with Marcel, advising him that I was the sole survivor of the Wouters family, and asking if he could assist them to restore what was rightly mine. He was obliged, he told them: he had utter respect for Dr Wouters and had been devastated to learn of his and his family's death. 'Such a great miss,' and yes, he did have documents that could assist the young girl. Not only did he have documents relating to Dr Wouters's will, but that of Helena Wouters. So, he would make enquires, he told them. He would also need evidence of the death of Derk Wouters.

This led Lucas to whisper to Sophia that they probably needed to visit Nina and Lars's farm in Lint, about twenty miles from the city. It was likely that they could get the confirmation there of Derk's death. The only information they had was what I had been told by the Nazis that he had been shot and killed. After discussing with Dr Peeters, it had been agreed that they would speak to me and see if I would wish to travel with them. When I heard this, I pondered on it for a moment, and then agreed: it was another part of my journey.

****

I had last visited Nina and Lars's farm about a year before war had been declared. I vaguely remembered it as a small holding with a few acres of land. Lambert very kindly loaned Lucas his car, which made the journey much easier. We had no idea of what we were going to find. As we drove along the short track towards the farmhouse, the first thing that struck us was that the fields looked unkempt. That was repeated once we reached the buildings. The farmhouse itself looked almost derelict. Windows were broken, the front door almost off of its hinges, and weeds were growing from the gutters. It had an eerie presence about it, and we stopped to have a good look about it before we entered. There was one thing that looked sure, and that was there was no one living within the property.

As we entered we were hit by a musty smell. There, amongst

broken furniture and scattered belongings, was evidence that this had once been a family home. I made my way through the mess and looked to see if there was anything worth salvaging. I was rewarded with a couple of photos, ripped out of their frames – and one been nibbled, probably by mice who had free roam of this building. I looked at the photos and recognised one of Lars and Nina on their wedding day. The second photograph made me gasp. It was one taken of the family when I was about ten. In it was Mama, Papa, Derk and me. I held it to my chest and showed it to Sophia and Lucas; whatever the outcome of our journey I had found a little piece of gold that I would treasure.

Lucas did his best to pull the front door to, and told us that he would return on another day to make the building wind and water-proof. He was amazed that no one had taken over the property. He would let the lawyer know about it, so that he could make enquires about whom it now belonged to. We knew that Nina was Estelle's cousin, but that was about all we knew about the connection to the Wouters family.

We decided to go into the village and make some enquires, hoping that someone could tell us what had happened to the residents. There was just one café in the village: it had some tables and chairs on the pavement. It was open, and inhabited by a couple of men who sat at one of the tables smoking and drinking beer. They stared at us with a certain interest, and not a terribly friendly one at that.

Sophia, Lucas and I sat at the other table, and ordered coffee from the café owner, who came out bustling with some interest in his new customers. When the coffees were delivered, Lucas posed the question, asking about Nina and Lars, explaining that I was a relative. That question brought immediate interest from the men at the other table, who were doing their best to listen in. One stood up and interrupted, telling us that they knew Nina and Lars very well. After introductions, they pulled their chairs across to join us.

I was fascinated by them; they were very vocal and animated when they described Nina and Lars as heroes. They should have been awarded a medal, they told us, for the work they had done for the Resistance, shielding many and helping them escape to freedom. They were part of an active line for getting people out of the country, especially Allied airman. I remembered all of those who had passed through Ramstraat, and so I was not unduly surprised by this information. The two men went on to recount that Nina and Lars had been given up to the Gestapo by a local collaborator – one man spat on the ground as he remembered – who, they told us, 'Has since been dealt with.' The night when the Gestapo came and raided the farm and killed Nina and Lars had been one of fury and sadness, and of course one said, 'Also Derk, the young lad, I think he was a relative. He was shot in the back as he tried to escape. He was a brave lad, took many risks and was one of the guides that travelled with the escapees to the next safe house.'

Sophia reached over and grabbed my hand, taking it in hers. She squeezed it, feeling me tremble.

'Have you any idea where their bodies are?' asked Lucas, holding his breath and hoping that these men would have an answer.

'They are all in the cemetery, along the road.' One of the men pointed with his finger. 'How are you related?' he asked me, realising from the way I was reacting that this news was impacting on me.

'Derk,' I told them, 'was my brother, and Nina, my mama's cousin.'

Both men bowed their heads in a kind of respect, and asked. 'Would you like us to show you where they are lying?'

We expressed our appreciation, and followed the two men along the road. We were shown some relatively recent graves;

we stopped in front of two, marked by two wooden crosses and showing names. One was carved with Nina and Lars Vison, with the date of their deaths, and the second grave, Derk Wouters, with his date of death. Seeing these, I fell to my knees, and picked up some of the earth and let it run through my fingers. Here was my brother, Derk. The brother I had shared so many memories with. And then I felt a huge surge of anger, that he was here in this graveyard when he should have been living his life to the full. It was so unfair.

The two village men stood back in respect, allowing us some time to mourn. Lucas went to join them, leaving Sophia and I to share our sorrow. Lucas thanked them for their help. 'Most of the village helped to place them here,' he was told. 'The priest would have their deaths recorded in the register, so that might be of some help if needed.'

The return journey back to Antwerp was travelled with mixed emotions. There was a sense of relief that we had discovered what had happened, and that the bodies had received a proper burial, while on the other, sadness and anger that lives had been wiped out before their time.

CHAPTER 34

I had been attending Dr Peeters for several months, when during one of my appointments he suggested a way of dealing with the trauma that I had suffered. When he first made the suggestion my immediate reaction was one of alarm. To write the details of my life, and what I had encountered along the way, and in English, felt a little beyond my grasp.

'You see, my dear...' He had a way of stroking his short beard when he was contemplating the best way to explain a concept. 'I am making this suggestion, not on a whim, but it is my belief that if you can externalise your memory by writing it, and not in your first language, that it will allow you to manage your trauma.' He bent forwards in the comfortable saggy chair where he sat for his consultations. 'You have the ability both to write, and your mama's teaching of English, and these give you an advantage over others.' He could see from my reaction that I wasn't convinced. 'You see, Elsa, what you have witnessed, and what you have had to endure since the war started, has been so extensive that the part of your brain that holds your memory has been damaged. So, by taking out the memory and putting into order can help repair the damage.' He became animated. 'I know that it is a strange thing to advise, but I will support you all of the way until it is finished.'

I sat back into the chair, not replying for a couple of minutes. 'So, doctor, the treatment that you are suggesting, has it worked with others?' I watched again as the psychiatrist framed his words.

'There are many studies taking place with survivors who

have experienced severe trauma, Elsa. The world of science is struggling to help people in your position and, well, if I am honest, there isn't any data to back my idea up. But frankly, my dear, it may help you and it could allow you to find a way to live your life.'

I trusted this man. He had provided a lifeline to me over the past few months. I wasn't sure I had made much progress; I was still tormented in my sleep, and often in the daytime. But if he thought it might help me to find a way out of this dark place and move on with my life, then it would be worth a try. 'Okay,' I hesitantly told him. 'When do we start?'

I was provided with notebooks, and Dr Peeters made his study available to me twice a week so I could have the peace and the space to write. He explained to me that I could write my account while he was on hand to support me, so that if I became overwhelmed, having him close by would provide a sense of safety. Also, it was away from home, and therefore an emotional distance could be provided. And so the experiment commenced.

I journeyed to Dr Peeters' study twice a week; some days were easier than others. I would write most days for just an hour and that was enough. He made sure he was available for when I had finished, and if I needed to talk, then he was there. On some occasions, I was very distressed and needed his counsel, on others I was able to give him a weak smile and let him know that I was okay.

On the days when I wasn't writing the journal, life with Sophia and Lucas fell into a routine. I helped Sophia in the mornings, and was also happy to stand in food queues for her. Sophia had procured an old sewing machine, and had set it up on the table in the main living room. There was real lack of clothing available, so with her skills and my help she set up a small business, repairing and making clothes. Word of mouth in the area brought people and their old garments to her, so that she could fix them with her adroit hands. It kept us both busy, although no matter how much I tried, I didn't have the natural skills required to make a good seamstress. But at least I could use a pair of scissors accurately, so was able to follow her instructions and cut out material for her.

I looked forwards to receiving letters from Harry. I read and re-read them. Reading about his sister Violet and his parents and how they were all working hard on the croft. I was amused when he described how he had got a job as the local postman, which meant that his nosy little sister had been thwarted in her badgering and teasing to know who it was who was writing to him. I was a little troubled that he had chosen not to tell his family about me. His words of love to me, though, reassured me and smoothed away my worries.

While Sophia was enjoying her newly formed business, especially given it brought a little money into help the household, Lucas was not content in his job. He found working in a shop claustrophobic, and longed to be out in the open. When he expressed any of this to Sophia, she reminded him how fortunate he was to have a job, when so many did not. Building work was more in evidence in the city, as it began to rebuild and repair the damage that had been created by the bombing, and of course the destruction that had been generated during the occupation. He longed to be outside, and missed the garden at Ramstraat, where he had spent so many hours growing vegetables. He also missed Papa, and the stimulation of helping him in his practice. He told me how he missed Papa more than he could express to anyone, his guidance and wisdom had, he thought, been more influential than his own parents had been. Lucas still had no knowledge of what had happened to his family, but he accepted that he was just one of so many.

I did start to feel more in control of my emotions, and so I accepted an invitation from Dominique to join her on a Saturday afternoon to visit the cinema. I enjoyed her company, and when she persuaded me to attend a hair salon to have my hair restyled I agreed, although somewhat reluctantly. Taking care of my personal appearance didn't feature much in my attentions. I had put a small amount of weight on, but remained slender. My hair had grown long, the curls had become intertwined and although I had tried to keep them untangled, it was often a real problem to do so. I had not given it much attention to it since it had regrown, after the hospital had had to hack it off to cleanse me when I had been admitted all those months ago. My skin had improved from the pallor that had been left by the prison and the camp. I still had my small, pointed nose, but my eyes seemed to have smaller dark circles underneath them as my sleeping improved. I did once ask Dr Peeters whether the lack of food had hampered my growth, as since I was a teenager, my height had remained the same. He assured me that it had not; I was naturally a person of small stature and delicate bones.

The day of the visit to the salon arrived. Dominique had insisted that this was to be a present from her, and so I was not to worry about the cost. Linking her arm with mine, she hurried me along the pavement until we came to a stop outside what appeared to be a high-class salon. I tried to calm myself. I didn't find it comfortable to be given so much attention as I was whipped away to have my hair washed, and then found myself sitting in front of a tall mirror. The stylist, started to cut away much of my hair, until it was just touching my shoulders. My hair had always been curly, and now it was much shorter the curls seemed to sit well and frame my face. The brunette colour seemed to have an extra richness about it. My face seemed fuller, and less pinched, and yes, I had to agree, it did make me feel a little better about myself. I thanked Dominique, who told me that the afternoon event was not yet over. She linked my arm again, and hauled me along the road where we entered a rather smart café. This, she told me, is a treat from her parents. 'We are going to have coffee and cake.'

****

Christmas of 1947 was a time for me to find a glimmer of joy. Firstly I had received a parcel from Harry, and I kept it until I could open it privately on Christmas morning. When I peeled back the brown paper, I found that it contained a small ring box. My heart raced as I opened it, to reveal a small gold ring sporting a small sparkling diamond. I reached back into the paper to open the card that had accompanied it. I read the thin piece of paper that flew onto my lap as I opened the card:

Well, my darling girl, it has been nearly two years since we were last together. I have thought about you day and night since. Will you marry me? I hope the answer will be yes, and you will place the ring on your left hand. If not, then please just keep the ring as a gift from an old friend. I cannot wait any longer, my love, please say yes and we can try and sort out you coming to join me.

I know you have had to do the work with Dr Peeters, but as you have said, you think that it is now going to come to an end. So come to me, my sweet lass.

I will walk along the river on Christmas morning, and be thinking of you, and hoping that just as I am looking at the hills, that you will be placing the ring, (I hope it fits) onto your finger, and wish that I could do it myself, while looking into those beautiful eyes, while I did it.

With my everlasting love

Harry.

The engagement was a surprise, and when I showed the ring to Sophia and Lucas that Christmas morning, they had both leapt up to embrace me. We had all been invited to join the Van Holden's for a meal later in the afternoon, and so we spent the morning talking about how they could help me to achieve my wish to leave Antwerp, and start a new life far away in Scotland.

Later in the afternoon we made our way across the city to the Van Holden's house, where the house had been decorated to reflect the festival. We were welcomed into their home, and hugged by all of the family. It was Lucas who announced that they had a special event to celebrate, as he grasped my hand and held it up to show the ring that sparkled on my finger. It brought a huge cheer, and more hugs as we were ushered into the large sitting room, where a fire blasted out heat. There were many congratulations, and Lambert and Cecily left the room, leaving their daughters to fawn over the ring, only to return with two bottles of wine, and a tray of glasses. They all stood and raised their glasses towards me, wishing me happiness for the future. The happiness they wished for me seemed to be working. They said later that it was the first time they had witnessed a genuine sense of happiness from me, since I had returned to the city nearly two years ago.

CHAPTER 35

The offer of marriage and the realisation that I could find another life spurred me on to complete the journals. Dr Peeters had been fulsome in his praise for his star patient. I had worked so hard, and apparently the procedure seemed to be having a positive impact. I was more relaxed and I was able to report that I was sleeping better and experiencing fewer nightmares. I also seemed to be more confident and able to deal with the occasional flare-ups of reliving the events. Dr Peeters suspected that these would take much longer to deal with. Dr Peeters told me that in his opinion the grief processes were also now moving more normally; he shared with me that he did not think he would have been able to deal with similar losses as well as I had.

Lambert and Lucas, together with Marcel Maes, had made excellent progress in dealing with the Wouters estate. They had also been able to raise the issue of the squatters, who had taken over the family house, with the court, and had success with this. Lucas had tried to keep me up to date with the progress, but until recently I suppose I had not shown any real interest. Perhaps it was with the plans that were starting to form about making the move to Scotland that had ignited more interest.

It was a on a cold Tuesday in late January when Lucas accompanied me to Marcels office. Lambert was already sitting in the room, nursing a cup of coffee. He got up to welcome us. He had become exceptionally fond of me and was always so kind. I admit I was quite nervous as Marcel offered me a chair, and handed me a cup of hot coffee. I needed the hot drink to warm me, and I wasn't convinced that it was due to the cold day that was causing me to shiver.

Once we who had gathered were sitting comfortably, Marcel announced what Lambert and Lucas already had some prior information on. He addressed me. 'Now, my dear, it has taken a great deal of time, and I have to say tenacity, to get us to this place. But we have now concluded the following. The house in Ramstraat is in the process of being returned to you. It has taken some considerable time to convince the people living in the property that they have no right to remain. The courts also took their time to agree that they should leave. This property is legally yours, Elsa, and it will be returned to you within the next couple of weeks as the current occupiers secure other accommodation. Thankfully the increase in building construction on the outskirts of the city has proved an attractive option.' He shuffled some papers. 'Now your grand-mama's property has been sold, as per your request. The sum has been invested. We have also recovered all of the bank accounts, and the share accounts, that were held by your father and your grand-mama, and the moneys have been transferred into an account that was set up on your behalf. There is a substantial amount, I have to say, and we would be happy to offer advice in terms of investment. I am sure some of the funds will be needed to restore the house at Ramstraat.'

'I have one last matter to advise you of,' he went on, taking his time to shuffle another paper, which he presented to me across the desk. 'It is the matter of the Neef estate. It has taken some time to explore and investigate whether any other person would have a claim on this estate, but it appears that you are also the sole heir. So while there is little money, the property at Lint, which I understand consists of a farm house, with several acres of land, now belongs to you.'

Wow, I was stunned. I had no idea that firstly Papa and Grand-mama's estate would be worth so much, and now on top of that I was to inherit Nina and Lars's estate as well. I was somewhat overwhelmed. I now had more money than I could have dreamed of, but I would give it all up if I could just have my family back.

The amount of money and wealth lay hard on my shoulders. I found that I regressed a little, some of the previous intense grief emotions resurfacing. My mind tried to process my new status from hardly having a penny to having a substantial amount. While I was really appreciative of the work that Marcel had done on my behalf, the wealth weighed heavy on my shoulders. There was something around the money and wealth that I could not help but feel was dirty money. I did not feel that I was entitled to it. I accepted it was legally mine, but I could not shift the sensation that I was not morally entitled to it.

I discussed my feelings with Dr Peeters who helped put them into context. 'It is survivor guilt,' he told me. That made sense, but it didn't make it feel any better, or take away the sense I didn't feel entitled to it. For some reason I didn't share the news about my wealth with Harry. There was a fear that if he knew it might change his feelings for me. Better he thought I was poor, although he knew that there was a family house, and that the lawyer had been attempting to establish that I owned it. Dr Peeters advised me to do nothing drastic, but to let the knowledge settle.

****

In the middle of February, I accompanied Lucas down to Lint to revisit the farm. It needed some urgent repairs, and Lucas offered to undertake these at the weekends. He turned and surveyed the land, telling me that it was fertile and would be good for growing things in. When I was in the village I made inquiries about getting a proper headstone fitted for Derk and Nina and Lars's graves. This was the least I could do. As the spring started to take hold, I presented Lucas with car of his own: he was grateful, although he objected to the gift, but I convinced him to accept it as it enabled him to travel back and forth to Lint to undertake the essential repairs on my behalf. Purchasing this for him did give me a small sense of relief that at least some of the money could help another. His loyalty to my family deserved some recompense, although he did not see it that way.

The plans for me to leave were progressing well. Marcel helped me gather the paperwork I required, and as my plans became clearer, I instructed Marcel on several matters on which he was sworn to secrecy.

One evening towards the end of February, Lambert arrived at Klapdorp. He was warmly welcomed, having become a good friend to both Sophia and Lucas. He refused refreshments, and explained his reason for the visit. There had been many discussions over the past months, about how the city could recognise and pay tribute to the Resistance workers who had done so much to assist with them regaining freedom. Now, it had been agreed that there would be a ceremony held at the *Stadhuis* the following month to honour these people. My father and brother, he told us, would be amongst the names to be remembered. He wanted to confirm with me that I would accept the invitation to attend as their representative. He appeared somewhat relieved when I said that I would do so.

The day arrived when the ceremony was to be take place. It was an anxious time for me, even though I was going to be accompanied to the *Staduis* by Lucas and Sophia. The great and the good of Antwerp were present, and many who had fought for the city and had survived were also in the audience. I searched the hall for any faces I could recognise. I had never known the names of those in the Resistance, but of course many of the local people had been part of it. The names of those who had taken a major part were read out; amongst them was Doctor Martin Wouters who, the audience were informed, had been a brave man, and who had helped many fellow citizens. 'He saved countless lives,' they were told, 'and assisted many brave citizens and Allied airmen to escape and survive.' I found that I was weeping quietly. Sophia held my hand to steady me as I listened. 'Doctor Wouters,' the speaker continued, 'was cruelly murdered at Breendonk Prison, on the 28th August 1944.' So that was the date. I had not known the exact date, and wondered again what had happened to his body. The other name that triggered my tears was Derk Wouters who, the speaker said, 'was a brave young man, who helped many Allied servicemen on their journey to escape across the country to Switzerland and Spain. Without him, and many others, then many men would not have survived. I now call on Doctor Wouters' daughter, Elsa, to come to the stage and receive these medals in the memory of their gallant and brave acts.'

I stood and tottered a little. Sophia helped to steady me. My legs felt like jelly as I made my way to the stage. My ears were ringing, and my heart racing. I tried so hard to compose myself. I managed to do so as I was presented with two medals, one each for Papa and Derk.

It was a touching ceremony, and one that gave me some comfort that somewhere their names would live on, and what they had done to help their country would be remembered. As we were leaving the event, we were approached by two men who introduced themselves as Victor and Mathis. Did I not remember them, they asked. I stared at them, trying to place them but could not do so. Then one man reminded me of when we had met before: they were two of the men who had been guests in the cellar. My father, they reminded me, had removed bullets from them, and they had gone on to survive. I felt emotional as they spoke about the cellar and how they had been cared for by Mama and me. I did now recall these two men, who had aged immensely since I had delivered food to them, and was humbled by their thanks. It had been an intensely powerful event, one that I was pleased that I had attended. It gave me tremendous pride to think that my family had done their best, and tried to help others. Nevertheless, in doing so it had been at a terrible cost to them.

****

Plans were made that I would leave and travel to Britain at the beginning of May. Harry was going to travel down to Hull and meet me off of the ferry. I felt energised to complete all of my tasks before I left. There was much to do, and in between the tasks, Sophia fitted me for my wedding costume, which I would carry with me. Sophia was also making some dresses and night wear to ensure that I did not arrive in my new home and life looking scruffy.

April was going to be a busy month, my visits to Dr Peeters had ceased a few weeks previously, as I completed my last journal. I had something that I wanted to discuss with him and so I arranged an appointment with him. I thanked him for his help, and told him that I didn't have enough words to do it the justice it deserved. He bowed his head, telling me that he needed no thanks, other than to know I was more able to live my life. He bundled up all of my journals into a leather suitcase so I could carry them back to Klapdorp. 'Now,' he explained, 'they record part of your life, and what I suggest is that these remain with you as witness to what you have achieved. But they remain locked away. You do not need to revisit them, in fact I suggest that you do not. Having them locked away, yet still accessible, gives you the power and control over them.'

This was an unusual concept, but I trusted him completely. I advised him that there was another matter that I wished to share with him but that he was sworn to secrecy.

The 8th April heralded my twentieth birthday. There was, I informed my friends, to be a small celebration. I had booked a table at a rather swanky restaurant for a dinner. There was something I wanted to share with them, I told them.

Sophia and Lucas's birthday gift to me was her trousseau, consisting of the clothes sewn by her, and some silk lingerie for my wedding day. I could not help but blush when I opened the package. I was too embarrassed to look Lucas in the eye, while being grateful for their kindness.

I dressed for the dinner, and decided to wear one of my new dresses, which fitted me like a glove. I pinned Grand-mama's brooch onto it, and then fastened the clasp of the small silver bracelet around my wrist. These two items signified to me that I was doing the right thing.

The arrival at the restaurant was jolly. My other guests, the Van Holden family, were already sitting. Wine was ordered, and then I was presented with several small gifts which made me both smile and shed a tear for their care and friendship. We ate a wonderful meal, and they all toasted my birthday and my forthcoming new adventures, which were now just three weeks away. At the end of meal I called for silence as I wanted to say something really important.

I felt a little shaky, but managed to control my emotions, as I addressed them. 'I cannot thank you all so much for the kindness and care you have all shown to me.' I drew a large breath to settle myself as I continued. 'Without you all, I do not think I would have been able to live. The past two years has not been easy, as you are all aware, and I know I have been so fortunate to have you as my friends. What I want to share with you is that I have instructed Marcel to undertake certain tasks for me, and one of these I would like to share with you tonight. The other will become evident after my departure, and Marcel has my instructions which, I am assured, he will carry out to the letter. But first,' I reached into my bag and withdrew an envelope which was addressed to Sophia and Lucas. I handed it to them. 'Open it.'

They did so, and gasped, looking at me in absolute amazement. 'Elsa,' cried Sophia, 'this is too much.'

The others around the table were silent waiting to hear what was enclosed in the envelope, Lucas told them, 'Elsa has gifted the farm at Lint to us, plus a sum of money to get us started in our own business. It is too generous,' he told me.

'No, my friends, it is not too generous, it will never be too generous for what you have done for me. I know it is what my family would want to happen. You are, and have been my family since I returned. So no, it is definitely not too generous. I want you both to be secure, and as for you, Lucas, it will allow you to develop all those ideas you have fantasised about, as you have worked on the building.' I couldn't help but laugh. 'Little did you realise that it was your own house you were repairing.' Sophia and Lucas got to their feet and hugged me tightly, thanking me again.

'Now, I have a further announcement to make. It is one that I have thought long and hard about. I hope that I am doing the right thing, but I believe that I am. What I have to say might be hard to hear, but, well, here goes. I have taken the decision that when I leave Belgium in three weeks-time I will leave my old life behind. *Totally*. I have a sense that this is what I need to do, to enable me to live a new life, in a new place, and hopefully with a new family, who will accept me for who I am now. Not remembering who I was. Apart, of course, from Harry, who met me at my lowest ebb. But no one else knows what has happened to me, and that is how I want it to remain. So, my dear friends, when I leave I will not return, and I will not correspond with you, apart to let you know that I have arrived safely.' The intake of breath around the table was audible. 'Before you protest, please can I ask you to try and understand, that I don't just *want* to leave my memories and old life behind, I *need* to.'

There were a few nods of acceptance, and an understanding that this was what I had to do. I agreed that they could all attend the train station on the morning of my departure for one final goodbye.

On the day of my departure, there were many tears. Lucas and Sophia packed my two suitcases into the back of the car, along with a basket containing food, and a flask of coffee for my journey. I was both nervous and excited. I would the following day reach Hull, and be reunited with my Harry. There were others gathered on the platform to see me off. As well as the Van Holdens, Dr Peeters and Marcel also arrived. I was surprised and grateful to see them. There was no time for any big speeches, but there were hugs and good wishes. As I clutched Dr Peeters to me, he whispered his thanks to me and bade me a fond farewell and hoped I would have a good life.

As I found a seat on the train, I looked out of the window, and saw the faces of those who had become my family, and hoped that my new family would be as supportive and caring as these people had been.

PART 3

CHAPTER 36

As I sit on my bunk on the ferry as it makes its way across the sea, I am writing my final statements in this last journal, and then I will place it with the others in this case, and then turn the key in the lock and then I will throw the key overboard. I will explain to Harry why I will not empty the contents. It might sound a little daft to him, but I think he will understand. I am excited that I am to see him in a few hours, and I do hope that that special spark that we found will be relit. He, thankfully, has been in my dreams more recently, but until I set eyes on him and feel his arms around me, I don't think I will actually believe it.

This is a new life for me, I will embrace it. I will never forget those who have been taken from me, my papa, mama, brother, Grandmama, they, I do believe, are travelling with me. They will always remain in my heart, and each day I will look at the sunrise and remember them, just as Mama had told me, that one day the sunrise will bring peace and hope. I do hope that I will achieve that when I start my new life.

Laura wiped the tears from her eyes. It was early evening and the darkness had crept upon her. She had been reading all day; this was the second day since she had prized open the suitcase. She was absolutely astounded at what she had read. Her granny's early life bound up in a suitcase. She had wept tears of sorrow, and sworn words of anger, and felt the despair of what Elsa and her family had suffered. She had kept it all hidden so well, and she wondered whether anyone, apart from Harry, had ever known about it. What a secret. It would take some processing to fully understand what had happened. What on earth would she do with these volumes of journals that powerfully documented part of a life, from nearly seventy years ago?

Bella nudged her, to remind her it was again well past her supper time. She had rather neglected her since she started to be engrossed in this fabulous find. 'Come on, then,' she told the dog. 'It is far too dark for us to go for a walk now, so you will have to make do with the yard for a pee.' She let the dog out, while she went to prepare her supper. Bella appeared after a short time; clearly, her supper was the priority and not sniffing around the yard. She quickly cleared her dish, and then looked at Laura as if she was asking for more. 'No way,' Laura told her. 'Now, what will I have for my supper?' Opening the freezer, she reached in and extracted a ready meal, not her normal eating regime, but she was pleased to have it tonight to save her thinking up a recipe. Her mind was full of the story, and she needed to phone someone to share the revelations.

As she used a small piece of bread to mop up the sauce from the so-called, luxury meal, she reminded herself why she didn't normally eat them. But it had filled a gap, and that, she supposed, was better than nothing. A glass of wine was what was she needed. She opened a bottle and poured herself a large glass, before returning to the sitting room and settling herself in front of the fire that she had lit that morning.

She just about had enough logs in the basket to keep her going for the remainder of the evening, thank goodness, and so didn't need to stumble around in the dark to get more. She texted her father, first to say she would make her way home the following day, and could he please make sure the heating was on. The text was returned quickly, saying *yes, of course and safe journey*. The next text was to Iona, asking if she was free for a chat. The answer came by her mobile phone vibrating and blasting out its ring tone. Iona's pretty face appearing on her phone contacts, to announce that it was her calling.

'Hello sweetheart, how are you?'

'I am fine, Mum. How are you? Have you finished reading the contents of Granny's suitcase then?'

'Yes I have. Goodness me, Iona, what a story,' Laura went on to give her a brief description of the story that had totally amazed her. 'She had been through so much, and left everything behind. I am still trying to get my head around how she managed to do that.' She stopped to think for a moment, while she placed another log onto the fire. 'I cannot recall anyone ever mentioning anything to do with Belgium, Antwerp, or Belsen. I wonder what happened to all the people who had helped her.'

'Blimey, Mum, that's some story. I wonder what she did then with all the money? As from what you say, she seemed to have inherited both money and property.'

'Well, she gave the farm and some money to this Sophia and Lucas. But she never said what happened to the family house. God knows. Anyway, darling, I am going to make my way back home tomorrow. I will lock everything up here, and take the important documents with me. I can contact the solicitor and make arrangements for things to be done.'

'You're not going to sell Birch End are you, Mum?'

'I don't quite know what I am going to do with it yet, it's too big a decision to take without a long think. Granny has left enough money to keep it going for some time. But there are other things I need to do at home, so I need to get back. How are things going with you, anyway?'

'I am doing fine, Mum. I would love to read Granny's journals.

Are you planning to take them home with you?' When she heard that Laura did plan to, she went on, 'Then I will come home for the weekend and read them. I will stay at yours if it's okay. Just let Grandad know I am not abandoning him, but I think I need to be with you when I read them.'

CHAPTER 37

The following morning, Laura opened the bedroom curtains to see that it was a bright autumn day. It was still early; sleep had eluded her for some time, and when she had eventually dropped off, the night was full of dreams. Bella had heard her move about, and had leapt up the narrow stairs to greet her. 'Hello, sweetheart. Now let me pass so I can go and have a pee, then you can go for one too.' Managing to avoid tripping over the dog, she reached the bathroom and sat on the toilet, looking around the bathroom. It needed work done on it. While the shower had been a fairly recent acquisition, the rest of it certainly needed a proper makeover, more than the temporary one that Grant had completed. She let Bella out before making herself a cup of tea. Scanning the sky outside of the window, she decided to finish her tea, and quickly get dressed. There was something she wanted to do.

Laura called to Bella, who needed no second calling, and they set off behind the house, down the pathway through the woods, until she came to the river. Bella was delighted, and thought this meant that her new mistress was going to play. She loved nothing better than sticks being thrown into the river so she could dive in and fetch them out. The collie waited, watching, but the new mistress hadn't got the grip of this game. She had taken herself to sit on one of the big stones, gazing around her. It took several attempts, dropping sticks at her feet, and looking hopefully, and still it took a final nudge before she got the hang of it.

The reason Laura was making this early morning walk was to contemplate and reflect what Elsa might have seen, on those early days after she arrived at Birch End. The scene she was currently seeing had not changed much in the seventy-one years since her granny had arrived in Scotland. The sun had recently raised its head, low across the hills, its strength weakened in the autumnal day. Laura thought about the ritual that her granny referred to several times in her journal: that of the sunrise bringing hope. Hope for peace, and hope that all those who she had lost would be at peace.

After a second soaking by Bella, as the wet dog shook herself over her, she decided it was time to go back, have some breakfast, and start packing the car. She hoped she would catch Maisie, to ask her if she would keep a close eye on the house for her. In the back of her mind, she did not trust either the laird or his land agent not to come poking around when they knew the house was empty.

It was late afternoon by the time she reached Broadsea. She emptied the car, and then took Bella for a quick walk along the beach. On her way back she called in to see her father. Grant heard the back gate click, so already had the kettle on when she appeared in the kitchen. Bella rushed in to greet him, sending a film of sand that had stuck to her coat across his neat kitchen. Tabby the cat appeared and Bella rushed over to give him a welcome sniff. The cat took little notice, apart from a certain distain that the black-and-white dog was disturbing his peace. 'Is Tammy settling in?' Laura asked her dad, watching as he filled two mugs with tea before placing them on the kitchen table.

'Seems to be fine, he has taken over a front spot in front of the fire, and there is no sign that he is worried or thinking of running away. To be honest, Laura, I have found him to be a bit of company, he's a couthie cat, likes being petted. So no problem, not so much work as this madam here.' Bella had sat herself by Grants side, and was eying the biscuit he was dunking into his tea, looking hopefully for some to drop off. 'So tell me, you have finished reading all of your granny's journals then?'

'Flipping heck, Dad, what a shock it was to read them. Granny suffered so much, and yet she didn't say a word, did she? Did Mum have any idea do you think? I cannot remember it being spoken about when I was a child.' She sipped her tea and replaced the mug on the table, reaching over to take another biscuit from the plate. 'I have been trying to think back, to anything being said about Granny's family, but it is all a bit hazy.'

Grant caught a soggy piece of biscuit before it fell into his tea. 'I do remember your mum saying that her mother's early life was all a bit of a mystery. I think she had grown up knowing not to ask, that it was a bit of a taboo subject. Of course her granny, your great-granny, was a great one for keeping things... not said, if you know what I mean. No one really questioned people about those sorts of things. Look at Harry: he must have also seen terrible things in the war, and never spoke about them either.'

'They were really close though, Granny and Grandad. I remember they were never apart, always went for a walk every day, and even finished each other's sentences off. I remember we used to think that was really funny. Even when we played a board game they could never play it independently; they always ended up being a team.' She broke off a small piece of biscuit and fed it to Bella as she remembered all those times when she was a child, and her mum was still alive. Many happy times spent around the table at Birch End with her granny and grandad.

'Your mum used say that it was the same when she was growing up. Do you know, she told me once that she felt a bit like an outsider. The fact that she had her own granny and grandad living in the same house helped, I think. I remember her telling me that her mother and father were joined at the hip, and sometimes she thought they didn't want her. That was rubbish, of course, they loved Estelle very much. She was doted on, not just by them but by the whole Kerr clan. Especially given that she was the only child in the family.'

'Yes, I have been thinking about that too. Granny was only twenty when she married grandad, and so Mum was born when she was just twenty-two. I wonder why she didn't have any more children? But then, maybe, because she had suffered so badly it may have affected her body. Oh, I do wish Granny was here so I could ask her. What a tragic life, losing all of her family, then to top it all, she lost her only child.' She hesitated, her thoughts taking her to the loss of her own Mum. 'She must have only been... what, about fifty-five, when mum died? I have little memory of how Granny took Mum's death. I suppose I was in shock.'

'I think we all were, including Elsa and Harry. Christ, we all walked round in a blur for ages. I do remember Harry saying something like, this was yet another painful loss for Elsa, and he hoped it wouldn't set her back again. But to be honest, l was like you in deep shock. We didn't see much of Birch End for a few months after your mum died.' Laura looked surprised. 'Well, you see love, I found that the most I could do was to just get through a day, make sure you were fed and watered, so we stayed here most of the time, and didn't venture far. Of course they could have come over, Harry was still able to drive, but Elsa, as you know, didn't travel far. That meant that it was a good while before we started visiting again. So I don't know how she was in the early days. It must have been hard for her, though.'

'I suppose it now makes sort of sense as to why Granny didn't like to travel. It was too much for her, and she loved Birch End so much. It clearly helped her to be there, and so it became the centre of her universe. There is one question answered, though. I have often wondered why Mum was called Estelle, and now we know.'

Grant invited her to stay for supper, and she was very happy to accept. She would have to do a shop tomorrow, especially if Iona was coming to stay for the weekend. She broke the news to her father that Iona was going to stay with her; she watched his face for disappointment, but he seemed fine. But, she told him, he was to come for supper on Saturday evening, and for Sunday lunch. That would give him time with his granddaughter, without feeling she was snubbing him.

****

Once back in her own flat, Laura carried the leather suitcase up and placed it in her sitting room. She would put the journals in the spare bedroom, so that Iona could read them at her will. She had always been a fast reader, so she suspected she would scan them quickly. She had brought the box with the important documents she had found with her, and intended to sit tonight in front of her log burner, with a glass of wine, and go through them in more detail. There were still some bits and pieces at the bottom of the box that she hadn't had a chance to sort out.

Much of what was in the box was, frankly, rubbish. Why they had kept so many old invoices and bills that had long ago become irrelevant were beyond her. She knew that her grandparents would have been considered self-employed, and there was a timescale for keeping accounts, but forty years was well beyond what was required. She put these in a pile, as while they were interesting, she didn't think that any of the family would be that interested in seeing how much they had paid for seed potatoes in 1979, or how much subsidy they had received from the government thirty years ago.

There were one or two things she found that would be worth keeping: the invitation to her parents' wedding, for example. This was the first time she had seen this. There were also her great-grandparents' wedding and death certificates. They would go into the pile for adding to the now increasing Kerr family history. She delved into the box again, and found an envelope that had within it two very faded and damaged black-and-white photographs. She looked closely at them. These must be the two photographs referred to in Granny's journal. One was of a couple in what was a wedding photo; this must be Nina and Lars, she concluded. The other had four people in it. She studied it closely: this was a photograph of her granny and her family. The only one apparently in existence, now. This was a real treasure. First thing in the morning, she would go down to her stock room, where she had the perfect vintage silver frame, and this photo would fit it perfectly. She couldn't wait to show it to Iona.

CHAPTER 38

Iona reached Broadsea just before lunchtime, and decided to visit her grandad before she went to her mother's flat. Iona worshiped her grandfather; he had, since her parents had divorced, been the father figure she had missed out on. This had become increasingly so, after her father had remarried and moved to the other side of the world. Reflecting on that time brought painful memories, a sadness mixed with anger that he had chosen Sally over her. Although it was eleven years ago when her parents broke up, it still affected her. There were times when she still felt like that nine-year-old girl when he had left. When she spoke to Tony about it, he had hinted that it was like she was still that nine-year-old girl and that she hadn't moved on. While that had caused a falling out between them, as she had insisted that was not true, she had since then pondered on what he had said and, just maybe, he had a point. If the truth were known, she was quite pissed off with Liam, as he rarely texted her now, and whenever he did it was all about Dad, and how they were doing great things. Was she jealous? Maybe she was, but she refused to travel to the other side of the world to visit him. Her father could continue to play happy families with his new family, and her brother; she would just get on with life here.

Finding herself outside her grandad's house was a bit of a surprise. She must have driven the final couple of miles on autopilot, her thoughts elsewhere. As she turned off the engine, she sat for a moment assessing the detached granite house in front of her. It was a bit big for one person, but she knew that there was no point suggesting to him that he downsize. It had been her family home after the separation, a real refuge, if she remembered rightly. Her bedroom remained as it had been; it was the room of a teenage girl. It held many happy memories, of spending fun times with her friends, listening to music, which her grandad had described as "just loud bangs", swotting for her exams, but more importantly it had provided her with safety and security. Just as her grandfather had done, with his wisdom and good humour. She could not bear to think of life without him in it. Reaching over, she gathered her bag and a gift for him, a bottle of his favourite single malt. He would admonish her for this, and she would lecture him to only have one dram a day, but it would all be in good humour.

Grant was delighted to see his granddaughter. He was exceptionally proud of her, and enjoyed her company. He totally got that she wanted to spend some time with her mum, and stay with her rather than in her old bedroom. He hugged her tightly, and held both her arms, looking her up and down, and announcing that she looked tired. 'Are you getting enough sleep?' he asked her.

This made Iona smile. It was hard to explain that being a medical student meant that of course she wasn't getting enough sleep. Did students ever get enough sleep? No, and she was no different. But she assured him she was fine, and was pleased to see that he looked well. 'Yes,' she told him. She would love to stay for lunch. She reassured him that she was more than happy that it was just going to be beans on toast, one of her favourite meals. She wasn't joking either; she was not one for cooking. Thankfully Tony enjoyed cooking, and she was happy to defer to him. She was very good, she had told him, at ordering a takeaway.

They spent an enjoyable time catching up. Grant was always interested in Iona's studies, and thought it was just wonderful that she was going to become a doctor, and was next year going to be starting on the wards in earnest, when she completed her fifth year. He knew she would make a good doctor, and listened as she told him that she was becoming more interested in paediatric medicine. She hoped to spend time next year at the Children's Hospital. Iona helped with the washing up, and then bid him goodbye, pleased that her mum had invited him to join them for supper tomorrow.

Laura had just returned from shopping when Iona appeared. She helped her put things away, although Laura did think it might have been easier to do so herself, given that Iona kept asking where everything went. Once they had finished, Iona couldn't wait until she could get her hands on the journals, to start to read them. It was so exciting, exciting, to find that there was a family secret unravelling before your eyes.

Laura could not stop herself from laughing at her daughter's energy. She was so full of life, and bounded through to the spare bedroom to dump her overnight bag, and return with two of the journals. She curled up on the sofa and started reading. Laura left her to it, and started on the supper. She had the weekend menus worked out: some of Iona's favourites, lasagne tonight, homemade chicken pie tomorrow, which was also one of her dad's favourites, and roast beef on Sunday. She loved having Iona to stay, and feeding her up; she had a sense that she didn't bother too much with cooking in the flat in Aberdeen, and thought she was looking a little tired. She knew that Iona also had a sweet tooth, so had bought a cheesecake for desert, and would make a trifle for Sunday. Bella wandered about sniffing, and looking at her in a way to remind her that she was due a walk. 'It's okay,' she told her. 'I will take you out soon.' She realised that it was getting dark already and it was only just after three thirty, such short days this time of the year. Never mind, just another four weeks and it would be the shortest day, and after that, it would be over the worst.

After Bella had been walked, Laura lit the wood burner; she had switched all of the table lamps on in the sitting room. Iona was fully engrossed in the journals, and she had just accepted the mug of tea and the biscuits by waving her hand in thanks, before she returned to her reading. Laura left her alone, set the table in the kitchen, and placed the lasagne in the oven to cook. She had to call Iona twice to let her know it was ready, and even then there was a lengthy delay before her daughter appeared.

'Well?' Laura enquired. 'What do you think?'

'Honestly, Mum, it's like reading a novel. There is so much to think about. I can't put it down, sorry I am not being very good company. But it's just, well, you know, you have read it. It's compelling.'

They ate their supper, sharing a bottle of wine as they did so. Laura was interested to hear what Iona had been up to, plus she wanted to hear how things were going with Tony. Iona was non-committal on how things were going with him. She seemed to prefer not to speak about him, other than saying, that he was fine. Yes, they were still in a relationship and, yes, she would arrange to bring him out for a meal in a couple of weeks' time. Laura refused her help to clear up, telling her that it would only take a moment to stack the dishwasher, and that she should just go and chill in the sitting room. By the time she had cleared the kitchen, opened a second bottle of wine, taking it into the sitting room to refill both hers and Iona's glass, there was little conversation, as Iona was again engrossed in the journals. She was already on to the second one, and Laura suspected she would have finished them all by this time tomorrow night at the rate she was going.

Turning on the TV didn't disturb her, and so Laura settled down to watch one of her regular programmes. She noticed that the wind was getting up by the whistling noise that circulated outside of the house. It made a very cosy scene; the fire was giving out a lovely heat, the logs burning brightly and sending reflections of light to bounce off the walls. Iona curled on the sofa, journal in one hand, a glass of wine in the other. Bella's soft snores as she lay in front of the stove, and lastly her own sense of wellbeing as she sipped her wine, feet up safe in her own home. She couldn't wish for anything better.

CHAPTER 39

Saturday morning saw a late rise for Iona. Laura had left her as she thought that her daughter probably needed a long lie. The wind was still howling outside, now peppered with heavy showers that almost felt a little wintery. As a consequence, Bella's walk was short, but still resulted in both of them being drenched. Laura took an old towel and did her best to dry the dog, before having to change into another pair of dry jeans. There was still no sign of Iona, but she did hear her getting up and using the bathroom, so she put the kettle on to boil. A few moments later, a very sleepy young woman appeared, her short hair standing in spikes. 'Well hello, love, did you have a good sleep?' She poured a mug of tea, and handed it to her.

Iona accepted the mug, and sat down at the table, curling her leg under herself, which brought the memory to Laura that her daughter had never been able to sit properly on a chair. She smiled. 'Now, what can I get you for breakfast, although to be fair,' she looked at the clock, 'it's more like brunch.'

'Just a piece of toast, and if you have it, some honey would be lovely thanks, Mum.' Iona took a sip of her tea. 'Sorry I am up so late, but I couldn't stop reading Granny's journal. I finished another one, so just one to go now.' She also looked at the clock, as Laura handed her a plate of toast accompanied by a jar of honey. 'It's absolutely fascinating. What an insight into what the war was like, and for poor Granny's family. Weren't they ever so brave?'

'They certainly were, and now we know where you got the gene for being a doctor, as well. Fancy that, eh? Your, great,

great, grandfather. I had no idea. Oh, wait a minute, I, entirely forgot to show you something.' She rushed into her bedroom and retrieved the silver photo frame, now with the old photo fitted in it. 'Look at this.' She handed it to Iona.

'Blimey, is that Granny then?' Iona pointed to the young girl. 'And that must be Derk, and their parents. How fabulous that you have it. I wonder why on earth this was hidden away? Surely that doesn't make sense. Some of this just doesn't make any sense at all, does it?'

Laura shook her head. 'No, it doesn't. But I suppose, as Granny said, she was acting on advice from this Dr Peeters, and she was so young. I am not going to give you any more information into what I think is one of the big mysteries.' Iona raised an eyebrow in interest. 'I will see what you think once you have finished reading.'

'On that note then, I will have a shower, and then get on with the last journal. It isn't quite as thick as the others, so shouldn't take me long.'

Laura used the afternoon to make her special chicken and leek pie, so that it was ready to put into the oven for their supper. Lunch had been a bowl of soup; Iona had briefly appeared to sup it, and then disappeared back into the sitting room to recommence reading. Laura left her alone, and before dark she and Bella ventured out for another walk. It was still blowing a hooley, and the rain had become more persistent, not the night for being out and about. Bella was somewhat relieved to have her supper and retire to her place in front of the stove in the sitting room, her long body fully extended to make sure she caught the full impact of the heat.

Grant arrived looking equally windswept and soaked. Laura helped him off with his coat, and produced his slippers he had left in her cupboard. She put his wellingtons in the back porch to dry off.

'Goodness, lass, what a night. It heralds the start of winter, I'm thinking. Where's Iona?'

Laura filled him on Iona's progress of reading her granny's journals, and asked whether he would also like to read them. He had to think for a moment, and decided that he might do in the future, but maybe not now. He was happy to listen, if she wanted to tell him what she had learnt.

Grant sat at the kitchen table watching his daughter cook the meal. As she bustled around, he wondered whether she would ever find a new partner. She was a good-looking woman, and young for her forty-six years. She hadn't as far as he was aware had any serious relationships since her marriage broke down. She had only been in her middle thirties then, and she was still far too young to spend the rest of her life on her own. She seemed happy enough, with her own flat and business, but he did worry about her being on her own. She had been so devastated when Guy left her. Grant couldn't help still feeling some anger towards his once son-in-law for the way he treated his daughter. She had so much to give, and now with both Iona and Liam had grown up, he hoped that she might just reach out a bit further and spread her wings.

Laura handed a bottle of wine to her father, and suggested he opened it and pour them both a glass. He did so, and was just about to take another through to Iona, when she appeared, a big smile on her face, and greeted him with a big hug. She took the glass he offered her, and joined him at the table. Laura placed the food in the middle so they could help themselves.

'So, that's me finished the journal. Grandad, you should read them, they are *amazing*. Mum, I know what you mean now: where did all the money go?'

'What money?' Grant looked bemused. He had been Elsa's financial advisor since he had known her, for nearly fifty years.

'Well, it seems that granny Elsa, had inherited her family's estate. She made reference to it in the journal, and that she was informed about this by a lawyer when she attended an appointment. Apparently it was a substantial amount, even in those days.' Iona helped herself to the food, piling her plate, which brought a smile to Laura's face: she still felt that warm glow of parenthood when she saw her child fill her plate with food. 'I know she gifted the farm to Sophia and Lars, but what happened to the rest?'

'What farm?'

'Grandad, you will have to read them. Not only she did she inherit a farm, but the family house, monies from her grandmother's house, and it seems quite an amount of money from her father and grandmother too.'

'Well, it seems whatever happened to the money, was at her wish. Didn't she mention something about leaving instructions for her lawyer... what was his name, Marcel or something?' stated Laura, as she cut through the crisp pastry that she had to admit had turned out well.

'That's right and, well, aren't you interested to know? I know I am.'

'I am not sure how on earth we would go about even trying to find out, after all these years, Iona. Anyway let's enjoy supper; there is still a large piece of cheesecake waiting for desert. I need you to eat it up, or else I will keep eating it.' She felt her midriff. 'And there is one thing for certain, I do not need it. I am hoping that now I have Bella, it will help me lose some of this.'

After they had all helped to clear the table and stack the dishwasher, they moved into the sitting room. Taking through the wine, Laura insisted her dad had a nice glass of single malt to relax with. Laura broached a subject that had been on her mind for a while: Christmas, and whether Iona would be able to come home to spend it, or at least, one, of the days with her.

'Yes, I think I will manage to come for Christmas Eve, but will have to go back for Boxing Day as I am on duty,' she told them. 'And no, before you ask, Tony will be spending Christmas in Orkney with his parents. But if it is okay with you, Grandad, I will stay with you. I think it will be nice to wake up on Christmas morning in my old bedroom.'

'I suppose you will be expecting the usual stocking at the end of your bed then?' he asked. 'So does that mean I have to do all the cooking as well?'

Laura could understand Iona wanting to have a Christmas in the home she had spent a great deal of her childhood in, and chastised herself for thinking any different. She had hoped that she might have stayed with her, but at least she was coming home. 'If it's okay with you, Dad, I am happy to do the cooking, but at yours of course. It will just be the three of us. Liam will be sunning himself on a beach somewhere, no doubt.'

Later, after Grant had left and they had retired to bed, and just as Laura was settling down to go to sleep, her duvet drawn up around her shoulders, she heard a tap on her door. 'Mum, are you still awake?'

'Yes.' She turned her bedside lamp back on and sat up. 'Is there something wrong?' she asked as Iona appeared at the end of her bed.

'No, Mum, but look.' She handed over her iPad. 'Look what I have found. I googled Ramstraat 45, and look what has come up.'

Laura read what was in front of her, *The Wouters Centre, Ramstraat 45, Antwerp, Belgium.*

'Crikey!'

'From what I can make out, this is some sort of place that offers counselling and other therapies for people suffering from psychological disorders. So that, Mum, gives us a little glimpse into maybe what happened to the money. How wonderful!. Tomorrow I am going to email them to see if I can find out more.'

It took Laura some time to fall asleep after Iona's visit. If it was true, then Elsa did more than she could ever have imagined. Yet another layer of intrigue.

CHAPTER 40

It was Monday afternoon before Iona texted her to say she had had a reply from the Wouters Centre, and she had replied, and had forwarded it to her. She would call her later, she told her. Laura opened her email box and read the email that had been forwarded.

To: Nicole@wouterscentre.com

From: iona.simpson22@hotmail.com

Cc: broadseagifts@gmail.com

Subject: Elsa Wouters

Hi Nicole

Thank you so much for your swift reply. My mother will be delighted to hear more about how the Centre came into existence. We have only just made the discovery that Elsa had had such a tragic life. She had kept it all a big secret. I have copied my mother into this, as I am sure she would love to be the one to be in contact with the person who you mention is a member of the family who directly knew my great-grandmother. My mothers' name is Laura Simpson.

Thank you

Best wishes

Iona Simpson

To iona.simpson22@hotmail.com

From Nicole@wouterscentre.com

Subject: Elsa Wouters

Dear Miss Simpson,

How wonderful to read your email, to tell me that you are the great granddaughter of Elsa Wouters. What a surprise. I have often wondered what happened to our benefactor, and am sorry to hear that she has so recently died. She lived a long life. I would be very happy to give you more details about this Centre's history, but I have only been the Director now for the past five years, so I will need to gather some information from others who would know more.

What I do know is that the Centre is run by a Trust deed, and that we have six people who sit on the board. One of them is a relative of one of the original board members, so I will speak to them and let you know.

I am sure the whole board will be delighted to hear that one of our founder's family members has been in contact.

Best regards

Dr Nicole Renard

Director of Wouters Centre

Laura felt a frisson of excitement run down her spine. She hoped that she would not have to wait too long before finding out who the person was that was referred to in the email. It was just the following day when she found out.

To: Broadseagifts@gmail.com

From felix@beckersassociates.org

Cc: Nicole@wouterscentre.come

Cc: iona.simpson@hotmail.com

Subject: Elsa Wouters

Dear Laura

I do hope you do not mind me emailing you direct. Nicole passed on your daughter's email to me, and I was so very pleased to receive it. I have copied them both into this, but thought it made much more sense to start by contacting you direct.

Firstly, I will explain that my great-grandparents were friends of your family. I do not know whether you will know the name of Van Holden, but Lambert and Cecily were my grandmother Dominque's, parents. They were good people, and my grandmother Dominque told me the story of the Wouters, and especially remembered Elsa, who was her friend. Dominque died about ten years ago, and up until her death she had spoken warmly of Elsa, and her mother Estelle, who I understand taught her during the war.

The story about how the Wouters Centre came into being was passed on to me; it is a very special story and our family have always had a continued involvement in the running of it. It has a very good reputation here in Antwerp as one of the places which help those who have suffered trauma. But you may be wondering how this came about. According to my grandmother, Elsa left instructions, when she left Belgium, that the family home in Ramstraat should be used as a place where people such as her could be helped. A Dr Stefan Peeters was the original Director; my grandmother knew him well. He built the Centre up, and carried on until his death in 1968. I only met him very briefly when I was a child. By then he was an elderly man, but he became a good friend of my great-grandparents, and also my own grandmother.

Your grandmother gave clear instructions that all of the money she had received would be invested so that this Centre could continue. As you can probably understand, it has been nearly seventy years since she left this instruction, and over the years it has been invested, but the Centre needed a great deal of other support to keep it up and running. Elsa wished that any therapy would be given freely, just as she had received it. She didn't wish for anyone suffering not to be able to receive help. So it has left to the board of trustees to find ways we can continue to do this.

We have a very committed group who believe in the Wouters Centre. It has now become a family tradition that at least one of us sits on the board. I currently do so; my father Axel also does so. I am *the chair of the board at the moment, and as I am an accountant by trade, you can probably appreciate that I have to use my skills to ensure that we remain financially stable. I have to report that we are such.*

I understand from my grandmother that Elsa left strict instructions that she was to have no part in establishing or running of the Centre, in fact, once she left Belgium, she dictated that she would not make contact with anyone from her old life again. That I feel is sad, especially as she left such a wonderful legacy. But I suppose, from what I know about the treatment of trauma (and I know very little), anybody who suffered as I understand your grandmother did had absolutely every right to do whatever they could to learn to live with what they experienced. It must have been terrible.

I would love to speak to you direct, and I have told my father that you have been in contact. He sends his best wishes to be extended to you, and thought that his mother, Dominique, would have loved to have had a conversation with you.

Yours faithfully

Felix Becker

Laura was delighted. Wow, she thought to herself. How about that, and how sad that Granny didn't get to find out how her money and especially the house in Ramstraat had been so successful. She sat down and answered Felix immediately.

To: felix@beckersassociates.org

From Broadseagifts@gmail.com

Cc: Nicole@wouterscentre.come

Cc: iona.simpson@hotmail.com

Subject: The Wouters Centre

Dear Felix

Thank you so much for your email. How great to hear that my granny's legacy has been so successful. I do think it was sad that she didn't wish to have any contact with anyone from Belgium. I have only very recently found out about what she and her family experienced during the war. Granny left some journals, they were written under the guidance of Dr Peeters who you refer to. Granny had left them locked in a suitcase, the same one I suspect that they were placed in when she left Antwerp. It was only after her death that I found the case and opened it, to find out about what had happened to her. She never spoke at all about any of it, so it has all been quite a shock.

Then my daughter Iona googled Ramstraat and hey ho, we found out about the Centre. It has left us all reeling a bit I have to say, so much to take in. Elsa mentioned your grandmother Dominique lots of times in the journal, and of course her sister Adele as well as your great-grandparents. From what she said they were very kind to her, especially your great-grandfather Lambert.

So, who would have believed that after all these years their great-grandchildren are communicating through this method? I would love to speak to you about the Centre, and hear about your family. I live in the north east of Scotland, beside the Moray Firth in a village called Broadsea. My grandmother lived about sixty miles across country in the Highlands. She loved it, I have to say, so I can imagine that living there helped her gain some peace. She certainly was a peaceful person.

My telephone number is 07891 221186

With many best wishes,

Laura

A few days later, she was unpacking her car following a visit to Aberdeen to do some of her Christmas shopping. She had managed to catch up for a quick lunch with Iona; it had been very quick as her daughter was due to attend a meeting, so they caught up in a café close to the university. Laura listened as Iona updated her on what she was doing. She was living a busy life, and one which meant that she was always on the move.

When she had heard that Laura and her grandad were intending to visit Aunty Vi before Christmas, she asked for a favour. She could not see how she would find the time to go down to Dundee before Christmas, so would Laura get something for her, and she would give her the money. Laura had been happy to do this, and suspected that although she knew her daughter was sincere about giving her the money, she would probably forget.

Laura had a number of bags, and tried to carry them all together to prevent her having to go back down to the car. Shopping was not her most favourite pursuit, and she hoped that she would not have to venture into the city again before Christmas. She put the bags down so she could unlock the door to the flat, and was just about to grab them again to carry them upstairs, when her mobile phone started to ring. She rummaged in her handbag for it, trying to find it before it rang off. She peered at the number on the screen, and didn't recognise it, so was tempted not to answer, but pressed the accept button before she changed her mind.

A male voice said, 'Is that Laura? I hope I have not called at an inopportune moment. This is Felix Becker. We have exchanged emails.'

Laura was taken by surprise. 'Felix, oh goodness, thank you for calling,' She bumped the door open using her hip, and with one hand pulled the bags inside the lobby, leaving them there she climbed the steps up to the flat. 'This is a nice surprise,' she told him, not sure really of what to say.

'I thought that I would give you a call, and say that my family are delighted that we have made contact. I spoke to my father, and he said that he hopes that we can meet up in the future.'

She sat down at the kitchen table and listened while he told her about the Centre, how every room was used. As well as counselling, there were also several alternative practitioners working there. This activity had increased over the past few years as alternative therapies became more attractive. He explained how the ground floor, and the first floors, were areas dedicated directly for therapists who were employed by the Wouters Trust, and the upper floors used to rent out. It brought in a little income to help, although no one was turned away from the Centre. Some were happy to pay a donation, and if they were referred by the health services then the trust received payment. Also private companies used them, he told her. As PTSD had become such a well-known illness, the Wouters Centre had become one of the most sought-after treatment centres.

'You speak excellent English,' Laura told him as she switched the phone to her other ear.

He laughed. 'Yes, most of us here in Belgium speak English, as well as our mother tongue. But I remember my grandmother telling me that the Wouters all spoke excellent English too. In fact it was your great-grandmother, Estelle Wouters, who taught it to Dominique.'

'Elsa had no sign of an accent: that is why it was such a surprise to learn that she was Belgian.'

They went on the exchange pleasantries for another few minutes, and before they ended the call, she thanked him again, promising to keep in touch. After the call ended she sat back on her chair for a minute, to mull over the conversation. He sounded nice. He had a deep warm voice, and his accent was definitely appealing. Sexy, but then she admonished herself for thinking that; that was stereotypical – weren't all European men who spoke English with an accent alluring?

She went back to sorting out the bags of shopping, and that kept her busy until her father arrived with Bella. Grant had helpfully looked after her for the day, and Laura could not help but think that they were becoming good companions.

'Looks like you had a successful trip then,' he said, pointing to the empty bags that littered the kitchen. 'So are we going to go down to see Vi next week? That's not going to be too soon, is it? You know how she goes on.'

'Yes, it is all arranged for next Tuesday; apparently that is the best day for her, and she can fit us in. I phoned her last night, of course she said the usual thing, about wasn't it sad that she was going to be on her own again for Christmas.'

Grant burst out laughing.' She is a character, is she not? Alone at Christmas? She is almost worse than that episode of the *Vicar of Dibley*... last year she bragged to me that she had had two Christmas lunches, one laid on by the sheltered housing complex, and the other by one of the families from the church. She didn't like to refuse, apparently, so ate both. So don't let her give you any of that old flannel. She couldn't manage the stairs to here, or mine, given that the toilet is upstairs. Any road, from the look of your bags here I think you must have bought the shop.'

They settled for sharing a hotpot that Laura had defrosted from the freezer that morning; there was plenty, she told him. Laura could not help thinking how lucky she was to have her dad living so close. They both had their own space, but she really appreciated his company, and had no desire to search for more. She had her two good friends, and others in the village who she would occasionally meet for a drink or a coffee, but she was content with her life, and had no hankering for any changes.

CHAPTER 41

Tuesday turned out to be a reasonable day, although the sun was low in the sky and caused Laura a little discomfort as she drove to Dundee. Grant was a good passenger; he was relaxed, and not one of those who had to interfere or give advice. He was happy to let Laura drive. He was even more relieved as he observed how she confidently negotiated the various one way systems until they drew up outside of the sheltered housing complex where Vi lived.

The plan was that they would collect her and take her out to lunch at her favourite gastro pub a short distance away. The elderly woman would no doubt be waiting for them. She was a stickler for time, and if they said they would be there by midday, then that is what should happen. Dare the traffic to have delayed them, or any other reason that might have impacted on their journey. They would receive no sympathy from Vi; she would have admonished them for not leaving earlier. Thankfully they were a little early, so they would not have to suffer Vi's wrath today.

She was waiting for them with the door to her small flat open, having been watching for them from her window that overlooked the carpark. Greeting them with her usual bluster, she hurried them into the flat. She wanted to see what they had brought her. Laura handed her two colourful Christmas gift bags, one from her and the other, she told her, was from

Iona. They both contained clothing. Laura's gift was a brightly coloured, two-toned cardigan, while Iona's was a pretty night-dress, and some of her great aunt's favourite chocolates. Vi accepted the bags, saying that she would open them on Christmas Day. It would give her something to do, as she would be on her own. Before she could launch into one of her tirades, Grant handed her his present, a shape that could not really be disguised as being anything other than a bottle. 'Oh,' she smiled, 'I think I can work out what this is, and hope it is a good bottle of gin.'

'Only the best for you, Vi. Now come on, get your coat on. I don't know about you, but my belly is rumbling.' She didn't need a second telling, and reached for her coat.

Soon they were settled at a table in the pub. Aunty Vi had refused the first table they were offered, demanding that they had the table by the fire. Even though the poor waiter tried to explain that one was actually reserved, this made no difference, and he gave up and allowed them to take that one. Laura and Grant hid their embarrassment, but then, they should be used to being in this position by now. This was a fairly normal occurrence when you were in the company of Aunty Vi.

Once they had ordered their main courses, as well as a glass of wine for Vi and a pint of larger for Grant, they sat back to wait for the food. Laura nursed her glass of water, refusing the suggestion from Vi that one glass of wine wouldn't hurt. 'So, Laura, what I want to know is, what you have decided to do with Birch End.' Vi asked the question peering over the top of her spectacles.

'I haven't made a decision.'

'So has that Hamish McKenzie sent you any further letters, or visits from that land agent lap dog, of his. Bloody cheek,' she uttered scathingly, before taking a large mouthful of her wine.

Laura watched as her aunt swallowed her wine, before setting her glass back down on the table. Her hand had a slight tremor to it; she had not noticed this before. Another sign that her eighty-six-year-old great aunt was becoming frailer. 'I had another letter from him,' she told her, 'suggesting that it would be in my interest to discuss his offer. The tone suggested that he was still willing to do me a favour. I have just ignored it, and am not going to bother to even give him the satisfaction of a reply. You are right, Aunty, he is a cheeky bugger. But I don't know what I am going to do with it yet. Granny left enough money for me to keep it going as it is, and Maisie Campbell is keeping an eye on it while it is empty.'

'I bet she is,' interjected Vi. 'She'll be sniffing about the place; I hope you didn't give her a key. She has always been a nosy blighter, and a gossip at that.'

'They have both been really helpful, Aunty. Charlie managed to drain all the water for me and turn everything off, just in case it freezes. I need someone to keep an eye on it, and as you know Maisie is at least reliable, and anything that is happening in the Glen, she would know. So she would also be first to notice anyone sniffing about.'

'Well, I hope you removed anything of a sensitive or confidential nature. I wouldn't trust the woman not to go through things that don't concern her,' sniped Vi.

Thankfully the food arrived to prevent any further slanderous comments could be uttered. The food was good and even Vi had no complaints about her roast turkey, which she claimed would be the only time she would have it this year. She didn't bat an eyelid when Grant reminded her that she had already told him that she was looking forwards to spending the day with that lovely family from the church. She had apparently forgotten that she had been singing their praises, about how they had adopted her under a local scheme to reach out to elderly people on their own.

Vi glared at him. 'Yes,' she told him. She was fortunate that there were kind people around, who were more caring than some family. The inference was that of course they were letting her down, but both Grant and Laura did not bite.

Instead, Laura changed the subject, and told Vi about what they had discovered about Elsa. Vi was spellbound, clearly amazed that someone she had known for seventy years had hidden so much from her.

'Good grief, I had no idea,' she responded. 'Fancy that. So that makes sense doesn't it? Harry rescued her from Belsen. Well I never. And you tell me she was a wealthy woman… now I wonder if Harry knew that, because my parents certainly did not. I can remember my mother saying that the poor quine had nothing to her name, and all the time she had property and money. I cannot understand why on earth she would give it all away. It doesn't make any sense to me at all. She and Harry could have lived in comfort instead of living in the draughty old house. She could have used it to help the croft, but chose to give it away.' She shook her head in bewilderment. 'Gave it all away, fancy that.'

Laura decided not to tell her any more about what she had found out about Elsa's life, or admit that she could understand why her granny had given her money away. As she had written, the money made her feel guilty, and she was following her doctor's advice by leaving all of her old life behind. She could only imagine how hard that had been for her, in so many ways.

Once Aunty Vi had scraped up the last traces of the sticky toffee pudding she had consumed for desert, and drank the last of her coffee, they suggested that they should make a move to begin their journey back north. Vi was quite happy to comply; she was a little woozy after the two glasses of wine she had consumed and, together with the large lunch, she could do with a nap. So she was quite happy to wave them off once they had helped her into her flat, and she had pressed some envelopes into their hands. 'They contain a little something for your Christmas,' she told them.

Once Laura had driven out of the city, and was on the A90 back up north, Grant looked at the envelopes. There was one for each of them, including Liam. 'I don't think this one will get to Australia before Christmas, but I am sure he will be grateful of it when it does get to him. '

'Yes, I will miss him. I sent him some money too. You know, Dad, what is really strange is that I feel I am losing touch with what he likes. I missed shopping for him this year, but what's the point? I am sure that he would prefer money.'

'I just sent him a cheque too. I know what you mean, lass. He seems settled, though, with Gus. I know it grieves you not to have him here, but it could be worse. He is safe and from what I can make out from the occasional texts he sends me, he seems to be having a ball.'

'I know, Dad. But, I do miss him; I have asked him to Facetime us on Christmas Day, so let's hope he does so. Now, do you think it's too late to call into Birch End on our way up the road, just to check it? I know that Maisie says its fine, but I think I would be happier to just have a look myself.'

'As long as you don't mind driving in the dark, lass, it's alright by me. Bella will be fine with Dorothy and Jack, they were only too willing to look after her and walk her today. So yes, lets' do a little detour and go home by the scenic route.'

They arrived at Birch End in enough light to see that all was well. It was late afternoon and they guessed they probably had less than an hour of daylight before the winter darkness closed in. Getting out of the car, they took a preliminary inspection of the two steadings; the doors were both secure, and there was no winter damage that they could see.

The house smelt fusty from being unlived in and closed up. Thankfully it was warm, as they had left the storage heaters on to keep the damp at bay. They couldn't, of course, have a cuppa as the water was turned off. Maisie had very kindly forwarded the mail to Laura, and so she was not expecting that there would be any correspondence, and knew that the post woman or Charlie, her husband, was going into the house once a week, just to check. They had also left a couple of lights on timers, to come on at night, just to deter any unwelcome visitors – although Laura suspected that this would not be much of a deterrent, as everyone in the area was well aware that the house was empty since Elsa had died, and no doubt anyone who wanted to target it would do so.

As Grant was checking all of the doors and windows, he spied an envelope behind the door, caught up in the draft excluder. It was addressed to Mrs Laura Simpson, and there was no stamp so plainly it had been hand-delivered. 'Look what I have found, lass.' He handed the envelope to Laura. She glanced at it before opening the seal. It took a few minutes to read what was enclosed, and then she handed it to her father to read.

'Hmm, he isn't giving up is he? Though I see has actually given you an offer this time, but I would suggest it is on the low side.' He handed the letter back to Laura who was just about to screw the paper up, but relented. Maybe it would be more prudent to keep these communications.

'The tone is becoming a little more intimidating, don't you think? Suggesting that if the property falls into disrepair that the Council may take action. I am not sure that is right, but he seems determined to get his hands on it. Although I have not made a decision about what to do with it, there is one absolute certainty. I will not sell to him. Bloody Hamish McKenzie, honestly, doesn't he own enough land?'

'I noticed you kept the news about the life insurance pay-out from Vi. I just bit my tongue in time, I almost blurted it out, but then realised you were not telling her.'

'No, I decided not to. Especially after she made those comments about Granny leaving her money behind. The insurance pay-out, was a nice surprise, and even you didn't know that Grandad had taken out the policy all those years ago, and the payments had continued.'

'Well, I knew that there was a policy, but the monthly payments were not excessive so hadn't questioned them when I had helped Elsa with her finances. So yes, it was a nice surprise, thirty-five thousand pounds, and what with the twenty-five thousand she had in her bank, that gives you a tidy sum to mull over what you want to do, as well as with the property. You have plenty of time, lass. '

They did another quick tour, checking the mouse traps as the winter attracted mice into buildings, looking for a warmer habitat. All were empty, thank goodness, and a sign that Grant's bit of handwork of filling holes when he had stayed a while back had been successful. They locked the house up. It was now dark and they were reassured when the outside security lights came on to flood the yard with light.

'I just need to stop off at Maisie's, and drop off the Christmas presents I have for her and Charlie. I know they will complain about me giving them to them, but I am thankful for their help, so it is the least I can do. I will avoid going in, I have a great excuse that I want to get home before the roads get icy.'

Just as they thought, Maisie tried to get them to join her for a quick cup of tea, but they were well aware that nothing was quick with Maisie. She thanked Laura for the gifts, and admonished her for giving them. There was no need, and yes, she and Charlie would let her know if there were any problems.

They escaped in just under thirty minutes, and began the journey across country, Laura taking care as it looked like the night would bring a sharp frost, and with it icy road conditions. She was somewhat relieved when she passed the sign to welcome them into Broadsea. A cuppa, feet up in front of the telly, would be what was on the menu for the evening.

CHAPTER 42

Christmas arrived in a blur of rain and wind. It was cold as expected, but not cold enough to turn the rain into snow. There were, no doubt, other places where it was snowing, but not by the Moray Firth. But the heavy rain meant that the long walk on the beach on Christmas morning she had hoped for had to be postponed. Laura had spent the night in her own flat; she had been tempted by the offer of staying with her father and Iona, but had changed her mind, preferring her own bed. Bella had been happy to accompany her home the previous evening, when she had left her father's at just after eleven. It gave the dog an opportunity for a final flurry of checking for new smells along the short walk between the two houses.

She had shared a pleasant evening, chatting in front of the coal fire, remembering all the previous Christmas Eves spent in the same room. Iona had teased her grandfather, that they were sitting on the same furniture, gazing at the same wallpaper as she remembered as a young child, and maybe he should consider updating. He had taken the teasing in good spirit, having heard it all before. He couldn't be bothered, he had told her, to have the mess and disruption, and for what when there was nothing wrong with the room.

Laura stretched, making a star shape in the bed. She heard the rain beating down on her bedroom window; no doubt the sea would be raging too from the sound of it. She snuggled down under the duvet for a little longer. It was just after eight, so no rush. Grant had said he would cook breakfast, but after a plea from Iona for it not to be too early, he had relented and agreed that breakfast would be at ten. She knew her father would have been up and about at his usual seven o' clock: he was a man of routine.

She reached over and checked her phone: there had been no texts from Liam, and she was a little annoyed. She did hope that he would honour her wish and Facetime them today as she had asked. She had suggested that he call them about 6.30 pm his time. If he did as she hoped, that would mean a call just after they finished their breakfast. With that thought, she forced herself to leave her cosy bed, and make a cuppa, deciding she would take it back and drink it in bed. Once she had her cuppa she returned to her bedroom and pulled the curtains back. She was able to sit up in bed sipping her tea while watching the sea waves pound the bay. She could just see the small harbour and the couple of boats that were tied up behind the harbour wall bouncing about, their masts swaying in the wind. She loved to watch the sea, and thought how much she would miss living beside it. Her thoughts turned to Birch End, and she wondered whether it would be greedy to have two properties. She would have the best then: one looking out at the sea, and the other to the hills.

Bella and Laura arrived at Grant's just a while before breakfast was due to be served. He had gone to town, preparing a full Scottish breakfast, including Iona's favourite potato scones. Iona was already up and sitting in her usual position, one leg under her, and sipping a mug of coffee. She screeched as Bella decided to shake the rain from her coat before Laura could dry her off.

Laura hugged them both, wishing them a happy Christmas, and offered her assistance to Grant.

'Just sit yourself down, lass, you will be doing enough for the rest of the day, cooking that large bird sitting over there.' He pointed to the turkey that had been prepared by Laura the evening before.

They just finished eating when Laura's iPad indicated an incoming Facetime call, and she excitedly answered it. 'Hello, love.' She smiled as the tanned face of Liam appeared on the screen. Laura positioned the device so that all three of them could join the call, and they chatted for a while, all adding a little about what they had been up to. Liam described how they had had a barbecue at the beach today, and how different it was from the usual Christmas dinner. Although, he added, he missed his mum's roasts. He appeared to be making the call from the kitchen, as in the background they could see the others move around. Gus poked his head into the camera view to wish them all a happy Christmas; he looked quite merry, plus he was also tanned. Laura could not help a little twinge as she saw him in the background grabbing Sally as she stood the kitchen counter, planting a kiss on her neck. How long was it since he had done the same to her? It caused a spike of pain, one that she thought had long been extinguished. They finished the call, with Liam promising that he would keep in contact more often; Laura, sadly, doubted that he would.

'He looks happy,' Grant commented, as he started to clear the dishes from the table. 'Very tanned, but I suppose it's the middle of summer there. I keep forgetting.'

'Yep, and by what he says, he is having a ball. Good to hear that my little brother is becoming a first-class mixologist, serving cocktails in a fancy bar. Well now, that's a good future.' Iona was not able to prevent a little sarcasm creeping into her voice. 'I thought he was supposed to be working with Dad, learning plumbing, so that he could join him in his empire.'

'That was a while ago, I think he found plumbing a little boring, or so he hinted. I had wondered whether, maybe, he and his dad were not hitting it off, but seems that they are. He is definitely adding to his CV, trying lots of different jobs. Let's hope that he sticks for a while at this one. Certainly seems to be enjoying the life.'

'Hmm, yes well, Mum, I suspect that his current position means he has lots of access to plenty of single Aussie girls, who he can chat up while he is shaking their cocktails.'

Laura was a little sad that her children seemed to be losing the closeness they once had. There was a time when they had been good pals as well as siblings but, according to Iona, she had given up trying to communicate with her younger brother. She was fed up with not getting an answer when she tried to contact him. Laura also suspected that she had not quite forgiven him for choosing to live with their father, when she had made a decision to have as little as possible to do with him. Iona had never quite forgiven him for, as she saw it, abandoning her when he chose to move to Australia.

After another coffee, it was time for the family tradition of opening their presents. Laura was delighted with the perfume she received from Iona, and with the other smaller presents they gave each other. She was taken aback by the present she received from her father; he told her that this was her main present, when he handed her an envelope. In it was a cheque for two thousand pounds. Iona received a similar one. 'Now do not argue,' he told them both. 'I had to move some money about, so I would rather you had it now. Before you say anything, I am not leaving myself short. I just hope that both of you have some fun with it – and that is what it is for.'

The day was very casual, and they ate their Christmas dinner in late afternoon. They were so full they could hardly move, and it had taken Laura and Iona a big dollop of willpower to make them stack the dishwasher before they collapsed in a heap before the fire. Just as they were contemplating whether they had any energy to get a board game out, Laura's iPad sprang into life, announcing a Facetime call. She wasn't expecting one, so was somewhat unsure whether to answer it, but then she recognised the number. 'It's Felix,' she told them.

She accepted the call and the smiling face of a bearded man appeared on the screen. She had spoken to him several times on the phone, but had not seen him before. 'Hello, Laura,' he said as he brushed his thick fair hair back off of his face. 'Happy Christmas to you, I just thought I would chance it, and make a call, as there are some people with me who would like to say hello to you all.'

Iona and Grant joined her on the sofa, so that they could also see the screen and shout hello. 'It is good to see you, Felix, and what a nice surprise.'

'Now then, I will introduce you to these people, who are all excited to say hello to you. Firstly here is my lovely daughter Anna.' The face appeared of a young woman with long blonde hair and bright blue eyes, similar to her father's. 'And here –' he moved the camera to show two older people who were sitting in the background, ' – these are my parents, Axel and Marie. They so much wanted to meet you.'

Axel moved his face toward the screen. 'Hello to you, Laura. Who would have believed that I would be greeting the granddaughter of Elsa. My mother would have loved to have spoken to you, she spoke with such love for her old friend. It is sad that they never met for so many years.'

'Thank you so much. Yes I agree, it is so sad, but at least we now know what happened to her. Now please let me introduce you to my father.' Laura moved the iPad slightly. 'Here is my father, Grant, and –' she moved it again, '– here is my daughter, Iona.'

There was a little more conversation, with Axel saying he hoped they could meet up in the flesh in the future. 'Maybe next year,' he shouted as Felix returned to the screen. 'Yes, I second that, why not come and see Antwerp?' Another, face appeared to say hello and introduce herself as Stella, an attractive redhead. This was Felix's wife.

They wished each other a good New Year when it came, and signed off. 'That was nice, wasn't it, Mum? He seems such a nice man, especially to take the time out to call us today.'

CHAPTER 43

January and February were months when Laura spent time getting her business ready to open, usually sometime in March. Every year since she had been in business, Grant helped her to give the premises a freshen up with a coat of paint. Laura always added a little extra to the interior. This year she purchased some pretty lemon and blue striped blinds, which could be pulled down to prevent the sun from dazzling customers when they tucked into their scones and cakes. It also protected some of the goods she was selling from the sunlight. The premises were not large. On one side, the area was set out with six tables that together offered twenty covers. At the height of summer, she added another couple of smaller tables on the pavement outside. But unless there was warmth in the sun, these didn't work. The serving counter was at the back, with the entrance to the kitchen area in the room that ran along the back of the building. The kitchen wasn't large, so it curtailed what she could offer on the menu. Mainly sandwiches, and soup, with of course home bakes, which was the main pull for the customers. Laura had help to make the cakes; two of the women in the village were excellent bakers, so they were commissioned every week to make a range of stupendous cakes, with a batch of fresh scones every day. It provided a little employment for them, and helped Laura as well. The sandwiches and soups were made every morning by Carol Templer, who was Laura's right-hand woman. Carol was an excellent worker, and also a good cook and manager. She could be left to sort out the tea room and order what was needed, and was happy that the work was seasonal. Carol also lived in the village, and her husband worked abroad for long periods, and she often joined him during the winter months. So she was quite happy to work through from March to October.

The other side of the premises was Laura's baby, the gift area. She had built up its stock over the past three years and now, like her flat, was quite eclectic in its choice. Some of the stock was from local crafters: wood carvings, art work, and she knew a lovely jewellery maker called Samantha, who lived in the next village and made some really unusual items. The local goods she sold on a commission basis, which allowed her not to have a big outlay, as well as being able to hand all the unsold goods back at the end of the season. It also gave the crafters time to create new and different articles for the next season. While she had a number of local handmade crafts, about half of the stock she purchased herself. She perused catalogues and visited warehouses during February to purchase a selection of interesting, and middle-of-the-road items that she could sell and make a good profit from. She wasn't one for selling expensive items – there was not the demand – but often people came in to enjoy a coffee and cake, and then spent several pounds on a nice little item that caught their eye. She was always pleased when she had all the stock laid out at the start of the season, and equally pleased when she tallied up how much she made by the end.

As well as Carol, she had a couple of young people who helped out at weekends. They came and went, and often she was approached by schoolgirls asking if she had any weekend jobs. Her dad also gave a helping hand when she was busy. Grant seemed to enjoy it, and his friend Dorothy was also happy to be drafted in during the busiest times, refusing totally any payment, but happy to be paid in cake and the occasional item in the gift shop that took her eye. They were a happy little team when they were all working together. They got on well and the place had a real buzz.

There had been several calls with Felix since the Christmas call, some on Facetime. He and Laura had chatted like old friends, and she was able on one sunny day to use her iPad and show him around her premises and the bay outside. He was very taken with it, and said he looked forwards some time to visit and to see it for himself. He had never been north of Edinburgh, and it had been on the list of places he wanted to travel, but he had never got around to it.

During one of their conversations, Laura had posed a question about what happened to Sophia and Lucas. Were they still at the farm, she asked. Felix promised to make some inquires. In fact, he said, it would be a good outing for him, to take his family to Lint to explore at the weekend. He did just that, and on a Sunday evening, her iPad announced a Facetime call.

'Guess what,' he said, as his face appeared on the screen. 'We have just returned from Lint, and you would never believe it, but the farm is still in the hands of the Neefs family. Even a bigger surprise, Lucas is still living there, with his son Christin, and daughter-in-law Ada. He is ninety-seven, and still bright, although his health is failing. That is why I am calling you so quickly. He remembers your grandmother, and her family, and would dearly love to meet you. I would suggest, though, that you do not leave it for too long; as I said, he is quite frail, understandably given his age. The farm by the way is a great family enterprise. Christin runs the business with the help of his two sons. It's a thriving market garden enterprise; they grow lots of potatoes and other vegetables, and seem to have made a good business. So, will you think about coming Laura, before it is too late to meet someone who was so important to your family?'

'Well, I am not sure really, as it's the wrong time. I am due to open up in the next couple of weeks. So I don't know how I could just drop everything and come to Belgium.' She paused, her hand running across her forehead as she thought. 'Let me have a think about it. And thanks, Felix, for finding Lucas for me.'

After the call, Laura took Bella for a walk along the beach, providing her with a little time to process what she had just learnt. She would love to meet Lucas; he was really the last person who was alive who had directly known Elsa. It would be special to meet him, but how could she go now? When she had walked the length of the shore, she made her way to her speak to her father, and get his view on what she should do. Grant was certain about what she should do. 'You must go,' he told her. 'Don't leave it, Laura, so you regret not having to the chance to meet Lucas.'

'But how can I leave the business, Dad? It's all ready to open at the end of next week. I can't just go rushing off.'

'Yes you can, love. I can, with the help of Carol, and Dorothy if need be... we can open up and get things going. It is unlikely to be busy yet any road. It never is at the start of the season. So you go, and call Felix back, and tell him. Then get on to the internet and book a flight. So go on, love, just do it.'

She took her dad's advice and did exactly that. Felix was delighted. He told her to let him know when she had booked her flight, and he would meet her at Brussels airport. He was adamant that she would not stay in a hotel, but stay with his family. So no more arguments, he instructed.

A week later she was packing her suitcase ready to leave the following morning. She was flying from Aberdeen, via Amsterdam. She was feeling a little nervous; she realised she had never travelled on her own before. It had been either with Gus, or later Iona and Liam: someone had always been with her when they flew to holiday destinations. It had been a bit of a whirlwind the last few days, as she got the shop ready for opening at the weekend. She had suggested that she could be back by then, but both Grant and Carol had assured her that they could manage and she should just stay for the complete week, and return the following Monday. They would manage perfectly, and seemed rather excited about taking charge. She was ready, and Bella had already moved in to her other home, and would no doubt be curled up beside her old friend Tammy in front of the fire.

She was off on an adventure, and was looking forward to walking in her granny's steps.

CHAPTER 44

The flight from Aberdeen was on time; in fact, the captain had just announced that they would be landing and on the stand in Schiphol ten minutes ahead of schedule. She was a little relieved, as she had flown before via Amsterdam, and knew how big the airport was, and, it took ages to travel to the next gate. She hoped she could find it easily, but if not, she consoled herself she would just have to ask. In the end it was an easy transfer, and the flight to Brussels was on time. She texted Felix to let him know, receiving an immediate reply to say that he would be at the arrivals to meet her. Laura was looking forwards to meeting him and the rest of his family. She of course had seen Anna, but was looking forward to actually meeting her, and of course Felix's wife Stella. Felix rarely referred to his wife, but then why would he? He had assured her that his family were looking forwards to meeting her.

The flight to Brussels was very short, just forty-five minutes; no sooner were you settled in your seat with the seat belt sign going off, when the captain switched them on again and announced they would be landing in ten minutes. She peered out of the window as the aircraft circled over Brussels, and thought of the Wouters family. She was going to find some of her own roots, and felt a buzz of excitement over what she was going to see.

The landing and disembarking of the passengers was very efficient although, as usual, it took a while before her case trundled into view along the carrousel. It was always a relief that it had arrived safely. She grabbed it, and set off towards the exit signs. The large doors opened, and there was the arrivals hall, full of people going about their business. She looked around, and heard her name being called. Turning, she saw a tall man waving his hand, and recognised Felix. Laura made her way towards him. He came and met her with his arms open, and crushed her to him in an almighty bear hug.

'You are much smaller than I expected,' he told her, hugging her again. 'It is so nice to meet you at last, Laura. Welcome to Belgium.' He took the handle of her suitcase, and told her that it was only a short distance to walk to the car park, and then they would be on their way.

Laura could not help glancing at his profile as she walked beside him. She had to quicken her pace to keep up with his long strides. He must have been nearly six feet tall, and she was only five foot five, so only came up to his shoulders. He was a well-built man, but not overweight, just well built, with broad shoulders that looked as if they could take on the world. She had always been struck by his blue eyes, but they seemed brighter and bluer in the flesh; his nose was slightly flattened, and she thought his beard probably hid a square, slightly protruding jaw. As he placed her suitcase in the back of the Audi, she noticed that his hands were enormous; he smiled, opening the passenger door and inviting her to take a seat.

'So, this is your first visit to the country of your grandmother's birth place. I hope you do not mind, but I have arranged that we will visit Lucas tomorrow. I thought it prudent to do so, as his son informs me that he has not been too well over the past couple of days. Just a cold, but he is so elderly, I do not think we should take a chance.'

'That's perfectly fine with me. I do hope I am not inconveniencing you and Stella.'

He turned his head sharply. 'Stella, oh my, I am stupid. I did not realise that I have never told you. Stella and I are no longer together. We divorced about three years ago, and she lives in New York with her new partner. A female partner, I have to say. Anna lives with me, and when I talk about my family, I am referring to myself and Anna. Plus my parents, who live about a five minute away drive.'

Laura was a little shocked. She had not questioned him about his status, and as he had mentioned Stella's name a few times, it hadn't crossed her mind that she was not part of the family he referred to. 'I am sorry. I hope that the break-up was not too painful.'

'It was a little at the time, if I am honest. It came more of a shock when she told me she had fallen in love with a woman at work. To add to that, she then announced that her friend had just been offered a position in New York, and she was going with her.'

'What about Anna?'

'Oh, she seems to have managed it okay. She decided to remain with me, and we sold the family house, and bought the present flat. Anna goes to New York during the summer for an extended period, and Stella returns to Antwerp twice a year. In fact, that it probably why you had not realised. She comes for Christmas every year and stays with us, with her now married wife Gemma.' He chuckled. 'I find referring to her wife still a little odd, but we have all become very civil and possibly good friends. It is a strange world, is it not?'

As Laura processed this new information, she wondered why she had not asked about Stella before, but then why would she? She listened as Felix pointed out various landmarks and gave her a running commentary on the towns they passed by on the motorway. It would not take long, he told her, around forty minutes or so. He was right, and it was not long before she noticed the first signs to indicate Antwerp. 'I am quite close to the centre,' he told her. She was fascinated to view the city as they glided along. He pointed out various places, and she enjoyed him telling stories of his early life rampaging, as he described it, around the city with his friends.

They drew up outside a building across the busy road from a river. 'That,' Felix told her, 'is the *Scheide*.' It was a famous waterway, full of history which he could update her on later. He turned the car into a driveway and, after he pressed a couple of buttons, a gate opened to reveal an underground car park. He parked in a space that appeared to be his private parking space. 'Now,' he told her, 'let us get your case, and I am sure you are now ready for something to eat and drink.'

She followed him to a lift. He pressed the fifth-floor button, and when the door opened they walked into a narrow hallway with just two doors off it. Felix reached for his keys, and unlocked one, and Laura was led into what was a huge apartment, full of light. 'So let me show you to your room. I hope it will be okay.' She followed him along a corridor, with several doors each side. He opened one to reveal a huge bedroom with a king-size bed, and very modern contemporary furniture. 'Your bathroom is just through there.' He pointed to another door at the back of the room. 'Now just unpack and join me, the living room and kitchen are just across the hallway. Would you like a nice cool glass of wine to celebrate your arrival?'

'That would be lovely.' Laura sat on the bed for a moment, and looked around. Blimey, this must have come at a price. She quickly emptied her case, had a quick pee, and then joined in him a huge open-plan room. There was a large kitchen area at one end, with an island with several stools around it, and then at the other side of the space was a huge sitting area, with comfortable sofas. The light was amazing, mostly due to the huge windows that overlooked the river. He handed her a glass of white wine, and she took it and walked over the look out of the windows. 'What a fabulous view.' She turned and gazed around to take in the huge living space. 'And what an amazing apartment.'

'Yes, it is very different from the house we once lived in, but Anna and I fell in love with this place when we viewed it. Plus,' he indicated to the spiral staircase at the end of the room, 'we are fortunate to have outside space, by the way of a roof garden. It is a bit too breezy to go up there today. You will see a fantastic view. Now I have prepared a little snack, and tonight we will eat out. Anna will be home from school in,' he peered at his watch, 'in about thirty minutes, she is so excited to meet you.'

'What about your work, Felix? I do hope that my visit hasn't caused you to take time off.'

'Laura, do not worry, please. I find that I am in a position to take as much time off as I like now. Our business is doing well, and as the senior partner, I now can sit back a little. To be frank, I do not really need to work, and could retire, but at aged forty-eight that is far too early to do so.' He took a mouthful of wine, swilling it around in his mouth before he swallowed. 'Don't get me wrong: I worked long, long hours for many years to build the company up to what it is, so now I can reap the benefits from it. That is important to me. I have loved living with Anna, and being her only parent who is present for the past three years. We have grown close. She is wonderful, I am sure you will love her.'

It was not long before they heard the front door open, and a moment later a tall young girl arrived in the sitting area, her long blonde hair tousled and her eyes shining. 'Hello, Laura! I am so pleased to meet you at last.' She ran over and hugged the older woman. 'Papa has lots planned for this week, I am just disappointed that he is insisting I attend school, but I will be able to join you at the weekend. Is that not right, Papa?'

Laura watched the bond between Felix and his daughter, and she looked forward to getting to know both of them over the next week, in what was clearly a luxurious apartment.

That evening the three of them went out to a restaurant for dinner. Anna advised that this was her favourite place to eat, and they made the most fabulous frits, which were to die for. The meal was eaten in a lively atmosphere, mostly due to the exuberant Anna. She divulged information about her father that he probably wished she had not done. 'Do you know, Laura,' she leant over the table, and said in an indiscreet manner, intending to embarrass her father, 'Papa sings very loudly and very badly when he is in the shower, so I would recommend that you have ear plugs.' Felix smiled indulgently, with a certain resignation; this was evidently not the first time he had been made to suffer by his mischievous daughter. 'Plus,' she went on, 'he has the most annoying habit of wearing clothes that do not match. Often it is different coloured socks, but he most definitely has no sense of fashion.'

'Unlike you,' Felix had interjected. 'Anna has great ideas, that she will be the most famous fashion designer in the future.'

'And so I will, Papa, once I am able to be free of school, then that is exactly what I am going to do. You see, Laura, when I complete my schooling in a few months- time, I am going to spend the next year in New York. Gemma, my mother's wife, works on a really big fashion magazine and has arranged for me to be an intern for a year so I can learn the business.'

'Well, at least you will have a good place to stay, and your mum will love to have you, I am sure.' Laura watched Felix. His face told a thousand stories, pride, and also sadness; he would find it hard to let Anna go, she was sure, but he would have to.

'Oh, and one more thing, Laura, don't go grocery shopping

with my papa if you can avoid it.' She glanced at him, her eyes glinting with amusement. 'He is hopeless. He might be the best accountant in the world, but he is terrible at shopping; he ends up getting all the wrong things, forgets what he went out to buy in the first place. There is just one word, hopeless.'

They all laughed at her description and Felix admitted that shopping was not on his list of enjoyable activities. The rest of the evening was fun, and Laura could not help but liken Anna to Iona when she was the same age. Full of energy and excitement, everything was going to be such fun. Now, she considered how much Iona had changed; she was so responsible, and at times serious, seeming to have the world on her shoulders. But then, the profession she had chosen, she supposed, needed those qualities. She just hoped that when she was with Tony, she was also having a little fun.

CHAPTER 45

Laura woke to the sounds of movement in the flat. She had slept really well given it was a strange bed and place. She stretched, and took a moment to wake up fully. Donning her dressing gown, she made her way tentatively out into the main room. Anna was sitting on a stool at the island, spreading something onto a thick piece of toast. Felix was sprawled on one of the deep sofas, his laptop on his stomach. 'Good morning, Laura, did you sleep well? Help yourself to breakfast, Anna will show you where things are.' He gestured towards his daughter. 'You must just make yourself at home.'

'I did sleep well, thank you.'

Anna leapt from her seat and showed Laura where things were, and then returned to finish her toast. 'I have to apologies for my papa, he is the most lazy host.' She gave him a look of annoyance. 'Do not pander to him, ever.' She crunched another mouthful of toast, but grinned and winked at Laura to let her know she was teasing him.

It worked. Felix took his attention from whatever he was doing on this laptop and joined them at the island. 'I am sure that Laura is quite capable of asking if she needs anything,' He went across and ruffled Anna's hair. 'And, young lady, if you do not hurry, you are going to be late for school again.'

Once Anna had left in a whirlwind, moaning about having to go to school, when she would much rather join them on their outings, calm resided over the apartment. Laura finished her second mug of tea, and began to tidy up.

'There really isn't any need to do that, Laura,' he stated. 'And please do not take any notice of Anna, she is always teasing me.'

'You will miss her when she goes to New York.' She watched his face cloud over a little, and he scratched his beard. 'Are you okay about that?'

'I don't really have any option. I really had hoped she would stay and at least attend a college or university, but as you have already witnessed, she is not a lover of school, and also she has a strong will. I suppose it could be worse; she could just say she wanted to go travelling, and at least I know she will be safe with Stella and Gemma. Who, I must say, are delighted to have her, although once they have experienced living with her full time, and her rather messy habits, that might change. I do admit, though, that I will miss her terribly. She and I have been a real team these past three years, and have done so much together. I am just going to have to get on with it. You have managed with both your children flying the nest.'

'I would not say it has been, or is, easy. Iona of course is reasonably close at hand, at least I can see her often, although she is caught up with her studies and life. But it is different with Liam. I do miss him very much, and he is not good at keeping in contact – but then, as you say, it could be worse. At least he is safe with his father. It takes a bit of getting used to.'

'Right, come on, let us get ourselves organised. I will have a shower, and then we can make our way out to Lint to visit Lucas. His son said late morning was the best time, and once we have visited, then we can find somewhere to have some lunch. Is that a good plan?'

****

It was a fairly short journey out to Lint. Felix turned the car off of the main road, and took a small single-track road, signposted to Neefs Market Garden. On each side of the track were fields which held polythene tunnels, with several people working in them. The farm house was at the end of the track, and there was a newer extension on the side of the house. 'That,' Felix said, 'is Lucas's accommodation.' As the car drew to a halt the front door opened and a small elderly man approached them in welcome. 'That,' Felix told her, 'is Lucas's son, Christin.'

Christin welcomed the visitors, and said how delighted he was that Laura was able to come. An elderly lady stood at the door and beckoned them in, introducing herself as Ada, Christin's wife. She told them that Lucas was so looking forwards to the visit, and yes, he was well today, just a little tired. But then, she stated, who would not be tired, at the age of ninety-seven?

The couple showed them through the house until they reached a doorway that took them into the new extension. This, Christin explained, was built several years ago, to give his father some independence, and of course it was all on the one level. They walked into a bright, modern room. In the corner sat a rather small and wizened old man. He attempted to get up, but Laura rushed forwards, telling him not to. He looked very frail, his skin wrinkled and covered in brown liver spots, but his eyes were still bright and interested.

Laura bent down, and took his hand. 'Lucas, it is so good to meet you at last.' She found herself getting a little emotional. 'I have read so much about you.'

Lucas too became emotional. 'Oh, my dear, you are so much like Elsa. Poor Elsa. I am so sorry she is no longer with us, but I am equally pleased she had a good life.' They were interrupted by Ada bringing a chair across so that Laura could sit close to Lucas. She told them she would bring some coffee, and Christin and Felix sat quietly to observe and listen.

'So tell me, Laura, did Elsa have a peaceful life?'

Laura went on to describe her granny, the croft and how she had spent the past seventy years. She reassured him that she had been happy and content. She went on to explain that until her death she had known nothing of the trauma and loss she had experienced during the war. It had been a huge revelation.

Lucas listened intently, and nodded. 'Yes, she suffered greatly. So much for a young woman. It was true that neither Sophia nor I knew the full extent of what she had suffered.' They had been aware though, that it was too much for her. 'Sophia would be grateful to have known that she was well and had a good life with Harry. She had wondered all of her life, up until she sadly departed this world over twenty years ago, whether Elsa had found peace. We were sad that she wanted to cut ties with us, but we understood.'

'Did you never hear anything from her, at all?'

'We had a postcard once a year, for several years.' He looked across at Ada. 'Did you find them, my dear?' Ada placed a small box that seemed to have once held chocolates on his lap. His arthritic fingers struggled a little to open it, but he managed. He pulled out several postcards, and handed them to Laura.

She realised they were postcards from her grandmother, 'oh me,' she uttered. She recognised the spindly writing and on each postcard was written exactly the same; the only difference was that the postmark indicated that they were sent in May, a year apart. She read

To dear Sophia and Lucas
I am well, and still looking at the
Sunrise to bring hope and peace
Love

Elsa

Laura found her eyes filling up with tears when she read this.

'She did not give us a forwarding address,' Lucas told her, 'so we could never reply. When the postcards stopped coming, we were worried that she was no longer living. But it seems she had just decided that enough was enough, and got on with her life. Sophia and I were forever grateful to her for giving us this.' He raised his arms up. 'Without her gift, we would have struggled very much to make a living. Now, we have made a living, not just for my son, but for our grandchildren too. There is much to thank her for.' He wiped his eyes with the back of his hand. 'Yet we were never able to thank her. Or for her to know how much difference she made.'

'I have another memento that you may like, my dear.' He looked again at Ada, who put a faded photograph in his shaky hand. He looked at it fondly, and then handed it to Laura. In it were three people, all looking as though they were in their early twenties. The younger of the women, who when she looked at closely she saw was Elsa, was holding up two medals. She realised that the other two people were Sophia and Lucas. She looked to Lucas for an explanation.

'That was taken not long before Elsa left. It was an event held to recognise the Resistance movement. One of the medals was for her dear papa, and the other for your great-uncle Derk. They of course were awarded posthumously: such a waste of life.'

Laura remembered reading in her granny's journal about going to a ceremony. 'Do you know where the medals are now?' she enquired.

'I am afraid I do not, my dear, what Elsa did with them I do not know. I do know that she found the receiving of them very distressing, but I have no idea where they are. But you must keep the photograph. It is much more important to you than for me. I have had it in my possession for so long.'

After drinking the coffee, they took their leave, realising that this visit had taken so much out of Lucas who was, it seemed, struggling both with his energy and with the emotions that had been stirred up by meeting Laura.

Once they had bid goodbye to Christin and Ada, and promising to keep in contact, they made their way back along the track. 'Do you think we could go and find Derk's grave?'

'Of course, we must do so. First though, I think we need to have a moment for you to process what you have learnt. And maybe we can find some flowers to place on the grave.'

After having a light lunch in one of the cafes, and finding a florist where she purchased two bunches of flowers, they walked to the cemetery. Christin had given them some directions to where Derk's grave was, and also where his mother Sophia was buried. They found hers first, and Laura stood at the end of the grave, and gave up a silent prayer, and a thanks for all that Sophia had done to help her grandmother. They walked further along the pathway, and found a grave which had been better cared for than many around them. It was clear that some of the Neefs family had taken on the responsibility to ensure it was cared for. Laura read the inscription that was carved on the stone headstone.

Derk Wouters
Born 5th September 1926
Died fighting for freedom
August 1944

Laura reached for a tissue. She had never known this great-uncle, but he was family. She remembered Elsa writing that she had found this grave, and that she had arranged for a headstone. She laid her flowers, and sent a silent thought, hoping that they were now reunited in the unseen world.
Wiping her eyes to stop the flow of tears, she felt Felix's arm

around her shoulder, and leant on him. She was grateful for his support, and for his silence.

CHAPTER 46

The next few days flew by, with several visits to various places, including her great-great-grandmother's grave, where she laid some flowers. There were other people to meet, including Felix's parents, Axel and Marie, who were delightful. They fussed around her, welcoming her into their home and insisting that she relaxed. Anna accompanied them for supper one evening, and Laura loved the way she bossed them around, and her two grandparents absolutely wallowed in the attention that Anna paid them.

The lunch and evening meal she shared with the older Beckers was relaxed and she enjoyed their company very much. Axel told her about his mother Dominique, and how she had spoken so warmly about Elsa and Estelle. They had, he recalled, always been present in the lives of Dominique and the wider family. His Aunt Adele, who had died many years ago, had also spoken about the lessons that Laura's great-grandmother had given them as young girls.

There was also, of course, a visit to Ramstraat, to meet Dr Nicole Renard. Laura was very taken with the attractive psychiatrist, who was well groomed, professional and in her late thirties. Her presence radiated a sense of safety and empathy. She noticed that Felix and she had a great rapport, and seemed to know each other very well, which got her wondering as to whether there was something more than a professional relationship between the two of them. The Centre was impressive, each room decorated in calm colours and furnished simply, yet warmly. As she was shown around, she could not help but to try to consider how it was when her family had lived here. She reminded herself of what her granny had written in her journals. The rooms on the first level would have once been her great-grandfathers work space, and were now transformed into a similar use. Nicole had one of the rooms for her consulting room, the other was the reception area; Laura wondered whether it was the same room as in Martin's time. At the back of the ground floor, what must have been the dispensary was now an administration room with two computers and filing cabinets. The final room on the ground floor, would, she remembered have be Martin's study. It was now another consulting room.

It was the next two floors that were probably the most different. The larger of the two front rooms was now used for group work, while the other, smaller room, likely to have once been the Wouters dining room, was now a consulting room. It was the large kitchen that probably was closest to the same use; it had become the staff room and still a kitchen. This was the room which caused Laura to have goose bumps; she could only imagine how Elsa had witnessed the shooting of Helena here. The back garden was very neat and tidy. The lawns were kept short and there was an abundance of plants, and she suspected during the summer it would be a blaze of colour. She saw an apple and pear tree standing at the end of the garden, and realised they were the same trees that would have been there when Elsa was a child. She wanted to go out and experience walking in the footsteps of her family. This was the real healing sanctuary, Nicole told her; patients often came to sit in the quiet place, and soak up a little of nature in the middle of a busy city.

Laura walked to the end of the garden. She saw that the back gate was no longer in use; it had been boarded up and plants had ivy had grown up the wall and almost covered the gate. She allowed her imagination to see those brave Resistance fighters and all those Allied service men sneaking though it, to freedom. What a story this was, and now she could see it and feel it. She wondered about Estelle's hens and her protection of them. As she wandered back up she saw that the door to the cellar was open, but checked with Nicole that it was okay to go inside. The cold hit her as she entered. It was no longer in use, apart for storage. She looked around, especially seeking the small hatch, the entry to the concealed room. Felix showed her where it was; he had to force the catch as it was rather rusted with age. He managed to pull it open, causing a hail of dust to burst out into the cellar. It caused Laura to sneeze, and as the dust settled, she placed her head into it to take a look. My goodness, it was narrow, and she suspected very uncomfortable if you were stuck in it for any length of time.

There was just one last storey to visit, and that was the top floor, which was once where the family bedrooms had been situated. She climbed the stairs, listening to Nicole explain that these were the rooms that were rented out to various complementary therapists. As it was the end of the day, and there were no patients visiting, she was able to open each door to allow her to see inside. She guessed from Elsa's description which had belonged to each family member. Standing now in what once had been Elsa's bedroom, she looked up at the ceiling, and imagined how many times her granny would have lain in her bed and gazed up, to look and dream.

After the tour, Nicole gave her a run-down of how the patients were referred, and the help they provided. It was humbling to know that it was due to Elsa that all these people who were suffering emotional pain were being helped. It was over a coffee in Nicole's consulting room that Laura certainly got the feeling that her earlier impressions, of there being a closer relationship between Felix and the doctor, were right. There was definitely some flirting going on, lots of smiles and reference to events they had both attended. Yes, and she wished them both well and could see them as a couple.

The remainder of her week's stay passed quickly. She found Felix's company both stimulating and relaxing. He was easy to talk to, a good listener, and quite funny. Anna's company was also welcome. A shopping trip was fun, it was ages since she had enjoyed a girly shop. Sunday arrived, her final day, and the weather was good, so Felix suggested a walk around the *Grott Markt* and a leisurely late lunch, which was accepted by both Laura and Anna. Laura loved Antwerp. It was lovely city. She had taken the opportunity to spend some time being a tourist, and had walked several times along Klapdorp, letting her mind wonder how many times Elsa had walked the same pavements.

Returning to Felix's apartment in the early evening, they were ready for a chilled evening with a glass of wine. The lunch had been long and extensive, a tradition it appeared for the Becker family. Laura excused herself to go and pack her case, as she was leaving early the following morning. Felix had insisted that he would drive her to the airport. She had texted her father several times over the weekend to check how things were going back in Broadsea, and whether they had managed to open the shop alright without her. His replies were short and to the point: everything was fine, so stop worrying.

Later that evening, Felix and Laura nursed a glass of wine; both were relaxed and sitting on opposite sofas. Soft music was playing in the background, and Anna had disappeared to her room to chat on her phone to her friends. 'It will be very quiet,' Felix announced, 'once you have gone, and I only have Anna here to taunt me. Even that will not be for too long, just a few weeks left, and she will be on her way to New York.'

'It's bound to be difficult for a while, Felix, but you seem to have a busy life from what I have heard and seen. Didn't you say that you had a trip to Paris, and one to Milan planned over the next few weeks?'

'I keep myself busy, yes. I like to keep a watch on what the company is doing, and yes, I still have some clients that I like to give special time to. But it will mean returning to an empty flat. I will have to be more focused on building up my social life again, I suppose. It is a part of my life I have neglected somewhat, since I became a single parent.'

Laura thought for a moment. She was a little surprised by this comment, as it seemed that he had a great social life, compared to hers, which was almost non-existent. 'I am so grateful,' she told him, 'to have been able to stay, and despite what Anna said, you are a very good host. I don't know how to thank you.'

'You have no need to. It has been a real pleasure to get to know you. I regard you as a dear friend, and anytime you wish to come, then you will be most welcome.'

'There is just one thing that has been niggling me: the medals. I wonder what Elsa did with them. I will have to look again at the croft, when I get back, but it is strange, don't you think, that they were not with her things. I would have thought they would have been very precious.'

'Your Elsa certainly turned out to have many secrets. I will check, if you like, whether any medals were found at Ramstraat, or whether there was any other place where she could have deposited them. I cannot believe that she would have discarded them.'

The following morning Anna threw her arms around Laura, kissing her on both cheeks and wished her a good flight. She would, she hoped, see her again. Shortly after, Laura sat beside Felix as he drove in and out of the busy morning traffic, to make sure she reached the airport in time for her flight. They had already agreed that he would just drop her off, rather than accompany her to the departure check in. When they arrived, he had some difficulty trying to find a suitable place to stop, given that the airport was busy. He managed to pull in, and insisted on getting her case from the boot. Handing it to her, they stood for a moment looking at each other, a little uncomfortably, for the first time since they had met. Felix reached over to hug her, kissing her on both cheeks, which she realised was a very Belgian thing to do. Turning, she pulled her case across the busy pavement, turning to wave, but realised he must have revved his car and left without a second glance.

CHAPTER 47

The next few weeks flew by. The weather was behaving, and that was good for business, as it brought people out from the towns to walk on the beach. Broadsea Gifts and Tearoom became the place to retreat to once the walk was completed. This pleased Laura, who relished having a busy shop, as well as the buzz of the tearoom and the chatter and rattling of cups. Carol was also in her element, as she found the start of the season and the build-up to summer still held an attraction for her. It was the middle of summer when it was really busy, and then in autumn energy levels fell off, and it became a bit more of a slog.

Grant also was full of revived energy. He was well into the bowling season now that the outdoor bowling had commenced. He still found time to help Laura if she needed it, as did Dorothy, who was a frequent visitor. She liked to be fully occupied and enjoyed helping out, especially as Jack was caught up with his bowls, and when he wasn't bowling, he was gardening. She kept reminding Laura that she was willing to help out at any time.

Life had regained a certain rhythm; the ebb and flow of daily routine gave her a degree of contentment. Often, in the evenings, she was too tired to do more that give Bella a quick walk, cook some supper, and then flop in front of the TV. She had made a mad dash over to Birch End the previous week, just to double-check that it was all okay, and gave a cursory search through the wardrobe and drawers, looking for the missing medals.

There were regular phone calls and Facetime calls with Felix. He seemed busy, and had been in Milan on business the previous week. He was bracing himself for Anna's departure next week. Anna's face often appeared on some of the Facetime calls, to shout hello, but mainly it was just Felix and her. It was strange, Laura reflected; she had known Felix that many months, but now he seemed part of her life. It was just like talking to an old friend, as though he had been in her life for ever. She could not recall ever having a male friendship such as she had with Felix, and it felt good.

When her iPad burst into life just after six on a Wednesday evening, she saw the request for a Facetime call from Felix and expected the usual catch up. She pressed the accept button and Felix's excited features came to life. 'You will never guess what,' he exclaimed, but before she could answer, he was waving a small wooden box in front of the camera. 'We have located the medals.'

'Wow, how, where?'

'You recall that Elsa instructed the lawyer, Marcel Maes, to deal with her family estate and all that; well, I spoke to Oskar Charlui, you remember he is the lawyer who is on the trust board. He, of course, still works in the original offices of Marcel Maes, and I asked whether there was anywhere Elsa could have left the medals. He first forgot to check, but he called me just yesterday to say that he had got his secretary to go up the loft area, which is where the old articles are stored. She found this in one of the filing cabinets. It was wrapped in a thick brown paper, but on the front Elsa's name was written so he took it and opened it. Now there are two medals, but also some other small items. But – now this is exciting – there is also a letter, which is sealed and says on it to be only opened after her death. We have not opened it, as I suggested that it should be you who did so.'

'Oh, my goodness, Granny, another pathway you are taking me. So, are you going to post it over to me?'

'That is what I need to discuss with you, Laura. Anna leaves in two days' time, so I was thinking after she leaves, that I could take a little holiday and come to Scotland. I can hand-deliver this, plus I get to see where Elsa lived, and of course get to catch up with you.'

'That would be fab, it would be lovely to see you.' Laura felt some excitement build. 'And you will get to meet my dad and Iona. I can put you up, but don't forget that my flat is not on the same scale as yours. When are you going to arrive?'

'I was thinking I would drive. I can get the ferry to Newcastle from Amsterdam, and then I would make my way up to you. I thought it would be good to have a little detour, perhaps spend a couple of days in Edinburgh. So I would say I would be with you, say, in ten days' time. Would that be okay?'

****

Laura looked around her flat, and tried hard not to compare it with the size and luxury of Felix's. Well, she could not do anything about the size, and her eclectic interior would maybe counteract the contemporary style of his penthouse. Nevertheless, she did find herself taking a critical view of the spare room. It was not big enough for a double bed, and it seemed quite cramped. Would his large frame even fit in there, she wondered. She did decide to purchase a new duvet cover; she had been using old ones she had scavenged from her dad's house. At least she could brighten the room up a little.

She felt a level of anticipation, and a tingle of apprehension. She could not quite work out why. Maybe, she counselled, it was about opening the letter, and seeing what else was in the box. Whatever the reason, she found that she was not sleeping well. The shop was busy; it was the middle of June, and so holiday-makers had started to make an appearance. The tea room had taken on a new level of noise, and the two ladies who baked cakes for them had to up their baking to keep the tea room supplied. Two young teenagers were taken on for weekends, and the school holidays, so really everything was under control. Dorothy had assured her that she would be happy to look after the shop when her friend arrived. Dorothy, and she suspected also Carol, had been chatting quite a bit about the arrival of Laura's friend, Felix. They had been questioning her about him, occasionally speculating between each other that he was maybe more than just a friend.

The day of his arrival came, and he texted Laura to say that he would probably reach her by around six. It was Friday evening, and the beach was still busy as it had been a warm sunny day. The shop and tea room closed at five, and while she could have continued to fill the tea room until much later, they had all had enough. Plus, they had run out of several cakes and scones until they could be replenished the following morning. Dorothy had insisted, backed up by Grant, that she should take some time off the following day; they would look after the shop, and they had plenty of help with the two weekend girls. Laura was grateful, as she would like a bit of time to show Felix around.

She was watching from the sitting room window when she saw a blue Audi drive slowly down the street, the driver looking about him. She rushed downstairs and out to the front and waved to him. He parked in front of the shop and got out of the car, stretching his limbs to shake off the tension of driving some distance… and he had forgotten that driving on the wrong side of the road, in his case, took a little getting used to. She went over and they embraced, he doing his usual three kisses on alternate cheeks. 'You look tired,' she told him.

'Well, I can certainly do with a drink, and yes it took me longer than I thought it would. Getting out of Edinburgh was a challenge, so much traffic.' He removed his two bags from the car boot, and another large gift bag, and followed Laura through the side gate to the back of the house, where she climbed the stairs to the flat.

'Well, this is nice,' he said as he looked around the kitchen. 'It is very cosy.'

'Would you like a coffee, or something stronger? I have beer and wine.'

'Actually, a beer would be very welcome. Thank you.'

'I will show you your room, but brace yourself, it is quite small. I hope you will be comfortable enough.'

'Laura, I am sure I will be. It is just good to get here and see you.' She opened the door to the spare room, and he passed her, looking around. 'This is fine,' he said. 'It is very comfortable. Thank you.'

She left him to sort his things out, and retrieved two beers from the fridge, and as they met up in the sitting room, she handed him one. Felix gazed out of the window. 'Wow, this is absolutely stunning, Laura.' He took a swig of his beer and turned. 'Now here is the box and letter. I am sure you are dying to open it.'

She took the rather faded envelope and sat down on the sofa. Carefully slitting the top of the envelope she withdrew a single piece of paper, firstly reading it to herself. Once she had finished she read it out.

To whom this may concern.
I am hoping that my wishes that this was only to be opened after my death have been adhered to. If so then I am of course no longer on this earth. Why, you may ask, have I left such a letter. It has to do with the contents of the box. The contents contain some heirlooms for the Wouters, and I had to make the decision either to take them

with me, or to leave them behind as I had done with all of my life. I chose the latter. So if this letter is now opened, then I hope that the contents will be dealt with appropriately. They were special to me, but to take them with me would have caused the pain of loss every time I would see them. Better, Dr Peeters had said, to leave the pain behind. They were too special for me to just disregard them, so I have asked Marcel to keep them safe.

I do hope that these can be given to someone who would value them, if not please sell them and give the money to a good cause.

Regards

Elsa Wouters

She opened the small wooden box to peer inside. Firstly, she removed two small boxes. They contained two medals. The inscription on the inside of the box read:

To Dr Martin Wouters, we are forever grateful for your bravery.

The other held a similar message, but for Derk. So here were the missing medals. She looked into the box and she retrieved a small silk pouch, and opening it she found a small silver bracelet, and the other was a sapphire brooch. 'Oh my,' she whispered, 'these are the two items that Sophia found after Elsa and the family were taken. Granny wrote in her journal that Sophia had given her these when she returned to Antwerp. Look, this was my great-great-grandmother's; she gave this to Elsa, as a gift, on her thirteenth birthday; and this is the bracelet that the Jewish family gave her. How absolutely wonderful.' Laura looked upwards. 'Well, Granny, wherever you are, I can assure you they will be treasured forever. What a lovely find, thank you so much Felix for bringing them across, and more importantly for finding them in the first place.'

The peace was interrupted with the entrance of an excited and bouncy black-and-white dog, Bella, accompanied by Grant. Bella went directly over to sniff, and say hello to Felix, closely followed by Grant, who remarked he would just shake hands as opposed to sniffing. Grant accepted a bottle of beer, and read Elsa's letter while examining the contents of the box. 'My mother-in-law has turned out to be an enigma. Goodness, since her death it has been like unravelling a puzzle. Is there anything else, I wonder?'

The evening was spent pleasantly, with Grant hearing about Felix's grandmother, Dominique, and how she had been a huge influence in his life. She had, he told them, given him the values that no matter what obstacles you were faced with, you could overcome them. All three raised their glasses to that sentiment.

CHAPTER 48

The next couple of days went well. The weather remained sunny and warm, which of course showed Broadsea at its very best. Felix was impressed by the set-up of the shop and tea room, and insisted that he help out by becoming a temporary waiter on the Sunday afternoon, when there was a rush for teas and cakes. Carol and the customers were quite taken with the tall, fair-haired Belgian. He was of course charming and was, Carol commented, 'Definitely an asset to the business.' This caused Laura to give her a rather withering look. Nevertheless, the weekend was a success, and Laura had even managed to drive Felix along the coast to sample some of the other villages.

On Sunday evening, after the shop was shut, Felix was interested in sampling the Broadsea Arms' pub supper. Laura didn't need any persuading; she was happy not to cook. There was only one condition – she was paying for it, as he was her guest and she wanted to repay the hospitality that he had shown to her. Bella was delighted to join them, and settled herself under the table at the pub, hoping that she could hoover up any bits of food that were discarded.

'This is lovely,' he told her, looking around at the busy lounge bar. Most tables were full, with couples and families tucking in to large portions of home-cooked food. He had chosen fish and chips; he had been promised that this was very much a local catch. When it came, he was impressed by the freshness, as well as the size of the portion. 'Wow, this is some plateful. I see, what you mean about not having a starter.' He tucked in. 'You have a great business, Laura, you must be very proud.'

'I suppose I am, but it is not easy. It brings in enough, though, for the season, so I can manage through the winter. Also, to be candid, I live quite a quiet life.' She dipped a fat chip into some tartare sauce. 'I own the property, so I do not have mortgage or anything. I am very fortunate.' He looked a little perplexed. 'You see, when my marriage broke up, the money from the sale of the family house came to me. I think that Gus's guilt got to him, and so he agreed that he would walk away. I have to add he didn't walk away with nothing; he sold his business and that probably gave him an equal amount. So I sold the house, and then moved in to live with my dad for seven years. My dad, like you, is a good finance man, and he invested the money. It allowed me enough to buy the property here outright. So it is special to me.'

'And you have never thought about re-marrying? It is some time you have been on your own.'

She felt herself blushing slightly, as although they found conversation easy and relaxed, they had not spoken about their personal relationships. 'No, to be honest, I have not found anyone I would want to give up my independence for.' She paused to take another piece of fish on the end of her fork. 'I suppose I haven't been looking.' She placed the fish in her mouth, watching him digest this information. 'What about you?'

He considered the question for a moment. 'I have been on several dates, and yes had a couple of, what might be described as serious relationships. But they did not come to anything. Anna became my dating manager for a while. About a year after Stella and I separated, she lined several dates up for me, via the internet I have to say. I think she felt sorry for me, with her mother seeming so happy and loved up with Gemma. She gave up, after a while, and claimed I was a hopeless case.'

'And now?'

He shrugged his shoulders, pushing his empty plate to one side, and taking a sip of his wine. 'There has been someone who I spend some time with. I have the feeling she would like it to be more serious than it is from my side. I think that maybe she may describe me as a commitment phobic.'

Laura decided to change the focus. 'So tomorrow you are happy for us to go across to Birch End? Dad and Dorothy are happy to look after the shop. It's usually quiet at the beginning of the week. So we can stay a couple of nights, and come back sometime on Wednesday. That gives you a couple of days back here, before you head back.'

'That sounds great, Laura. I am looking forwards to seeing the place that your grandmother made her home. Also, to meet Iona. Is she still up for coming out?'

'Yes, she and Tony are intending on coming out on Tuesday. I am really looking forward to introducing her to you. Plus, to be honest I am looking forwards to getting to know the elusive Tony a little, too. Iona seems to be keeping him very much to herself.'

****

Felix was delighted with the drive across country to Glen Gavin. Bella was quiet in the back of the car: that lasted until Laura turned into the drive of Birch End, when she sat up and started whining. The view of the croft always tugged at Laura's heart, bringing with it so many childhood memories. It now looked sad and unlived in, and she wondered yet again what its future would be.

Felix was expansive in his first impressions. 'Wow, this is remarkable, what a setting.' He turned to take in the whole vista of the hills in the background, with the sun causing the granite to glint and sparkle. 'This is fabulous.'

Laura laughed; this was just as she expected. The better she got to know Felix, the more she became prepared for his exuberance when he was faced with something that moved him.

Bella was also moved. She ran around in sheer excitement of being back – in her small doggy mind – home. As she reunited herself with the smells, Laura unlocked the door, and she felt the heat. While she had arranged for Charlie to turn the water back on, she had completely forgotten to ask him to turn the storage heaters down. She immediately opened all the windows to let in some air and the stuffy heat out, before turning them off.

Felix's enthusiasm continued as he moved around the cottage. 'This is so quaint,' he commented as he gazed around him. 'Like a little time capsule.' He was also enthralled by the walk down through the woods to the River Dee, which was rather low due to lack of rain. Sitting on her favourite rock, Laura watched him throw sticks in the water so that Bella could swim out to retrieve them before they disappeared into the flow of the river. She was enjoying immensely Felix's reaction to Birch End and, looking about her now, she admonished herself for leaving it to its own devices over the past few months. She would need to make a decision soon about its future.

Iona and Tony arrived the following day. Laura had made a lunch and as they were running late it was ready on their arrival. She introduced Iona to Felix and watched how he grabbed her daughter and did the usual welcome of three kisses, taking Iona by surprise. Tony shook his hand, and they spent a congenial time eating and catching up. Laura was taken by Tony; he seemed to be a perfect fit for her daughter, and going by the glances he stole at her, he was in love with her. She wondered whether Iona reciprocated this love, or whether she was being slightly cooler due to being in her mother's company. Laura was slightly confused as to why that might be.

Iona and Tony stayed until late afternoon, and then explained that they had arranged to meet up with some friends tonight, given that they were both off duty together which, according to Tony, was unusual. Felix and Laura waved them goodbye, and returned to work companionably together to clear and wash the dishes. He was rather amused that there was no dishwasher. He had been rather perturbed the previous day, when he realised that there was no TV or Wifi, although thankfully Laura's dongle worked and he was able to check his emails, and do a little business: but no dishwasher? Now that was deprivation.

Once they finished and returned from walking Bella to the river, they grabbed two glasses of wine, and sat together on the bench outside the cottage. 'Now then,' she told him, 'we may not be out here for long. Once you have been introduced to the scourge of Scotland, known as midges, we will have to escape back into the house, and batten down the hatches.'

As they took in the peace, watching Bella chase flies, and then lie panting from the exertion, they relaxed. 'Have you any idea what you will do with all this?'

'No, I have no idea. That is not exactly true: I have thought long and hard, and so far I seem to have three options. One is to sell it, which I would be loath to do, the second, keeping it for the family to use as a holiday home, and lastly to rent it out, which I think would be the most sensible option. Then it could stay in the family and also provide a home to someone.

'Hmm, have you thought about making a business from it?"

'What sort of business are you thinking about, a holiday rental?'

'A little bit more. What has struck me more than anything since we arrived here, is the sense of peace and tranquillity. I can totally understand why your grandmother continued to stay here, it must have been balm to her soul, after her experiences. It made me think, and thinking about the Wouters Centre, and I started to wonder whether this could become something along the same lines.' He noticed her raising her eyebrows and about to interrupt. 'Before you say anything, I was not going to suggest that you have a centre for counselling, but more like a retreat.' He stood up and walked across to the two steadings. 'Here,' he pointed to the building, 'these could be made into two self-contained units. I have looked at the buildings and they would need a lot doing to them, but they are still sturdy. Then over there in the paddock, you could maybe have, say, another two wooden chalets.' He turned and pointed to the cottage. 'And the house could be where staff person lived.'

She drained her wine, and smiled. 'Hmm, that's a lovely idea, but how would it work, plus the biggest issue would be where would the money come from to renovate it and build the chalets?'

'As for where the money would come from, I have an idea about that which I will share with you, but firstly, how it would work. For example, the people who came to stay would of course have to contribute to the hire of the units, but it could be marketed on how this retreat could provide... all of this – ' he threw his arms up in the air to demonstrate, ' - this nature to help them find peace. Now I know that might seem a little hippyish, and maybe I have spent too long at the Wouters Centre, but that is often what people suffering from trauma need. I am sure many of the users at the Centre would come, and possibly they could be assisted with finance if they needed it. But there must also be many people in the UK that have a similar need. There would be limited need to intervene, in terms of running it, just someone living in the cottage to ensure they were booking in and out, and helping them access local amenities. That is how I imagine it might work.'

'Very interesting, Felix, but as I said earlier, it would take a lot of capital to do it all up to standard. Where would the money come from?'

'Ha, now that is where I come in. I think that given all we know about the background of how the Wouters Centre came into being, that there would be agreement that some of the finance to support this could be given by the trust. I have never outlined it to you, but the trust is a very secure and, I would say, a wealthy fund. Not only with the money that was invested by your grandmother, but when Stefan Peeters died, he left his whole estate to the trust. That money was also invested, as was that of several other donors. So I am sure that the board would be interested in investing in a satellite centre of healing. If there was any further finance needed, then I would personally wish to invest.'

She looked astounded. 'Why on earth would you wish to do that?'

'I am seeing myself perhaps living in the cottage and being the person to book them in and out,' he joked, 'but seriously, I think it would be a good investment. So what do you think?'

'Just one word: wow!'

The rest of the evening became a torrent of ideas and suggestions of what this project, if it actually became a project and not just a fantasy, would look like. Laura went to bed with a huge bubble of excitement surging through her, meaning that she had little sleep.

In the morning, they took their breakfast mugs outside and continued to pursue the idea. Felix pointed out where he thought the chalets could be situated, giving them a full view of the hills, and then poked about the steadings, suggesting a possible lay out. They didn't hear the sound of the post van making its way down the track, until it drew up in the yard. 'This is Maisie, please do not share any of your ideas with her;

it will be round the whole of the Glen if you do.'

'Well hello, Laura,' shouted Maisie. 'I was just passing, and thought I would drop in and see if all was well. You are locking up today, aren't you?' She stood and looked Felix up and down. 'Oh, now then are you going to introduce me?'

'Hi Maisie, yes I was going to stop by and let Charlie know we are away. I won't turn the water off, I think it will be safe enough to leave it on. I will plan to come over more often, and this,' she turned to Felix, 'is Felix, a friend of Elsa's family in Belgium.'

'Belgium, oh of course I remember you saying at the funeral that Elsa was born in Belgium. Fancy, that, and you have tracked down an old friend, mighty me, that's interesting.'

Felix moved over and shook her hand. Laura was relieved that he hadn't greeted her in his usual manner; she was not quite sure how Maisie would have reacted.

'Yes, it's been lovely. Thanks again though, Maisie. I suppose all is well in the Glen?' Laura successfully managed to change the subject to one which Maisie could never resist, that of gossiping about her neighbours.

CHAPTER 49

The following few days of Felix's visit to Scotland were busy. He took a number of photographs of Birch End and its surroundings, including several of the exterior and interiors of the steadings. He had several contacts of various professionals all over Europe, some of whom had become close friends over the years. He emailed some of the selected photographs to one of his close architect friends, asking what he thought about the possible future project. While he waited for a reply he spent time surfing the web, looking at costs for chalets; this gave him something to focus on while Laura worked in the shop. By the time she appeared at the end of the day, he had news that the idea might just be becoming a little more like a reality.

'Would you mind if I went back over to Birch End?' he asked a day after they had arrived back in Broadsea. 'I know I was due to go back to Belgium at the weekend, but I can extend my stay if it is okay with you. I have received a reply from my friend, who has put me in contact with an architect colleague of his – he lives in a place called Stirling – anyhow, to cut a long story short, he is willing to meet me and survey the buildings and the idea.' He scratched his beard, smiling. 'Who knows, Laura, our idea might be gathering momentum.'

'That's absolutely fine with me. I can give you the keys, and I will phone Maisie to let them know you are not a burglar. But a word of caution, we would need planning permission before anything could be built.'

'Yes, I see that, I have read about it. I will get James, the architect, to make enquiries, but according to what he might say, there may be something I can take back to put before the Trust board. Just to see if they might be interested. Don't look so worried, I have been looking out for a new project, and may just have found something to keep my mind off missing Anna.'

Felix returned three days later, saying how chilled he was and the second stay at Birch End had cemented the idea. He genuinely believed that it could become a fantastic healing place. James the architect had agreed with him and he was away to draw up some plans, and some projected costs. He would email them to him once they were ready. Laura could not help but be stimulated by Felix's energy; when he got an idea, flipping heck, did he get going. He was, however, due to leave to return home the following day. Business appointments beckoned him, he told her, although he wished he could stay longer.

The final evening Laura had invited her father to join them for supper. She cooked one of her specials, a fish pie with green vegetables. This went down well with the two men, who continued on the theme of how Birch End could become a viable business. Why not make it into a non-profit business, Grant suggested, and once he had uttered those words that was him inveigled into the idea, and given a job to check out the best way to do so.

After her father had left, they sat in the sitting room, Felix nursing a large glass of single malt, and she a Baily's. 'Blimey, Felix, who would have believed that a few days ago I didn't have a plan for the croft, and now we almost have a business plan. You are like a tornado when you get going.' She laughed.

'Ha, well, I hope that if I am a tornado, I do not end up damaging anything. I will miss you. I do think we make a good team, Laura. I will be back, especially now I have hopefully a project.'

CHAPTER 50

Life for Laura returned to normal once Felix had left. She missed his energy. She also realised she missed his company. A couple of weeks passed before she got an email from him, telling her that he had received the drawings from the architect, and he had attached them. He went on to say that he had had a word with the rest of the board, and they seemed sympathetic, but of course would need a proper business plan, which he and Grant had had further discussions about. He gave her the figure for the projected costs, and this was eye-watering to her but, he had reassured her, not to him. So the Elsa Wouters Retreat seemed to be taking one step further along the line to becoming a reality.

Laura was restless. She had no idea why; the days in the shop were busy and earning her a nice little income. The tea room was functioning well, with lots of return customers. Even the weather was good for a Scottish summer. Liam occasionally sent a text with a photo attached, usually of him with a bunch of pals drinking beer, or surfing. Iona was also busy, but still managed to visit and even brought Tony out for lunch one day. So, there was no reason at all for her feeling as though she was missing something.

It was late August when she had a Facetime call from Felix, his face full of excitement as he told her that the Wouters Trust board had agreed to back the idea of the retreat. He was going to try to come to Scotland, and spend time over September and October to get the project up and running; was that alright with her? In the meantime, James was going to submit the application for planning permission. They would, then, have to hold their breath about that one. She decided it was time for a visit to Birch End.

Grant and Dorothy were only too pleased to take over the reins for the shop, which allowed her the time to go over and stay for a couple of nights. She awoke in the back bedroom of Birch End the following Monday morning, having packed up and driven over after she had closed the shop up on the previous evening. The drive over had been the usual wonderful journey on a summer evening, with the heather now in abundance. She had a plan for this morning, and that included a chat with Maisie.

She had the kettle boiling as the red post van made its way along the track, and Maisie didn't take a second asking to share a cuppa. The post woman was interested and had worked out that there was something up. When Laura outlined the idea about the retreat, Maisie was delighted. 'That sounds a great idea, and bringing a new enterprise to the Glen. I am sure the Council will agree, and I am absolutely sure others in the Glen will think it a good use, better than the old bugger Hamish McKenzie getting his paws on it for another one of his holiday houses and more money in his pocket. At least yours will bring in people to the area, and give them a chance to experience what we have every day. The clean, Scottish air!'

Laura knew that once Maisie had completed her round everyone in the Glen, and probably half of Deebank, would know about it. She also knew that if there was going to be anyone who would object, then Maisie would no doubt hear about it, and let her know.

As it turned out, the only feedback was positive, although, Maisie had informed her that Charlie had heard that the laird's land agent had not been so impressed. Charlie also had a couple of good contacts with local builders. Maisie assured her that if any work went to local people, it would keep any petty mouths shut. Laura agreed. It would make a lot of sense to keep work local. In the meantime, she looked around the cottage and started to pack up some of her old bits and pieces that were no longer of use.

It was with some sadness that she placed more and more items onto a pile to throw away. She bagged the rest of Elsa's clothes, and decided that she would drop them off at the Red Cross charity shop; this seemed appropriate given the references to the Red Cross in her granny's journals. Much of the bedding and towels could also go. Some of the sheets were so worn you could almost see through them. Looking around she tried to see the cottage through fresh eyes. It needed a good makeover, so she grabbed a notebook and made a list. If there was going to be builders on the site, she would maybe get some work completed in the cottage. At the top of the list were new windows with proper double glazing. A couple of years ago, Grant put some secondary glazing in to keep the drafts out over the winter, although that had almost caused a row with Elsa, who was determined that she was used to drafts, and there was no need. The second item on her list was the bathroom; it really needed a complete new one, perhaps a wet room, and last on the list for a major upgrade was the kitchen. It would look so much better if the units all matched. Then, it just needed a complete re-decoration, some newer and more comfortable furniture. Goodness, she realised she was feeling energised just thinking about how the cottage would look. It even crossed her mind about what it would be like to actually live here. Although she couldn't see how that could be, given her flat and business in Broadsea.

True to Masie's word, one of the local builders turned up. He had heard that there might be some work in the future. Laura just gave him a few details, advising him that once they had got planning permission, then she would get Felix, who was insisting he would be the project manager, to call him.

When she returned to Broadsea, she found that everything

was in order. There had been no calamities in her absence, and Carol, Dorothy and Grant had everything working perfectly. Grant described how they had been really busy, and takings had been excellent, so it just proves, he exclaimed, that you can take time out, and it doesn't all fall to bits. Grant had been unobtrusively observing his daughter over the last few weeks. Her demeanour had left him a little concerned. To his mind, she needed to have a little fun; it was all work with her. So he told her – working a seven-day week is no use, you get tired. 'So why don't you think about taking at least one day a week off. You know, lass, take a day and go and do something fun.'

'Hmm.' She looked at him strangely. 'Maybe, but I have had two days off now, so back to work tomorrow.' That evening she Facetimed Felix, and when he answered it seemed that he was in a restaurant. She apologised, and said she would call him back another time. He was obviously out with friends. He confirmed this when he turned his phone so that Nicole could say hello, and to congratulate her on the future of the Retreat, which she said, she was so looking forwards to visiting at some point in the future. Laura was a little embarrassed, as she undoubtedly had interrupted a cosy dinner between the two of them. Felix told her he would call her back the following day, as there was something else he wanted to speak to her about, and the noise in the restaurant was making it hard to hear.

After the call, Laura tried to analyse her feelings. It was a feeling that she had not experienced for some time, but she had to name it: jealousy. But why, she admonished herself. Of course Felix spent time with other people, and Nicole was plainly the woman he mentioned he was seeing. So stop it, she told herself. But was she worrying that she would lose the close friendship they had built up, or was it something else? She would just have to get her act together and stamp out the daft feeling. 'Come on, Bella,' she called. 'Let's have a nice long walk along the beach.' The sun was just going down, and it was a fine evening. A walk would sort her out.

The following evening just after five, the Facetime call came through from Felix. 'Hi,' he shouted. 'Sorry about last night, but Nicole and I were just putting some final touches to an event, that is what I want to speak to you about.'

'Oh?' Laura was all ears. 'What event it that?' she enquired, propping her iPad onto the kitchen table so she could continue to pour herself a cup of tea.

'You realise, don't you, that it is seventy years, since the Wouters Trust and the Centre was established. So we were discussing that we should have an event to mark this. It is even more relevant given that we now have contact with Elsa's relatives, so we wondered if you would be able to attend. We were setting it for September 8th.'

She had a moment's thought, before she replied, 'I would love to. But I would need to check with Dad to see if he and his merry band of troops, could look after the shop.' She picked up her diary and flicked through it. 'That's a Saturday, so I could come for the weekend.'

'Yes, but I have a proposition to put to you: why not take a week? I know you will say no, that you cannot possibly do so, but let me explain. I have a little confession to make. As you know I speak to your father often about the project, and he told me, just last week, that he, and as you call them his merry band of troops, are only too happy to look after the shop for a week or so. So I am sure he is true to his word. Now here is what I was going to suggest. If you fly over, say on the Monday, then I could come back with you the following week. I was planning to come over for an extended period, so we could maybe drive back, and get the ferry over to Newcastle. How does that sound?'

She only had to ponder on it for a moment, before she replied, 'Yes I think that would be good, especially as it seems you and my dad have it all worked out anyway. So what will be event be like?'

'Just a few people who have been assisted by the Centre will be in attendance, as well as some of our supporters and donors. They would all love to meet Elsa's granddaughter. Just one other thing.' There was a longish pause. 'I know that you have one other place that you said you very much wanted to visit. Bergen Belsen.'

'Yes, but I think we thought it was too far to go in a day?' She sipped her tea, and pulled her fingers through her hair, as she began to contemplate a visit to the terrible place where her grandmother had been taken.

'But what about if we went up and stayed the night in the area, that would, as you say, kill two birds with one stone. Have I got that saying right?'

Laughing, Laura assured him that he had, and he was getting used to British sayings. 'If you are sure about it, then that would be good. To be honest, I don't think I would want to visit it on my own. So would really appreciate you being with me.'

They agreed that she would speak to her dad, and then book the flight. A quick call confirmed that Grant was only too happy with the plan. Especially as Dorothy's friend Agnes, who had helped out a few times, had expressed a hope she could do so again. Laura was also very aware from the way her dad spoke that Felix had already briefed him, so it seemed like they had been conspiring behind her back. Still, she felt a tingling of anticipation at the thought of having yet another visit to Antwerp, and spending time with Felix. Thank goodness for her dad's Christmas money; it was certainly being put to good use. The cost of the flight was no doubt going to be pricy. But then hey ho, life was for living.

CHAPTER 51

The flight to Brussels was delayed. It landed forty minutes after the scheduled time. Laura had only brought hand luggage this time, so once she had disembarked, she walked at pace to the arrivals. She was very aware that Felix would have been waiting for some time. As the large automatic doors opened, she saw him waiting by the barrier, waving to her. She felt her heart quicken, just a little, when she saw him. A minute later she was in a bear hug, and kissed on the cheeks, in the welcome she had come to look forwards to. He grabbed her bag, noting that she was travelling light.

'Well, you did say not to bother with bringing lots of toiletries, that Anna had left enough to fill a chemist, so I took you at your word. I can always use your washing machine if I run out of clothes.'

He laughed loudly, exclaiming, 'Of course, Laura, you must just consider my home yours. After all, I will do the same when I come to you.'

The conversation was easy; it was exactly as if they were very old friends. This time there was no need for him to point out landmarks, and the traffic was not too busy, so they arrived in Antwerp before she knew it.

She was in the same room as the last time. He referred to it as "your room", and it gave her a lovely feeling when he referred it like that. It took her only a moment to unpack, and returning to the kitchen she was handed a large glass of chilled white wine. Following him to sit on one of the sofas, she took in the view of the river. 'This is such a lovely apartment, Felix.' Sipping her wine, she felt a real sense of bonhomie.

'So, if you are okay about this, I suggest we drive up to Bergen tomorrow morning. It should take about five hours, the German autobahns are fast, as long as there are no hold ups. I have booked us rooms in a hotel in Celle, which is just a few miles from Bergen. I have never been to Celle before, but according to what I read online, it is an attractive town, so we can have a little holiday.' He raised his glass in a toast.

'Are you absolutely sure you don't mind driving me? It's further than I thought, plus I can pay for the hotel.'

'You will do no such thing,' he remonstrated with her. 'This is my treat.' His face lit up, with a mischievous grin. 'I have booked a two-night stay, I thought it would give you better time to process the area. Plus, I am looking forwards, as I have already said, to exploring Celle. Then if we get back on Thursday, my parents are hoping that we will go for dinner. Therefore, it is going to be a busy time, Laura.' He reached over and placed his glass on the coffee table, peering at her as though he was considering how to continue. 'Saturday is all set up for the event, even the local press have expressed an interest. I hope you will be okay about speaking to them.' He hesitated again before continuing, 'Sorry, I should have perhaps checked, before we agreed to publicity.'

'It's fine Felix, do not worry. It is the least I can do, and if it helps to promote the Centre, all well and good. Just as well I bought a new outfit, so I won't appear like some country bumpkin.'

'Laura, you would never appear like a county bumpkin, you look good in anything you wear.'

She raised her glass, her face turning a little pink with a blush.' Thank you, kind sir.'

****

The drive to Celle was a little hair-raising for Laura. Everyone drove like they were on a motor race circuit. Apparently, according to Felix, there was no speed limit, apart from on some parts of the road where there were bends. She was somewhat relieved when they drove into Celle, and with the help of the satnav, which directed hem around the one-way systems, they arrived at what looked like a lovely hotel. They were allocated rooms next door to each other, and Laura was impressed with the size of hers. She had just hung up a few items of clothes, when the knock at the door heralded Felix. 'This is lovely,' she told him. 'Is yours okay?'

'Yes, it is all good. What do you want to do? Shall we go and have a wander, and maybe a drink somewhere? We could go to the camp tomorrow morning. I can check with reception, to see if there are specific opening times. Do you think that is a plan?'

'Sounds good to me.' Laura picked up a wrap, just in case it became a little cooler in the afternoon.

'We can check out the restaurants for dinner tonight while we are at it.' Laura thought he was like an exited puppy dog. 'Let's go and explore.' Taking her hand he propelled her along.

They spent a lovely afternoon, wandering around the old town, which indeed was very picturesque, with lovely old buildings and facades. The *Schloss* was striking but they decided to forgo a visit into it, in favour of sitting in an outside café drinking a beer. They located a restaurant in the Ratskeller, which looked like it had a good menu. 'What a strange name,' she stated.

'Yes, well, Rathaus is the German name for town hall. I am thinking that a restaurant in the old town house might be quite atmospheric.'

'As long as there aren't any actual rats' she joked, 'I am sure it will be fine.'

Later, they walked back to the town centre, to the restaurant. Laura had chosen to wear a dress, and had her wrap around her shoulders. She wore her comfy flat sandals, and as she walked beside Felix, her head just about came up to his shoulder. She wasn't sure how or when, but he seemed to be holding her hand again. It felt natural, but well, it was Felix, and she just accepted that this was his normal tactile conduct.

The dinner was lovely. The price was eye-watering, but she did not dare to make a comment; this was what Felix was used to. They just chatted about all sort of things. Felix regaled her with Anna's stories about New York, where she seemed to be having a great time. 'Although,' he commented, 'reading between the lines, there was the occasional reference to a little tenseness, living for an extended period with her mother and Gemma.'

They had consumed a bottle of wine, and had already drunk a couple of beers in the afternoon, so Laura was feeling a little tipsy. She felt relaxed, so having Felix's hand in hers again as they walked back seemed the most normal thing to do. It was as they neared the hotel that he stopped, and turned to her.

'Laura,' he said as he looked down at her. 'I am so pleased you are here.'

'That's good,' she giggled, raising her head to look up to him, realising as she did so that she was definitely a little drunk.

'I hope that what I am about to do is not going to ruin our friendship, but I am going to do it, and hope it will not.' He reached down and lifted her chin, bending down at the same time to brush his lips against hers. As he felt her respond and not pull away he pressed his lips harder, and then they were into a passionate kiss. Breaking off eventually, he smiled. 'So, I am guessing that I haven't ruined it.'

Laura was all of a tizzy, her tummy was doing somersaults, her heart beating like a drum, and she was just a little breathless. 'No' She too smiled. 'Not at all.'

He took her hand again, and they walked into the hotel, and as the lift doors closed to shield them from the public, there was a second, more passionate kiss. The lift doors opened, and they found themselves outside of their rooms. She unlocked hers, and looked at him. There were no words needed. He followed her in, and closed the door behind him.

CHAPTER 52

They woke the following morning and gazed at each other. 'Any regrets?' he asked, smoothing her hair back off of her face, and kissing her on her forehead. 'No. Have you?'

'Not one. It was a very special night, and I think we make a very good team in bed, as well as outside of it.' He reached over and held her. 'I am, I have to say, a little relieved. I did not know whether you were feeling the same way as I was. I think that the wine helped me overcome my nervousness.'

She looked surprised. 'I had not realised that you were nervous.' She turned to look directly at him, stroking his beard. 'I think I had started to realise that my feelings towards you were a little more than just friendship. But then, I thought you were involved with someone else.'

'Not really. Well, I think I told you that there was someone, but it was more of a casual thing... well, for me that was. I broke it off when I returned from my trip to Scotland. It was during that trip that I realised that you were becoming more important to me, more than just a friend. I did not wish to pursue you, though, if you only wanted to keep it platonic. But yesterday, spending time with you in Celle, and when you did not loosen your hand from mine, it felt so good. That was when I became a little reassured that if I made a move, it would be reciprocated. Lucky for me, it was.'

After they had eaten a leisurely breakfast, they made their way to Bergen. The actual village was a few kilometres from the camp. As they drove through the village, they came to a military camp, Bergen-Hohne. 'Oh look,' Laura pointed out. 'That must be the camp where Elsa was taken after liberation. I read about it; it was until recently a British Garrison, that was until they closed it.' Felix drew the car to one side, so she could look at it. 'It was where Granny's life was saved, and she and Grandad got together. I am going to take a photo, if that's okay, so I can show Iona and Dad.' She leapt out of the car, and took several photos on her phone.

They drove along the road until they reached the sign for Bergen Belsen, concentration camp. She felt her stomach tighten. Felix parked the car, and they first went into the visitor centre. It was full of horrific images. She could hardly believe that within these terrible images her grandmother and great-grandmother had existed. Felix was interested in reading and looking at the exhibits, but after a while she told him that she was going to retreat outside, but for him to remain. He shook his head. 'I think I have a good understanding of this.'

They walked outside to where the camp had once held so many people. It was difficult to picture it, as now it was an open landscape in a forest. There were several memorials, but what was more heart-breaking were the large mounds of burial grounds, with signs giving approximate numbers of bodies buried. Five thousand, four thousand…, so, so many poor souls. She could not help but wonder which one held the body of her great-grandmother, Estelle. Although so many people had suffered in this place, there was now a sense of quiet, if not peace. She watched as several other visitors wandered around looking, as she was, sad and reflective. This was such a sad place. The thought of her dear granny, so young, so frightened in this place brought tears.

They walked around the area, until they believed they had come to the place where the women's camp once stood. 'It must be about here,' she told him 'where Granny was put, and where Grandad found her. It is quite hard to believe how he found her alive, especially after seeing those images in the visitor centre. She was lying with Estelle, trying to warm her up. But she was already dead. Poor Granny, can you even imagine what it must have been like for her? Then the one soldier who found her turned out to be Grandad. That surely was a love destined to happen.'

'Just as, they have now brought us together.' He held her to him. 'I do not believe in coincidence; we were meant to meet, Laura.'

They turned just as a beam of sunlight came from behind a cloud, sending its rays across the trees and causing a flicker of light that seemed to dance between the branches, as though it was alive. Laura remembered how Elsa had written about her mother's mantra, of looking at the sunrise and praying that it would bring hope and peace. She felt a shiver run up her spine, and she got the feeling that she and Felix were not alone, but surrounded by unseen spirits, who had all lived with that hope. She placed the flower she had brought with her on the ground and said, 'I am laying this in memory of Estelle Wouters, my great-grandmother: may you please be at peace.'

They stood for a moment, soaking up the atmosphere, the sense of sadness penetrating their souls. She took Felix's hand. 'I think that I have done what I needed to do. Thanks for being with me.'

Apart from the joy of finding each other, a degree of sombreness surrounded them as they drove away from Celle the following day. 'Celle will always hold a special place in my heart. It is a lovely city, but so close to the sadness of what happened to my family. It is like two worlds.' Laura searched for her sunglasses as the sun hit the windscreen, blinding her for a moment. 'For now, though, I am going to keep the hotel in Celle at the forefront of my memory.'

He smiled, and reached over and took her hand. 'I think that hotel will be a lasting highlight in my memory as well. I had no idea that we would fit together so well, and this is just the start. When we get back to my apartment, the room I had designated as yours is now redundant.' He stopped, and glanced at her. 'Although, if you wish to have your own space, then of course you must remain in it.' She did not reply, but just looked at him with a sexy grin.

CHAPTER 53

Saturday arrived, with Felix and Laura having a leisurely lie in. He made coffee and brought it back to bed; they leant up against the pillows to drink it. 'So tell me again, what is the itinerary for today? You have been a little vague about who will be there.'

'As I said, we are due to be there at two, and there will be a small gathering in the garden. There will be a little ceremony of planting of a rose in the garden, in memory of your family. If you recall I said that a Belgian flower grower has named a rose after the Wouters family. It will be you who will plant it. There will be some drinks and snacks, and,' he reached over and pressed the remote that drew up the blinds,' if the sun stays out, then we can talk with those who are attending.'

'And tell me again, who will be there?'

'Oh, just a few people, as I said. Some who have used the Centre, and others who are supporters and donors.'

They arrived just on two, and Nicole met them in the reception area. She gave them both a warm welcome, and advised them that guests had already arrived. She led them up the stairs to the kitchen, where several plates of canapes were placed on the table; they looked delicious. As Laura followed Nicole out of the back door and down the steps, she realised that there was quite a gathering of people. She recognised

Axel and Marie, and then spotted Christin and Ada, she waved to them, and went straight across to hug them, and ask how Lars was.

'He had wanted to come,' Christin told her, 'but then changed his mind. I think we are thankful that he had, it may just be a little too much for him to return here on such a day. He misses Mama so much, and this would bring back so many memories.'

Felix shouted, his voice loud, trying to reach all of those present. 'Good afternoon, everyone. Thank you very much for coming here today. I am speaking in my capacity as the chair of the board of the Wouters Trust, and am very pleased that we have here, today, the granddaughter of Elsa Wouters, who of course is the founder of this place. Many of you know the story of how the Wouters Centre came into being, and how Elsa disappeared to start a new life in Scotland. Laura,' he reached over and brought her to stand beside him, 'had no knowledge of what her grandmother and other family members had endured, until after Elsa's death. The Wouters assisted many people during the German occupation, and without their help many people would have not survived. Today I am humbled to say that we have some of the descendants amongst this gathering.'

Laura looked a little bemused, and thought he must be referring to Christin.

'So, first could we ask you, Laura, to plant this special rose, in memory of your family.' She took the small spade from him and did as he asked. 'Now then, Laura, do you recall reading in your grandmother's journals about Rachel Cohen, who was your father's receptionist, and then lived with the family?' Laura thought for a moment, then nodded that she did. 'Well, for those who do not know the story, Rachel's husband David was part of the Belgian forces, and managed to get away to Britain on D-Day. Rachel did not know whether he had survived, and when the Nazis started to get interested in the Antwerp Jewish community, Martin Wouters considered that it would be safer if Rachel left. She was helped by the Resistance, I have to add, and also by Derk Wouters, to escape across the border into Spain, where she remained until the war was finished. With the help of the Red Cross, she located David, who in turn had been searching for her. They were reunited, but did not return to Antwerp, but instead settled in Holland. They,' he turned to Laura, 'went on to have three children, who then went on to have children of their own. So I would like to introduce you to the Cohen family.'

Laura's hand flew to her mouth. She was stunned as several people walked towards her. There were two elderly men, who introduced themselves as Rachel and David's sons, and they in turn introduced the other members of their family, their own children. Jacob, the oldest of the two brothers, said, 'I have to say that we are eternally grateful for what your family did, Laura. My dear parents always remembered the Wouters, and they were certain that it was due to them that our mother, Rachel, survived. Without that happening, none of us would be here now.' He took her hands and drew them to his mouth to kiss them. 'We thank you.'

Laura was overcome. Jacob introduced the family members, two of his own daughters, with their four children, and his brother also introduced her to his son and grandchildren. They explained that sadly their younger sister was unable to travel, but introduced her son and daughter who were there to represent her. Laura lost count of how many were in the family, but it was quite startling that due to her family, so many had been given the chance of life.

Just as she was starting to regain her composure, Nicole came to stand beside her. 'There is someone else who would like to meet you,' she whispered, and guided her across the lawn to another group of people. An elderly woman sat on a chair, her wavy white hair framing a wrinkled face. With the woman sat a younger version of the old woman, gripping her hand. When they saw Nicole and Laura approach, they both broke into wide smiles. 'Laura, I would like to introduce Martha Altman, and her daughter, Marion.'

The old lady started to rise from her seat, but Laura rushed to tell her to remain where she was, and bent down to her level to take her hand. 'You will probably not know who I am,' Martha spoke in broken English, 'but I was born here in this house, and my family were saved by your family.'

Laura looked at the woman, trying to recall whether Elsa had mentioned anything, and then it suddenly came to her. The baby that was mentioned in the journal, who Martin had delivered, had been named Martha. Surely, it couldn't be! Laura stood back up. Marion said, 'My grandparents arrived one night, and sought refuge. My mother was born that night, and they spoke often about how kind your family were. They took a huge risk, and sheltered them until they could be led to safety, by the Resistance. After the war they went to Israel, where my mother grew up, married and had me.' She laughed. 'And I went on to have four children, and have eight grandchildren.' She bent to hug her mother. 'So you see, saving one small baby has resulted in thirteen more lives, at least.'

Laura felt a little overwhelmed, and was relieved when she felt the strong arm of Felix placed around her shoulders. 'I don't quite know what to say,' she told them, 'other than my grandmother did write about you in her journal, but I never expected to meet you.' She bent down again to take the old lady's hand in hers. 'Did you come all the way from Israel?'

Martha looked to her daughter to speak, as she became quite emotional. 'I contacted the Wouters Centre a couple of years ago, as I was doing some searching for my mother. I found the Centre on the internet, and we have been in correspondence ever since. Mother always wanted to come back at some point, and so when Nicole contacted us to tell us about this event, we could not resist. I am so pleased we have done so, and to meet the granddaughter of one of the direct family.' She moved to take Laura into her arms and hugged her tightly. 'What your family did for mine means so much, they were exceptionally brave people.'

The afternoon became a jolly affair. Many stories were shared. Laura was introduced to some of the previous patients who had been treated by the centre; all of them were full of praise for the support they had received. When they heard of the retreat project they were eager to know more. They would love to visit Scotland, and experience the peace of the mountains, they told her.

As the afternoon moved into early evening, the guests dispersed, hugging and kissing Laura's cheeks, and saying they wanted to be apprised when the retreat was opened. Laura felt quite washed out with the emotion, and thankfully Felix planned a lazy evening with a takeaway. Nicole walked with them to the front reception, and hugged Laura, whispering in her ear, 'I am so pleased that Felix has found you. He has been lost and now I can see the sparkle in his eyes again. I wish you both every happiness.'

Later that evening, curled up on the sofa listening to music and sipping wine, she asked him, 'So can I ask you, was Nicole the woman who you were seeing?'

He looked surprised. 'How did you know that?'

'Just had a feeling, I think she is maybe a little in love with you.'

'Yes, I did feel a little bad about that, but I can assure you, I did not lead her on. When I told her how I felt about you, she told me that she also believed in destiny, and I should not lose time in delaying telling you. Good advice, and thankfully I followed it.' He picked his glass up. 'Here is to a long life together, my darling.'

Epilogue

1 year later

Laura woke and looked at the clock on the bedside table, it was showing 6 a.m. She looked around the newly decorated bedroom; the new curtains hung just a few days ago went well with the soft lemon walls. She stretched and climbed out of bed, dressed quickly and grabbed Bella before anyone else in the house woke. Creeping downstairs, she grabbed a jacket from the peg, donned a pair of boots and whisked an excited collie out of the house. The sun had just started to appear over the hills and she took in the full view. It was still quiet in the yard of Birch End, but much had changed over the last year. The two steading conversions looked fantastic, and they were both currently occupied. One had just one bedroom, and the larger steading two bedrooms; they were both very modern units, with all mod cons, and furnished to a high standard. Her eye followed to the field beside the cottage, and took in the three wooden two-bedroom lodges. They were also smart and had been finished just two weeks ago. So far, they had not been hired, but there were bookings that stretched right up until after the New Year. However, today, all three were currently occupied.

She called softly to Bella to follow her. Walking quietly past the lodges, she took a quick look into the large marque that was sitting proudly in front of the lodges. She had been surprised at how quickly this had been erected and furnished. The company that they had hired had so far been excellent, and professional to the highest degree. The wooden floor had been provided just in case the Scottish weather didn't behave, to prevent the whole event turning out to be a festival of mud. But so far, looking at the sky, they were in for a good day. There were no clouds to destroy the September sunshine.

Bella followed her down through the woods to the river, where she dashed about collecting sticks and waiting her for mistress to throw them. It was a game she never tired of, even though she was now nearly twelve years old and should be slowing down.

Laura sat on her favourite rock, and reflected on the past year. So many changes, some almost unbelievable, and today she was going to make a lifelong commitment to the love of her life, Felix. He certainly was a mover and shaker. The Elsa Wouters Retreat had been finished on time, and officially opened just three weeks ago. How he had managed to get the whole thing finished, she had no idea, but he had. Felix was the one person who was actually not in residence today, having been banished to a hotel in Deebank for the night. Anna had been insistent that the Wouters family had had enough bad luck in their time, so it was the least he could do on the eve of his wedding night not to see the bride until the ceremony. Anna, Stella and Gemma were currently resident in the two-bedroom steading. The others were occupied by other guests, while Iona, Tony and Grant were staying in the house. The biggest surprise was the person staying in the one-bedroom Steading: Liam, who had arrived unexpectedly with a very attractive young woman who he had introduced as Bridget, his fiancée. That had been a lovely surprise. They were planning to travel around Europe, and being at his mum's wedding had been the trigger for starting their travels in Scotland.

Deciding that Birch End was going to be their main home had been a decision that she had wrestled with. But she realised how fortunate she was; they had two homes, one in Antwerp, but Birch End was something they had created together. Felix promised her they were not going to be tied to it, but at least they could put down their roots here. That felt right to her. She had rented out the flat in Broadsea, the shop and tearoom would continue, but had changed its focus slightly as several of Dorothy and Carol's friends had offered to run it as a community project, with a small sum to her for the rental of the building. That felt right too. This meant she and Felix could devote their time initially to the Retreat. Birch End had been renovated in so many ways; the cottage had had the best makeover, and was now a mixture of tradition with modern facilities, a home she had created with Felix.

As she sat, she watched the river roll and bubble over rocks, and wondered what Elsa would think about the changes. She wasn't convinced that her granny would agree with them all, and she was pretty sure she would have objected with the name given to the retreat. But as much as Elsa had done her best to leave all of her past behind, and to all intents and purposes she had been successful in doing so while she was living, her past had become Laura's future.

So many of their guests who had travelled to be with them today bore witness to that. The second-generation families of Rachel and David, Sophia and Lars, Martha, were all here because of the sacrifices that Elsa's family had made. That would surely have been balm to Elsa's scars.

The chain of events had taken life of their own since she had opened that old suitcase and found Elsa's journals. So many life changes, and the one she was most amazed about was the love she felt for Felix. Destiny, fate, or whatever the name was for it, it worked.

As she looked towards the hills, she saw the sun make its way above the summit of the hills, the streams of light catching on the granite and sparkling like small diamonds. Laura felt the presence of others standing beside her, but when she turned there was no one there. At least, not in their bodies, she thought. They were all here with her, though, in spirit. 'So, Granny, I am looking at the sunrise, and it has brought peace, and so much hope.

'I will always think of you when I see the sunrise, and remember to always hope.'

Printed in Great Britain
by Amazon

49351559R00208